ENEMIES OF THE CROWN

BOOK 5 IN THE SAXON WARRIOR SERIES

PETER GIBBONS

Boldwood

First published in Great Britain in 2025 by Boldwood Books Ltd.

Copyright © Peter Gibbons, 2025

Cover Design by Head Design Ltd.

Cover Images: Adobe Stock and iStock

The moral right of Peter Gibbons to be identified as the author of this work has been asserted in accordance with the Copyright, Designs and Patents Act 1988.

Every effort has been made to obtain the necessary permissions with reference to copyright material, both illustrative and quoted. We apologise for any omissions in this respect and will be pleased to make the appropriate acknowledgements in any future edition.

A CIP catalogue record for this book is available from the British Library.

Paperback ISBN 978-1-83518-250-5

Large Print ISBN 978-1-83518-251-2

Hardback ISBN 978-1-83518-249-9

Ebook ISBN 978-1-83518-252-9

Kindle ISBN 978-1-83518-253-6

Audio CD ISBN 978-1-83518-244-4

MP3 CD ISBN 978-1-83518-245-1

Digital audio download ISBN 978-1-83518-248-2

This book is printed on certified sustainable paper. Boldwood Books is dedicated to putting sustainability at the heart of our business. For more information please visit https://www.boldwoodbooks.com/about-us/sustainability/

Boldwood Books Ltd, 23 Bowerdean Street, London, SW6 3TN

www.boldwoodbooks.com

For my family. Love and support is everything.

Swa stemnetton stiðhicgende
hysas æt hilde, hogodon georne
hwa þær mid orde ærost mihte
on fægean men feorh gewinnan,
wigan mid wæpnum; wæl feol on eorðan
Stodon stædfæste.
So they prevailed, sternly determined,
the men in battle, they directed their thoughts
 eagerly
as to who first at weapon point
would win a life from fated warriors,
men at arms; the dead fell to the earth.
Steadfast they stood.

— AN EXCERPT FROM 'THE BATTLE OF
MALDON', AN ANGLO-SAXON POEM
WRITTEN TO CELEBRATE THE BATTLE
FOUGHT AT MALDON IN 991AD

1

994AD

Fear hung over the kingdom like a death shroud. War loomed. Talk of raids, battles and slaughter travelled on the wind like smoke from burned thatch. War needs warriors like fire needs kindling, and so Beornoth and Ealdorman Alfgar reached Winchester on a blustery late spring day when gusts of wind snapped their cloaks about them and Beornoth frowned as grit from the dry road stung his eyes. Two of Alfgar's warriors rode ahead to clear the road for the ealdorman and his retinue. They carried ash-shafted spears from which the banner of Cheshire stood proud, golden wheat sheaves on a square of wool dyed blue. Churls stood by the roadside, heads bowed in deference as the ealdorman and his ten-man retinue trotted slowly by. The warriors' armour, weapons and bridles clanked and jangled. Big men on big horses, grim-faced, scarred and terrifying. The churls stood before their carts of onions, cabbages and cut peat with downcast eyes, afraid of the spears, swords and shields but understanding that the fearsome riders and their ilk were all that stood between them and destruction at the hands of bloodthirsty men. Men who would come to raid, steal and kill should the sheep find themselves unprotected by the dogs of war.

'We'll reach Winchester today,' said Alfgar. He tossed scraps of hacksilver to the common folk with their dirty faces, greasy hair and rough spun jerkins. The churls waited until the horses had passed before scrabbling to grasp for the ealdorman's alms.

'Aye,' Beornoth replied, 'and find out why they summoned us.' He shifted in the saddle, rump aching after the two weeks it had taken to ride from Alfgar's home at Mameceaster to the king's capital at Winchester. Alfgar was the ealdorman and ruler of a wide swathe of land in England's north-west. As ealdorman he answered only to the king, which made Alfgar one of the most powerful men in the realm.

'Danes again. That's why the king has sent for you, Beo.'

Beornoth's frown deepened, the lines upon his forehead creasing like a furrowed field above the hard, flat crag of his face. Scars and old wounds pulsed at the mention of the cursed Vikings. His shoulder ached, stomach knotted and his thigh throbbed. Too many wounds to remember. The cold stab of steel had cut at Beornoth his entire life. Swords, axes, spears and arrows slashing and stabbing at him as he hewed at the kingdom's enemies with his monstrous strength and savagery. Terrible wounds suffered fighting brutal Viking warriors come south across the Whale Road from the wild lands of Jutland, Kattegat and the Vik. Beornoth frowned because Alfgar was right. A summons from King Æthelred meant trouble, battle and blood.

'Maybe King Æthelred is getting married again?'

Alfgar leant back in the saddle and cocked an eyebrow at Beornoth. His beard was neatly combed, and his eyes shone brightly. 'So the king sends for you, Beornoth the famous Dane-killer, to pick some flowers for his bride?' He laughed, and Beornoth curled his lip.

Beornoth glanced around him at trees bursting with bright leaves, lush meadows and blooming wildflowers. 'It's late spring. Time for war. The time when the Danes sail their dragon ships south looking for trouble. Bastards must be back.' Beornoth had fought the Vikings since his first beard had grown like dandelion fluff on his chin. They had taken everything from him, his children, his heriot – the land and weapons his father had left him. War had made Beornoth what he was, and in truth he had known it must be the Danes when the message came north summoning him to the king. Beornoth was not the sort of man to invite to a wedding. He was a king's thegn. Thegns were warriors who held land and weapons in an ealdorman's service, oathbound to fight for their lord whenever he called. A king's thegn was different. There were only a dozen such men in the kingdom, warriors of equal rank to an ealdorman, who answered only to King Æthelred. Equal in rank, but not in lands and power. The king's thegns were his protectors, the wolves he called upon for the grim work, the sword work beyond his own warriors and nobility. Beornoth had felt the Vikings return in his bones, but hoped it was not so. He had prayed to God before leaving Mameceaster to let the summons be something else. When Beornoth had kissed his wife Eawynn goodbye, he had whispered that it might not be the Danes this time, but she had stroked his bearded cheek and stared up into his face with sad eyes. It was always the Danes.

'Time for war indeed, old friend. Thanks be to God that the northmen do not trouble us in Cheshire. But we must heed the king's call, and if necessary, help our brothers in Wessex, Essex and Mercia. So let's see what work the king has in store for us.'

Alfgar clicked his tongue and urged his bay gelding along the road.

The Danes craved the fertile lands of England's south. They had won much of the north already. Descendants of Norse raiders ruled everything north of the old Roman road known as Watling Street, which ran from Lundenwic to the River Mersey. Lands known as the Danelaw. The Vikings had settled there, becoming part of the kingdom. Folk referred to the invaders from Norway, Denmark and Sweden as Vikings, Danes, northmen or Norsemen, irrespective of their actual homeland. They came south every year on board *drakkar* warships with sleek hulls and snarling-dragon carved prows, sailing up England's wide rivers in search of blood, silver and glory.

Beornoth leant forward and stroked the neck of his warhorse, Virtus. The horse whickered and followed Alfgar's mount at a canter. Virtus was a roan mare, a gift from the king himself, and trained for war in the royal stables. Virtus meant courage and strength in Latin, the tongue of the Church and of old Rome. She was not as large or vicious as Beornoth's old warhorse Ealdorbana, but she was fast and strong. Beornoth had always felt a closeness to horses. He enjoyed their company. There was a bond between a warrior and his mount, the care and respect of the rider for the horse's strength and willingness to carry his burden.

They reached Winchester after noon, riding alongside the shining River Itchen. The king's capital city emerged from the rolling hills and farmland, grey, brown and formidable amongst the grazing meadows and farmsteads. Beornoth noticed with approval that the king had maintained the city's walls and fighting palisade. A ditch, bank and timber palisade on which spearmen glowered along the muddy roads reaching to north, south, east and west had strengthened the neat, dressed stone left by the Romans. Alfgar sent his men ahead to announce his arrival at the gate, and Beornoth rode beside the ealdorman as the familiar city smell of smoke, tanned leather, livestock and shit drifted on the breeze. A cloud of grey smoke hung above the walls, rising from hearths, forges and cook fires.

Two of Alfgar's warriors bought steaming strips of roasted meat from one of the crudely built market stalls clustered outside the walls, and another bought a leather necklace set with a small teardrop of amber for his wife. The gate guards waved them through and bowed their heads to both Beornoth and Alfgar, and a bent-backed steward wearing the king's livery of the green dragon of Wessex met them inside.

'Welcome, my lords,' said the man, bowing deeply. He wrung his hands and peered nervously at Alfgar's men. 'Could I ask your men to make camp beyond the walls for now, Lord Alfgar? Once your meeting with the king is over, we shall find rooms for them at a tavern. You, of course, will be welcome to spend the night inside the king's palace.'

Alfgar nodded and his men left through the north gate. Two boys took Beornoth's and Alfgar's horses, and Alfgar gave them each a scrap of hacksilver. The ealdorman was expected to pay such small offerings to the common folk, and Beornoth had seen Alfgar give away a small fortune on the journey south.

'Brush them, and make sure they have clean hay,' Alfgar said with an easy smile.

The steward led Beornoth and Alfgar through a winding mass of timber-framed houses and buildings with wattle and daub walls and thatched roofs. Some leaned precariously against one another along narrow, winding streets whilst other, larger buildings boasted painted gables and carved window shutters. The stone church and hall within King Æthelred's palace grew closer, grand and magnificent above the mud, wood and thatch. More guards waited at the royal enclosure, and they took Beornoth's sword and seax. Beornoth and Alfgar handed over their weapons without challenge, for it was customary not to bring weapons into a home or feasting hall, and certainly not before the king's presence. Beornoth's heriot, his trappings of warhorse, sword, spear, seax, byrnie coat of chain-mail armour and helmet, were all gifts of King Æthelred, provided upon his appointment to the rank of king's thegn in reward for his service to the throne. The gate guard's mouth dropped open when he noticed the ring on Beornoth's finger. The band was deep yellow gold, inlaid with a green stone etched with the dragon banner of Wessex, the mark of his rank, which Beornoth also wore sewn into the leather of his sword scabbard.

The steward left Alfgar and Beornoth with the palace guards and scuttled off to meet more visitors in the king's city. They followed the palace guards, both wearing hard-baked leather breastplates and carrying leather-covered shields daubed with the grasping dragon, who led them inside the royal enclosure, a place of rose gardens, Roman water fountains, clean stone and bustling servants. The king's hall rose tall, its doors oaken and as broad as five men, flanked by the old minster, an iron-grey stone cathedral from which the praying and song of priests lilted above the city's din. They passed through a side gate and into a bright courtyard filled with bright flowers of yellow and blue. It was a garden haven set within the hard stone and drab wattle buildings. The city had long been the seat of the kings of Wessex, and there were reminders of Alfred and Athelstan, and the other great Wessex lords in tapestries and carvings all over the palace. The courtyard was a small square spread between the hall and minster. A cobblestone walkway linked the build-ings and meandered its way around bright plants and bushes, which smelled fresh in the afternoon sunlight.

'Wait here, please, my lords,' said a guard, leaving Beornoth and Alfgar alone.

'I have been here before,' Beornoth said. He stared at a small stone bench. 'Ealdorman Byrhtnoth sat there. Leofsunu of Sturmer and Aelfwine of Foxfield stood beside me.'

'Good men and stout warriors. We miss them,' said Alfgar. He clapped Beornoth on the shoulder and smiled sadly for their friends, who had perished in the battle of Maldon.

'My lords?' said a croaky voice from the shadows, thankfully interrupting Beornoth before he slipped further into melancholy thoughts of lost friends. 'The king will see you now.'

Beornoth followed Alfgar up a narrow set of mottled steps and into a shadowed corridor. They emerged into the king's great hall, a vast space with high ceilings and ancient, smoke-darkened roof beams. Heavy tapestries hung from the walls and a hearth fire crackled and spat at one end. Beornoth's footsteps echoed around the great chamber and his chain-mail byrnie clanked against the buckle of his thick leather belt. Two dozen men huddled at the centre of the hall, talking in whispers. They fell silent as Beornoth and Alfgar approached.

'Ah, my ealdorman and my Dane-killer!' said King Æthelred. He emerged from the crowd with a beaming smile. The king had lustrous auburn hair and wore a circlet of gold upon his brow. His long, lantern-jawed face had gained more lines than the last time Beornoth had seen him, and there were streaks of white in the king's thin beard. He wore a large silver crucifix on a thick chain over a finely woven purple tunic.

'Lord king,' said Alfgar, and inclined his head. 'We received your summons and came at once.'

'Lord king,' Beornoth said as he bowed his head. The men about Æthelred crossed themselves and made pinched faces at Beornoth. Most of them were narrow-shouldered men with soft, pale faces and gentle hands. Most wore the brown and black robes of priests, others wore the vestments of higher office: greens, whites and reds, heavy cloaks and soft scarves. Beornoth bit his lip to avoid snarling at the little bastards. They flocked about the king filling his ears with softness and the word of God, or the word of God as they saw it.

'It has been, what, two or three years since that dreadful day at Maldon?' said the king. He tutted sympathetically and made the sign of the cross. Beornoth did the same. 'We all miss Ealdorman Byrhtnoth.'

'Not all of us,' hissed a thin voice, scraping and hushed like a winter wind across dry, fallen leaves. It came from the shadows, beneath the lowest eaves of King Æthelred's hall. A small, grey-haired woman shuffled from the darkness flanked by two huge warriors. Beornoth stiffened. She was bent-backed, but kept her head high, her lips pursed and her gnarled knuckles showed white upon the black staff she used for support as came with short, scuffing but determined steps. 'Byrhtnoth was too power-ful. He was a supporter of your brother's crown. You would do well to remember that, my son.'

'Ealdorman Byrhtnoth was a hero of the realm, who stood fast against our Viking enemies, Mother. We have raised my dear late brother to sainthood, and shall remember the fallen ealdorman just as fondly.'

'He was a proud fool.' The king's mother banged her staff on the floor and pointed its tip at Beornoth. 'He was there. He knows. Byrhtnoth could have slaughtered Forkbeard and the Danes at Maldon, but he let them come ashore. The tide stranded them on Maldon island. He wanted to fight a great battle, to be the noble warrior, to face them in a fair fight on firm ground. Well, he got his comeuppance. And as for your brother, your half-brother…'

'Enough!' King Æthelred shouted, but his voice came out high-pitched, like a cat screeching in the night.

'Lady Ælfthryth has kindly joined us to share her wisdom on the problem with the Danes,' said one of the bishops. The king's mother glowered at Beornoth, and he returned her stare with a sharp look of his own. Her sour talk of Maldon made his fists bunch, for it had not happened that way. Beornoth knew. He had been there. The last Beornoth had heard of the old queen was her exile to a convent, an exile she had earned through the failure of dark plots and deep cunning. She was old King Edgar's second wife, mother to Æthelred, but not to his older brother Edward. After King Edgar died, Edward became king, but was then murdered and replaced by Æthelred. Many, including Ealdorman Byrhtnoth, believed Ælfthryth arranged King Edward's murder so that her own son might become king. Æthelred had been but a boy and she had ruled in his stead until the king came of age. She was powerful and ruthless, and had once tried to have Beornoth killed.

'My lady,' said Alfgar, bowing deeply to the wizened old battleaxe. Beornoth said nothing.

'You have missed my counsel. The kingdom withers and suffers at the hands of weak men. Despite my son's payment of a kingdom-crippling gafol to the Danes after the crushing defeat at Maldon, Sweyn Forkbeard has returned with ninety-four ships,' said Ælfthryth. She stalked amongst the priests and bishops, tapping her staff and staring up into their pale faces with her challenging eyes. 'For those of you with minds like mice, which, unfortunately, is most of the lackwits in this hall, that means he brings six and a half thousand Vikings to our shores. He is in the Thames Estuary as we speak with this vast fleet and does not come to pay us homage. There are many in the north who would welcome Forkbeard's return, who would rejoice to see a Dane on the throne of England. We stand on a knife edge, my lords.'

Æthelred chewed at the fingernails of his left hand, thought better of it, and stuffed his long fingers into the sleeves of his luxurious tunic. 'So you see, Lords Alfgar and Beornoth. We face war again.'

'How can we be of support, lord king?' asked Alfgar. Beornoth stood straight-backed and kept his eyes on Ælfthryth. Though small and frail, malevolence pulsed from her like heat from a fire. She had been Byrhtnoth and Beornoth's enemy, and to see her returned to the king's presence filled Beornoth with dread. The priests bowed their heads, exchanging nervous glances at what the king might suggest, and Beornoth knew the gentle churchmen would advise any path but violence, but if Forkbeard had returned, then violence was upon them whether they chose it or not.

'King Sweyn Forkbeard of Denmark makes for the City of Lundenwic,' said the king, turning to Beornoth. 'We must defend the city. If he gets a foothold behind its walls, we might never get him out again. We have Vikings north of the Danelaw, and now King Sweyn is back with a mighty army. Despite the vast sum we paid after Maldon to ensure that he would never come back again. Enemies surround us, my lords. Sweyn Fork-beard and an army of Vikings have already raided the east coast. We must defend Lundenwic, Lord Beornoth.'

'Yes, lord king,' Beornoth replied, knowing what must come next. After the battle of Maldon, the priests had counselled the king to pay off the Vikings, hoping that a horde of silver would be enough to keep them from England's shores forever. But the gafol had simply given the wolves a taste of blood. So whenever Viking warlords needed silver, they would sail to King Æthelred's kingdom. Row their sleek-hulled warships up a long river, burn some villages, kill a few lords and then wait for the offer of silver to pay them off.

'They are lying, cheating murderers and must be stopped, Lord Beornoth, and who better than the greatest Dane-killer in the kingdom?'

'Yes, lord king,' Beornoth repeated, waiting for it.

'So you will go to Lundenwic and help its people defend the city against the cursed invader. Ealdorman Alfgar, you will return to Cheshire and raise a third of your shire fyrd and march them south to help defend Wessex and East Anglia. The rest of my ealdormen shall do the same. We shall build an army and show our enemies what it means to threaten our kingdom.' Æthelred looked around at his advisors. Some nodded vigorously, but others, the men in church robes, kept their heads bowed and would not give the king the approval he sought.

'My men will go with you, Beornoth,' said Ælfthryth, and a smile played at the corner of her wrinkled lips. The two warriors at her side stared flatly at Beornoth. Both big men clad in bright chain-mail byrnies with scars on their knuckles and hard faces. They wore their hair shaved high at the back of their skull, and cut short on top, brushed forward like a cap. 'This is Robert de Warenne and his brother, Odo. They have fifty spearmen and will accompany you to Lundenwic.'

'I have brought them back from exile,' said the king, and then seemed to catch himself. He glanced at the Norman warriors from across the sea in Frankia and his long face turned ashen grey.

'You must ride with all haste, Lord Beornoth,' said a heavy-jowelled bishop. 'The Danes are already in the river!'

Beornoth and Alfgar left the hall and the sound of whispered talking behind them.

'Much has changed since we were last in Winchester,' said Alfgar, once they had marched through the oak doors.

'Much and more,' Beornoth replied. 'Not for the better. I had hoped never to see Ælfthryth again. And who were those Norman bastards with her?'

'I don't know, Beo. But I know someone who might. I did not see Bishop Nothhelm in the king's presence. We must find him before we leave Winchester.'

Nothhelm had been the bishop of Essex when Byrhtnoth was ealdorman, and had led the prominent monastery at Ely. Byrhtnoth had trusted the old man, and so did Beornoth. They found Nothhelm praying in a small chapel in a southern corner of the royal enclosure. He heard their heavy boots approaching and rose from his knees, smiling.

'Ah, friendly faces,' Nothhelm said with a tired smile. He was a small, wiry man with tightly curled grey hair sprouting from either side of his otherwise bald head. 'I wish you visited under better circumstances. But here you are, and I am glad to see you. Come, I have some freshly brewed ale in my rooms.'

Nothhelm led them through a labyrinth of narrow corridors until they reached a pine door hung with a large crucifix. He ushered them inside a room with a ceiling so low that Beornoth had to bend his neck to get inside.

'Sit, please,' said the bishop, fussing as he grabbed a milking stool for Beornoth to sit on. Alfgar sat upon the small pallet bed, for there was no other furniture in the room save for a small table on which Nothhelm poured two wooden cups of ale from a stone pitcher. His hands shook as he poured and handed the cups to his guests. 'Forkbeard has returned and so they have called for you, Beo.'

'I am surprised to see you still in Winchester,' said Alfgar, smiling but unable to keep his eyes from Nothhelm's simple priestly woollen robe belted with knotted hemp rope. 'The last time we met, the king spoke of you becoming archbishop?'

Nothhelm held on to the ale jug and stared at Alfgar, as if he were frozen in ice. The awkward silence lasted for a dozen heartbeats until Nothhelm seemed to remember where he was and set the jug down on the table. 'Much has happened since last we met, Lord Alfgar. These are difficult times. But I am glad to see you both. Have you eaten?'

'Why is Ælfthryth here?' Beornoth asked.

Nothhelm wagged a thin finger at him. 'Never a man to beat around the bush, eh, Beornoth? Ever since Maldon, the king has become convinced that God sends the Danes to punish him and his people for our sins. Some of my colleagues have encouraged him in this, those who supported the late Bishop Sigeric's belief that the best way to be rid of the Vikings is to pay them off. These men seek higher office, and they pour whatever velvet words they can connive into the king's ear to promote themselves in his service. The king has embarked upon a journey of repentance and reform these last two years. He has returned land to the Church, land taken by him and his father in the years when they wished to shift power away from the clergy, monasteries and abbeys. The king has pardoned some men for their past crimes. The king's brother, Edward, has been martyred, and the king has brought Lady Ælfthryth back from exile and restored her to his favour.'

'Æthelred tries to wash away the guilt of dark deeds with martyrdoms and forgiveness?' asked Alfgar.

'I am afraid so. And promotes those who aid him down that path. Those who advise against it find themselves...' Nothhelm gestured at his homespun robe and meagre quarters.

'So you will not be archbishop?' asked Beornoth.

'I think my chance at high office has passed me by. It is a

relief, in many ways. I devote myself now to prayer and the service of the Lord.'

'Ælfthryth killed King Edward to put Æthelred on the throne. We all know it. No amount of repentance can change that. She wanted Byrhtnoth dead and tried to kill me. Returning her to Winchester is not the pathway to heaven,' said Beornoth.

Nothhelm flinched at that truth. 'We do not know who was behind King Edward's murder.'

'They killed him on her lands, and her son became king. She ruled for ten years until he came of age.'

'Yes, yes. Even so, Beornoth. She is the king's mother and has returned to favour. There is little you and I can do about it. You are for Lundenwic, I hear?'

'Aye. To fight Forkbeard. Who are the Normans with Ælfthryth?'

'Ah. The brothers de Warenne are the sons of the man who slew King Edward. He fled to his kin in Normandy afterwards, and now his sons are back and in the queen mother's service.'

'Normans are just Danes who settled in north-west Frankia. They give succour and safe harbour to the very Viking fleets who attack our shores. How can the king bring such men into his trust?'

'I am afraid that's not the worst of it, Beo.' Nothhelm fussed at his rope belt and lifted the jug to offer his guests more ale.

'What is the worst of it?'

'The king's advisors have seen fit to recommend that the crown employ mercenaries to help fend off the Danes. Fight fire with fire, so to speak.'

'Mercenaries from where?' Beornoth felt the warm curdle of fear turn over his stomach.

'Northmen. Danes. Vikings. Five hundred of them, commanded by a man named Pallig Tokeson.'

'God save us,' said Alfgar, and made the sign of the cross over his chest. 'Danes in the king's service. Who allowed such a thing?'

'The king has advisors from within the Church. Men who supported the late Archbishop Sigeric. If our warriors cannot defeat the Danes, then we should use Danes to fight Danes. That is their logic. Pallig and his warriors will march with you to Lundenwic, Beo. They are men with which you will defend the city from Sweyn Forkbeard.' Nothhelm offered Beornoth an upside-down smile of understanding and Beornoth shuddered.

'I go to raise the fyrd of Cheshire,' said Alfgar. 'I wish you were coming with me, Beo. You will remain here alone, marching to battle with men we neither know nor trust.'

King Sweyn Forkbeard had come with ninety-four warships and six and a half thousand blood-hungry Viking warriors. They sailed for Lundenwic's crumbling Roman walls and Beornoth had to defend that ancient, wealthy city. But to do it, he must fight alongside mercenary Danes, Normans and allies of a wicked old queen who wanted him dead. *In it up to my bloody neck*, he thought, and went to retrieve his sword.

2

Beornoth reached Lundenwic on a bright day, entering its north-eastern gate beneath a sky the colour of a frozen lake. His cloak billowed behind him as he ducked beneath the gate's lintel, and Virtus' hooves clopped on the cobbled road. Beornoth wore his byrnie and carried a spear in his right hand. He wore his sword at his hip and an antler-hilted seax in a sheath at the small of his back.

'We have come from the king,' he said as a warrior took the reins of his warhorse. 'Who is in charge of the defences?'

'Aldhelm, the city thegn, lord,' said the man. He was a tall man in a leather breastplate, and he could not take his eyes from the green dragon on Beornoth's scabbard.

Robert de Warenne thundered in behind Beornoth on a white stallion. He wore a black cloak over his chain mail and snarled at the man who came to help with his horse. 'Ale and food,' he barked in his Frankish accent tinged with Norse.

Beornoth climbed down from Virtus and stroked the beast's nose. He pressed a small silver coin into the warrior's hand. 'Find her some clean hay and oats. Where can I find Aldhelm?'

'Yes, lord, thank you, lord. Aldhelm is on the river wall. Watching the Viking ships. Them that's with you, lord. Are they Danes?'

'Aye. But they're on our side.'

De Warenne jumped down from his horse and sucked in a large breath. 'This place stinks of shit and foul water,' he said. He was the same height as Beornoth, and few men were so tall. Pallig came through the gate alongside Odo de Warenne, followed by Pallig's five hundred Viking warriors. The Saxons at the gate made the sign of the cross to see Danes, men they knew only as enemies, inside their city. The Vikings rode to Lundenwic on horses provided at the crown's expense, and the sound of so many mounts clattering along the stone road sounded like a thunderstorm. Pallig's men wore their hair long and braided, many bore tattoos of ravens, wolves or eagles on their arms and faces, and all carried axes and shields. They spoke in Norse, laughing and joking as they dismounted, staring up at the Roman gateway and its neatly dressed stone.

'There must be plenty of whores in a place like this,' Pallig said in Norse with a wolfish grin. 'We should hump them free of charge whilst we defend the city.' The Vikings laughed and Beornoth stalked off towards the south wall. Pallig was a broad-faced man with a balding pate. He wore his remaining hair in two long plaits on either side of a face framed by a beard roughly trimmed into the shape of a shovel. He wore a byrnie patched in places with rings of dark metal, carried an axe at his belt and walked with an easy swagger. Beornoth had avoided Pallig and his men on the road. It had taken four days to ride from Winchester to Lundenwic, and Beornoth rode alone. He had camped alone and refused all offers of ale and food from the Danes or Normans. Robert de Warenne and his brother Odo had brought fifty of their own retainers, all armed with spears, shields and swords, and they spoke Norse just like the Danes. The Normans and the Danes had drunk, thrown knucklebones, wrestled, and had a merry time on the journey eastwards towards battle.

'Time to earn your silver,' Beornoth called in Norse to Pallig. Beornoth spoke Norse because he had grown up amongst the descendants of the Great Heathen Army which had attacked Northumbria a century ago. Those men had made peace with King Alfred and settled the Danelaw, leaving the north a melting pot of Saxons, Danes, Norsemen and Swedes. The Normans spoke Norse for the same reason. Vikings had settled in north-west Frankia and made their own kingdom two generations ago, and their royal court still spoke Norse, even though they had married into Frankia's noble families.

'Come on, lads, our grim leader has spoken.' Pallig and his warriors followed behind Robert and Odo de Warenne. Much to his mother's disgust, King Æthelred had pronounced that, as a king's thegn, Beornoth would lead the company and assume command of Lundenwic's defence. Lady Ælfthryth had pressed for her Norman champion to take command, but the king had thankfully refused.

'I am Huna, lord,' said a man with a face mottled with red spots. He was short with a mop of greasy chestnut hair. 'I'll bring you to the wall.'

'The Danes are here already?' asked Beornoth. He followed Huna through a snarl of alleys and narrow streets. Frightened faces peered at him from behind shutters and darkened doorways. 'Why have the people not left?'

'They have, lord. The old city was abandoned when the Rome folk left, lord. People only came back when King Alfred repaired the walls and turned the place into one of his burh fortresses. Some folk still won't live in the Roman walls. Old women tell the children stories that the ancient buildings are haunted, and the old stone buildings are hard to keep warm. The people you see here are scavengers, come to steal from the merchants' stores by the quays, and to loot the dead when the attack begins. Most of our people live in the new part of the city, outside the old fortifications. The traders, merchants, smiths, thatchers and potters who live in Lundenwic have taken refuge outside of the city. The Vikings arrived yesterday. They've already thrown up a few ladders and filled the river with their ships.'

'How many men do we have?'

'Five hundred warriors, and then the men of the fyrd, lord. Two thousand of 'em. Most never jabbed a spear or swung an axe. But we have the walls, lord. Twice as thick as a man is tall, and four times as high. The walls run across the northern bank of the river and old King Alfred built new wooden palisades and an earth bank for us to fight upon. We've kept it in good repair, lord. You'll see. The gates are all sturdy. Aldgate, Ludgate and Bishopsgate can hold until the end of days.'

Beornoth grunted. He stared around him at the old stone patched here and there with wattle and daub, a mix of timber strips, mud and straw. Grey thatch covered one roof, and red cracked tiles on another.

'Have they got past the bridge?' Beornoth had been to Lundenwic before, and had seen the wooden bridge first constructed by the Romans, which men had repaired and kept in place to aid trade and traffic between the north and south shores. Its foundations rested upon natural embankments of sand, gravel and clay. The northern shore lay upon higher ground, and at low tide that part of the river was said to be fordable, though Beornoth had never seen the wide river so low.

'No, lord, she holds firm. Aldhelm thinks their ships are anchored before the city and that they intend to scale the walls.'

They reached the foot of the high rampart, and Beornoth laid a hand upon the cold stone. Above him, spearmen hurried about upon the fighting platform. Shouting filled the city and Huna led Beornoth into the base of a wooden tower which began at the foot of the walls and stretched higher than the rampart. A dozen such towers stretched across the length of the defences Beornoth looked left and right and saw bowmen leaning from the heights, peering at the enemy in the river beyond their defences.

Beornoth's boots banged on wooden stairs like hammers. He moved carefully so that the heavy shield slung across his back did not hit the tower's narrow walls. Beornoth took his helmet from where it hung on his belt and pushed it onto his head. The leather liner was warm and cushioned over his hair, and as the full-faced helmet pressed down over his face, the stink of old leather and iron filled his nose. It was a magnificent piece of armour, with a boar-shaped nasal and a long black horsehair plume hanging from its top. Robert, Odo and Pallig followed Beornoth into the tower and the sound of their feet banging thrummed inside Beornoth's helmet.

A gust of cold air hit Beornoth as he emerged from the tower. A wall of horns and war drums sailed up across the walls from the wide River Thames and took Beornoth's breath away. The noise was deafening, like the crunching, crashing, all-consuming joining of battle. Shouting, the clang of iron, the hammer of wood on wood all came together to make a roar like the sound of a bear charging from its cave. Beornoth stared down at ninety-four dragon-prowed warships covering the water from its south-eastern bend to the straits leading up to the long wooden bridge. The tide was in ebb, leaving the Viking fleet wallowing in shallows close to the wall. Most of their ships huddled in the central, deeper waters to keep their hulls free of the rock and debris which littered the riverbed. Warriors and common folk filled the walls, leaning upon the ramparts to stare down at their hated Viking enemies. An arrow sailed over the wall and thumped into the tower a foot above Beornoth's head.

'You there!' Huna grabbed the arm of a boy carrying a sheaf of arrows. 'Where is Lord Aldhelm?' The boy stared up at Beornoth and swallowed hard. He pointed a trembling finger to where a group of warriors peered over the wall at the Vikings.

Huna led Beornoth, Robert, Oda and Pallig to where the commanding thegn scratched at his beard, pointing down as the Vikings rowed their ships into a line directly below the Roman wall.

'Lord Aldhelm,' Huna said.

'Not now,' barked the thegn.

'But, lord...'

'I said not now.'

The men about Aldhelm turned and looked up into Beornoth's helmeted face. He was taller than each of them by a full head, and despite his grey beard he was still broader across the chest and shoulder than any other man upon the wall. Aldhelm sensed the uncomfortable silence around him, a blanket of quiet above the din of six and a half thousand Vikings in the river below. He turned slowly and stared directly up into Beornoth's eyes, dark eyes hidden in the shadows of his helmet. Aldhelm saw a monstrous warrior armed with sword and spear, with an iron-bossed shield slung across his back. He saw the king's dragon upon Beornoth's scabbard, a shining byrnie coat of mail, and a warrior to fear.

'I am Beornoth. King's thegn. Come to take command of the city defences by order of King Æthelred.'

Aldhelm ground his teeth and glanced at Robert de Warenne and Pallig Tokeson. 'Then you are welcome, Beornoth. I have heard of you. You keep strange company.' He was a heavyset man with blue eyes so sunken and ringed with dark circles that it gave his face a skull-like appearance.

'We have five hundred Danes with us, men taken into the king's service. Your man tells me you have a similar number of warriors, and two thousand fyrd men?'

'Aye, we do. The five hundred are my garrison plus warriors taken from every thegn and reeve in the shire. We called the fyrd four weeks ago when the first of Forkbeard's ships arrived. They've eaten over half our food stores already.'

'The farmers and churls of the fyrd won't stop Forkbeard's Danes from breaching the walls. But we can put them to other uses.' Beornoth leaned over the wall and stared down as a dozen ships waddled in the shallows as close to the riverbank as their hulls allowed. Three ladders wobbled from ships' decks and came to rest against the Roman stone, and every other enemy ship's crew fumbled with ladders of their own. 'They're going to attack during the ebb tide. When the river floods, they won't be able to keep the ships steady enough to assault the walls. How long until the tide changes?'

'I don't know.' Aldhelm shrugged, and looked to his warriors for support but found only blank faces.

'Find someone who does. That's how long we need to hold out until the men can rest. What missiles have you assembled up here?'

'All the arrows and spears we could muster. Some rubble.'

'Scour the city and bring up all the pots and cauldrons you

can find. We'll heat river water, well water, or whatever you can carry up here. Heat it to boiling and we'll throw it on the Danes as they climb the wall. Are there any shipyards in the city?'

'Yes, beyond the bridge to the west.'

'Good. Bring up all the caulking tar you can find. We'll melt the skin of the bastards' faces.'

The men of the Lundenwic fyrd grinned. They had shuffled slightly closer to Beornoth as he spoke, their eyes widening.

'Forkbeard is a savage warrior, and cunning. I've fought him before. At Maldon. He has six thousand warriors, and he outnumbers our warriors six to one. But he has to climb these walls to enter the city, or break down our gates. He won't breach these walls whilst I breathe. Are you ready to fight?'

The men gulped and exchanged nervous glances.

'I said, are you ready to fight? If Forkbeard enters this city, his men will rape every woman and sell every child into slavery. All that stands between your families and that fate is your courage and your blades. So I ask you again. Are you ready to fight?'

'Fight! Fight! Fight!' The warriors on the walls roared as one. Even Aldhelm drew his sword and held it aloft.

'Then let's see you do it. Aldhelm, take one hundred men and hold the river gate. Pallig. Bring up your men. It's time for them to earn their silver.'

Pallig grinned wolfishly. 'A fine speech. Short, just how I like them. Odin watches us, Beornoth. I can feel his eye upon me.' He strode towards the tower and drew his axe from a leather loop at his belt.

'Sorry, my lord,' said Huna, standing at Beornoth's elbow. 'I didn't want to interrupt. But I have an idea.'

'Out with it then, the Danes are coming,' said Beornoth.

Raucous shouting and cheering from the river below thundered around the city. He glanced over the parapet. More ladders rested against the walls and others wavered as Vikings struggled to lower them from the decks of their ships towards the high ramparts. War horns blew and Forkbeard's army roared their defiance at the defenders.

'Piss, lord.'

'What?'

'Piss, lord. Lots of it.'

'Do it away from the walls, man. The fight is upon us.'

'No, lord.' Hunna dragged a trembling hand down his beard. 'There are a half a dozen tanneries in the city. They use piss to tan the leather. If we bring the vats up here, we can boil it and throw it on the bastards.'

'Good. Take fifty men and see to it.'

'Here they come!' called a warrior further along the line.

Horns blared from Forkbeard's vast fleet, and Viking war drums began their deep, foreboding music.

Boom, boom, boom ba boom. Boom, boom, boom ba boom.

Six thousand Danes roared their malice and their bloodlust, and Beornoth swallowed down the burn of fear in his guts. He wrapped his hand around the leather-bound hilt of his sword and dragged the blade free of its fleece-lined scabbard. He slipped the shield off his back and passed his left hand through the leather strap, and grabbed the wooden grip inside the bowl of its iron boss. The tips were missing from three of the fingers on that hand, but it did not stop him from holding the shield tightly. The shield was heavy, linden-wood boards riveted to an iron boss and edged with an iron rim. Leather painted with the king's dragon sigil covered Beornoth's shield, and men stared at him in his war finery. Most of the soldiers on the wall wore leather breastplates or padded wool tunics. They carried spears, axes, seaxes or long knives. Some, like Aldhelm, wore byrnies, carried swords and wore bright helmets. But Beornoth came to battle like a lord of war and he let the men see him. He stalked amongst them so that the defenders could see that a king's champion stood with them, ready to fight and die to defend their city and families.

Beornoth rolled his shoulders and raised his weapons high in front of him twice to prepare himself. He pushed his tongue through the gap in his teeth where an arrow had once ripped through his face. Beornoth's chest rose and fell beneath the iron links of his byrnie and he brought forth dark memories, the blood and carnage of a lifetime fighting Viking raiders. He remembered his dead children and the pain his wife had suffered at Viking hands. Beornoth recalled his friends, slaughtered by Forkbeard and Olaf Tryggvason's warriors at Maldon. So much pain, so much suffering. That pain now became Beornoth's ally, flooding his ageing limbs with strength. Pain turned to hate, and it broiled within his monstrous frame and became rage.

'A rousing speech,' said Robert de Warenne. 'You barely spoke on the road. I had you pegged as a quiet man.'

'Shut up and draw your sword,' Beornoth spat. The time for words had passed. Six thousand Danes came with ladders, axes, spears, swords and bloodlust. Beornoth waited for them, and he was a being of violence and strength. He was the Dane-killer, the man who had killed Viking champions in single combat. 'Let's see how you Norman bastards fight.'

Robert de Warenne scowled at Beornoth's harshness, but he drew his sword and made ready. His brother, Odo, joined him. Two men with shaved skulls and bright swords. Pallig and his Danes streamed from the tower's stairway. The Saxons on the walls crossed themselves, confused to see Vikings ready to fight alongside them. Pallig roared at his men in Norse, and they let out a wild cry in response.

'Bring up braziers,' Beornoth said, grabbing a warrior by the arm. 'Find the men with the water, the tar and the piss and get them up here. Now!' The warrior nodded so vigorously that his pot-shaped helm slipped off his head.

A clash of iron to Beornoth's left caught his attention. Danes swarmed up the ladders and hacked at the men atop the walls.

'Archers!' Beornoth roared and waved his sword. Fifty bowmen stepped forwards, sidling between the warriors. Each man took a goose-feathered arrow from the cloth quiver hanging from his belt and nocked shaft to bowstring. 'Draw!' The archers stretched their yew war bows until the string reached their ears. 'Loose!'

Arrows shot low and fast, whooshing over the parapet to slam into the climbing Danes. Men fell from the ladders, dragging others behind them to splash into the river or smash onto the decks of their ships. The city defenders howled with delight to see so many of their enemies die.

'Loose at will,' Beornoth ordered. 'Use your arrows wisely. Aim for the men at the top of the ladders. If you see Viking captains aboard their ships giving orders, kill them.'

'Arrow flight,' a voice called along the wall. For a moment, the sky turned to shadow. Beornoth raised his shield just in time to catch three arrows. The missiles hammered into the linden-wood boards, jarring up Beornoth's arm. Men screamed in pain with arrows jutting from shoulders, chests and necks. One of Pallig's men lay twitching with an arrow in his eye. Beornoth cut the arrows from his shield with his sword and laid his weapons down. He bent and lifted Pallig's dead warrior bodily from the timber fighting platform and hurled him over the side. Men gaped as the corpse sailed through the air, smashed through a ladder and thumped onto a ship's deck below, crushing two men beneath it.

The war drums continued their relentless thunder. *Boom, boom, boom ba boom. Boom, boom.* The battle for Lundenwic had begun.

3

A snarling face appeared over the parapet, blue-eyed and framed with braided blond hair. The Dane reached a meaty hand over the wall to haul himself up and onto the walls of Lundenwic. He opened his mouth to shout his war-fury at the Saxons and died with Beornoth's sword in his maw. Beornoth ripped the blade free, sending teeth and blood splashing onto the walls. The Dane swayed at the top of his ladder and Beornoth kicked him in his dying face, sending the man flying backwards to tumble onto the ship below.

A man of the fyrd on the wall vomited. Beornoth turned to him and snarled, just as another fyrd man pissed his trews. They were farmers and woodsmen, unaccustomed to the horror of battle.

'If you can't fight, get back from the walls,' Beornoth growled at them, his sword held before him dripping gore on their boots.

The Danes attacked Lundenwic's walls for hours and the defenders held them at bay. No Viking made it over the walls, but more than a hundred of the defenders died as the climbing Vikings hacked at the men on the summit with axes and stabbed at them with spears. Beornoth's shoulders ached from the effort of killing so many of Forkbeard's men. He had cut and slashed and hacked with his sword at every head, hand and arm which appeared over the wall. He had pushed ladders away only to see them replaced again, and so the battle raged on.

'They still attack,' gasped Robert de Warenne, his face wet with sweat. He had lost his helmet in the battle and his broad face was spattered with the blood of his enemies. His brother Odo rested with his back against the tower stairway, an arrow protruding from his shoulder, his face ashen.

Beornoth risked a glance over the wall and saw that Forkbeard had sent more of his ships towards the walls. They used their oars and seal-hide ropes to squeeze a long line of fifty warships together at the base of Lundenwic's walls. Aldhelm had brought a pinch-faced fisherman to the rampart who said the tide would flood before the sun went down.

A Danish warrior hooked his bearded axe into a defender's jerkin and hauled him over the wall. One of Pallig's men took his place and died as the axe flashed again and slashed through his throat. Robert de Warenne darted forward and stabbed down with his sword, killing the axeman with a well-timed thrust. De Warenne sidestepped and killed another Dane on the next ladder, and blood dripped from his sharp sword. Odo and Robert de Warenne fought well. Despite being Lady Ælfthryth's pets, Beornoth fought beside them, protecting their flank as they protected his. They were stout warriors and had both taken wounds in the fighting.

'Time for the boiling oil and water,' Beornoth said. The Vikings were attacking the wall in as great a number as they could from the river, so there would never be a better time to hurt them. 'See to it.'

Robert de Warenne grinned and dashed towards the fires

where men heated dozens of cauldrons along the length of the wall. Forkbeard massed his men for one huge assault before the tide forced his ships away from the walls. Hold that attack and the city was safe for the night. The drums beat continuously and horns blared anew. A great roar erupted from the river as more ladders clattered against the walls as thousands of Vikings began their climb to death or glory.

Beornoth slammed the boss of his shield into a Dane's face as it appeared over the wall. A spear jabbed at him and he batted it away with his shield, and killed the Viking spearman with a sweep of his sword. The part of the wall where Beornoth fought was slick with dark blood. Blood of both attackers and defenders pooled sticky and foul on the timber palisade sat above repaired Roman stone. Above them, the wooden tower gave archers the chance to loose their arrows at the attackers and sweep them from the ladders.

'Ready,' said de Warenne.

'Wait,' said Beornoth. He watched as the Danes swarmed up their ladders like insects. The sun glinted off their weapons and their hungry, fearful faces peered up at the defenders. They were men who had left their cold northern homes to brave the wild seas and bring their weapons and their malice to King Æthelred's kingdom. Forkbeard and his warriors were men of daring and courage, men who would stop at nothing in their quest for wealth and reputation. So hungry were they for glory, women and wealth that they would climb from their *drakkar* warships on makeshift ladders and attack one of England's greatest cities. They knew the defenders had the easier task, that they must hack at defenders whilst they balanced at the top of rickety ladders lashed together with hemp rope, whilst the defenders cut at them from above on firm footing. They came for death, rape and silver, and now they would die.

Beornoth waited until the ladders were thick with enemy warriors, until he could see no stone beneath their climbing bodies clad in leather, wool and iron.

'Now. Burn the bastards.'

Robert de Warenne repeated the order and Pallig's men hefted the heavy, steaming cauldrons towards the edge of the palisade. The contents slopped onto the fighting platform and Pallig's men groaned as they heaved and turned the cauldrons over. Boiling water, tar and piss poured from high walls to wash over the climbing Danes. Their screams made even Beornoth wince. High-pitched shrieks like foxes crying out in the night. The Vikings fell, clutching at burning faces and chests, and the decks of Forkbeard's ships writhed with bodies and steamed like slaughterhouse blocks. Still, the Danes came on and Forkbeard himself urged his men onto the ladders soaked with water and tar.

'There he is,' Beornoth called. 'Have the archers loose whatever shafts they have left at that man!' Beornoth pointed his sword down towards Forkbeard on board the largest longship, floating calmly on the River Thames. It was a beautiful ship, dragon-prowed with at least sixty oars, and in her bow stood a man of middling height with a round face. He wore a golden torc around his neck and waved a shining war axe around his head as he urged his men to make another deadly climb. Forkbeard. King, ruthless warlord and master of deep cunning.

Arrows flew from the towers and walls, but the supply was low, so only a dozen white-feathered shafts raced towards the king of the Danes. On the king's longship a big warrior with a bald head hefted his shield and caught any arrows which came close to his king, and Forkbeard snarled up at the walls. Beornoth pulled off his helmet so that Forkbeard could see him. The king glowered at the defenders and then his clever eyes rested upon Beornoth, and a smile of recognition played upon his cruel mouth. Beornoth pointed his bloody sword at the king and waved at him, goading the enemy king to make the treacherous climb himself. Forkbeard raised his hand in salute, and clasped a fist to his chest, banging on the huge silver and gold cross he wore around his neck.

Beornoth closed his eyes and remembered Forkbeard coming from the sea at Maldon. He had come dripping with water and fought like a demon, and the memory of Beornoth's dead friends made him shudder. Fresh warriors replaced the screaming, burned men. Unbloodied Danes, howling and ready to make a renewed attack upon Lundenwic's walls. Beornoth met them, cutting at the faces and hands of any who reached the parapet. Robert de Warenne hurled a gigantic piece of masonry from the walls, and its weight crashed into the deck of a Viking warship and sent its crew into a panic as water rushed in through the gaping hole.

Men cried out to Beornoth's right. He peered over the spears and moving heads of the defenders and set his jaw.

'Robert, Pallig,' Beornoth called. 'With me.' He pushed his helmet back on top of his sweat-soaked hair and strode towards the wall's northern edge. Axes flashed there, men died and blood flowed. Danes had breached the wall and a dozen of them fought with their axes and their fury to drive the defenders back. They fought above the bridge gate, and if those men could clear that section of wall, more Danes would pour up ladders and flock into the gap like ravens on a corpse. From there, they could attack the defenders of the gate. If the gate fell, the city would be lost. So Beornoth hefted his shield and charged.

The defenders in front of him moved out of his way, and Beornoth ran with his shield held before him. The Vikings saw him and shook their axes, roaring and bellowing with wide-eyed fury. Beornoth crashed into them at full charge. No pity, nothing held back. His shield hammered into the first three Danes with all the weight of his monstrous frame behind it, and they fell back like reeds blown over by a storm. Beornoth lifted his shield and brought the rim down on the shin of a fallen Dane and his leg broke like a chicken bone. He lifted the shield and brought the iron rim down again, and crushed the throat of another enemy. An axe thudded into his shield as a scarred-faced Viking snarled and spat at Beornoth, cursing in Norse.

'Saxon whore!' he roared. 'Die, you stinking piece of goat turd!'

Beornoth stabbed his sword beneath the rim of his shield and opened the man's groin. The Viking's face sagged and Beornoth sawed the blade back and forth until the man fell clutching at the terrible wound, his lifeblood gushing out to soak the fighting platform with dark blood. Three of the enemy charged at Beornoth and the first of them died with Robert de Warenne's sword in his belly. Beornoth beat them back, but more Danes pressed him. They drove their shoulders into his shield, shoving at him, hacking with their axes. A blade struck his helmet, and another sliced across his forearm. Pallig and his men pushed Beornoth and Robert de Warenne from behind so that the fight for that section of wall became like a small shield-wall battle.

A spear point stabbed at his face and Beornoth twisted away. A Dane raked his boot down Beornoth's instep and a knife stabbed around the edge of his shield, poking its sharp tip at his ribs, but the rings of his byrnie held. Beornoth tried to lift his sword, but the press of men held it fast. He released his grip on the sword and instead reached around to the small of his back and whipped his antler-hilted seax from its sheath. It was a wicked weapon, broken-backed, single-edged and as long as a man's forearm. He slashed the seax across the eyes of the closest Dane and drove the point upward into the soft flesh beneath the next man's chin. The pressure upon Beornoth's shield relented, and he set about the enemy like a demon from hell. He cut at them, smashed them with his shield. Beornoth kicked and bit and howled like a madman until the enemy fell back from his fury.

Beornoth sagged to one knee, exhaustion suddenly reminding his body how old he was. His limbs ached and his muscles burned. His breath came in ragged gasps and every joint, tendon and fibre in his body screamed at him to rest. Bodies littered the battlements, dead Danes and dead Saxons. One of Pallig's men rocked back and forth, holding in the purple coils of his own entrails. A Lundenwic warrior clutched at his half-severed leg. The iron stink of blood mixed with the rank stench of men who had voided their bowels as they died. Such sights were as familiar to Beornoth as the sunrise, but he had never heard a bard sing of those horrors. Young men dreamed of bright swords, glory and brave deeds, but the blood-soaked carnage atop Lundenwic's rampart was the true face of war.

'They are falling back!' came a shout from behind. Beornoth forced himself to rise. Forkbeard's ladders withdrew from the walls and his ships backed oars. The tide was in flood. It was over for the day. Beornoth slid his seax back into its sheath and picked up his sword. He had a dented shield, stuck with arrows, and the iron rim warped and twisted. His hands shook from the effort of battle, and Beornoth could barely move his muscles were so tired.

'Well done, king's thegn,' said Robert de Warenne. He clapped Beornoth on the shoulder and went to find his injured brother.

'We live to fight another day, eh?' said Pallig.

'We do,' Beornoth replied.

'I had heard you spoke our tongue, and you speak Norse like a Viking.'

'Heard from who?'

'From King Sweyn himself. Forkbeard is my brother-in-law.'

'You are married to Forkbeard's sister, Gunhilde?' Beornoth's jaw fell open as he stared incredulously at the Viking mercenary.

Pallig shrugged. 'That is what brother-in-law means. No?'

'Yet you fight against him?'

'I do. I fight wherever I can earn silver. Your king pays me. So I fight for him. Forkbeard cares not who I fight for. I am a jarl, and my wife is much younger than her brother. My mother, Frigg protect her soul, proposed the marriage and King Sweyn accepted. His father, old king Harald being dead by then. My father and uncles are powerful men at home. I think Forkbeard was glad to be rid of the girl, to be honest. She has a pretty face and broad hips, and I think myself a lucky man to be married to a princess, and daughter of the great Harald Bluetooth.' Pallig shrugged as if it were the simplest thing in all the world. That simplicity was at the heart of Beornoth's feelings for the Danes. He both hated and loved them. He hated their cruelty and the violence they had brought to his life, but he loved how they lived. In their world, a man succeeded or failed by the strength of his arm. Men would fight for a good leader, and desert a weak man. Only the strong ruled, for the warriors, the *drengr*, would slay a weak man. Even if that man was the son of a king. A fight to the death could settle any dispute, and their gods had no churches and no priests. Beornoth had found solace in God in his later years, after a long time of hating him for the deaths of his daughters, though he had little love for the Church and its power. The word of God had found its way to Sweyn Forkbeard's court. Both he and his father Harald Bluetooth worshiped God and Jesus. 'You see that big bastard down there?' Pallig pointed his axe to a black-painted ship on which stood a man, head and shoulders larger than any other on his *drakkar*.

'I see him.'

'That is Thorkell the Tall. He worships the old gods, like me. I saw him once before, at a feast in Jutland. A great champion, perhaps champion of all the northmen. He leads the Jomsvikings. I believe you know of the Jomsvikings?'

'I know them. I killed their leader Palnatoki, the man who was as a father to Olaf Tryggvason.' Beornoth remembered that grim fight, and how the old boar had died on the end of Beornoth's blade. The Jomsvikings were a band of warriors for hire. Their home was a fortress at a place called Jomsburg. They lived for battle. They allowed no women inside their fortress, and people feared them worldwide for their skill and ferocity.

'I heard the tale. Men in our lands call you Beornoth Reiði. The wrathful. You have killed many famous warriors. Skarde Wartooth, Palnatoki. I even heard that you and Forkbeard once played a game of riddles. You have reputation, but I must admit that you are much older than I expected.' Pallig winked mischievously.

'You hear a lot, Dane. Tell me more about Thorkell?'

Pallig laughed. 'I keep my ears open. Thorkell comes to make his legend. Be careful of him, Saxon. Come. The fighting is over. We must find some ale and some food. You will need your strength again tomorrow, I think.'

Beornoth staggered from the walls and down into the town. The men of the fyrd gathered in the streets and lanes behind the walls, and they moved out of the way as Beornoth and Pallig trudged wearily by. Blood spattered their bodies, and they looked wounded and grim, like wraiths from a nightmare. Pallig ordered one of his captains to fetch someone to tend their wounds and bring ale, bread and meat. They found an empty house and sat on two benches on either side of a wooden table. Pallig's man came back as Beornoth cleaned his sword on a scrap of cloth and the Dane poured ale and laid down a loaf of dark bread, a fistful of cheese and some dried fish.

'It's the best I could find,' the man said. Pallig broke off a chunk of bread and a piece of cheese and handed them to the young warrior, who grinned from ear to ear. He left the room, striding with his head held high. A good leader of men understands that such gestures bind men to him. They steel men's hearts and make them stand firm in the line of battle when their lord commands it. Men will fight fiercely for a commander they love, and will flee more readily from battle if led by a man they loathe. Beornoth had loved the dead Ealdorman Byrhtnoth, the greatest leader of men Beornoth had ever known.

'So, Saxon,' Pallig said, talking around a mouthful of bread. He paused and raised a thick finger, swilled a mouthful of ale, swallowed so hard he squirmed on his stool and then sighed with relief. 'My men fight well, no?'

'They fought well,' Beornoth allowed. Many had died, and Pallig's warriors had fought just as hard as the Saxons who defended their homes and families.

'You are from the north? The Danelaw?'

'I am. Cheshire. I have a Norseman who is like a brother to me. Brand Thorkilsson is his name. He is a thegn to Ealdorman Thered of Northumbria.'

'You would make a good Viking, Beornoth Reiði.'

'Pass me the fish, and close your cheese pipe for a while.'

Pallig threw his head back and laughed at Beornoth's surliness. Beornoth was exhausted. He needed food, quiet and sleep before the fighting resumed when the tide changed. He cared little for what other men thought of him. They ate in silence for a while, drinking ale and examining their wounds. One of Pallig's men brought a bucket of heated water and some clean cloth, and the two men bathed their cuts and wiped the grime of battle from their faces, armour and clothes. Beornoth unstrapped his scabbard and sword and laid them down on his shield.

'Here you are!' boomed a voice in Norse as the door burst open. Beornoth's shoulders sagged when he realised it was Robert de Warenne and his brother Odo. 'I have found some wine in this shithole. Wonderful wine from Frankia.'

'My Norman friends,' said Pallig warmly. 'Come, share your wine and we shall share our meal.'

Beornoth ignored the Normans and ate a mouthful of cheese. Pallig and the brothers talked and relived the day's fighting. Odo's arm was bound to his chest within a woollen shawl and he told Pallig how a priest had cut the arrow from his shoulder and sealed the wound closed with a red-hot iron. Beornoth listened to the men boasting for a while, finished his ale, and stood.

'It's still early,' said Pallig. 'Where are you going?'

'To sleep,' Beornoth said. He picked up his sword and shield. 'We have set watches for the night and men know to wake me if the Danes attack during the night. But we are safe until the tide changes. You should all get some sleep.'

'A fine blade,' said Odo de Warenne. 'A gift from the king, no less.'

Beornoth ignored him and stepped around the table.

'Are you trying to insult us?' said Robert de Warenne as he took a sip of wine from a clay jug. 'Is it because we are not Saxons that you dislike us so?'

'You fought well today. That is enough. We don't need to be

friends,' said Beornoth. He kept walking towards the door, hoping to find a quiet room somewhere to lie down and rest.

'My Lady Ælfthryth warned me about you, Beornoth.'

Beornoth stopped. 'I'm surprised she didn't ask you to put in a knife in my back whilst I sleep.'

'We are proud to serve Lady Ælfthryth. You should speak better of her in our presence.'

Beornoth turned slowly to face the Norman brothers. 'Your lady once tried to have me killed. I speak as I find.'

'The lady has nothing but the interests of king and realm in her heart. She is a godly woman, and my brother and I shall be forever in her debt for bringing us home.'

'Home?'

'After King Edward's death, they exiled our father and took our lands for the crown. Lady Ælfthryth will return our lands to us, although our father is dead and cannot see justice done.'

'Your father was a king slayer, and your mother a Norman.'

Robert de Warenne rose slowly and placed his hand on the hilt of his sword. 'Careful.'

'By some craft of the devil, Ælfthryth has returned to the king's favour and brought you two sons of an assassin home to do her bidding. I know you, and I know her. If you touch your hilt to me again, I'll kill you both.' Beornoth didn't wait for an answer. He stalked out into the night to find somewhere to lay his weary bones.

4

The tide changed before the sun came up. Beornoth woke stiffly to the sound of blaring war horns and the beat of Forkbeard's drums. He had slept on a bed of old straw in an abandoned house close to the walls. He stretched his back and kneaded the knots and cramps from his thighs, arms and shoulders. Beornoth winced at the soreness in his muscles as he pulled his byrnie over his head. The cut on his forearm had stopped bleeding, and he left the cloth bandage in place. He collected his sword, seax, shield and helmet and ducked beneath the low door lintel and strode out into a morning hazed by drizzling rain. It dripped from grey thatch to make puddles between the cobblestones, and Beornoth drew his cloak closer about him.

Pallid yellow sunlight tried to light the cauldron-grey sky and men came from their beds coughing and yawning. Captains barked orders, the nightwatchmen retired to rest and men hurried to their posts clutching spears, bows, axes, whilst the less fortunate men of the fyrd carried clubs, scythes, hammers and shovels. Beornoth found Aldhelm on the wall, staring down at Forkbeard's ships. The *drakkars* turned slowly in the flooding river, their oars splashing in the brown water as shipmasters tried to avoid hulls clashing or oars fouling.

'Bastards know their business,' said Beornoth, admiring the seamanship and skill to bring ninety-four warships to order within the bend of the River Thames.

'Can we stand against another attack?' Aldhelm's face was swollen, with a purple and blue welt discolouring the left side.

'We must. Ready the men. How many arrows have we left?'

'Precious few, lord.'

'Then bring up as many spears as you can find. If we have used up all the tar, piss and water we can get our hands on, then demolish some inner walls and have the fyrd men carry the rubble up here. Forkbeard cannot afford another day like yesterday. He lost too many men. His jarls will be restless. They sailed from their northern homes for plunder and women, not to die with boiled piss poured on their heads. Give them enough of a beating today, and Forkbeard might just sail away in search of easier prey.'

'Yes, lord. Me and my men are fresher than those who fought up here beside you yesterday. I'll send those men to hold the gate, and I shall fight on the walls with you.'

'Good.' Beornoth stuck out his hand and took Aldhelm's wrist in the warrior's grip. 'Then let's kill some Danes.'

Aldhelm hurried away, bellowing orders at his men. The walls turned into a kicked beehive. Warriors ran to their posts with armfuls of spears, bleary eyes and nervous faces. Some bore wounds from the previous day's fighting. Boys scrubbed the fighting platform free of blood, and one handed Beornoth a skin of ale which he took with a nod of thanks.

'I've never been fond of early mornings,' said Pallig, appearing at the top of a set of stone steps. He yawned so loudly that every man on that section of wall turned to look. He farted just as loud, and the boys on the wall sniggered. 'Better get these lads off the battlements. Looks like Forkbeard means to attack again.'

'Where are your men?'

'Coming, they gather in a courtyard, yonder. They'll be up here before the ladders come. Don't worry. Our Norman friends have taken a bit of a disliking to you.'

'They don't need to like me. They just need to fight.'

'That's what I love about you, Beornoth Reiði.'

'What?'

'Nothing.' Pallig laughed at his own jest and then leaned on the palisade to peer down at Forkbeard's ships. 'Wait a moment...'

'Lord Beornoth!' came a shout from along the wall. 'Lord Beornoth!' A young warrior with a red face and a spear in his hand came running along the fighting platform, gesturing wildly towards the river.

'What is it, lad?' asked Beornoth.

'Lord Aldhelm says you must come to the bridge. The Danes do not attack the walls. They are massing upon the bridge.'

Beornoth cursed under his breath. 'Pallig, get your men and follow me to the bridge. The rest of your Lundenwic warriors stay here in case the bridge attack is a feint.'

He marched to the bridge gate and found Aldhelm there amongst a press of warriors. Beornoth shouldered his way through the throng. Men huddled together in a narrow street with two-storey stone buildings on either side. They tried to shift out of Beornoth's way, edging backwards into their fellows, staring up into his scarred face as he towered over them. The shield on his back banged into the warriors on either side of him, but Beornoth pressed forward through the stink of their leather armour, the rank foulness of their breath and sweat.

'Forkbeard himself is on the bridge,' said Aldhelm, peering through a shutter. The gate was constructed from stout planks of oak reinforced with iron nails and strips. They called it Bridge Gate, and it controlled the flow of people and goods entering Lundenwic. A gatehouse rose higher than the surrounding walls and Beornoth glanced up to see half a dozen spearmen in the tower and more lining the walls. Aldhelm moved aside and Beornoth peered through the shutter. Forkbeard stood with his arms folded, hair and beard dripping wet with rain. Thorkell the Tall stood beside him with a double-bladed war axe turned upside down so that he could rest his forearms upon the haft. Hundreds of Danes clambered from the ships up the bridge's sides to form up behind their king like swarming rats.

'He wants to talk,' said Beornoth wearily.

'Talk about what?'

'They always want to talk before a fight. Make threats. Exchange insults.'

'What fun is a battle if you don't get to call the enemy leader a whoreson to his face?' said Pallig, who had arrived with his men.

'What do we do?' asked Aldhelm.

'I'll talk to him,' Beornoth replied. 'Open the gate.'

'But what if he kills you?'

Beornoth frowned at the thegn and Aldhelm nodded his understanding. Men pulled the heavy door open, creaking on its iron hinges. Beornoth stepped out onto the bridge where a brisk wind from the wide river whipped the drizzling rain about his face. He marched towards the king of the Danes and tossed his cloak over his shoulders to stop the wind blowing it about his legs. A smile played at the corner of Forkbeard's cruel slash of a mouth, and when Beornoth drew close, his round face stretched into a wolfish grin.

'Beornoth Reiði,' he said, raising a hand in greeting. Silver arm rings clinked as they shifted upon his wrists and the crucifix upon his chest glittered.

'King Sweyn,' Beornoth replied.

'Open the gate. I'll give your people until noon to flee, then I'll march my men inside the city.'

'The gate stays closed.'

'And you'll defend it with your life?'

'I'll defend it. Like I did the walls yesterday.'

'We could settle this with a riddle, like we did before our last fight.'

'No riddles today. Just steel. Take your ships and sail away. I hear that there is good raiding in Frankia this year.'

Forkbeard laughed and turned to Thorkell the Tall. 'This is the famous Beornoth the Wrathful. I killed his lord and his men when Olaf and I took ten thousand pounds of silver from their king.'

'You killed Palnatoki?' said Thorkell in a deep, slow voice. He was taller even than Beornoth, with long, lank hair that hung about his face like seaweed from a rock.

'I killed him. If you attack today, I'll try to kill you too.'

Thorkell made a growling sound deep within his throat, and his right eye twitched. 'I'll fight you here. Now. On the bridge. Saxon son of a whore.'

'Your giant has rocks in his head,' Beornoth said, looking at Forkbeard instead of Thorkell. 'He's slow-witted. Did his mother drop him on his skull when he was a bairn? Or was she addled by the pox whilst he grew in her belly?'

Thorkell snarled and took a step forward until Forkbeard put a hand on the Jomsviking's brawny arm.

'Just open the gate,' said the king of Denmark.

'Come and open it yourself. You can use this one's thick head as a battering ram.'

'Bastard!' Thorkell shouted.

Forkbeard smiled and then glanced up at the churning sky. 'If you don't surrender the city, I'll let my men loose when we take the walls. I'll let my men kill, rape, burn and butcher their way through the streets until nothing is left alive.'

'If we surrender the city, you have a foothold in England. More Danes will flock to your banner when they hear of the victory. Before summer's end, another fifty ships will sail up the Thames to join your army. Men who smell the kill and come looking for land and wealth. They'll swear oaths to you, and you will try to make yourself king of the Saxons and of the Danes.'

'Your King Æthelred is a weak-minded fool. There is good land here. Your people should welcome a new king. A strong king.'

'Danes have dreamed of England since the days of Ragnar Lothbrok. Ivar, Ubba and Sigurd Snake-in-the-Eye came. Guthmund came. Olaf came. Now you have returned. You won't win. So tuck your tail between your legs and find a monastery to raid or some nuns to slaughter. There are warriors upon these walls, not unarmed priests. Attack again and more of you will die. Keep on attacking and you won't have enough men left to row your ninety-four ships home.'

'Did you see Byrhtnoth die?'

'I saw.' Beornoth stiffened, noting the gleam in Forkbeard's eye and determined not to let the king get under his skin.

'He was the last of your kingdom's noble warriors. All that remains now are lickspittles, nithings and cowards. I thought you had died that day at Maldon. You should have died beside your lord. You should have defended him with your life.'

'Yet here I am.' Beornoth slowly drew his sword. 'Keep your

teeth together. No more talking. Send your men to die. I'll soak this bridge with their blood.'

Beornoth turned and stalked towards the gate. A great war horn blew behind him and the Viking army erupted into roaring cheers. The gate slammed closed and Beornoth found Aldhelm, Pallig and Robert de Warenne waiting for him.

'How is my father-in-law?' asked Pallig cheerfully.

'He's going to attack. Ready the men.'

Beornoth ignored Robert de Warenne and climbed the stairs to take a place in the gatehouse. Thorkell the Tall stalked amongst his warriors who carried a great battering ram cut from the trunk of an oak tree, its fresh timber still golden in the sheeting rain. The Danes came on in a fury. Their ram hammered at the gate, whilst Beornoth, Aldhelm and the defenders hurled rubble down upon their heads. The fight at the gate was a bloody, desperate struggle. The Vikings hurled spears and loosed arrows at the gatehouse and palisade wall in a constant hail of death. Men tumbled from the defences or fell back, screaming with arrows and spears embedded in their bodies.

Robert de Warenne and a dozen warriors carried an enormous piece of masonry up onto the gatehouse, so large that it took them half of the morning to struggle up onto the battlements with its bulk. They tossed the rubble over the gatehouse and it smashed the ram into the bridge, sending slivers of wood in all directions and crushing three Danes beneath its weight. Thorkell roared in anger and threw his men forwards to resurrect the ruined oak trunk. But the defenders killed those men with spears and yet more blocks of rock and rubble thrown from above. Thorkell turned to retreat, and as an afterthought, he snatched a spear from one of his fellow Danes, turned and launched it at the gatehouse. The leaf-shaped blade raced in a low arc and crunched into Aldhelm's chest, sending the thegn spinning backwards. Beornoth caught him and lowered Aldhelm to the ground. Blood seeped from the wound and coughed from his mouth in dark bubbles. His eyes searched about him frantically, hands tearing at Beornoth and at the weapon embedded in his chest. Then he went still, staring at the heavens with dead, glassy eyes.

Beornoth set his jaw and grabbed his sword.

'They are retreating!' called Robert de Warenne from the palisade. Forkbeard's men were falling back to their ships, climbing from the bridge to slink back aboard their *drakkars*. No more horns blared and the war drums fell silent. Now it was the Saxons' turn to cheer wildly. They shook their spears and stamped their feet. Men embraced one another, some wept, and others sank to the ground with relief.

'Why does he break off the attack?' Robert de Warenne asked Pallig.

'It will cost Forkbeard too many men to take the city. Lundenwic would have made a fine prize, but he can find easier silver elsewhere. We have won a glorious victory. Time to get drunk, I think?'

'They can't get off the bridge quick enough,' Beornoth said. He strode down the steps and waved to the men gathered beneath the gatehouse to haul open the oaken doors.

'Quick enough for what?' Pallig asked, leaning over the gatehouse to stare down at Beornoth with raised eyebrows.

'To stop us from killing them as they flee.' Beornoth raised his sword aloft and gazed over the faces of the celebrating warriors who thronged the Bridge Gate street. 'Charge with me now, men. Strike a blow at the enemies who would have burned your city and enslaved your families. Kill them as they run. With me!'

The gate edged open, and Beornoth slid through the gap. He was so full of rage that he could not wait for the gate to fully open. He came out onto the bridge and clambered over the shattered ram. Beornoth unslung the shield from his back and broke into a run. He did not wait to see how many men followed him, but felt the thrum of their footsteps through the wooden bridge. The Vikings climbed onto their waiting ships, but scores were stuck on the bridge as they waited for their shipmates to climb down the vertical piers where their decks awaited. They called out in panic, pointing at Beornoth. Thorkell the Tall appeared amongst the throng, bellowing at the men in front to form a shield wall. Some ignored the order and leaped from the bridge down onto the ships; others, the braver warriors, hefted shields and prepared to meet the defenders' charge.

Beornoth crashed into them with full force. The weight of his shield drove the Danes backwards and he hacked at them with his sword. A Viking cried out in panic and died as Beornoth swung his sword with such strength that he cut the Viking's head from his shoulders. The enemy clamoured away from that terrible blow. Blood spurted from the corpse and Beornoth kicked it into the Danes. He stabbed his sword into a Viking's stomach and then hammered a man from his feet with his shield. A hundred Saxons charged into the Danes with vengeful fury and that fight upon Lundenwic Bridge turned into a slaughter. Beornoth pushed through the fighting, searching above the heads of the Vikings for Thorkell the Tall.

Thorkell was crouched at the edge of the bridge when Beornoth found him, about to make the climb down to his waiting ship. They locked eyes and Beornoth heaved himself through the press of men.

'You run from battle like a whipped dog,' Beornoth shouted at him and raised his bloody sword in challenge.

Thorkell snarled and climbed back onto the bridge. He snatched his double-bladed war axe from one of his men and came at Beornoth in a wild charge.

'Bastard!' Thorkell spat, and Beornoth caught a swing of that monstrous axe on his shield. The force of the blow was like nothing Beornoth had felt before. It drove the shield back into his body like a smith's hammer beating metal. Beornoth staggered backwards and swung his sword at Thorkell's legs, but the big man skipped away with a litheness belying his size. The axe came around in a wide sweep and Beornoth ducked beneath the blow.

Saxon warriors and Pallig's mercenaries hacked at the Vikings all around him, desperate to strike at the men who had come to take their lives. Beornoth stabbed his sword upwards, aiming to drive the point into Thorkell's throat, but he parried the strike with the haft of his axe and hooked its bearded blade over the rim of Beornoth's shield. Thorkell wrenched the shield with monstrous force, ripping it from Beornoth's grasp. Beornoth, dragged forward with his falling shield, stumbled and back-swung his sword. Thorkell blocked the blow with a ringing clang as metal strips inside his boot caught the blade.

'You are old and weak,' Thorkell said, eyes blazing and teeth bared. 'You fight like a toothless grandfather. Die now and let Palnatoki be avenged.' He laughed and the axe flashed out underhand. Beornoth just caught the attack with his sword blade. The sheer power behind those monstrous axe blades, curved like the shape of a butterfly's wing, banged the sword from Beornoth's hand. Everything moved slowly then. Beornoth's heart thumped at half of its normal rhythm. Men moved around him as though they were underwater. The sword fell to the bridge and Beornoth stared into Thorkell's triumphant eyes. The giant Jomsviking reached out and grabbed the neck of Beornoth's byrnie. He dragged Beornoth towards him and lifted his axe to slice open Beornoth's throat with its sharp edge. The world sped up again. The din of battle raged about them, shouting, cries of desperation, the clash of weapons. Death came for Beornoth on the edge of Thorkell's axe. The weapon was so well honed that all the giant had to do was slice it across Beornoth's throat. It would be as easy as cutting through roasted pork. Beornoth was not yet ready to die. Eawynn waited for him at home. There were more sunrises for them to share, more warm nights beside the fire. So Beornoth fought.

He grabbed the axe haft with his left hand, using all the old-man strength in his corded muscles. Beornoth pushed the axe away from his neck and Thorkell matched his power, so that they became locked in a test of strength. Beornoth drove his knee up into Thorkell's groin. The Dane groaned and bent at the waist. The axe moved further away and Beornoth drove two outstretched fingers into Thorkell's eyes. Thorkell howled in pain, dropped his axe and pulled away from Beornoth's savagery. Beornoth reached behind him and whipped his antler-hilted seax from its sheath. He slashed the blade across Thorkell's face, and all that stopped the weapon from blinding Thorkell was the big man's hands, which he had clamped over his poked eyes. The seax cut a bloody slice into Thorkell's cheek and across the back of his hands. Thorkell kicked Beornoth away from him, dropped his axe, and dashed to the edge of the bridge, where he jumped onto the deck of a waiting ship.

Beornoth dropped to his knees, sucking in huge gasps of air. Thorkell had come within a hair's breadth of killing him, as close as he had ever been to death, and he shook his head to clear the panic. He rose, retrieved his sword and shield, and watched as Thorkell's ship rowed away from the bridge to join the rest of Sweyn Forkbeard's retreating fleet. Thorkell stood amongst his warriors, towering over his Jomsvikings like an ogre. He pointed at Beornoth, and then at his own chest. Thorkell balled his fists and crossed his forearms, signalling Beornoth that their fight was not over. Beornoth hoped it was. His body screamed at him to rest, muscles burning and his old wounds throbbing. The Saxons on the bridge roared their victory, and the men defending the walls joined in. Robert de Warenne picked up Thorkell's mighty war axe and raised it above his head, shaking it as the defenders cheered wildly.

'The city has survived,' said Pallig. He stood beside Beornoth and watched the ships row away around a wide bend in the river. 'Thanks to you.'

'Thanks to all of us,' Beornoth replied. 'Lundenwic and its people are safe. But someone else will suffer. Forkbeard will find somewhere less well defended and those people will face his warriors' ire. This defeat will only stoke the flames of their wrath. I pity those people. We should follow the ships. Head them off.'

'We cannot ride as fast as that fleet can sail. Once they reach the Whale Road, they can go where they please. But you are right, there will be a reckoning. Thorkell the Tall won't forget you.'

'He should have killed me.'

'He nearly did.'

5

Beornoth returned to Winchester, riding alongside Pallig and doing his best to avoid Robert de Warenne and his brother. He enjoyed Pallig's company. The Viking was a warrior, brave and skilled, and his men loved him. Pallig led hard men, warriors who sailed to wherever in the world the fighting was most fierce and sold their blades to the highest bidder. They were ruthless, and some might say without honour, but they had fought for Lundenwic as hard as any of the Saxons.

King Æthelred and his court celebrated the victory with a feast. It was a long, dreary affair. Bishops preached for hours about the glory of God, and how God and Jesus had triumphed over the heathen and rewarded Lundenwic's people for their pious prayer and devotion. Beornoth endured the ceremony beside Pallig, and the Viking sniggered because Æthelred's bishops seemed ignorant of the fact that Forkbeard himself was a Christian. The ceremony went on and included a parade through the streets of Winchester where Robert de Warenne rode a white horse and held Thorkell the Tall's captured axe high for the common folk to marvel at its brutal size and shining twin blades.

'You'd think he took the bloody axe from Thorkell's grip,' said Pallig, as he and Beornoth shared a jug of ale later that night in the king's hall. Robert de Warenne sat at the king's top table during the feast, with the axe set behind him like a battle trophy. Lady Ælfthryth sat between her son and her Norman champion.

'This king's court has turned into a nest of vipers,' said Beornoth. He turned away from the king's table, unable to look at Ælfthryth without the sight of her curdling his stomach. He didn't care that Robert paraded about with the axe Beornoth had taken from Thorkell the Tall. Beornoth was too old to care about position and influence. Ælfthryth sat with pursed lips, enjoying every second of her return to favour and power. She leaned to whisper into her son's ear, turning to her champion Robert de Warenne with glowing appreciation. 'The sooner I can go home, the better.'

'What is keeping you here?'

'I cannot leave whilst Forkbeard threatens the kingdom. Æthelred will want his king's thegns close until the men of the fyrd arrive from the shires to swell his forces. It will take the northern ealdormen, like Alfgar and Thered, weeks to assemble their armies and march them south.'

'You haven't heard then?'

'Heard what?'

Pallig shook his head and took a long draught of ale. 'Forkbeard has gone.'

'Gone? Where?'

'Home to Denmark. The threat is over.'

'How?' Beornoth asked slowly and glanced again at the king. The bishops and the queen mother who shared his table ate and drank with smug looks on their pale faces. Beornoth's hands curled into fists, understanding then what the king's advisors had done. There could have been no battle to drive Forkbeard away. No force could have repelled Forkbeard's army without the royal forces lending their support.

'They paid him.' Pallig laughed and clapped Beornoth on the back. 'They paid the gafol again. Forkbeard is rich. He has enough silver to make his jarls and *drengr* happy. Enough to make his attempt to become king of Norway and Denmark. Who knows what could be possible with the fortune Forkbeard has at his disposal?'

'How much?' Beornoth seethed with frustration. They had learned nothing. Bishop Sigeric had once urged Æthelred to pay off the Vikings after Maldon. It had worked for a while. Until the Danes realised that the gafol payment came from a place of fear, designed and supported by weak men who had never seen or fought a battle. All the daring men, the Vikings, killers, slavers and ruthless warriors, knew that if they sailed their ships to England, that if they could menace the king enough, that they could return home rich without even fighting a battle.

'Sixteen thousand pounds of silver.'

It was a staggering amount. A fortune. The last gafol of ten thousand pounds of silver had crippled the kingdom for years. 'Forkbeard will come back. The Vikings will never stop coming unless they fear us. Alfred made them afraid, and we had peace. For a time. Now there can never be peace.'

'I hear Forkbeard fancies taking on his old friend Olaf Tryggvason, who is king of Norway. He can hire as many crews as he wishes with the wealth he carries from England.'

'Will you join him?'

Pallig winked at Beornoth. 'I might. But I am well paid here. The king has rewarded me generously. I am to have land. My wife likes it here, and she is with child. Some of my men will go, and I will not stop them.'

'So you are a king's man now?'

'I am.' Pallig puffed out his chest and smiled. 'Perhaps I will get a gold ring with a green dragon, just like you. How has the king rewarded you?'

'I have not spoken to the king since our return to Lundenwic.'

'Ah.' Pallig sensed the frustration and returned to his ale.

Beornoth left Winchester the following morning. There would be no thanks for the victory at Lundenwic, Beornoth knew well. Ælfthryth had seen to it that Robert de Warenne bathed in the king's glory and that men believed the Norman had led the defence of Lundenwic. There could be no place for Beornoth in King Æthelred's new court. The king had forgiven those he had once banished. He sought repentance and reform to atone for his brother's murder and the land taken from the Church. All Æthelred had achieved was to restore his court to its feral, decaying state of old. Beornoth feared for Æthelred, he worried how the bishops and the poisonous Ælfthryth would weaken the kingdom and leave its coasts and rivers open and inviting to the ever-hungry Viking threat.

He reached home on a sun-drenched afternoon. Beornoth dismounted and walked Virtus slowly along the stream which babbled through reed-filled meadows until he reached the small hall he shared with Eawynn. To call it a hall was generous. It was more like a large wattle and daub cottage. Alfgar had granted Beornoth the land from his estates close to Mameceaster. It was a smallholding between an orchard and the stream, and Eawynn loved the place. He found her knelt in the garden, tending to her roses. The sun shone through her hair, making the grey gleam like polished silver, and Beornoth allowed himself a rare smile.

'Can you spare a few morsels of food for an old soldier, my lady?' Beornoth said.

Eawynn turned and laughed. She hitched up her long dress and ran to embrace him. 'I was so worried,' she said.

'I missed you.'

'Thank God you came back.'

Beornoth remembered Thorkell's axe and the horrors of the defence of Lundenwic. Survival had been a close-run thing. 'How have you been?'

'Alfgar sent a man to check on me every few days. I have been fine. Are you hungry?'

'Starving.'

'I made bread this morning, and there's a broth in the pot.' She hooked her slender arm through his heavy one and led Beornoth towards their home. Bees hummed about the garden, and the smell of fresh flowers filled Beornoth's senses with contentment. He loved Eawynn beyond words. She was everything to him, though they had been estranged for a long time during the dark days. A memory came to him of her running amongst wildflowers, young and beautiful, playing with their two golden-haired daughters. They had lost those daughters in a Viking raid, and Eawynn had suffered viciously at the raiders' hands. Beornoth bent to kiss her hair, and his eye caught the lurid scar across her neck and face where the raiders had cut Eawynn's throat and left her for dead.

'Let's eat out here,' he said. 'We can sit in the sun. I must tend to Virtus first. He needs brushing and some food.'

'We can do it together. I don't want to be apart again, Beo.'

Beornoth watched her as Eawynn brushed Virtus and whispered gently into the horse's ear. Wrinkles creased her top lip and crow's feet pinched her eyes. Her hair was iron grey and her hands wrinkled, but she was beautiful. Later that afternoon, they ate broth and warm bread and watched the late summer breeze in the orchard trees. Beornoth hoped Æthelred would forget him, that his new advisors would not recommend that the king call for his Dane-killer when trouble returned. The years were growing long for both Beornoth and Eawynn, and he wanted to spend what time remained at her side. He put his sword, shield, helmet, spear and seax in a wooden chest at the end of his bed, and wrapped his byrnie in an oily fleece. Beornoth hoped his days of battle were over, that it was time for him to be at peace. But deep down, he knew there would never be peace. Not as long as there were men in the world. Men always craved more. More land, silver, women and glory. He just hoped they would forget about him at his little home beside the orchard. A man can hope, but the sea-wolves rage and the dangerous men are ever restless for blood and war.

6

1002AD

'Here you go, my love,' Beornoth said. He knelt beside the grassy mound and winced at the pain in his knees. He carried a small bundle of cowslips and primroses in his gnarled fist, freshly cut from Eawynn's garden. Beornoth had done his best to tend the flower beds, roses and vegetables in the two years since her death, but he was no gardener. He laid down the flowers and brushed the wooden cross which marked her resting place. Beornoth had carved the grave marker himself in the cold winter in which she had died from a wracking cough. Eawynn had died in her sleep, peacefully. Beornoth had awoken to find her cold and still, without pain, for which he was thankful.

A chill in the spring air blew cold against Beornoth's neck, carrying with it the earthy smell of damp soil and new leaves from the orchard beside which he had buried his wife. A hawthorn tree beside her grave bloomed with pale white flowers. Beornoth stared at the branches swaying softly in the breeze. She had loved to sit beside that tree, so he had buried her there, close to her garden and the orchard where she had loved to walk. The song of robins and blackbirds lilted from beside the stream, tinged with melancholy like the ache in Beornoth's chest.

It had been two years since she had died, but Beornoth still came to be with her every day. The path from his home to the mound was worn and free of grass. He would spend time each morning talking to her as if she might hear him, sharing the unimportant details of his day – of how Virtus had fed, what Beornoth cooked for his supper, news from Alfgar and the goings-on in Mameceaster. They were the things they would have talked about as they sat together on long, dark evenings. Now, Beornoth talked to the wind, hoping that somehow his words would reach her, carried on the gusts which rustled through the orchard, briars and river reeds. Theirs was a life of sorrow, but filled with a love strengthened by all that they had endured.

Beornoth stared at the mound. The emptiness within him was a hollow space where her smile used to make him warm, where the warmth of her touch once gave him a reason to live. She was with God, Beornoth was sure. Alfgar had brought a bishop, priests and mourners to mark Eawynn's burial. The ealdorman came to call on Beornoth from time to time and always extended an invitation for Beo to live with him at Mameceaster. Beornoth had helped make Alfgar ealdorman and taught him to fight. When Alfgar's father, the old Ealdorman Aethelhelm, had first asked Beornoth to take Alfgar under his wing, he had been a callow youth fresh from studying at the Church, his fingers stained by ink and his arms and shoulders unused to the weight and use of weapons. Alfgar was the second son of the old ealdorman, and a bastard. As was usually the case for most second sons, Aethelhelm had steered Alfgar into the Church, but he had failed at his studies, stating that he did not feel close enough to God to preach his word. The ealdorman reluctantly took Alfgar from the Church and gave him to Beornoth to turn into a warrior, which Alfgar struggled with at first, but he was now the veteran of many battles against the Vikings, and had been instrumental in the defeat of Olaf Tryggvason's forces outside Folkestone nine years ago. Beornoth thought of Alfgar as a friend, and the offer was a kind one, but Beornoth was content to remain alone in his home by the orchard.

A flower fell and Beornoth reached to fix it. His hands, strong and calloused from years of battle, hefting shields, swords and spears, felt clumsy as he straightened the flowers beneath the grave marker. He had held Eawynn for hours on the morning of her death, just to be close to her for one last time. For years she had tended his wounds, cleaned his mail and given him the benefit of her sharp mind with advice and guidance. Her presence had been a salve to his warrior's bluntness, a quiet, steady love that anchored him. Without her, the silence was a weight pressing down upon his broad shoulders, leaving him stooped, with an ache in his heart to match the ache in his bones.

Beornoth had thought he would die once Eawynn was gone. He was not afraid of it. He almost welcomed it. His massive body was criss-crossed with scars, his beard as grey as an old helmet. He had come close to death so many times on the battlefield, and he dreamed of dying in that quiet place, in the home they had shared. Beornoth hoped he would join Eawynn in heaven. He prayed to God for that each day before sleep. A priest in Mameceaster had washed Beornoth free of sin and had assured him that the men he had killed would not bar his path to heaven. Beornoth was not so sure. He rose, old bones protesting, kissed his fingers and touched them to the wooden cross. He trudged through the wild grass toward his sparse home, but he would return tomorrow with more flowers, more words, and a dream that perhaps Eawynn could hear him from beyond the veil.

A horse whickered from the direction of Beornoth's home, and it was not the sound of his warhorse. Virtus rested in a stable twenty paces from the house, and he knew her sounds as well as he knew his own voice. Beornoth straightened, forcing his shoulders back. He quickened his pace and was surprised to see a young warrior in a green cloak waiting on his wooden porch.

'Lord Beornoth,' the man said, rushing to his feet, face reddening.

'Who are you?' Beornoth asked. 'Calm yourself, lad.'

'Thank you, lord. Sorry, lord.' The warrior fussed at his jerkin and straightened his cloak. 'Ealdorman Alfgar requests you join him at Mameceaster.'

'Why?'

'There are men there, lord. For you. From the king.'

'Is it war?' Æthelred had not sent for Beornoth since Lundenwic eight summers ago. There had been war since, endless war. Viking attacks had been relentless in that time, and the people of England had suffered. Beornoth simply assumed that the king had no more need for him, that he had been put out to pasture like an old nag. Beornoth had accepted that fate. He had no hunger for more violence.

'I'm just a warrior, lord. They don't tell me why. I just follow orders.'

'Are the men who came to Alfgar carrying weapons? Wearing armour?'

'Yes, lord.'

'How many?'

'A score of them.'

'Wait here.'

Beornoth went to the chest at the end of his bed and wiped the dust from its lid. He opened it and took out his weapons and armour. Beornoth pulled on his chain-mail byrnie, kept clean of rust by its oily fleece. He strapped on his thick leather belt and slid the sword into a scabbard bearing the king's dragon. Beornoth eased the seax into its sheath and went to ready Virtus for the ride. He placed his leaf-shaped *aesc* spearhead in a saddlebag along with his helmet. The byrnie was tighter around the gut than it had been eight years ago, and Beornoth feared he looked like a grandfather in a younger man's war gear. But he could not refuse a summons from the king.

After the short ride from Beornoth's home to Mameceaster, Beornoth met Alfgar in his feasting hall. The ealdorman smiled and pulled Beornoth into a warm embrace. A steward brought bread and ale and placed them on a feasting bench beside the hearth fire.

'Thank you for coming,' said Alfgar. 'I asked them not to bother you, but the king's man insisted.'

'You look tired,' Beornoth replied, and regretted his bluntness as soon as the words escaped his lips. 'I mean, you have grown more dignified since last we met.' Alfgar's beard showed white at his chin and his hair was thin on top.

'Time waits for no man, Beo. Except you perhaps. I know men your age without a tooth in their head. You have the strength of a man half your age.'

'No need for kind words between old friends. How are the children?'

'They are children no longer. They ride and learn to fight, they disobey their mother and flee from their Latin instructor. You have not visited this year. How have you been?'

Beornoth thought about that for a moment. 'Quiet. Resting.'

'I've said it before, but I'll say it again to make sure that you understand. You are always welcome here, and nothing would make me happier than if you came to live with us. You could help train the young warriors, pass on your experience. It must be lonely out there on your own.'

'I am not alone, and never lonely.' Beornoth smiled. He was with Eawynn, and the memories of his life lived with him. Good and bad. He could awake to hear his daughters' laughter, or sleep through dreams filled with the faces of men he had killed in battle. The faces of his past haunted him. 'The king sends men here to speak to me?'

'Yes. I am afraid so, Beo.'

'The Vikings have returned?'

'They have never left. Which seems to be the problem. You know the man who has come, I believe.'

'There he is!' called a voice from the hall door. A heavily accented voice. A Norman voice. 'Lord Beornoth, scourge of the Danes.' Robert de Warenne strode into Alfgar's hall like he was the ealdorman of Cheshire. He walked with an easy swagger, tall, broad-shouldered and a thick silver chain about his neck. He wore a finely woven blue cloak tossed back over one shoulder to reveal a tunic embroidered with a double-headed axe.

Alfgar rose and Beornoth followed. 'Lord Robert comes from Winchester with a message from the king,' said Alfgar.

'Lord, is it?' said Beornoth. 'The years have been kind to you.'

'I am a king's thegn now,' said Robert de Warenne in a voice both silky and confident. 'Just like you. Only the king himself is my superior.' He glanced pointedly at Alfgar, as if the ealdorman wasn't aware what it meant to hold the powerful office of king's thegn.

'Lord Robert is modest, Beo. He is also lord commander of Lundenwic and its environs, and commander of the king's royal guard.'

'You have come far for the son of a man exiled for murdering King Edward. How is the Lady Ælfthryth?'

Robert de Warenne smiled at the barb. 'You must not have heard. The kingdom wept as one, for she died a year past. The king was distraught.'

'I had not heard,' said Alfgar. 'Please pass on my deepest sympathies to the king.'

'I will. She was a noble and remarkable woman, a great queen.' Robert de Warenne stared at Beornoth. He met the Norman's gaze but offered no sympathies. She was a murderer, a manipulator, and Beornoth was not sorry that Ælfthryth was dead. Robert de Warenne would love nothing more than for Beornoth to express his feelings for the late queen mother openly, so that he could scuttle back to Winchester and inform the king and condemn Beornoth to death.

'There must have been many a mass said in the lady's honour?' said Alfgar.

'A full week of prayer. And then a royal wedding.'

'The king has a new wife?'

'He does, and we should all rejoice. It is regretful that the king could not invite his northern ealdormen to grieve at his side, but we find ourselves in dark days, my lords.'

'How has that news not reached the north? A new queen. We should feast and pray in celebration!'

'It was one of the last great deeds of Lady Ælfthryth. Faced with treachery, and assaults on the kingdom from men who enjoyed the king's trust, the marriage is truly groundbreaking. A union of necessity, promise and alliance. I played a small part in the bridal negotiations.' Robert de Warenne waved a hand dismissively, as though the part he had actually played was nothing at all. Beornoth shifted uncomfortably. If Ælfthryth and de Warenne were involved, Beornoth expected a sting in the tail.

'Please tell us, Lord Robert, who is the new queen? Of what noble family is she?'

'She is Emma of Normandy, daughter of Richard the Fearless, count of Rouen.'

'A Norman wife?' Alfgar gasped and then turned his lips in on themselves as though to stop any further ill-advised comments escaping from his mouth.

'Richard the Fearless,' said Beornoth. 'Or Jarl Rikard, son of William Longsword, as he is known to his Norse kin.'

'That's the chap. A relative of mine on my mother's side,' said Robert de Warenne.

'Jarl Rikard, who offered shelter and succour to both Sweyn Forkbeard and Olaf Tryggvason the last time they invaded England.'

'A regrettable incident, and one which is remedied by this happy union. No longer will Danes find a safe port to our east. We have allies in Normandy now. Kinsmen. It was not an easy marriage to broker, but a wise and cunning move. I am sure you will both agree. The count of Rouen prefers to be called Richard, not Rikard.'

'I'm sure he does,' Beornoth snapped. 'I imagine the king rewarded you handsomely for finding his new wife?'

'I have been lucky, I must admit. But we must talk about more pressing matters. There is a reason the king did not invite his northern ealdormen to the wedding celebration.'

'Please, Lord Robert,' said Alfgar, 'share it with us. I have always served the king well and am surprised to have fallen out of favour.'

'You are not out of favour, Lord Alfgar, rest assured of that.

The king's advisors thought it prudent that we keep the invites for those lords south of the Danelaw. There has been trouble, my lords, dark deeds, oaths broken, and the kingdom ravaged.'

A shiver passed across Beornoth's shoulders as Robert de Warenne fixed him with a steely stare. 'Danes?' Beornoth asked.

'Yes. A most heinous act, an attack from within. Danes sworn to the king's service and honoured by him with silver, grants of land, titles and wealth turned against the kingdom and raided Sussex and Defnascir. They invited Vikings from across the sea to join them and laid waste to those shires. These were trusted men. One of them is a friend of yours, Beornoth.'

'Who?' Beornoth realised his hands had curled into fists and he forced himself to relax. His first thought was that his old friend and brother of the sword Brand Thorkilsson was involved. Brand was a Norseman who had fought beside Beornoth countless times. He had saved Beornoth's life after Maldon and was now a landed thegn in the service of Ealdorman Thered of Northumbria.

'Pallig Tokeson, or Pallig the Traitor, as he is now more widely known. He invited his kinsman, Kvitsr War Raven, with a score of ships to his treacherous enterprise. You remember Pallig, Lord Beornoth?'

'I remember him.'

'You and he were friends, as thick as thieves as I remember it.'

'He fought well at Lundenwic, so did you and your brother. That does not make him, or you, my friend.'

'Quite. He ravaged the south-west shires and had to be stopped.'

'Who stopped him? You?'

'I rode against the enemy, yes.'

'So they are defeated and dead?'

'They are not. They remain on those lands, but are pacified.'

Beornoth laughed and shook his head. 'They were paid?'

'In the end, we deemed a gafol was a more godly option than more loss of good Saxon lives.'

'How much?'

'Pallig and Kvitsr were paid twenty-four thousand pounds of silver, and now we have peace.'

It was a staggering amount of silver. Pallig, the rogue, was now as rich as a king. 'You should have killed them both. Not paid them.'

'Which brings me to the reason for my visit. After the awful treachery of last year, King Æthelred, through the counsel of his leading men, issued a decree.'

'Of which you are one, no doubt?'

Robert de Warenne paused and rewarded Beornoth with a dead-eyed, sly grin for his unhelpful comment. 'All the Danes who have sprung up on this island, sprouting like cockle amongst the wheat, are to be... forgive me. Sometimes I struggle with my Saxon words. *Necarentur...*'

'Slain,' said Alfgar, translating the Latin.

'Yes, slain. All the Danes who have sprung up on this island are to be slain. This is a *iustissima exterminacione...*'

'A most just extermination.'

'Thank you, Lord Alfgar. These Danes are to be slain by a most just extermination. This decree is to be put into effect as far as death. So, you see, Beornoth, there is work to be done for the most famous Dane-killer in the kingdom.'

'The king had ordered that every Dane in the kingdom is to be killed?' asked Alfgar incredulously. 'Vikings have settled north of the Danelaw for over one hundred years. They are landholders, married to Saxon families, virtually indistinguishable from us. The rivers will run red with their blood. There will be war, for the Danes will not sit idly by and allow themselves to be slaughtered.'

'Not all the Danes, Lord Alfgar. The ones who have given oaths to the king, the ones who betrayed him. Those Vikings who are new to these shores and have grabbed land and wealth for themselves. There is a list, and Beornoth is going to help me kill them.'

'A list?' asked Beornoth.

'Compiled by the king and his most trusted advisors.'

Beornoth used his thumb to turn the gold ring upon his finger around and around as he thought about Robert de Warenne and his list of death. Beornoth did not wish to ride across the kingdom killing Danes, though he did not doubt that most of them deserved it. He had liked Pallig, and from the day that King Æthelred listened to his priests and weak advisors and paid the first gafol payment, this day was inevitable.

'When Pallig raided Defnascir, did his men kill women and children?' he asked quietly.

'Any folk they didn't enslave they raped and killed. I am surprised at your question, Beornoth. You, more than most, have seen the face of Viking raids. Their cruelty, their barbarism. These men are heathens, they do not worship the one true God. The king has issued his decree, Lord Beornoth, and we ride at dawn.'

Robert de Warenne turned on his heel and marched from the hall. Alfgar warmed his hands close to the hearth fire and stared into the flames.

'Dark times,' he said. 'There is to be a slaughter.'

'Some deserve it,' Beornoth replied. 'But you and I both know that list won't only contain the names of men who took part in Pallig's raid.'

'No.'

'There will be others in there, folk who have made enemies of the king's advisors. Land will be stolen, titles taken, people butchered.'

'Which is why you must go, Beo. To punish the guilty, and make sure that the innocent do not suffer.'

So it was to be war again, and Alfgar was right. Beornoth had to ride, whether or not he wanted to. It was his oathbound duty. Murderous Danes had to be found and punished, and someone had to make sure that Robert de Warenne and his Dane-killers did not butcher half the landholders in England to make themselves rich. Beornoth's sword had slept, the cold steel dormant, and Beornoth had rested. Eawynn was dead and Beornoth had hoped that it was his time to wait beside her grave for death to come for him, to see out the twilight of his years in peace. But peace was for other men. Beornoth was a king's thegn, a warrior. He needed a shaft for his spear and a fresh edge upon his sword and seax. Danes had slaughtered innocents in the south-west, and Beornoth must punish them.

7

Robert de Warenne rode beneath his banner of the double-bladed war axe. He led two hundred men mounted on fine horses. Each man carried spear, sword, shield and wore half-helms and chain-mail byrnies. They waited for their commander a day's ride from Mameceaster, camped beside a village where their horses cropped at the heather and the warriors ate fresh fish from the river. Beornoth rode Virtus from Mameceaster, riding behind de Warenne and two warriors who served as his escort.

'Brother!' Robert de Warenne called as their horses cantered into the village. The villagers ducked inside their hovels and a scrawny dog barked at them from behind a small barn.

Odo de Warenne emerged from a hovel fastening his belt, his face flushed red. A young woman with dark hair ran from the building like a scolded cat and Beornoth shifted in the saddle. Odo raised a hand in greeting. He wore his hair shaved close at the back of his skull in the Norman fashion, and a long red scar ran from his forehead, through his left eye and down to his black beard. Where the scar ran into his beard, the hair grew white. He walked with a limp.

'Welcome, Lord Beornoth,' called Odo. The warriors lolling about the village looked up at the mention of Beornoth's name.

'Who are these men?' Beornoth asked, reining in beside Robert de Warenne.

'Good men. Warriors. My men,' he replied.

'Normans?' Beornoth noted the shaved heads and short beards of the men who wore dark tunics bearing de Warenne's double-headed axe sigil.

'Some are my brethren from across the sea, others recruited from my estates here in England. All thrilled at the prospect of fighting alongside a warrior of your reputation.'

'We cannot fight an army with two hundred men.'

'There's no army to fight. The Danes have settled. They raided, killed, made themselves rich, and now grow fat on their stolen land. As is their want. They have disbanded into crews. Each jarl has his own land on which to feed his own men. Lands ripped from the king and his subjects. So this won't be a battle, Beornoth. We ride to punish the sea-wolves. We take them one by one, stolen hall by stolen hall and we put them to sword. We attack them with the same cruelty which they brought down upon the people of the southern shires. What we do will serve as a warning to all oathbreakers, to all the warriors in the Skagerrak, Jutland and the Vik who turn their hungry eyes to England's shores.'

'Are you going to give me the names on your list?'

Robert de Warenne turned to Beornoth and fixed him with his cold blue eyes. 'We should get something clear from the outset, Lord Beornoth. I command this force of men, and all who ride with it. I do so with the king's full authority and at his order. You will follow my orders. I decide where we go and in what order we exterminate the traitors identified as requiring justice. Do you understand?'

Beornoth climbed down from the saddle and stroked Virtus' long nose. He dug deep into his saddlebag and found a carrot, which he fed to the warhorse, smiling as the hairs around her mouth tickled his fingers. He thought about Pallig, of his open, smiling face and how much he had liked the Dane. But a warrior is a warrior, and Pallig was a killer. Beornoth did not relish the thought of fighting a man he had liked, a man he considered a friend. Virtus shook her powerful head and Beornoth stroked her mane. This was to be a summer of death, a ride across England to punish Vikings who had slaughtered innocent Saxons. It would be bloody, savage and ruthless. Which was the tale of Beornoth's life, he thought. Beornoth sighed. He was tired. Too tired to spend months in the saddle hunting killers, but it was his duty to the king. He also knew how the innocent folk had suffered. He understood the pain of death, loss and despair. His sword would strike back for those people and try to bring them justice for the Vikings' brutality.

'Do you understand?' Robert de Warenne repeated.

'When do we ride?'

Robert de Warenne's jaw quivered as Beornoth avoided his belligerence. His horse scraped the earth with its foreleg and made a half-turn. Robert sawed at the reins to bring the beast back around to face Beornoth. 'On the morrow.'

Beornoth led Virtus away to find some hay to brush her down with, leaving de Warenne seething behind him. They were equal in rank and so Beornoth was not about to take orders from a man who had wheedled his way into the royal court through the favour of the poisonous king's mother, and who had taken for his sigil the axe Beornoth had plucked from the hands of Thorkell the Tall on a blood-drenched Lundenwic bridge.

The war party spent the night camped in between the hovels, barns and stables of the village on Cheshire's borders. They had leather and sailcloth tents, but the de Warenne brothers slept inside a timber-framed house commandeered from the village headman. A warrior offered Beornoth a berth beneath his cloth tent, and Beornoth accepted.

'Wiglaf is my name,' said the warrior, offering Beornoth a piece of goat's cheese. 'But folk just call me Wigs.'

'You're no Norman,' Beornoth replied. 'Thank you for the cheese.' He took a skin of ale from his pack, which he had brought with him from Mameceaster, and offered Wigs a drink.

'I'm from Mercia, lord. From lands which Lady Ælfthryth left to Lord Robert in her will.'

'She leave him much, did she?'

'Yes, lord. Land, silver, lordships, men. Robert is one of the wealthiest men in the kingdom now.'

'I bet he is. A reward for his father's dirty work.'

'Don't let the Normans hear you say that, lord.'

'How many Normans are there here?'

'There are two hundred of us in this company, and seven score of them are Normans.'

'I like your sigil there.' Beornoth pointed at the axe sewn upon Wigs' tunic. 'What does it stand for?'

Wigs' face beamed with pride. 'We all wear it so that men know we are warriors sworn to Lord Robert. Even when we wear our byrnies we wear these underneath. It's on our shields as well. Look.' He pointed to where his shield lay upon the ground, and sure enough, it too bore a painted version of the axe.

'Robert does not fight with an axe, though?'

'It's a symbol of the glorious victory he won at Lundenwic. That's where Lords Robert and Odo made their name. They saw off an army of Danes, ninety-four ships of the bastards, led by

Sweyn Forkbeard and Thorkell the Tall.' Wigs leaned forward, excited to tell the tale. 'Lord Robert fought like a bear. He defended the walls and not one Dane set foot inside the city. He crossed blades with Thorkell himself, men say. Thorkell fled and Robert still has his axe to this day. It's hung in his hall. I've seen it there. Bloody huge, it is. Too big for any normal man to wield. Thorkell must have been a monster.'

'He was a big man.' Beornoth took a swig of his ale.

'You were there?'

'I was.'

'Did Lord Robert fight like a bear?'

'He was very brave.' Beornoth was tired from a day in the saddle and he didn't have the strength to give Wigs the true story of Lundenwic. Robert de Warenne had fought well that day. That was true enough, but that was about all Beornoth could find that was true about de Warenne's legend.

A man poked his head around Wigs' tent and glanced first at Wigs, and then at Beornoth. He stumbled and almost put his boot in Wigs' small fire. 'You are Beornoth Reiði?' asked the man in Norse. Lurid red spots showed on the back and sides of his head, freshly shaved bald in the Norman fashion. He had a long face with a hooked nose and teeth, which seemed too big for his mouth. He belched, releasing a gust of ale-stinking breath into the tent.

'I am.' The Norman had not addressed him as lord, but Beornoth decided to let him get away with it.

He ducked back under the tent. 'It is him.' Then appeared again. 'Come out. The lads would like to see you. We've heard of you.'

'I'm tired. Go back to your ale.'

'Tired? Come on out. We are all friends here.'

'I said I'm tired.'

'Don't be like that, grandfather. Come and see the lads. Don't be a miserable whoreson.'

'Mind your tongue.'

He belched again. 'Just come out.'

'You should go,' said Wigs. He glanced from Beornoth to the Norman and licked his lips. 'Before there's trouble.'

Beornoth sighed and pushed himself to standing. He ducked beneath the tent flap and stood to his full height. He looked down at the long-faced Norman, who was a small man whose head barely reached Beornoth's shoulder.

'Big bastard, isn't he?' said the long-faced man. A dozen Normans gathered about Beornoth. One whistled, and another stroked his beard thoughtfully.

'He's older than I expected,' said one, appraising Beornoth like a prize bull.

'Much older,' said another. 'He's as wrinkled as your mother's arse.'

They laughed.

'Which one is it to be, then?' Beornoth asked.

'Which one for what?' asked long-face.

'Which one of you is going to face me now and pay for your disrespect?'

'Hold on there, greybeard,' said the second man. He was tall with close-set eyes and a wide mouth. 'We meant no harm. It's no insult to say an old man is old.'

'I am Beornoth, king's thegn. I won't be shamed. So I must punish one of you.'

'We don't need ignorant old whoresons like him anyway,' said long-face. 'He's too old for war. Probably too fat as well. We're warriors here, off to kill Danes and traitors. He's big all right. Might have been handy in a fight twenty years ago, but doesn't look like much of a champion to me.'

Beornoth hit the long-faced man hard. He punched him full in the face with his right hand. The knuckles connected with the long, hooked nose with a crack. Gristle and bone crunched, and the long-faced man crumpled, unconscious, into the mud. The other men sprang back. One drew an eating knife from his belt. The second man swung a fist at Beornoth, but he stepped in so that the blow fouled against his shoulder. Beornoth's left hand snaked out faster than the man could see and grabbed a fistful of his jerkin. Beornoth yanked him into a savage headbutt and then butted him again before tossing the rag-limp body on top of the long-faced man.

A knife flashed at Beornoth's midriff and he batted it away with his forearm.

'Bastard,' the knife man snarled and pulled the blade backwards. Beornoth backhanded him across the face, kicked him in the groin and, as the knife man bent double, he drove his knee hard into the man's face. The knife man folded into an unconscious pile.

'Anybody else want to be disrespectful?' he asked. The Normans backed away from him warily.

'Come, now,' said Odo de Warenne, stepping between Beornoth and the Normans with his extravagant limp. 'Stop teasing Beornoth. He's a king's thegn and would kill six of you before anyone could stop him.' He smiled at Beornoth, his scar twisting around the creases in his face. 'They are sorry. Too much ale and too little to do. We ride tomorrow, and our task will keep them busy.'

Beornoth grunted and ducked back into Wigs' tent. No harm in cracking a few skulls, he thought. It had to happen eventually. The Normans clearly had no respect. It did not bode well for the rest of the time he had to spend with Robert de Warenne's war band, but Beornoth didn't care. He had lived too long and fought in too many shield walls to be disrespected by young warriors still green to the ways of war. Wigs appeared beneath the folds of his tent. He glanced nervously at Beornoth.

'It's your tent, lad,' Beornoth said. 'You've nothing to fear from me. Come in and get warm.'

'They shouldn't have spoken to you like that.'

'No. But they won't do it again.'

'I don't suppose they will.'

Beornoth woke early the next morning. He went to Virtus and gave her another carrot and an oatcake from his pack. He took a fistful of hay from the village barn and brushed her coat until it shone. The Normans were wary around Beornoth as they prepared to ride. The three men Beornoth had fought had bruised and swollen faces. They kept their distance and would not meet his gaze, which suited Beornoth well enough. He rode beside Wigs, who introduced him to two of his Saxon companions. The first was a squint-eyed man with an easy smile named Gis, and the second a portly warrior with a reputation as an excellent cook named Ecga. They were cheerful, and chattered between themselves as the column rode south from Cheshire towards Robert de Warenne's targets. De Warenne gave no orders or any indication of who they were or where they would find the first name on his list. He simply gave the order to mount up and ride, when to rest the horses and when to make camp.

They followed the remnants of Roman roads that had once stretched across Mercia into Wessex, but over the years had become well-trodden and little more than dirt tracks winding their way across the country like a brown scar. They followed Watling Street for a time, its stone remains clattering beneath their horses' hooves. Nettles and wild grass filled the sides of the road, and the common folk hurriedly moved aside as the black-cloaked riders thundered past with spears in their fists and shields upon their backs. It took three weeks to travel to the kingdom's south-western borders, slowed by the need to find grazing for the horses and rest them at regular intervals. Each day, they travelled until late afternoon, careful not to over-burden their mounts. Each man carried a sack of food, mostly oatcakes and dried meat, which they replenished whenever the column stopped for the night at a lord's keep or a village on the road. Robert de Warenne's and Beornoth's gold rings were enough to secure supplies and hospitality wherever they demanded it.

They passed through rolling hills and dense woodlands, the countryside alive with the scent of wildflowers, heather and the sweet smell of freshly cut crops as the churls worked their fields. Oaks, elms and beech trees lined the edge of their path, offering welcome shade in the heat of late summer. The sun shone hot for an entire week and Beornoth baked in his byrnie. Clouds of gnats buzzed around the men and their horses, especially when they passed marshes close to river fords where the men whooped for joy as their horses splashed in the shallow waters. On the second week thunderclouds rolled in from the west, dark and malevolent. They brought short but heavy downpours that churned the paths to mud and left the air thick with the smell of damp soil and wet horse.

Where they could not find a fortress or village to spend the night, Robert de Warenne would send riders ahead of the column to find defensible spots to make camp, either on high ground, by streams or in clearings within woodlands where the trees would provide both cover and firewood. They softened hard bread in ale, which the men ate with their dried meat and cheese, if they were lucky. Half a dozen men carried hunting bows and would hunt for rabbit, birds and any other game which they brought to Ecga for his pot. He carried a pouch full of herbs and spices, which he used whenever the opportunity arose. He carried that pot clanking and banging against his saddle as he rode. In the villages, folk spoke of bandits and outlaws roaming the country. Masterless warriors of disposed lords, or of thegns killed by Viking incursions.

Further south, the land changed from hills, forests, valleys and dales and turned to gentle chalk downs and wide fields. By this time the men's faces were sun-darkened and dust-smeared from so long in the saddle, but they rode with a steely determination with their spears held firm and their shields emblazoned with their lord's axe sigil banging upon their backs. They spent a night in a reeve's barn at the bottom of a shallow valley, and a storm ravaged the countryside. Wind and rain lashed the thatch, doors and window shutters banged, children cried and dogs whined as the wind howled about the barn and the warriors huddled together for warmth. It was late summer, bordering autumn, and the wind made the night cold and the men had no fire for warmth, for fear that a stray ember would light the dry hay and sheaves stacked inside the barn. Robert and Odo de Warenne slept in the reeve's small hall along with their captains and ate beside a warm hearth. Beornoth sat with Wigs, Gis and Ecga and listened as they told riddles, jokes and mocked each other's appearance. It was good to be in the company of warriors, and Beornoth enjoyed the banter compared to the silent solace of his Cheshire home.

Beornoth awoke the next morning to find the valley still and calm, as though the storm had washed the countryside clean with its fury. Branches and fence posts littered the farmyard and thatch had blown off the reeve's hall in clumps. A donkey, loosed from its pen by the high winds, munched lazily upon the damp thatch as men grumbled and yawned, emerging from the barn to pull on their armour and ready their horses. It was a still morning with an ice-blue sky and a bright sun which warmed Beornoth's face. Robert de Warenne came striding from the hall, fastening his thick leather sword belt.

'Ready your horses, men!' he called in a bright voice. 'We ride at once. A foul Dane lurks half a day from this very farm. A bastard named Leif Hjalmarsson. He shall be the first to meet God's wrath. We must be ready, for he will have stout warriors with him.'

The warriors cheered and shook each other by the forearm. The prospect of battle thrilled them. This was what they trained for, what defined them. The farmyard rang with the noise of blades being sharpened and the clip-clop of horses as men saddled and prepared their mounts. Beornoth led Virtus to the rear of the reeve's hall and fed the warhorse some oats from his pack.

'A fine-looking horse,' said a woman. She sat behind the hall amongst a pile of freshly shorn fleeces. The woman was young, perhaps close to marrying age, with long dark hair tied back from her hair by a strip of cloth. She had rolled up the sleeves of her dress to her elbows, and her forearms were red like raw meat. She sat beside a tub of water in which she washed the raw wool, filthy and full of lanolin. Three fleeces hung on wooden pegs beside her, dripping with water and cleaned of dirt, sweat and grease.

'Her name is Virtus,' Beornoth said.

'She's huge. Much bigger than any of our horses.'

'Virtus is a warhorse. Trained, so that she is not afraid of battle.'

'Can she fight?'

'She'll kick and bite at my enemies, and I wouldn't want to get in the way of one of those kicks.'

The girl laughed and wiped a strand of hair away from her

face with the back of her hand. 'You go to fight the Danes? The ones who raided last year?'

'We do.'

'The Norman thegn told us all about it last night over supper. He says that the king sent you to make the Danes suffer for what they did.'

'That's why we've come.'

'They should suffer. God should punish them. They killed my uncle and took his daughters, my cousins. Men said that they burned another of my cousins in his house, and that his family's bodies were shrivelled and shrunken in the ashes when they found them. Babes and all. Dead. Burned. What if they come here next?'

'They won't come here.'

'How do you know?'

'Because we won't let them.'

'My father says Robert de Warenne is a great warrior and so is his brother. They told us the story of the siege of Lundenwic last night. They are brave and strong. Odo de Warenne tried to kiss me after my father had gone to sleep, but I ran away from him.'

'Good for you.'

'Are you brave?'

Beornoth thought about that for a moment. 'Sometimes.'

'Then you are lucky to have Robert and Odo to protect you.'

Beornoth laughed. 'Thank God for that mercy.'

'My mother cried every night after my uncle's family was killed and taken. She still cries. Why does God let the heathens butcher us so?'

'Some of them aren't heathens. But we cannot understand the will of God. All we can do is pray and hope that he hears us.'

'When I have washed this wool, we will comb it and spin it

into thread. All women do is spin. We spin from when we wake until we go to sleep again. When I work my distaff, and I twist the wool between my fingers, I will pray that you bring death to the Vikings. I'll wind my threads onto a spindle and make yarn and, from that, we'll make our fabric for clothes. I shall make a cloak for you, or for the de Warenne brothers. You can have it when you pass this way again. It will keep you warm in the winter. I want to make you something to thank you for killing the Danes. For stopping them from coming here. The Vikings live in my nightmares. I dream of their axes and their snarling faces and I wake up crying. What has become of my sweet cousins, warrior? I don't think I shall ever see them again.'

Beornoth climbed into the saddle, the leather creaking under his weight. 'We'll punish them. Do as your father tells you. Spin yarn, find a husband, have children. The Danes who killed your uncle's family will pay for what they have done. I'll make sure of it.'

Beornoth urged Virtus back towards the barn and took his shield and spear from Wigs. Two hundred warriors left the farmhouse, and they went to kill Leif Hjalmarsson.

8

Leif Hjalmarsson had stolen himself a fine swathe of land on the north-eastern borders of Defnascir. The hall and farm buildings, which had once belonged to a Saxon and were now home to a crew of Danes, lay on a gentle rise overlooking a meandering stream. Beornoth stared down at the buildings from a northern hillside, watching as fifty warriors milled about the collection of barns, granaries, animal pens and a small earth-topped hall.

'They know we're coming,' said Ecga. His horse became skittish, sensing its rider's nervousness.

'Two hundred horses make a lot of noise,' Beornoth replied. 'News of our arrival will travel faster than we can ride.'

'How many are there down there?'

'Fifty, maybe a handful less,' said Gis in his slow, drawling voice. Robert de Warenne had sent Gis, Wigs and four other men to scout the hall and farm. They had ridden ahead of the larger column and returned to report a crew of warriors living in the various buildings.

'What are those?' Ecga pointed his spear to a line of poles set at thirty-pace intervals along the road leading to the small settlement.

'You don't want to know,' said Wigs.

'I do want to bloody know. There are crows nibbling at them. They aren't...'

'They are. Corpses of the people who lived here before.'

'Why would they do that?' Ecga made the sign of the cross.

'They do it because they can,' said Beornoth. 'They've sharpened those staves and shoved the ends into the insides of those dead men and women and staked them there to show that this land belongs to Vikings now. Their gods do not forbid such things.'

'What gods don't make such cruelty a sin?'

'The same gods who would chain one of their number, Loki, with fetters crafted from the entrails of his own son. The Viking gods lashed Loki to a rock where a serpent will drip burning poison onto his face until the end of days. Loki's wife catches that poison in a bowl, but when she goes to empty it, the poison burns Loki's face and his cries make the very earth shake. Men governed by such gods do not shirk from cruelty.'

'God save us,' said Wigs, and he crossed himself three times.

The settlement overlooked a slow stream which curved around high banks, further east that stream flowed into the greater river Exe, but here it was little more than gleaming brook winding its way through meadows and fields heavy with summer crops. Leif Hjalmarsson's warriors waited behind a palisade with sharpened spikes on the end of each fence post. It was only chest high, little more than a fence offering some protection against wolves and small bands of roving outlaws and masterless men. Leif's men had dug a ditch around the outer edge of the palisade and set a bank beyond it. They formed three loose ranks inside the wall, spears bristling above their heads.

Beornoth glanced around at grazing fields dotted with sheep and cattle, and the patches of rich land where the previous owner had sewn barley and oats.

'Leif must feel like a fortunate man to have been rewarded with such a fine piece of land,' Beornoth said.

'Aye,' replied Wigs. 'Better than his rocky home full of goat shit and fish guts in Dane land, or whatever it's called. That's why they come, isn't it? For our fields and our grain?'

'Amongst other things.'

'Aye, well, they can't bloody have it.'

'Stop whining,' barked a Norman soldier, his black stallion stomping the hill with its forelegs. 'You Saxons mew like pigs for the slaughter. The commander wants to talk.'

Beornoth held his tongue and leaned forward to rest against Virtus' neck. Beornoth ignored the first part of Robert de Warenne's rambling. He stared instead at the heather-covered moors stretching away to the west, and a woodland to the north, where oak, ash and hazel provided firewood for the settlement beyond. A small orchard of apple trees grew close to the hall, their blossoms just beginning to fade in the last of the summer's warmth. It reminded him of home, and he thought of Eawynn and how much he missed her.

'...and so we Normans have come to slay the thieves and robbers who occupy this place. We fight today at the command of King Æthelred. I fight for the king and am sworn to his service, just as many of you are sworn to mine. We are no Saxon weaklings who quiver inside their halls when the Danes arrive. We are the descendants of Rollo Ganger and William Longsword, ourselves the grandsons of northmen, warriors and beloved of God...' Robert called to his men, riding slowly about them, a look of fervour on his face, not caring that he insulted the sixty Saxons under his command.

The bleating of sheep and the lowing of cattle mingled with Robert's speech and Beornoth flexed his fingers around the ash shaft of his *aesc* spear. This place could have been the home of the uncle and cousins of the girl at the last farmstead. He imagined the children running and splashing in the stream, of the celebrations at Yule and spring, and then of the Vikings descending on the place with their axes and their malice. Beornoth's breath became deep, his thick chest rising and falling beneath his heavy chain-mail byrnie. He took the helmet from his saddle and pushed it onto his head. Its boar-carved nasal and metal cheekpieces covering his face in cold iron. The people who had lived here were dead, their rotting corpses impaled on stakes for all to see. The raiders had captured the girls and sent them to be sold into slavery, and Beornoth could not contain the rage within him for much longer. There must be vengeance for that brutality, that blood, that suffering.

'Beornoth and Odo will attack the gate on foot,' said Robert, the mention of his name snatching Beornoth from his thoughts. 'I will take fifty men, ride around the settlement, and attack them from the rear. Walter and Hugh, take another fifty riders and form a ring around the place. I want no survivors.'

The plan made sense, and Beornoth made no comment. He did not enjoy being told what to do by Robert de Warenne, but his hunger to strike back at the Danes outweighed his desire to slap Robert, or to dispute his right to command warriors in England. England belonged to the Saxons, who had taken it from the Britons hundreds of years ago. Men had always fought over these lands, and the Vikings kept on coming. Beornoth slid from his horse, unslung the shield from his back and strode towards the settlement.

'Where are you going?' called Robert de Warenne. 'I have not finished.'

'You've finished. I'm going to kill this filthy rat's nest of stinking scum.' Beornoth realised he was shouting. He was deep in his anger and he did not care. He clashed his spear against his leather-covered shield and marched on.

'I command the shield wall!' called Odo in a shrill voice. Beornoth heard men hurrying to form up behind him. 'I lead the attack party, Beornoth, wait.'

Beornoth did not wait, nor did he look behind to see who followed. Robert de Warenne set off with his fifty riders at a canter, their hooves thundering down the hillside, and another fifty led their mounts to form a perimeter. Beornoth strode onwards, gnashing his teeth, gripping his spear and shield tight. He glanced at the Saxon corpses and let the horror of their torture fill him with vengeful fury. Men ran to catch up with him, the metal of their spears, shields, axes and swords jangling against the armour.

The warriors inside the settlement made their shield wall. They carried shields, axes and spears and knew the attackers must clamber through the ditch, up the bank and over the gate and palisade to kill them. They shouted in Norse, encouraging one another, threatening their enemies. Half a dozen arrows soared from beyond the defences and rose high in the sky, but Beornoth did not break stride. The shafts came down and thumped into the shields behind him. Men with grizzled beards and hard eyes stared at him from beyond the waist-high ditch and Beornoth marked them. They were killers, rapers and slavers and he was coming to bring justice for the victims of their wickedness.

Beornoth marched straight at the gate. Another volley of arrows whistled into the air and Beornoth raised his shield to catch one heading for his chest. The shaft thumped into the linden-wood boards and Beornoth continued on.

'Form shield wall!' hollered Odo de Warenne, but Beornoth ignored him. It was a foolish order. They must break formation to scale the ditch or gate. The men behind Beornoth followed the order and banged their shields together, each man overlapping his shield with the man next to him.

He came within ten paces of the fortifications and broke into a flat run.

'Beornoth, wait!' screamed Odo de Warenne like a fishwife, but Beornoth's blood was up. The old age and tiredness were gone, and he charged like a man half his age. A spear flew from beyond the gate, its sharp point driving towards Beornoth's chest like a thunderbolt. He dropped to one knee, raised his shield and deflected the spear over his head. Beornoth surged up and charged again. The Danes had thought to fortify their position after taking possession of the land, but they had been lazy. The ditch was too narrow and Beornoth leapt it in one stride. They should have made it deeper and wider, and the bank twice as high. But they had not, such was their disdain of the Saxons, and Beornoth was glad of that laziness. The gate itself was not thick oak, not riveted with iron or built to double thickness. So Beornoth hurled himself at it, shield first. He crashed into the timber with all of his massive body weight at full run, shoulder couched into the shield, and the gate shattered around him as though hit by lightning.

Beornoth checked himself, stumbling as he smashed through the gate, and then continued with his relentless charge as enemy shields and spear points loomed before him. The Vikings roared, but Beornoth noted the fear in their eyes. They saw a single man make quick work of their defences. A warrior in expensive mail, shining helmet with a dragon-painted shield on his arm and a spear in his hand. They saw an enormous man charging their shield wall alone, and they were afraid. These same men had slaughtered the Saxons in this place, folk who would have died terrified as they watched their loved ones die around them, or be shackled in chains for the slave markets. Beornoth thought of Eawynn again as he bore down upon his enemies. He thought of how much he missed her, how he wanted to be with her again in the afterlife, and he charged recklessly at a fifty-man Viking shield wall.

Beornoth hammered into them, shield first. He drove the point of his spear into the enemy shield facing him. His muscles bunched as the Viking tried to heave back at him and Beornoth drove his legs, muscles burning, forcing the enemy backwards. The enemy fell back before Beornoth's ferocity and Beornoth wrenched his spear from the man's shield. The leaf-shaped blade sprang from the wooden boards, bringing a shower of splinters with it. Beornoth reversed his grip, spinning the spear and driving it backwards into the spine of the enemy warrior behind him. That man screamed in agony as his backbone crunched and Beornoth twisted the spear, baring his teeth in an animal grimace.

Beornoth was amongst them. Faces snarled and spat at him. Men tried to heft weapons and cut at him, but it all happened too fast. They were so surprised and daunted by Beornoth's sheer ferociousness that the Danes could not react quick enough. Beornoth turned, smashing his shield into a bearded face and down onto a man's boots. A blade hammered into his back, but the links of his byrnie stopped the blow from cutting his flesh. He whipped the spear about, spraying the surrounding men with blood and drove the point between two shields, punching the point into a Viking's guts. He pushed that man backwards and let go of the spear as his sheer force tore through their ranks. Beornoth emerged at the rear of the enemy shield wall, stumbling into open space.

Odo de Warenne's men used Beornoth's mad charge to follow him through the broken gate. Leif Hjalmarsson's men were so stunned by Beornoth's onslaught they failed to react to Odo's attack and so the Normans poured through the gate and over the earth bank without resistance. Odo screeched at his men in his high-pitched voice, urging his Normans to form their shield wall. Shields banged together, Normans roared their battle cry in Norse and attacked the Danes.

Beornoth turned to find four men facing him, big Danes with shields and bright axes. They came on slowly, warily, surrounding him like a pack of wolves. A short, swarthy man with a thick beard and a sword in hand roared at them to attack, then he turned and beat at his men with the flat of his sword, urging them to hold the attacking Norman line. The short man was Leif Hjalmarsson, Beornoth assumed. The man who had come to England with Kvitsr War Raven to plunder and take everything they could get their hands on. Beornoth dragged his sword from its scabbard and as the four Vikings watched the sword catch the sunlight, he flicked the sword's tip out. The stroke came from his wrist, just a flick with the strength built over a lifetime of hefting weapons, and he slashed open the face of a blond-haired warrior. Beornoth surged left and banged his shield into the enemy on that side, swung his sword right where it crashed into a shield. He turned, always to the left, so that he led with the shield and an axe thundered into it, clanging off the iron boss.

'Saxon turd!' said one of the Danes, a big-nosed man with thinning hair. 'Shields! Pin him with our shields.'

Beornoth tensed his muscles, readying for them to come. The big-nosed man knew his business, if the four warriors could pin Beornoth with their shields, enclose him so that he could not swing his sword, they could hack at his face and neck with their axes and Beornoth would die in a welter of blood and pain. But he was no stripling warrior new to the shield wall. So Beornoth dropped his shield and whipped his seax free from the sheath at his back. The shields came at him like a wall of wood and iron and Beornoth raised his left hand just as the four shields clattered into him, pinning his sword arm to his side. The blond Dane with the cut face roared with a mad fury, and spittle from his maw flecked Beornoth's face. Beornoth stabbed with his seax, the blade high and above the ring of shields. The point of the broken-backed blade crunched into the side of the cut-faced man's head, a full thumb's length of the blade punching into his skull. Beornoth yanked the blade free, sliced across the eyes of the next man who screamed and dropped his shield to clutch at his ruined face. Two shields gave way and Beornoth spun away from his enemies. He crouched and levelled his sword, and the big-nosed man ran onto the blade, gaping in surprise as the point cut beneath his leather breast-plate. Beornoth pulled the sword free and rose slowly to face the last of his four attackers. He was young, blue-eyed, his face contorted in terror at the scene unfolding around him. Beornoth grinned and the young Dane dropped his weapons and ran like a hare.

A thunder of hooves reverberated around the valley and Robert de Warenne's riders came galloping from the south. Their mounts easily jumped across the too-small ditch, over the bank and leapt the fence palisade to bring fifty horsemen inside Leif Hjalmarsson's defences. The Vikings groaned in fear. Odo's shield wall pressed them backwards, and the warriors in the rear ranks glanced nervously at the baleful figure of Beornoth waiting for them, face and byrnie spattered with blood, his sword and seax waiting like the murderous fangs of a dragon. The front rankers died beneath Norman blades and the rear-ranking Danes threw down their weapons and howled for mercy. Leif Hjalmarsson killed one of those kneeling men, his own man, with his sword and was about to strike at another when Beornoth parried the blow with his blade. He cracked the antler hilt of his seax into Leif's face and the Dane staggered under the crushing blow.

'He's mine!' Odo de Warenne screeched. 'The victory is mine, Beornoth. Leave that man.'

Beornoth ignored him. He cut his sword down onto Leif's sword hand, cutting into the fragile finger bones, and the Viking's sword clattered to the floor. The Normans fought the bravest of Leif's men, the warriors who would not surrender, who chose Valhalla over shame, whilst Robert de Warenne and his riders milled about the settlement on their mounts, stabbing at any of the enemy who tried to flee. Beornoth sheathed his sword and grabbed a fistful of Leif Hjalmarsson's hair. He dragged the Viking leader to the closed building, hauling the roaring Leif, who bucked and struggled but could not free himself from Beornoth's implacable strength. He pinned Leif against a timber stable and stared into his furious eyes.

'What became of the slaves you took in this place?' Beornoth asked in Norse.

'A pox on you, Saxon. Your women are all whores and your warriors are...'

Beornoth stabbed Leif in the shoulder. The seax point shattered the links of his chain mail and Leif groaned with pain. 'I am Beornoth Reiði. You will tell me where the enslaved women have gone, and I will kill you before these Norman curs have their way with you.'

Leif sneered. 'Give me a blade. Let me go to Valhalla, and I will tell you.'

'Tell me first.'

'Unhand that man, now!' Odo de Warenne shouted, his voice now so ridiculously high-pitched that he sounded like a vixen in heat.

Leif peered over Beornoth's shoulder at the scarred, limping, vengeful Odo and then back to Beornoth. Beornoth had but moments to get what he needed from the Viking warlord. Robert and Odo de Warenne were on a campaign of vengeance and justice, sent by the king to slaughter the Danes who had broken their oaths, or who had come with Kvitsr War Raven to ravage the south-western kingdom. They had not come to find and rescue the women, girls and boys captured and enslaved by the Vikings. Meeting the girl that morning at the farmstead had unsettled Beornoth. He wanted to punish the Danes as much as, if not more than, the men in the war band, but there were families affected by the Viking raids. There were innocent people held in chains, battered, brutalised and filled with terror at what lay in store for them. One day, they had lived in this fertile valley and lived a simple life. Now they awaited that cruellest of fates, to be sold to the highest bidder at slave markets in Dublin, Mann or Hedeby, into God only knew what horrendous fate. Beornoth could not shake the thought of his own dead daughters, and what he would do to rescue them had they grown to womanhood and become enslaved by Vikings. There was little the common folk could do, next to nothing a Saxon churl could do to save his captured daughter. But Beornoth was no farmer, and he had to help those who could not help themselves. To do that, he must be merciless. He must act with the same brutal cruelty as the raiders and slavers. So he took his seax and cut off

Leif Hjalmarsson's ear. Leif grunted and ground his teeth as blood splashed upon the barn.

'Where are the slaves?' Beornoth snarled. 'Tell me or I'll make a heimnar out of you. You have heard of Ragnar the Flayer and what I did to him?'

'I have heard. All men know of you and your brutality. Beornoth the Wrathful. The slaves are gone.' Leif laughed. 'Pallig and Kvitsr rule this entire shire. Your people are like cattle to be herded, used and sold.'

'Beornoth. Give that man to me now!' Odo was close, his voice making Beornoth's shoulders tense. He had mere moments left to question Leif.

Beornoth threw Leif Hjalmarsson to the ground and stamped down hard with his boot. Leif tried to stop him, writhing on the ground, scratching at Beornoth with his hands and kicking with his legs, but he was not strong enough to stop Beornoth's foot from smashing into his midriff. He doubled over and Beornoth stamped on him again and again until Leif's ribs broke like dry kindling.

'Enough!' Leif cried, weeping at the pain. 'The slaves have gone to Watchet. Where Kvitsr's fleet awaits. From there they go to Dublin.'

'He's all yours,' Beornoth said to Odo, who stared at him with malevolent rage.

Beornoth found Wigs, Gis and Ecga thankfully unharmed. One of the Saxon warriors found a side of bacon drying in the rafters of a barn and brought it to Ecga, who roasted it over a fire and made a broth from the bones. The Saxons amongst the company watched the meat cook in silence, whilst Robert de Warenne, his brother and their Norman warriors butchered the surviving Danes. Beornoth turned his back. Wincing at the sound of men crying as the Normans tortured and did their foul work. The meat roasted, and Beornoth had to find a way to get to Watchet before the slave ships set sail for Ireland. Pallig, Kvitsr and the others must face justice, but Beornoth couldn't allow the Vikings to take the captives away to their fate.

The Normans hooted with delight as their Viking captives suffered. Soon it would be Pallig's turn to face the wrath of Robert de Warenne's war party, and even though Pallig had betrayed his oath to the king, Beornoth did not relish the thought of his friend suffering at the hands of the Normans. He rode in a company little better than the Danes themselves, led by brothers he neither respected nor trusted. Robert was the creation of Lady Ælfthryth, son of a traitor raised up by a woman who had once tried to kill Beornoth.

Beornoth was certain that the Vikings must be punished. He would see that mission completed, but the Normans made him uneasy. There was a taint upon anything connected to Ælfthryth, and Beornoth could not get that suspicion out of his thought cage. There were Saxons amongst his company, and they were good men. Beornoth watched as Ecga, Gis, Wigs and the others winced at the awful suffering of the Danes. Beornoth wondered if he could depend on the Saxons if things turned bad, if the battle lines were drawn between Norman and Saxon. He also wondered about Watchet, where he had once killed Palnatoki of the Jomsvikings in a desperate battle. Slave ships lay there, waiting for the Danes to fill their hulls with captured Saxons. Perhaps Robert de Warenne would agree and ride the company to Defnascir's northern coast to rescue them, but Beornoth wasn't so sure. De Warenne was eager for slaughter and to rise in the king's favour, but Beornoth had to try, for the sake of those who suffered.

9

The war band rode across Defnascir's northern border for a week. They hunted Kvitsr War Raven's jarls, the leaders of his crews rewarded with stolen land for their service. Each settlement suffered the same fate. Robert de Warenne's war band butchered four Viking crews, beating down their defences just as they had Leif Hjalmarsson's. Beornoth played his part. He fought in the front line, hacking at the fearsome Danes with his spear and sword until they crumbled. Then Robert de Warenne, his brother and their Norman warriors set about the captives with gruesome and unflinching tortures. Beornoth and the Saxons watched with disdain as the Normans crucified Danes, locked them in barns and burned them alive, and made them suffer other equally unspeakable acts unworthy of men of honour. After the fourth skirmish, Beornoth approached Robert de Warenne as the company camped for the night in the buildings of a liberated settlement. He waited until after the cries of suffering had ceased and the men of the war band sat around campfires and ate looted meat and grain from the settlement's stores.

'We push north,' Beornoth said, finding de Warenne sharing a roasted cut of beef with his brother. 'The sea is but a day's ride away.'

Robert de Warenne turned and stared at Beornoth as though he were something disagreeable on the bottom of his boot. 'What of it?'

'Kvitsr's fleet is at Watchet. We could reach Watchet harbour tomorrow if we ride hard.'

'We aren't going to Watchet. Kvitsr himself is at Cantuctone. We go there tomorrow.'

'Kvitsr is at Cantuctone?'

'That's what I said.' Robert went to take a bite of his food, and then paused, frowning when he saw Beornoth was about to speak again. 'We had it from a man who died today. The jarl's son. The one who wept when Odo peeled the skin from his body like an apple.'

Odo smiled at the memory. 'So much for Viking courage,' he said through a mouthful of food. 'He cried like a child and begged for his life. No Valhalla for that dead whelp. Cursed heathens.'

'Men fought a battle beside Cantuctone a hundred years ago, in King Alfred's day. Cynuit, they called it,' Beornoth spoke wistfully, trying to ignore Robert de Warenne's disrespect. 'Ubba Ragnarsson died and the men of Wessex won a glorious victory.'

'And now Kvitsr is there with three crews. Kvitsr and Pallig are the reasons we ride, so tomorrow we will go to kill Kvitsr.'

'With three crews, Kvitsr's force could match our own.'

'It could. We have lost a dozen men since we set out, and we may lose some more. But we are warriors. This is the life we chose.'

'Watchet is close to Cantuctone. We can defeat Kvitsr and get there before his fleet sails for the slave markets.'

Robert de Warenne threw his meat away and picked the scraps from his teeth with his fingers. 'What is it with Watchet that you feel the pressing need to keep harping on about it, ruining my meal after a hard day's fighting?'

'The Saxons, captured and enslaved by the Danes, wait at Watchet on board Kvitsr's fleet. From there they'll go to Dublin or beyond, never to be seen by their families again.'

'So?'

'So we should free them. The fleet will sail when they hear their leader is dead. Why stay here when they know we hunt them? They could rally their army and try to kill us, but surely the Vikings realised the king will eventually muster an army and march against them. Kvitsr's remaining jarls will sail away with their plunder and their captives and return home rich men.'

'Raising an army is no simple matter, as I am sure you are aware. The king must dispatch riders to his shires and command his thegns to bring their warriors south. The ealdormen are required to summon their fyrds. Those armies will need food and ale, enough to keep them fed not only on the march south but also throughout the duration of the fighting. One does not simply assemble an army overnight. It would take months for the army of England to assemble. Kvitsr and Pallig are no fools. They'll flee before the army even gets to Defnascir. Or they'll demand a gafol from the king. You Saxons hate the gafol, but how much do you think it costs the crown to keep an army in food, ale, horses and weapons?'

Beornoth sighed and shook his head. None of this was news to him, and everything Robert de Warenne said was true. But when a force of Danes ravaged a country, the matter went beyond straightforward thinking. A king must stand up for his people, or others would see him as weak and more *drakkars* would arrive the next summer. People were dead or captured, and that must be remedied. 'We have this one chance to free our captured people before they disappear forever.'

'Your people.'

Beornoth tucked his thumbs into his belt and shifted his feet. 'You are a king's thegn, a warrior of the king of England. They are your people, too.'

'They banished my father for serving the crown, and I was born in Normandy. I owe nothing to your people.'

'Then why are you here?'

De Warenne took a step closer. He was a big man and met Beornoth's gaze at eye level. 'I am your commander, Saxon, and do not answer your questions. I lead, you follow.'

'That is clear. But attacking Kvitsr's fleet at Watchet is still punishing the Danes, is it not? Destroy his fleet and we trap Kvitsr in our country. He has nowhere to go but face our blades.'

'I swear to God on high, if you mention Watchet one more time...' Robert de Warenne made a fist, flexed it open and closed, and then made the sign of the cross.

Beornoth stared flatly at the Norman, whose face flushed red. 'Let me at least take a detachment to the ships.'

'Since we left Cheshire, you have shown nothing but defiance and disrespect to my brother and I,' Robert de Warenne shouted, and the warriors nearby turned and looked at their angered leader. 'We have come from Normandy to help you Saxons do what you cannot do for yourselves. We are warriors, and you need warriors if you are to defeat the Danes. Lady Ælfthryth was right about you. Ealdorman Byrhtnoth indulged you. You drank away your heriot and became little more than a cattle reaver and retriever. The late ealdorman rose you up because you are a killer. I've seen you fight, Beornoth, and you are little better than the Danes you so despise.'

'I don't torture men who have surrendered.'

'You cut off their ears and smash their ribcages in with the heel of your boot. You make heimnars and slaughter churchmen. All at the king's court know how Archbishop Sigeric died, and how you butchered Godric of Essex.'

'What I do, I do for the right reasons. Godric betrayed us all at Maldon, as did Sigeric. They deserved to die.' Beornoth said nothing of the cruelty he had laid upon the Vikings. His only excuse was that he treated the invaders the same way they treated his people. With ruthless and brutal violence. But that only served Robert's argument, so he kept quiet.

'Who determines the right reasons for your actions? You?'

'We can't allow those ships to carry innocent captives to a life of slavery. Not whilst we have men and blades to stop them.' Beornoth raised his own voice so the watching warriors could hear. He was no fool, and much of what Robert de Warenne said was true. Beornoth knew what he was, acknowledged the things he had done. He was an instrument of violence and destruction, but he was necessary. Without him, Vikings and other strong men preyed upon the weak, and Beornoth would not apologise for that.

'He has undermined us at every turn, brother,' said Odo de Warenne. He limped close to his braver brother. Odo's lip curled at Beornoth, and he looked him up and down like he was covered in pig shit. 'He challenges you. He despises us. What shall we do with him, brother? Cut him out like a poxed growth.'

Robert de Warenne's eyes blazed in response to his brother's malevolence. His fingers edged towards the hilt of his sword. Beornoth readied himself. If the fingers curled the hilt, he would kill them both. The rest of the Normans would rush him, and he could not fight against one hundred and forty angry Normans. But the de Warenne brothers were close to Beornoth. They would die, and that would be enough. Robert stared into Beornoth's eyes, and then down at the scars on Beornoth's face.

'There are enough enemies for us to fight without fighting each other,' Robert said with an easy smile. He clapped Beornoth on the shoulder. 'We'll see about the ships after Kvitsr is dead. How does that sound?'

Beornoth nodded, not believing for a second that Robert de Warenne had any intention of riding to Watchet after they had dispatched Kvitsr. Robert put a heavy arm around his brother's shoulders and the two walked away. Odo hissed into his brother's ear, gesticulating angrily in Beornoth's direction, and if he didn't know it before, Beornoth knew it now. The brothers were his enemies. They fought for the same cause, and Beornoth was useful to them, but that would change once their quest to kill the men on King Æthelred's list was over.

Norman faces glowered at Beornoth as he marched through their campfires to join the Saxons.

'It's almost like you want to rub them up the wrong way, lord,' said Wigs, handing Beornoth a cup of ale.

'We'll go to Watchet. Whether the de Warennes like it or not,' Beornoth replied.

'Us four against Kvitsr's fleet, lord?' asked Gis incredulously.

'Would the other Saxons not follow us if we did?'

'Some would,' said Wigs. 'Maybe they all would. But you'd have to talk to them first. They admire you, lord, but they're afraid of the Normans. Once you've opened your mouth about it, there's no going back. It only takes one weak heart, one of our lads who's afraid to follow you to Watchet or sees a chance to get himself in de Warenne's good graces. One slip of the tongue and we are dead men.'

'First, we must deal with Kvitsr. He has three crews at Cantuctone. That's almost as many men as we have. It won't be as easy as our last attacks. Everybody in this company seems to think Kvitsr will roll over and let us kill him. He is a Dane, ferocious and cunning enough to capture the shire of Defnascir and make himself a warrior of reputation and wealth. Once we have fought him, and if we can kill him, then we'll see about Watchet.'

Beornoth stayed awake for much of that night. He lay down with his seax in his hand, covered by his cloak, wary of a Norman attempt to slit his throat whilst he slept. But no attack came, and in the morning the company rose and left their camp in good spirits. Robert de Warenne rode up and down the riding column, talking to the men of their chance to kill a Viking war leader and earn fair fame to last a lifetime. Beornoth rode with the Saxons and kept his own counsel. There was much to admire about Robert. He fought well, led his men from the front, inspired them with rousing speeches and encouragement. But he was also a piece of stinking weasel shit who had once served Lady Ælfthryth and was more likely to leave Beornoth dead in a ditch than allow him to earn praise before the king.

Cantuctone lay on Defnascir's northern coastal border with Somersaete, and as the company rode north, the terrain rolled gently, dotted with a patchwork of grazing meadows and woodland. They rode past hawthorn bushes heavy with late summer blossoms and stopped to rest the horses beneath the twisted branches of a sprawling oak tree whose boughs stretched over the rough track to give shelter from the late summer heat. Riders watched them from distant hilltops, their spears catching the afternoon sun. Robert de Warenne sent Odo and fifty men to chase them off, but the riders were too far away and easily outran them.

'Who are they?' asked Ecga, pointing at the distant watchers.

'Danes,' replied Beornoth.

'So they know we're coming?'

'Unless he is a fool, Kvitsr knows we are coming. Word will have spread. He knows we've hunted his jarls. That's why he's at Cantuctone. There's a ring fort of the old folk there. He'll use that to defend himself against us.'

'A Roman fortress?'

'No, older than that. Built by the folk who lived in these lands before the Romans came. Before our Saxon forefathers came across the sea. The Britons. They made forts from the earth, of steep banks and deep ditches. Kvitsr will make his stand there with whatever crews he can gather before we arrive. He's a Dane, a Viking warlord. He'll fancy his three crews can beat our two hundred men.'

'Why doesn't he just sail away? Bastard's rich already,' asked Wigs, who, just like Ecga, could not take his eyes off the watching riders. There was fear in the Saxon's eyes, fear learned from a century of Viking raids. Mothers told stories of Ivar the Boneless and Ragnar Lothbrok to children to frighten them. Do that again, and Ragnar will steal you away in the night. They were heathens who worshipped fierce gods. They fought with skill and tactics beyond anything the Saxons could match until Alfred and his sons built their burhs and organised their warriors. Then the raids stopped. For a time. Æthelred's father, Edgar, ruled for many years without suffering Viking depredations. Æthelred had not been so lucky. It was as though the Danes sensed the weakness, the open wound caused by Lady Ælfthryth's murder of the king's chosen successor in favour of her own son. England was a kingdom riven by feuds over land, torn loyalties, the power of the Church and the ever-present shadow of the Danelaw.

'Kvitsr wants to hold on to the lands he's won. He probably believes the king will pay him to stop his raids, maybe even make him an ealdorman. His people can settle here. Kvitsr will be a great hero. His men are out enjoying their new land. They have spent a year living like lords with crops, woodland, cattle, slaves and wealth. Kvitsr can't just sail away and leave his jarls here to die. The families of the men he abandoned would hunt Kvitsr forever. He's made his bed, now he must lie in it.'

'Can he beat us?'

'We'll find out when we get there. They are Vikings raised to the blade, bred to fight. That's true enough. But they are just men and we are warriors. You three can heft a spear as well as the next man. You've nothing to fear from them. They are desperate, in a foreign land, fighting with their backs against the sea. But we are men defending our people, fighting for those who cannot do it for themselves. We fight for this.' Beornoth showed them the ring of Wessex upon his finger, and pointed to the dragon sigil on his scabbard. 'Our king, our kingdom, and our kinfolk. So yes, Kvitsr could beat us, but we can beat him too. Victory lies in the strength of your shield and the speed of your spear.'

They sat a little straighter in the saddle, and Beornoth set his jaw. They rode to kill a raider, a Viking warlord, but Watchet and the thought of women and children weeping and shivering in the bilges of Viking warships distracted Beornoth's mind.

They reached the low hills around Cantuctone's hill fort mid-afternoon. The ancient earthworks loomed over a deep valley where a series of steep ditches and high banks encircled the summit of a wide hill. Age had weathered the defensive embankments, grass covered, eroded and broken in places, but the ramparts remained foreboding. Campfire smoke rose from within the ancient structure, and Beornoth's eyes narrowed against the glare from a low sun. Viking banners fluttered in the wind, snarling dragons, wolves and ravens, where three crews of Vikings waited behind the earthen fortifications.

'Three ships there, see?' Gis pointed west, and Beornoth shielded his eyes and gazed across the summit of the hill where the Severn estuary was at ebb and three *drakkars* lay beached on the muddy silt banks. The river shone in the distance like a carpet of silver, a grey-blue line that cut across the landscape towards the distant sea. Men shouted from within the fortress as Robert de Warenne sent men to ride around the hill and scout for any weaknesses in the fortifications. A few Danes clad in iron helmets and brightly coloured cloaks climbed up the bank to stare at the riders, hands resting on the hafts of their axes. The Viking camp sprang into activity. Through a gap in the bank, Beornoth watched the Danes pluck their shields and spears from where they rested in neat stacks. The ships were within marching distance, and if Kvitsr thought his men would die in Robert de Warenne's onslaught, he would retreat behind a wall of shields to his ships, heave them into the water and sail away to fight another day. Which made Beornoth frown, because Kvitsr believed he could win.

Robert de Warenne ordered his men to dismount. They readied shields, checked straps, tested the heft of their spears, fastened helmets and prepared for battle. Beornoth led Virtus to the six men ordered to keep the horses away from the battle. The war band would attack on foot and Beornoth sought Robert de Warenne amongst the Norman warriors. They spoke in Norse, praying together, helping each other tighten straps on their byrnies or taking practice blows against their shields.

'Beornoth, lord,' said a squat Norman as Beornoth approached.

Robert de Warenne turned and eyed Beornoth warily as he

fastened his helmet's strap beneath his chin. 'Do not mention Watchet. By all that's holy, do not.'

Beornoth opened his palms to show he did not intend to resume that argument. 'Did you see how the Danes reacted when our scouts rode about their flank?'

'We are going to attack head on,' Robert began, ignoring Beornoth's question. 'I'll march in the front rank with you. Odo will wait until we have engaged them on the ramparts and take fifty men around to their left flank, where the bank has collapsed and filled in much of the old ditch.'

'Kvitsr will expect you to do that. He's had time to prepare for arrival. He wants you to attack that part of the wall. They would have repaired it otherwise, or at least made some sort of makeshift barricade where the bank had collapsed.'

'I did not ask for your advice, Lord Beornoth.'

'No, but here I am.'

'Here you are.' Robert de Warenne picked up his shield where it rested against his brother's. He tested the weight and nodded approvingly.

'Send fifty riders around the defences and make for their ships. They won't be able to help themselves. Even if Kvitsr does not order it, his men will follow. Their ships are their lifeblood, their only means of returning home across the sea. They'll come charging after those riders and we'll split their force.'

'You and I will attack in the front rank, as I said.'

'Lord Robert, we have had our disagreements. But listen to me, attack the ships and we shall make a great slaughter here today. Like we did at Lundenwic.'

Robert's right hand touched the axe sigil beneath his byrnie without thinking. 'That was a glorious victory.'

'It was. And we shall have another today, if you let me attack their ships.' Beornoth did not mention Thorkell's axe, and how he had taken it from the giant Viking's grasp, and how Robert de Warenne had stolen his valour.

Robert looked deep into Beornoth's eyes, turned and gazed at the fortress and the glinting curve of the estuary beyond its ramparts. He licked his teeth and turned back to Beornoth. 'Very well. Take your sixty Saxons and ride for the ships. When Kvitsr's men follow, if they follow, kill them and attack Kvitsr from the rear. I'll still send Odo around their flank so that Kvitsr believes we shall attack the damaged bank and ditch.'

Beornoth nodded slowly and then set off, shouting for Wigs to get the Saxons organised to ride. De Warenne was many things, but he was no fool. Despite loathing Beornoth, the Norman had seen the sense in his plan. Men were never as simple to read as the flight of an arrow. Wicked men could show kindness, and kind men could be wicked. De Warenne and his brother took pleasure in torturing helpless men, and they were clearly only on English soil for the riches and opportunity presented to them by Lady Ælfthryth. But they still risked their lives to fight for King Æthelred, and Beornoth had certainly not seen Robert flinch from a fight.

Beornoth hefted his bulk into Virtus' saddle. 'Be brave today, old girl. Carry me with sure footing.' He stroked her ears, and the warhorse whickered. Sixty mounts milled about on the hilltop as the Saxons tried to group their mounts together.

'Where are we going, lord?' asked a Saxon warrior, a red-faced man with a thick beard and clever eyes.

'We are going to burn their ships,' Beornoth said. 'Then we're going to kill some Danes. Bring whatever kindling you can find and follow me.'

Beornoth dug his heels into Virtus' flanks and clicked his tongue. He led his riders down from the hill. They came in a disorderly line, some horses turning and failing to respond to their rider's command. The horses thundered down the hill, hooves throwing up clods of earth as they went. Beornoth carried his shield on his back and his spear in his hand. He wore his chain-mail byrnie, his helmet, and his cloak billowed as he cantered Virtus close to the enemy fortifications. The black and white horsehair plume flowed like a serpent from the crown of his helmet and Beornoth lifted his spear towards the enemy. The Danes peered at him as he went. Some thrust their groins at him, others made lewd gestures with their hands. One man pissed from atop the rampart and Beornoth smiled at him, because battle loomed. Those Danes who had come to England in search of glory and silver were about to meet Beornoth's fury. Beornoth laughed. It was a strange moment. But he laughed because in battle the rest of his worries, his longing for Eawynn, suspicion of the Normans, grief for his lost family, all became dulled. The thrill of battle was intoxicating. The moment where a man balanced on the blade's edge between life and death elevated him above the humdrum of life. A warrior soared like an eagle as the blades clashed about him, and God forgive him for it, but Beornoth enjoyed it. There was glory in killing one's enemies, in slaying a man who tried to kill you. Those feelings, that heightened joy, was upon him, and so Beornoth laughed, because it was time to kill Vikings.

10

Twelve men guarded Kvitsr War Raven's warships. Beornoth rode towards them at the head of fifty mounted Saxon warriors. Behind him, Vikings and Normans bellowed their war cries. A horn sounded from within the old earthworks and Robert de Warenne's men beat their spears against their shields to create a rhythmic war music, one that would fill hearts with bravery. They had all drunk their fill of ale since arriving at Cantuctone, and no war leader would begrudge his men that small mercy. The Normans were about to scale steep, grass-covered banks and attack a force of Viking warriors. Those men waited atop the ramparts to hack at the Normans from above as they tried to run up the grassy mounds and defend themselves at the same time. It was grim work. Men would die and suffer terrible injuries. To march into a forest of sharp blades, a man needed all the courage he could get, including a belly full of ale to dull his wits and embolden his spirit.

Hoofbeats pounded the earth around him and Beornoth drove Virtus hard towards the three Viking warships moored in the estuary of a wide-mouthed river. Afternoon sun cast a warm golden light across the water, glinting off the iron-studded shields carried by the dozen Kvitsr had left to guard his most prized possessions. The Danes had left their warships in the shallows, so that now the tide was at ebb, their hulls sat awkwardly on grey banks of silt. Beast-headed prows turned towards the distant sea. The *drakkars*, sleek and fearsome with their weathered wooden planks stained by salt and brine, would float on the flood, but for now they presented Beornoth with an opportunity to anger and frighten the Danes, to rob them of reason and ready their ranks for slaughter.

The estuary was vast, its mudflats stretched far into the distance, beyond rolling banks of glistening mud. Thin streams of water wound through the exposed flats, and twelve men stood on a heather-covered bank, glancing nervously at each other as sixty spearmen charged towards them on galloping horses. Virtus snorted and Beornoth growled, readying his spear for contact. He wanted to look over his shoulder, to see if Kvitsr's men had broken their ranks inside the ramparts to chase him down to their ships. But to look was to falter, and the twelve men he charged towards grew closer with every pound of Virtus' muscled legs. Hooves drummed in time with Beornoth's heartbeat, ringing inside the metal of his helmet to fill his head with war music.

Wigs, Ecga and Gis were with him. Beornoth trusted them and the rest of the Saxons to maintain the charge. He could not see or hear them through the confines of his helmet, but he charged on, believing in their steadfastness. The air was thick with the stink of the sea and the rich, pungent smell of the estuary at low tide. Debris and foam moved slowly through the muddy seawater rivulets, snaking their way towards the open sea. Marsh grasses sped by as Virtus galloped alongside reed beds. Wind whistled through his helmet's face to make Beornoth's eyes water, and he couched his spear for the charge.

A fire burned behind the dozen Danes, a small blaze of driftwood and willow branches between a circle of salt-stained rocks. Beornoth caught a whiff of cooking fish and he knew luck was on his side. A fire waited for him, and all he had to do was kill twelve boat guards to win the battle. Virtus slowed as the terrain became soft beneath her hooves, riverbank merged with mudflats in a sticky and uneven mess and every time the warhorse lifted her legs it made a slurping, sucking sound. Beornoth urged her on, digging his heels in and rising in the saddle. The twelve Danes backed slowly away from him, their spears wavering and their shields held low. One of them shouted something and pointed at the ships, and the others exchanged nervous glances.

Virtus picked up speed, finding purchase on the knoll upon which the twelve Vikings waited. They were close now, so close that Beornoth saw a hammer amulet around one man's neck, and the Viking runes etched into the shaft of another man's spear. Beornoth threw his *aesc* spear. He brought his arm back and hurled the weapon with all the strength in his upper body and the iron-tipped length of ash hurtled through the air. The point took a sallow-skinned warrior in the stomach, throwing him backwards with its sheer force. The Danes shuffled back further. One threw a spear at Beornoth, but there was no heart in the throw and the weapon fell wide of its mark. He urged his warhorse up the knoll and drew his sword. Beornoth preferred fighting on foot, not trusting the unpredictable nature of fighting upon horseback. But a warhorse is frightening. Virtus was an enormous animal, a gift from the king himself. She stood fifteen hands high and towered over most men. Virtus, built for strength and endurance rather than speed, had a muscular neck, broad chest and powerful legs. She could carry Beornoth in his byrnie and his war gear into the thick of combat. Virtus' thick hide protected her from injury, and her training allowed her to charge into enemy lines.

Beornoth drove Virtus into the remaining Danes. He roared his anger and slashed at their necks and shields. His sword cracked into the skull of one man and clanged off a shield rim. The Danes shouted and screamed at him, trying to stab at both horse and rider with their spears. Virtus kicked out with a foreleg and shattered a Dane's shield, her huge teeth bit an enemy on the shoulder and he twisted at the pain, leaving his neck unprotected. Beornoth stabbed his sword down into that exposed flesh and muscle and there was blood beside the wide river estuary. Gis and Ecga had dismounted and charged into the Danes behind their shields. Two Vikings fell to the ground and Beornoth let Virtus trample them, her heavy legs destroying their faces and torsos with terrible force.

'Burn the ships!' Beornoth called, waving his sword aloft. 'Use the fire and burn the ships.' More Saxons reached the knoll and smashed the twelve Vikings. One dropped his shield and spear and ran towards the river. He leapt into the thick mud, squelching through it in great strides as he tried to reach the water and escape the Saxons' fury. Beornoth tugged on the reins and Virtus turned. A stream of Vikings poured from the fortress like ants in summer. They came running in chaos, under-standing that Beornoth meant to burn their precious ships and leave them stranded in a foreign land.

Gis and Ecga chased the running man. They plunged into the thick mud, runner and hunters moving ridiculously slowly through the thigh-deep silt. Beornoth left them and rode Virtus to the beached ships. Men brought burning faggots and kindling from their packs. They cut branches from nearby trees and tossed them onto the Viking ships. Burning logs followed, and Beornoth waited to see if the flames would catch fire inside the ships' hulls.

'Mount up,' he ordered. 'Get on your horses and kill the bastards in the open! Look for men on their own and don't let them drag you from the saddle. Ride away if they make a shield wall. On me!'

It didn't matter if the ships caught fire or not. What mattered was that Kvitsr's men saw Beornoth try to burn them. It had worked, and three score Vikings dashed from their ancient fort to save their only means of escaping from England's shores. Robert de Warenne and his Normans reached the summit of the outer bank. Beornoth saw their shields, spears and helmets catching the sun like jewels on a bishop's fingers. He urged Virtus towards the running Danes, not in a wild charge, but in a controlled canter. He held his sword low and left his shield slung across his back. The Saxon riders followed him in ragged order, fanning out to pick off the Danes as they came. If the Vikings formed ranks, the horses would do no good. Only a trained warhorse would charge a line of spears and shields, the rest would shy away. So they rode for the stragglers to pick them off and spread fear into the hearts of Kvitsr War Raven's men.

Beornoth glanced to his right and saw Gis and Ecga catch their man and hack him to bloody ruin in the muddy filth. He did not pity the man, nor any of the Vikings who were about to die. They deserved their fate. They knew the risks when they left Jutland and the Vik on their dragon ships. And now they would suffer Beornoth's wrath. A long-legged man tried to avoid him. He ran from the other Danes, veering left, hoping to flee around the fighting, but Beornoth pulled Virtus into his path and swept his sword down. The Viking cowered, raising his hands, eyes wide in horror. Beornoth's sword cut through his fingers and chopped into his face. He ripped the blade free and wheeled Virtus back towards a pack of running Vikings. Beornoth came behind them, slashing his sword across one Dane's back and driving the point into the spine of another. The Saxons rode about the Vikings, killing them as they tried to run for the safety of their ships. Smoke rose from the *drakkars* in thin columns, but it was enough.

A group of Danes caught a Saxon rider and pulled him from the saddle. They hauled him to the ground and hacked at him with their axes. The man screamed for help and died with an axe buried in his chest. One tried to mount the horse, and another dragged him away and clambered into the saddle himself. Beornoth led his Saxons in a charge against those Danes, killing the first man with a sweep of his sword and then stabbing overhand into the back of another. Wigs killed the mounted Dane with a cast of his spear and the horse ran away nodding its head, terrified by the violence and the iron stink of blood. More Vikings streamed from the fortifications, and still they did not form a shield wall. They ran like madmen towards their burning ships and found vengeful Saxon blades waiting for them. The din of battle sounded from inside the high ditch banks where Robert de Warenne and his Normans met Kvitsr and the bravest of his warriors.

'Kill them all!' Beornoth roared at the Saxons. 'Leave no man alive. Any who tries to reach the ships must die.' He left them to the slaughter and instead rode Virtus towards the old earth fort. He saw Odo de Warenne's men at the breach where the fortifications had collapsed. A hail of arrows and spears met them, launched by Danes from behind a makeshift wall of thorn bushes and briar. Beornoth wheeled away from that struggle and came about the fortress' eastern edge. Virtus leapt the ditch and Beornoth dismounted. He slapped Virtus on the haunch and set her trotting away from the violence as he clambered unopposed up a high ditch.

Beornoth reached the summit to find a desperate fight raging within the old fort. Two shield walls clashed, heaving and cutting at one another. Six Normans lay dead or dying and the clatter and bang of shields, spears, axes and swords melded with the shouts and cries of men desperate to kill their enemies. A man fought at the centre of the Danish line, a tall man with a conical-shaped helmet and long, drooping moustaches. He wielded a strange, curved sword and roared at his men in Norse to stand their ground. That man must be Kvitsr, Beornoth thought. A man who had brought a fleet of warships full of Viking warriors to England, dangerous men who trusted him to lead them to wealth and glory. He was a brave man, and Beornoth watched him keep the Norman shield wall at bay. What Kvitsr could not see whilst he fought for his life was that men peeled away from his rear ranks like wax dripping from a burning candle. They were the weaker men, the ones who waited for the shield wall to break before they would strike a blow at the enemy. The champions, the lovers of battle, fought at the front. The men who lived for the clash of arms, the violent ones, the men to fear.

As Kvitsr's rear rankers fled the shield-wall fight, his battle line edged backwards under the pressure of the Norman shields. Kvitsr had begun the fight with equal numbers, with three crews of vicious Danes, but already at least one crew's worth of warriors had run to find their fate on the end of a Saxon blade. The runners could not see what awaited them beyond the high earthworks. They could see the masts of their ships where tendrils of smoke twisted into the sky, and that sight filled their hearts with fear. Beornoth unslung his shield and marched down the bank. It was time to fight, to punish the men who had slain so many of the innocent people of Defnascir. Beornoth came about the rear of Kvitsr's battle line, into the heart of the ancient fortress, and the noise of battle rang in that place, filling Beornoth's helmeted ears with the song of war.

A Dane peeled away from Kvitsr's left flank, dropping his shield and running. He carried a long spear and a tunic of padded wool. He was young, blond-haired and tears streamed down his dirt-smeared cheeks. The Viking glanced over his shoulder at his shipmates, looking to see if any of them saw him run, then he turned to look at the smoke coming from his jarl's ships. Beornoth strode quickly to cut off the Dane's escape. The young man's face was drawn, his mouth hung open and his eyes widened. His friends died horribly about him, and the vessel that could carry him back to his mother, his wife, or whoever waited for him in the cold north, burned before his eyes. He noticed Beornoth too late. His head turned and he flinched in terror. His eyes closed tightly, and he tried to veer away, not even bothering to strike at Beornoth with his spear. Beornoth lunged low with his sword, slicing open the young Dane's calf. He tripped and cried out, snot and spittle in his scant beard. He turned on the grass and shook his head, mouthing a silent prayer at Beornoth. The young Dane died quickly. Beornoth drove the point of his sword down hard into the Dane's heart and twisted the blade. There could be no pity for the sea-wolves. Even the soft-faced ones, the young ones with their lives before them, were killers. So Beornoth wrenched his sword free of the young Dane's corpse.

'The ships! The ships!' shouted two Vikings running from the shield wall carrying their shields and axes. Beornoth met them head on. They slowed their run, exchanged glances, unnerved to see a huge Saxon behind their battle line. Beornoth slammed his shield into the first Dane with so much force that the man fell to the ground. The second Dane swung his axe but without conviction, still running from the fight. Beornoth swayed away from the blow and drove his sword beneath the axe arm and into the soft skin beneath the warrior's armpit. A Dane charged at Beornoth, smashing into him with shield raised. Beornoth took the blow, and the man staggered backwards, surprised at Beornoth's strength. The Viking recovered and hooked the bearded axe of his blade over Beornoth's shield and dragged it down. His left hand came over the shield's rim and punched Beornoth full in the face. The man cried out as his fist crunched against the boar-shaped iron nasal and Beornoth threw him backwards. He let go of his shield and reached behind his back for his seax. The Dane bellowed and threw Beornoth's shield away. He swung his axe and Beornoth parried it with his sword and stabbed the Viking with the seax in short, sharp bursts, piercing his guts beneath his leather breastplate.

More Danes streamed from the shield wall, and Beornoth hacked at them. He roared incoherently, cutting with sword and seax at legs, arms, necks, faces and torsos. The Danes ran first in ones and twos, and then in groups of five until their shield wall broke and Kvitsr's three crews descended into an all-out, desperate retreat. They flowed around Beornoth like a river around an immovable boulder, fearing his bloody weapons and his fearsome grimace. The Normans followed, whooping at the triumph and chasing the Danes over the ramparts towards their burning ships.

'We've done it!' said Robert de Warenne as he reached Beornoth, chest heaving, shield dented and smeared with blood. 'We've beaten the bastards.' He grinned, teeth stained with crimson where a Dane had split his lip during the fighting. He left Beornoth and followed the Danes.

Beornoth let them go. He sighed, his old wounds and ageing

limbs suddenly stiff and aching. Men groaned and writhed, the injured of both sides begging for help or mercy. Beornoth sheathed his sword and seax and picked up his shield. He removed his helmet and fastened it to his belt. Beyond the ramparts, the sounds of slaughter fouled the afternoon air as two hundred war-Danes died before their smouldering ships. A Norman reached out to him, lying on the grass ten paces from where Beornoth stood. The Norman's chain mail was torn, and dark blood soaked the grass around him. Men's boots had turned the inside of the old fort to mud and filth, and a Dane with a blood-sheeted face crawled through the filth towards the injured Norman. It was over. They had won. Beornoth counted the Norman dead and dying, and a score of men had paid the ultimate price to bring Kvitsr and his men to justice.

As Beornoth looked over the carnage, he noticed a warrior whom he had thought dead sit up straight. He was a big man with drooping moustaches. He clutched a dented conical helmet to his midriff like he was a starving man and it was a loaf of bread. It was Kvitsr War Raven, his face filthy with mud and blood, bright blue eyes staring right at Beornoth. Beornoth walked to him.

'Your men are dead and your ships are burning,' Beornoth said in Norse.

'My men are dead. I think I am killed. I have more ships, though, many more ships,' said Kvitsr. He smiled then, a pained half-smile.

'Are you wounded?'

'Aye. I think I'm done for.' Kvitsr slowly lifted the helmet. Beneath it his chain mail was ripped open, and blue-black foulness showed there. 'You are a warrior. Hand me that axe there.' He gestured to an axe lying in the mud, just out of his reach.

'You worship the old gods?'

'I am no worshipper of the nailed god, Saxon.'

Beornoth nodded and kicked the axe haft so that Kvitsr could pick it up. He sighed with relief and clutched the axe to his chest above his helmet. He coughed up a gout of blood and stared at Beornoth.

'You know of our gods, Saxon?'

'I know you must die in battle with a blade in your hand if you want to go to Valhalla when you die.'

'Yes,' he said. Kvitsr swallowed hard and stared up at the sky. 'Who are you? What is your name?'

'I am Beornoth, whom your people called Beornoth Reiði.'

'Beornoth the Wrathful. I have heard of you. You have reputation. I had reputation, I dare to say it, now that I am before Odin's mercy. Always I fought in the front, always I struck with the axe. When my father died, he left me two ships and a rusty sword. I die now having sailed to England with sixty warships at my back. I could have been a king here.'

'And now you are dead.'

Kvitsr grimaced at the pain of his wounds. 'And now I am dead. I await the clouds to part and the Valkyrie descend and carry me to Asgard. There I shall feast and swive with the great corpse host, fight and die each day and rise again each night to do it again. Or perhaps it will be Thor's hall, Thruthvangr, or Sessrúmnir, Freya's mighty hall upon the fields of Fólkvangr. I am ready.'

'You might not die. You might struggle on with that wound for days and die of the infection. You won't have your axe then, and you'll weep like a baby for its mother before the end. No Valhalla, if that happens, no Sessrúmnir. The skuld world will be your fate then, Kvitsr War Raven. Or perhaps the corpse shore, where the serpent Níðhöggr will gnaw upon your dead body until the end of days.'

Kvitsr thought about that for a moment. Beornoth had grown up in the Danelaw and knew the Norsemen's beliefs as well as he knew his own. Theirs were cruel gods, hard gods, gods which made the Vikings the men they were. 'Do you have any ale? I am thirsty. So thirsty.'

'No ale. But I have this seax.' Beornoth drew the blade and showed its fine antler hilt to Kvitsr. 'I could give you a good death, a warrior's death. Or I could wait until the Normans have slaughtered your men and let them crucify you, or leave you here to rot for days.'

'You want something, Saxon? Spit it out. I choose the warrior's death, but what must you have in return for that favour?'

'Why did Pallig break his oath to King Æthelred?'

'So small a request for so great a prize?' Kvitsr smiled, and another thick gloop of blood slipped from his mouth to foul his beard. 'They treated Pallig well here at first. He defended Lundenwic, where you fought with Thorkell the Tall. I have heard the tale. The king granted Pallig lands here, and he was happy. He fought for your Æthelred many times. But then the Normans grew in power, and bishops spoke against him. The king took half of Pallig's land and gave it to the Christ priests, the black crows, who have so much power over your people. You Saxons might not know it, but Pallig is well known amongst the Danes. A great warrior of reputation. He must be. He married Forkbeard's sister! We know of Pallig in the Skagerrak, the islands where I come from. One of his brothers married a cousin of mine.

'A trader sailed north from England and I heard of Pallig's woes. So, I paid a visit to Pallig two years ago, and we struck a bargain. I told him I would bring a fleet of warriors if he could tell me of the ripe places to pluck. I brought my ships and Pallig

brought his warriors and knowledge of England. We raided the
south coast, made ourselves rich on Christ-priest silver. Then we
came here to Defnascir. What land there is here, Beornoth. No
wonder men have fought for it for a thousand years. Pallig broke
his oath to King Æthelred, but I think your king also broke his
word to keep Pallig as his man, to be his ring giver, his lord. So
both men broke their peace. Your king is weak. He listens to
priests and Normans when he should listen to men like you.
Midgard is a place of war, and only warriors can survive. To be a
king, a man must be the strongest of his people, the most ruthless. Otherwise, he won't last long. Forkbeard is a good king, a
strong king. He will fight Olaf Tryggvason this year, or maybe
next year. The winner of that battle will be the king of the Danes
and the Norsemen. What glory, Beornoth!'

'Where is Pallig now?'

'Pallig took lands at Pinnock. South of here, at the end of a
river and the beginning of an estuary. He still holds the land the
king granted him at Oxenforda. Last I heard, he was at Pinnock
with two, maybe three hundred men.'

'Has he granted his men land?'

'Of course! He is their ring giver. All of his captains hold land
in south Defnascir.'

'Why did you settle your men here, send them out to take
halls and farms when you must have known that the king would
send men to destroy you?'

'I should have kept my army together. Is that what you
think? You think I am a fool? Ha! Have you ever tried to feed two
thousand men? To stop the jarls from killing each other? Half of
my jarls sailed home with ships heavy with plunder. The rest
stayed. So I sent them off to feed themselves and hold their new
lands.'

'You wanted to stay here, to make yourself a king's man?'

'I am Viking. I am a sea lord, a warrior. I would have left here before the winter. Until you came.'

'What of the slaves you captured?'

'Some fine wenches there. Some strong young lads and virgin maids. Worth a fortune in slave silver.'

'Where are they?'

'With the rest of my fleet at Watchet. I was going to sail three weeks ago. I should have gone to Dublin and sold the slaves. I would be rich by now.'

'But you are a greedy, bloodthirsty savage and you wanted to wait for more. And now you are dead.'

Kvitsr smiled at the insult. 'It's time, Saxon. You have your questions answered. Now, send me to Valhalla.'

Beornoth was tempted to leave him to his fate. It was all Kvitsr deserved for the suffering he had brought to so many Saxon families. He stared into those blue eyes, so pale they were almost white. Beornoth stepped forward and cut Kvitsr's throat with the edge of his seax. Kvitsr lay back, holding the axe haft so tightly that the knuckles on his hand showed white. He died, staring at the clouds with a smile on his face, and Beornoth wondered if the Viking gods had come for him, or if the priests were right, and the Danes would go screaming to hell for their heathen beliefs. He stood and sheathed his seax, and noticed Odo de Warenne staring at him from the top of a high grass-topped bank. The Norman had seen him kill Kvitsr. The sour little man would be angry that Beornoth had killed the Viking leader, that he had denied Odo his chance at torture. But there were plenty of other Danes captured or wounded in the battle on which he could practice his malevolent punishments.

Robert de Warenne would want to ride south to attack Pallig next. Pallig and Kvitsr were the leaders, the most prominent names on King Æthelred's kill list. Beornoth had not still come around to the idea of killing a man he liked, a man he had fought alongside. Odo disappeared from the rampart and Beornoth wondered how he could get to Watchet before the slave ships left, because he could not leave those people to a life of misery.

11

Robert de Warenne let his Normans celebrate after the defeat of Kvitsr War Raven. They found barrels of ale in the Viking camp, along with flitches of bacon, cheeses, fish and honey. Afternoon turned to a balmy evening as the Normans rounded up any of the Danes who had surrendered or were not too badly wounded to walk. They put those men on board the only one of Kvitsr's ships which had not burned during the fight. They tied the Danes' wrists and ankles with seal-hide rope found aboard the ship and left them there as they enjoyed a makeshift feast on the riverbank. The tide rose, flooding across the mudflats as the sun dipped to cast the hill fort in a flame-coloured hue. Beornoth found Virtus cropping wild grass close to the river, and he fed the horse with some oats found amongst the Vikings' supplies and brushed her coat with a handful of grass.

The Normans drank and ate, talking and laughing louder and louder as more ale flowed. They spoke in Norse and so the Saxons kept their distance, forming their own group to celebrate the victory. Once he had seen to Virtus, Beornoth joined them.

He sat with Gis, Ecga and Wigs to share some ale, meat and cheese.

'You drink little for so large a man. If you don't mind me saying so, lord,' said Ecga, with beads of ale showing in his beard.

'I have drunk enough ale to drown Winchester itself,' Beornoth said. 'I spent many years lost in it, drunk and wretched and no good to anyone.'

'You, lord? I don't believe it.'

'When that time was over, I stopped drinking ale altogether. I only took it up again not so long ago.'

'What does a man drink who does not drink ale?' asked Wigs. 'Water makes your arse as runny as churls' piss.'

'Lord Beornoth!' called Robert de Warenne, saving Beornoth from explaining himself further. He came striding from the Norman celebrations with a Viking horn of ale raised, its contents sloshing with each step. He still wore his byrnie, which was smeared with blood, and carried a cut on his cheek which had a crust of dried blood around it. 'We are lucky when we fight together, you and I, are we not?'

'We are, Lord Robert,' Beornoth said. He groaned, muscles protesting, and pushed himself to his feet.

'Another splendid victory today. Though we have lost some good men to do it. We should drink in their honour, and remember their names.'

'We should, you are right.' Beornoth tried to smile, but feared that his face only twisted into a look of discomfort. They had beaten the Danes, but only because Beornoth has set fire to their ships. If they had followed Robert and Odo's plan, it would be the Vikings celebrating over the corpses of their dead enemies.

'Come, join us. My brother and I have found some wine we

can share. Come.' He beckoned Beornoth on, and he could not refuse without insulting the Norman.

Beornoth followed Robert through his Norman warriors. They laughed and clapped one another on the back, their shaved heads pale in the dim evening light. They lit fires using wood from the burned Viking ships and cooked meat as they shared stories of their valour on the battlefield. It was a glorious victory, Beornoth could not deny that. They had killed a powerful Danish warlord, and the Normans had fought well. But the slaves at Watchet would not leave Beornoth's head, and as he watched Robert de Warenne strolling confidently, he wondered how Robert would react if he asked him again for men to ride west to the slave ships. It was only twelve miles to Watchet, less than a morning's ride away, and whilst there might be a stout force there to protect the ships, all Beornoth wanted to do was free the slaves, not fight another battle.

They reached the corner of the riverbank where Odo and Robert de Warenne had set their saddles to lean on and enjoy the celebration, along with a dozen of their captains. The merriment subsided as Beornoth approached and he stiffened under their gaze.

'Give old Beornoth here some of that wine,' said Robert de Warenne.

Odo frowned, the fire casting shadows upon his scarred face. He stood, poured a horn of wine and limped over to Beornoth. 'I serve you with my own hand, Lord Beornoth. Here, enjoy the fruits of our victory.'

Beornoth accepted the horn and inclined his head in thanks.

'We should all raise our cups now, and say thanks to God for what we achieved this day,' said Robert.

'But won't that insult our guest?' said Odo. He turned and gestured to a grisly sight Beornoth had not noticed. It was Kvitsr's severed head pushed onto a spear point, with the spear's shaft set into the ground so that the head stared out at the Normans. 'Perhaps we should thank Odin for turning his back on his people?'

The Normans laughed, but Beornoth turned away.

'Is it my jest that offends you, Lord Beornoth? Or that we have taken Kvitsr's head?'

'Congratulations,' said Beornoth. 'You do yourself great honour, Odo.' He turned to leave, unable to look upon Odo's gruesome trophy any longer.

'I saw you,' Odo shouted, his voice screeching. 'I saw you kill Kvitsr. You gave him an axe before you slew him. I saw you give the Viking what he wanted more than anything in all the world. Comfort for his soul. Do you love the Danes, Lord Beornoth? Are you loyal to your king?'

Beornoth stopped and let his horn of wine fall to the grass. He turned slowly. 'Choose your next words wisely.'

'Beornoth is famous for killing Danes,' said Robert, placing a calming hand on his brother's shoulder.

'He's a turgid old Saxon bastard,' Odo spat, and shook free of his brother's hand. He limped towards Beornoth, unsteady and slurring his words under the influence of the strong wine, which was far more effective at loosening a man's wits than the ale brewed in England. 'Beornoth has dogged me at every turn. He thinks himself the noble hero.'

Beornoth surged forward with a speed which belied his age. He punched Odo so hard in the side of his head that the Norman collapsed, as if his soul had been snatched from his body. The Norman warriors flew into uproar, throwing their ale into the air, pushing Beornoth and shouting insults. Beornoth stepped back with his hands raised. He should not have hit Odo, should have controlled his anger. But it was too late for regret now. Robert de Warenne barged his men aside and threw his horn of wine at Beornoth. Beornoth batted it away.

'How dare you strike my brother!' Robert shouted. He came at Beornoth, lip curled in a snarl.

Beornoth set himself, and was ready to fight, but the Normans grabbed their lord and held him back. Beornoth was uncertain that they did so because they did not want him to act rashly, or because they feared what might happen if the two big men came together.

'Go, malinger with your Saxons,' Robert de Warenne spat. He shook his men off and mastered his temper. 'I won't let you take the shine off my victory.'

Beornoth stalked away and rejoined Gis, Wigs and Ecga at their campfire.

'That went well,' said Wigs, and the others sniggered.

Beornoth ignored them. It had been a mistake to hit Odo, one that Beornoth feared he might come to regret. The Normans drank themselves into a stupor, and once darkness fell, they tossed burning planks and branches onto the last surviving *drakkar*. It was afloat on the flood tide, and the tied-up Danes aboard screamed in panic as flames took hold. The Normans capered about on the riverbank in their cups, shouting of their victory to the heavens, clapping one another on the back and rejoicing at the defeat and suffering of Kvitsr's warriors. Rigging, benches and sailcloth caught fire, and soon the entire ship became engulfed in flames, along with the forty Viking prisoners on board. The stink turned Beornoth's stomach and, as the blaze lit the entire estuary, he gathered his fellow Saxon warriors close to him.

'Drink no more, lads,' he said. 'Get some sleep. We ride to Watchet before dawn. We'll free the slaves and return before our

Norman friends have nursed their sore heads and roused themselves to ride.'

'We can't just ride to Watchet without the Normans,' said one man, searching the faces of his Saxon comrades for support. They huddled around Beornoth like a wolf pack. 'Lord Robert won't like it.'

'Look at them,' said Beornoth, jutting his chin to where the Normans leapt about in the glare of a burning dragon ship. 'They'll drink until there isn't a drop left and won't wake until noon. When they do, they won't be fit to ride. Tomorrow will be a day of rest and preparation to ride against Pallig. We'll be back from Watchet before they know we've even left.'

'The ships might not even be there,' said another Saxon. 'They might have sailed for Dublin already.'

Beornoth stood to his full height. 'Our people are aboard those ships. Somebody's wife, daughter, son or mother. What if it were your wife or daughter huddled, shivering and full of fear aboard those ships? What if they were about to be shipped off to some unknown shore to become a slave to a cruel master, where their bodies are their only thing of value? How hard would you fight to free them? How hard would you want the warriors of your shire to fight for them? We are warriors, and we have a duty to save them if we can.'

'The ships will be guarded. The Danes won't leave their fleet unprotected. How can the fifty left of us fight those men? There could be hundreds or thousands of warriors waiting for us at Watchet.'

'There could. And the ships might not be there.' Beornoth drew his sword slowly, so that the blade scraped against the wooden lip of its scabbard. The Saxons leaned away from him, staring at the cruel steel weapon, fully aware of what Beornoth was capable of with the sword in his hand. He showed them the blade, part of the heriot granted to him by King Æthelred as part of his elevation to king's thegn. He scowled at them and locked eyes with each warrior gaping up at him. 'I am a king's thegn. I am going to Watchet. If there are ships there, I will free our people or die trying. It doesn't matter how many Vikings await me there, I go anyway. Not to fight and kill the Danes, but to free the slaves. Any guards will watch for an attack, but there will be no attack. I'll free those poor souls and be back here whilst our Norman friends are still nursing their sore heads. If the Normans object, then they can face me. I ride before first light. Any man who loves his people is welcome to ride with me. I won't hold it against any man who does not.'

At first light the next morning, fifty Saxons rode away from smouldering, charred warships and snoring Normans. The riders cantered along the riverbank, their silhouettes dark against the dawn. They rode in tight formation, the air already warm before a steady wind from the dark, open sea. Beornoth was proud to see all of his countrymen waiting for him when he woke. They were grim-faced and pale with worry, but they were ready. Beornoth had gone amongst them, especially those who had questioned him the night before. He had clasped each man's forearm in the warrior's grip, saw the looks of pride and determination upon their faces.

The riders kept a steady pace westwards, moving briskly across open pastureland and through the small forests that dotted the countryside. It was twelve miles to Watchet as the Rome folk measured it and they varied the pace, trotting and walking to conserve their horse's strength. The track followed an old Roman road for a stretch and then diverged along narrower pathways carved into the earth by local use. The fields about them swayed heavy with barley and wheat and hedgerows thick with hawthorn and bramble marked the boundaries of farmsteads where churls peered at them as they worked their fields in the early morning light. Cattle and sheep grazed in soft meadows and birds sang to add their song to the peaceful hum of a late summer morning disturbed by the sound of fifty sets of hoofbeats, rattling tack and the bang and clatter of swords, spears, shields and chain-mail armour.

Virtus splashed through a shallow ford in the River Parrett as its shallow waters glittered in the sunlight. Willows and rushes lined the riverbank and Beornoth urged his warhorse up a hillside, following the track above marshlands to the south. Further east, the Quantock Hills loomed on the horizon in a dark green ridge against the brightening sky. They rode in silence, each man following Beornoth, fearful of what awaited them at Watchet's burh and harbour. Beornoth knew the way, remembered the landmarks from his last visit to Watchet, when he had fought fearsome Jomsvikings and killed their leader in a desperate battle. He knew the river, the distant hills and ancient hill fort of Dumnoc and thought of the brave men he had fought beside that hard day in Watchet. Virtus' hooves drummed the earth and memories of dead friends and brothers thrummed in Beornoth's mind. He thought of Eawynn and his slain daughters. Though fifty men surrounded him, it was a lonely ride, and the more Beornoth tried to banish unwelcome memories from his mind, the more they haunted him.

The riders thundered through villages and gated farms where churls, farmers and villagers bowed respectfully. The caw of gulls announced their arrival at the coast before Beornoth saw the grey rolling sea to his right. Fishing boats bobbed in the swell and the fortified town of Watchet and its timber palisade hugged the cliffs like a limpet, and the masts of *drakkar* warships filled the harbour like tree trunks stripped of their leaves and boughs in winter. Beornoth set his jaw and glowered at the

Viking ships. The warriors guarding the ships hadn't sailed, which meant they either didn't know their lord was defeated, or they hadn't decided what to do or who should lead them. Kvitsr's death left his newly conquered lands in uncertainty. He had granted stolen land to jarls and captains, but all remained oathsworn to him. Kvitsr was the rope that bound them together. Without him, their loyalties fractured and the strongest amongst them would challenge for power. They would never be weaker than at that moment, so Beornoth wheeled Virtus around to address his men.

'The ships are here,' he said. 'Wigs and Ecga come with me. The rest of you wait here with the horses and keep out of sight. I go to see what king of force defends Watchet and how many ships are in the harbour.'

Beornoth led Wigs and Ecga along towards Watchet, cantering their mounts and keeping to the coastal path. He took his helmet and pushed it onto his head. In his byrnie, cloak and helmet he looked like a Dane, and so did his men. There was little to separate Dane and Saxon but the way they wore their hair and beards, the pagan or Christian talismans they wore around their necks, and the arrogance with which they carried themselves.

'We are riding towards the fort, lord,' said Wigs, bringing his mount alongside Virtus.

'We are,' Beornoth replied.

'There are Danes there, lord.'

'There are.'

'And we are Saxons.'

Beornoth rewarded his empty statements with a frown.

'We can't just ride through the gates and count them.'

'Just don't open your mouths when we get there. Leave the

talking to me. Count the ships in the harbour and the spears you see inside.'

Beornoth rode ahead, understanding why Wigs and Ecga were nervous about approaching a captured Saxon burh held by Viking invaders. Beornoth followed the path as it led away from the sea and around to Watchet's landward-facing gate. He recalled the twin oak gates and timber palisade, and the horror of scaling those walls to kill the men beyond made him shudder. It was mid-morning and the path leading into Watchet's open gates was busy with folk pushing handcarts, coming to and from the settlement with food and goods. Half a dozen spearmen lolled on the palisade's fighting platform, and no guards stood beyond the gate. So Beornoth simply rode in. He led Virtus through the open gates and reined her in amidst a busy courtyard. Stables and houses faced the open square, reached out of it in a snarl of lanes and pathways. A Dane strolled from behind the gate, he was a tall man with blond hair and a beard so long that its braid reached below his chest. He looked Beornoth up and down and leaned on his spear with a tired look on his youthful face.

'Are you Kvitsr's men?' Beornoth asked in Norse. He spoke as though he owned the place. He looked like a lord in his war finery, and any hint of fear or apprehension would arouse suspicions amongst the belligerent Danes.

'Yes,' he replied. 'What's your business here?'

'Yes, lord,' Beornoth said. He tugged slightly on Virtus' reins so that the beast's great chest and neck veered towards the guard, forcing him to take a step backwards.

'Yes, lord,' said the guard, and bowed his head in deference.

'I am Harald Haraldsson. Come from Jarl Pallig to speak with Lord Kvitsr.'

'My Lord Kvitsr isn't here. He is a half-day's ride to the east.

You'll find him at a place named Cantuctone. Bloody Saxons are as bad at naming their towns as they are defending them.'

'Who commands here?'

'Jarl Hvitserk. Shall I send for him, lord?'

'How many men does Hvitserk command?'

'Two crews, lord. One here and another ranging to the south. They say a Saxon war band is on the loose.'

'That's why I'm here. There are hundreds of them three days to the south. Pallig sent me to warn Lord Kvitsr. Did Kvitsr take his fleet with him?'

'Just three ships. We have a dozen ships here, and the rest are spread out along the coast. We're lucky though. Ours have the captured womenfolk aboard. You should stay the night before you ride east.' The Dane winked at Beornoth and his two riders. 'Hvitserk lets us use the old ones.'

'We ride for Cantuctone. Tell Jarl Hvitserk I would advise him to send a score of men riding south to watch for the Saxons.'

Beornoth didn't wait for the warrior to reply. He wheeled Virtus about and galloped the mare through the gates.

'Well, what news?' asked Ecga as they raced away from Watchet.

'Only one crew inside the walls guarding a dozen of Kvitsr's ships.'

'But that could be as many as seventy Danes. How can we free the slaves?'

'Have either of you ever sailed a warship?'

'No, lord. Gis is from a fishing village and he might know his way around a ship. Why?'

'Because we are going to steal a Viking *drakkar*.'

12

Beornoth would have preferred to take the ship at night, but he wanted to return to Robert de Warenne and the Normans before the day was over, which meant he had to steal a Viking warship in broad daylight. The Saxons had baulked when Beornoth had explained his plan, but none had refused to follow him.

'Could we not use cunning to free the slaves?' asked Gis.

'We could,' Beornoth replied. 'What do you have in mind?'

The Saxon scratched his beard and stared about him as though he could find the answer to his problem in the trees or out at sea. 'Why don't we capture a fishing boat? Sail towards the warships, climb aboard, and be away before the bastards know what's hit them?'

'We would need four or five fishing tubs to carry our men, and perhaps the same again for the freed slaves. Even if we can find so many ships and relieve the fishermen of their liveli-hoods, the Danes would notice a fleet of fishing ships sailing towards their harbour.'

'When you put it like that...'

So Beornoth led his fifty riders slowly along the coastal path towards Watchet. They did not like the idea of what Beornoth intended, for it was brutal and desperate and some of them would surely die. But they rode, and Beornoth was proud of their bravery.

'If each man plays his part,' Beornoth said as the Saxons mounted their horses, 'we'll free the slaves and escape before the defenders are even aware of us.'

When he was within two hundred paces of the fortress, Beornoth urged Virtus into a gallop. The Saxons followed his lead and their horses thundered towards the oak gates at full tilt. Beornoth held his spear in his right hand and leather reins in his left. The noise rumbled inside his helmet and his black cloak flared out from beneath the shield strapped to his back. Spearmen on the ramparts stared at the riders, and Beornoth was sure that some of those men would raise the alarm. It would not matter, for they wouldn't have time to stop what he intended. The Vikings were confident. Sure that they had vanquished the callow Saxon defenders and any warriors in Somersaete and Defnascir who might challenge their presence. That confidence made them lazy. Beornoth had noted spots of rust on their spears, the open gates, the lack of a robust guard outside. They weren't concerned about an attack, and now Beornoth came for them in all his vengeful fury.

Virtus raced into the open gates and Beornoth did not hold the beast back. The Dane he had met that morning gaped at him and died with a spear in his chest. Beornoth led Virtus along the primary thoroughfare leading from the town square to the harbour. Warriors came from lanes and pathways and fell back as Beornoth and his huge warhorse galloped by. People ran and dived to get out of Virtus' path and Beornoth rode her hard. He kept his spear ready, couched in his right hand, but did not slow the beast to strike. The Saxons followed him, under strict orders not to engage with the Vikings unless they tried to bar their path to the ships. But so quick was the attack that the Vikings presented no obstacle, and Beornoth reined Virtus in when the warhorse's hooves clattered on the stone cobbles of Watchet's harbour.

Three Danes came from a crowded street where warriors and people cowered from the charging horses. They ran at Beornoth carrying spears in their fists and he climbed calmly down from the saddle as the rest of his riders hurtled from the main street. The ground inside Watchet shook and Beornoth let go of Virtus, trusting that his men would follow their orders. The first Dane met him in a wild charge. He ran with his spear held in two hands, running with such force that the spear point would tear through Beornoth's body as though it were soft butter. Beornoth parried the spear with the stave of his own weapon and lunged at the rightmost Dane. His reach surprised the enemy and the *aesc* spear slashed open a wide gash in the Dane's throat. Beornoth spun, whipping the spear around to parry a second thrust from the first spearman and meet the third. That man came on half-heartedly, stunned by the blood pumping from his shipmate's neck, and Beornoth drove his spear hard into his belly. A blow struck Beornoth's shield upon his back and he turned, leaving his spear in the third man's guts. The first spearman roared like a bear and thrust again. Beornoth swayed away from the attack, grabbed the man's head in his two powerful hands and twisted it savagely. The Dane's neck broke like a brittle twig beneath Beornoth's towering strength and he dropped the dead man to the cobbles, drew his sword and made for the jetty.

Vikings came streaming from alleys and lanes, armoured men with spears, others in trews and jerkins brandishing axes.

Beornoth's riders swarmed around the harbour, the clip-clop of their horses' hooves drowning out any other sound.

'Dismount!' Beornoth roared above the din. 'Ecga, lead the riders, go now! Go!'

Ecga waved his spear about his head and bellowed at the Saxons. Just as Beornoth had ordered, half of the warriors dismounted and the man next to them took their reins. Those on foot hefted shields and spears and joined Beornoth on the harbour front and jetty, whilst Ecga led the riders away. Each horseman spurred his own mount into a canter and led a rider-less horse behind him. The Vikings stared at the horsemen and at Beornoth's warriors. They were leaderless at that moment, unsure what to do or who to attack. Beornoth's bold, surprise attack would never have succeeded had Watchet's gates been closed and properly guarded. Beornoth would not have made the attempt. He could never scale the walls and attack the burh with fifty men. But the Vikings' overconfidence made his daring raid possible and now Beornoth made ready to implement the second part of his plan.

'Get the slaves, quickly,' he said. 'Wigs, go ship by ship and take them to the boat furthest from the harbour. Get the oars ready. Do it now!'

Wigs set off at a run with ten men at his back. Beornoth listened as their boots thumped on the jetty and trusted that his men would follow his orders. More Danes flooded from the shadowed spaces between the wattle and daub houses, and a man came forth in a byrnie, brandishing a sword and howling at his men to attack. He was red-faced, narrow-shoul-dered, bald and furious. It had to be Jarl Hvitserk, the leader Kvitsr had left in charge of Watchet and its valuable harbour. The Danes came together, shields clashing as they at last became organised into something resembling a shield wall.

Hvitserk strode forward, sword pointed at Beornoth and his men.

'So many,' gasped a Saxon at Beornoth's side.

'Wait here,' Beornoth said. The enemy needed their leader to organise them. That was clear. They were not the highly organised and battle-ready men Beornoth had fought before. A Jomsviking, a warrior of Olaf Tryggvason or Sweyn Forkbeard, would know immediately what to do if their town came under attack. But those men would not have left the gates open and unguarded. Beornoth strode forward and pointed his sword at Hvitserk. 'Come and fight,' Beornoth shouted in Norse so that every Dane at the harbour could hear him. 'You are a stinking whoreson who left his gates open. I challenge you, come and fight me. Show your men how brave you are.'

Hvitserk's lip curled and his face turned from red to purple as anger overwhelmed him. Every moment counted, and Beornoth resisted the urge to turn and see if Wigs and his men had freed many slaves. Beornoth banged his sword against his shield twice and stepped forward to fight. Hvitserk was in an impossible position. He had organised three score of his men into a shield wall five ranks deep, but now Beornoth challenged him to fight single combat. If Hvitserk refused, he would lose face in front of his men, and a Viking's power came from his reputation. With so many men, the Danes could charge and overwhelm Beornoth's small force in moments. So Beornoth had to create a distraction, to undermine the jarl who could lead that force. Kill him, and the Danes would be a leaderless rabble, and that might just give the Saxons time to escape.

Beornoth banged his sword upon his shield once more and showed his teeth beneath the closed cheekpieces of his shining helmet.

'Move to the ships,' Beornoth called to the Saxons behind

him in their language so that the Danes would not understand. 'When I kill this bastard, we go. Cast off. Don't wait for me.'

'But lord,' Gis shouted. 'If you don't make it, they'll cut you to pieces.'

'Do as I say!'

They set off and the Danes behind Hvitserk shouted their anger, edging forward so that their jarl took a step closer to Beornoth. A broad-shouldered Viking handed his jarl a shield, and then it was too late. There was no way for Hvitserk to avoid the challenge and he came on carefully, sword resting on the upper edge of his shield. Beornoth lashed out with his blade and Hvitserk caught the blow on his shield. Beornoth banged the jarl with his own shield, and Hvitserk met it with strength. A man does not rise to become a leader amongst the sea-wolves without knowing how to fight, and Beornoth kept his shield raised, waiting for the vicious attack he knew must come.

'For Odin!' Hvitserk said, and his sword snaked forward across the top of his shield and over Beornoth's. It was a clever blow and Beornoth had to twist his head away to stop the sword from taking his eyes. Cold, sharp steel lanced across his cheek and opened a gash. Beornoth veered away as blood gushed into his beard. Hvitserk followed up with an overhand sweep of his blade, and the sword slammed into Beornoth's shield with a strength Beornoth had not thought possible from the Dane's slight frame. He kicked Beornoth in the knee and Beornoth stumbled backwards. The Vikings let out an almighty roar to support their jarl and Beornoth tried to rise, shield held before him and sword ready to strike. But Hvitserk kept up his vicious onslaught, his sword battered Beornoth's shield like a hammer and Beornoth tried to bully the smaller man backwards, but Hvitserk hit him a glancing blow with his shield which rang Beornoth's helmet like a bell.

'Hurry, lord!' called Wigs from the ships, but Beornoth dared not look for fear that Hvitserk would strike a killing blow. The jarl's face streamed with sweat and his eyes blazed with a feral fury. Beornoth caught a sword cut on the edge of his blade and trapped Hvitserk's weapon between his sword and shield. Hvitserk tried to haul it free, but Beornoth turned him, and as he came about, Beornoth released the sword and punched his blade's hilt into Hvitserk's face. The jarl rocked backwards and Beornoth slammed his shield into Hvitserk's own to drive the jarl backwards. Hvitserk tried to hunker behind his shield, but Beornoth stabbed his sword over the upper edge and the tip of his weapon opened a gash down Hvitserk's back. The crowd of Danes groaned to see their jarl bloodied, but Hvitserk came up roaring like a wounded beast. He cut low at Beornoth's legs, caught a swipe of Beornoth's sword on his shield and lunged with his sword through the gap between Beornoth's defence and the edge scraped across Beornoth's ribs. The byrnie held, and Beornoth stepped backwards in two long strides. Hvitserk's battle-rage consumed him, and he charged forward uncontrollably. He saw blood on Beornoth's face, and that he had broached the big Saxon's defence more than once. Hvitserk saw a chance to kill a Saxon warlord whilst his warriors looked on. He smelled glory and his Viking heart swelled with hunger for it. So, he came on quickly, the skin on his red face drawn taut with anticipation of the death blow.

Beornoth met him with all the strength and power in his huge frame. He drove from his legs, hunched behind his shield so that he powered ahead like a battering ram. He crashed into Hvitserk like storm waves against a cliff. The smaller man fell backwards onto his arse and gaped up at Beornoth in surprise. Beornoth snarled, and without pause or hesitation he stabbed the point of his sword into that open mouth, pulled the blade free and stabbed again into Hvitserk's chest.

Without waiting for a response from the Danes, Beornoth turned and ran towards the jetty. His days of actually running were long behind him, so Beornoth moved in a hurried walk, limping slightly from an old leg wound. The Danes were quiet behind him, shocked and unsure what to do now that their leader was dead. Beornoth reached the first warship and clambered on board. He slung his shield over his back and ducked beneath the rigging, relieved to see that none of his men, nor any slaves, were on board the boat. He reached the bow of that ship and climbed onto the second vessel, and the Danes in the harbour erupted into a storm of anger and hate. The Danes charged up the jetty all at once, pushing some shipmates off the narrow wooden platform into the shallows.

'Lord, hurry!' called Wigs. Beornoth glanced over the sheer strake to where his men waited aboard the last ship in line. Unfamiliar faces stared back at him from amongst the armour and weapons. Women and girls with frightened eyes, faces thick with filth and stained with tears, hair lank and greasy. Beornoth dropped onto the second ship. His muscles ached from the fight and the effort of climbing and his breath became ragged and short. Beornoth reached the third ship and the Vikings' din came closer. Beornoth risked a glance behind him. Six Danes were in the first warship, charging around the mast and over rowing benches, axes in their hands and hate on their faces. They were young men, fresh-faced and fleet of foot. Beornoth's foot slipped in bilge water and he landed heavily on a rowing bench. Pain seared in his ribs and Beornoth pushed himself up and over the bow to land in a heap on the fourth ship. His chest burned with the effort. He rose and a young Viking flew at him. He leapt from the third ship and crashed into Beornoth. Beornoth wrapped his arms around the Dane and tossed him like a rag into the rigging. Another man jumped and met Beornoth's sword blade.

Beornoth lumbered to the edge of the boat, and the first Dane came howling back at him. He swung his axe, but the head caught in the rigging ropes and Beornoth sliced open his belly. Beornoth was gasping for breath now, stumbling to the edge of the ship.

'Go!' he shouted to his men. 'Row!' It would take precious moments for the Viking warship to move quickly under oars, and Beornoth feared the Danes would swarm the ship before his men could get away. He readied himself, sword levelled, prepared to stand and fight so that his men could escape with the freed slaves. But no more Danes came. They milled on the jetty and on the first ship, and Beornoth realised his men had been clever. They had cut the moorings of each ship and they had begun to drift away from one another. Without their leader, the Danes argued about whether to pursue Beornoth or secure their precious ships.

Hands reached out to help Beornoth clamber aboard the last ship. They hauled him over the sheer strake and he collapsed inside the hull. He pulled off his helmet to help him breathe easier. Sweat plastered his hair to his head, his face ached from Hvitserk's blade cut and his ribs screamed in pain. The ship lurched and Wigs strode along the deck, shouting at the Saxons to pull the oars. Beornoth could not see the oar blades dip, but the rowers did not move in unison like the Vikings would. Their backs moved in disorder, each man pulling for himself rather than as one. The ship moved, but the dragon-headed prow shifted left and right, waddling like a lame duck as the boat glided away from the harbour.

'We did it, lord,' said Wigs. He bent, grinning into Beornoth's face.

'We're not done yet,' Beornoth said. 'Help me up.' Wigs grabbed Beornoth's outstretched hand and pulled him upright. The Saxons strained at the oars, heaving and doing their best to keep the warship moving. Some of their strokes missed the water, and others struck out of time. Beornoth stared over the prow beast as they edged away. The Danes piled aboard their first ship and others dived into the water to swim to the ships drifting away from shore. The Danes were the finest seamen on God's earth. They braved unforgiving storms in the wild North Sea where the whitecaps reached higher than the highest hall. Vikings had sailed further west and south than any man had been before, and when their warriors took up the oars, there would be no fouled strokes, no oars striking against each other. They would come fast and, within fifty strokes, the ships would come alongside the stolen boat and drag her close with axes and ropes. Then Viking warriors would cross the bows and hack the Saxons and their rescued slaves to pieces.

'Here they come,' said a Saxon woman. Her hands gripped the ship's timber and her face showed utter terror at the prospect of recapture.

Beornoth unslung his shield and hefted his sword. 'If we don't row, we die,' he said. 'When I bang my shield, you pull. We row as one. Every pull is a pull for your life, and the lives of these people we have freed. As one! Ready?'

The Saxons grunted their readiness, leaning forward with oars at the ready. They sat with their backs to the open water, facing towards Watchet so that they could see the Danes board their ships, lifting their oars from their crutches and slipping each length of ash into its oar hole.

Beornoth bashed his sword against his shield. 'Pull!' The

Saxons pulled in time, each of their backs straining as one, and the ship raced ahead, its sleek hull carved from a single piece of oak slicing through the water like a knife. Its clinker-built timbers creaked and the seal rigging groaned. 'Pull.' Beornoth beat time again. The *drakkar* picked up speed. The Saxons found their rhythm and the ship left Watchet, cutting through the increasing swell and heading out to sea. Wigs stood on the steerboard platform and leaned on the tiller, guiding the ship along the coast rather than out into the wild, deep sea. The pursuing ships also raced forward, but their crews rowed twice as fast as the Saxons, and their ships seemed to fly through the water like birds, oars rising and falling like wings.

Beornoth beat time and kept his eyes on the shore. The Danes closed in with every stroke, but the Saxons had already done most of what Beornoth required. He glanced at Wigs and pointed his sword to the grass-topped cliffs where a line of horsemen galloped along the heights. Wigs grinned and guided the warship towards a shale-strewn beach. The women, boys, girls and children shrieked, peering over the side as the Danes closed in. Beast-head prows rose over the waves, painted in green, white and red, teeth grimaced, and the Danes hung over the sides brandishing their axes.

'Pull for shore, lads,' Beornoth shouted. 'Reach the shore and we ride for freedom.'

The Saxons shouted, half in triumph and half out of fear. It had been an audacious raid, almost foolhardy. Six Saxons had lost their lives, but a warrior fights for his lord and his people and they had sacrificed their lives to free helpless captives from a life of horror. Beornoth quickened time, and the oarsmen responded. In thirty strokes, Beornoth felt tiny stones on the seabed scrape against the hull.

'Five more strokes, just five more strokes,' he urged them on.

They pulled and Beornoth ushered the captives towards the bow. 'We must jump over the side,' he said. 'We wade through the water to those waiting horsemen.'

'What will you do with us?' asked a young woman with raven-black hair.

'Set you free.'

She stared at him blankly, as though Beornoth spoke a language she could not understand. 'Free?'

'Free. But you must jump into the water when I say and wade ashore. When we reach the beach, each of you will climb up behind one of my riders. Do you understand?'

She just stared at Beornoth. He was a lord, huge and fierce and smeared with blood, and she was a churl. Perhaps a farmer's daughter or a young woodsman's wife. She was a victim of the Viking war and a woman who might never expect to travel further than a few Roman miles from where she was born. She would never expect to be spoken to by a lord, and had been through so much trauma that she could not form the words to react.

Beornoth bent and stared into her face. 'Do you understand?'

'Yes,' she replied.

The warship slowed as stones and sand crunched beneath the hull. Horsemen raced down a hillside path towards the beach, just as Beornoth had planned.

'Over the side,' Beornoth said. The ship slowed, its hull rising on the sandy seabed, and the Saxons leapt into the shallows. They turned with outstretched arms whilst Beornoth and others lowered the women and children from the prow. The Vikings came on, singing their fearsome rowing songs as their *drakkars* sped towards shore. Beornoth lifted the dark-haired woman and lowered her into Gis' arms. She gasped as she plopped into the rolling grey water and waded towards shore. When the last freed slave was in the water, Beornoth climbed over the side. The water came up to his waist, cold enough to take his breath away as he waded towards the waiting horsemen. A small boy wept as the water lapped at his face, so deep that he could not make it to shore. Beornoth lifted the lad high and placed him on his shoulders. He came from the water soaking wet, boots crunching on the shale, and turned to see the Viking longships turn bows on to the beach. Bearded faces stared at him as the Danes understood their pursuit was over.

'That was close, lord,' said Ecga, beaming down at Beornoth from the back of his horse.

'Almost too close. Make sure each slave sits behind a rider, and then we push hard for Cantuctone,' Beornoth replied. He lifted the boy from his shoulders and placed the lad on the back of Ecga's horse. The boy wrapped his arms about the warrior and Ecga patted his small hands.

Beornoth climbed into Virtus' saddle, wincing at the pain in his ribs. He held out a hand to the black-haired woman. She stared at him again, face full of fear and misunderstanding. There was pain in her eyes, and Beornoth could only wonder at the horrors she had suffered at the hands of her Viking captors. He nodded and beckoned her towards him. She took his hand and Beornoth helped her climb up behind him. The riders set off at a canter, leaving their Viking pursuers and the dragon ships in the churning waters.

'Where will you take us?' asked the woman. She wrapped her arms around Beornoth's midriff and he felt strange to have a woman other than Eawynn so close to him, guilty almost. Her body warmed his shivering limbs, wet and heavy with seawater. Virtus pounded up the cliffs and onto the pathway and forty-four Saxons rode west, away from Watchet. Beornoth had thought no further than rescuing the slaves. That task in itself had consumed his thought cage. How to get to the ships, how to free the women and children and do it without the deaths of every warrior in his war band. Now it was done, but he could not return to Robert de Warenne with the freed Saxons. They were mouths to feed, in need of clothing and care. The Normans were like all warriors, cruel, hard and without pity. Just as they should be. They would not understand the need to care for the Saxons, and nor would Beornoth have as a younger man.

'We'll find a village,' he said. 'Somewhere safe. Where the Danes have not reached. That's the best I can do for you.'

'Thank you, lord.'

They were free, that was enough. Theirs was the fate of so many innocents who paid the true price of war. Men fought for glory, wealth and power. They always had. Beornoth knew that better than most. He was a beast of war, created by it, moulded by it. As a boy, he had longed for it, and now it was at the core of his very being. Vikings came across the sea with relentless violence, and many Saxons believed that the Viking scourge was God's punishment for the sins of his English flock. But there would still be war without the Vikings. Men raided other shires for cattle, silver and women. Brothers fought over thrones. Neighbours fought for access to water, over who owned a field, or over slights and insults. Men fought for pride and power, and women and children suffered. Eawynn and Beornoth's daughters had suffered, had paid the price for greed and the hunger for violence. As he rode with the churl woman clinging to his back, Beornoth hoped he had tilted the scales of justice in his favour. So that when he died and his soul passed beyond the world and the almighty judged him for the deeds of his life, the souls of those he had rescued would speak for him and, perhaps, then he could join Eawynn in heaven.

13

Beornoth returned to Cantuctone as the sun touched the western coast, casting the land in soft shadow. The Saxons rode in grim silence, bleary-eyed, clothes stained with dry seawater and other men's blood. The riders had left the rescued slaves in a village west of Cantuctone and doubled back towards where burned Viking ships lay in the water like blackened skeletons. Beornoth gave the churls in the village a fistful of hacksilver with orders to care for the women and children. The raven-haired woman had waved to Beornoth as he had mounted Virtus, and he had nodded curtly. That was all the goodbye he could muster. They were free and that was enough. There was no room in Beornoth's hard heart for kind gestures and waves goodbye.

The riders found the Normans in camp, cleaning their mail, tending to their horses and preparing an evening meal. They stood as the riders approached, staring with stern faces and flinty eyes. Beornoth reined in and dismounted.

'I'll take her, lord,' said Wigs, reaching to take Virtus' reins. 'You'd better go to Lord Robert.'

'Make sure she's brushed,' Beornoth replied. Wigs led her away, his chin so low it almost touched his coat of mail. 'Wigs?'

'Yes, lord?'

'Don't forget what we did today. Don't feel shame just because our Norman friends disapprove.' Beornoth spoke loud enough for all of his men to hear. 'We are here to fight for our king and our people. We kill our Viking enemies, and we rescued people who needed our help. I won't apologise for what we did today, and neither should you. We did God's work, warrior's work. The Normans follow the king's orders, and so do we. So keep your heads up, and let your hearts swell with pride.'

'Lord Beornoth,' said a familiarly high-pitched voice.

Beornoth closed his eyes, exhaled and turned to face Odo de Warenne. 'How go the victory celebrations?'

Odo smiled, but there was no joy in his face. 'We prepare to ride tomorrow. My brother wishes to speak with you. I trust your little... outing was fruitful?'

'Horses and men must be exercised if they are to be ready to fight.'

'Just so.'

Odo kissed his teeth and turned on his heel. He led the way and Beornoth followed to Robert de Warenne's leather tent. They found the king's thegn sat outside upon a log beside a fire, and Robert de Warenne rose when he saw Beornoth approaching, a scowl splitting his handsome face.

'You have returned, then?' said Robert.

'You wanted to speak to me?' Beornoth replied, following Robert de Warenne's lack of pleasantries.

'There was a rumour in camp that you had the Saxons away, that you had fled our company. Where have you been?'

'Riding.'

'To where?'

Beornoth returned Robert's scowl and tucked his thumbs into his belt. 'I don't answer to you.'

'You do whilst we ride on this campaign, Saxon. By order of the king. So I ask you again. Where have you been with my warriors?'

'Last time I looked, I am a king's thegn, as are you. Do I ask you when last you went for a shit, or what you ate to break your fast today?'

'Your belligerence is not helpful. We ride on the king's orders, and tomorrow we strike camp to ride south. Your horses are tired from a day in the field where ours are fresh. We rested today in order to prepare for the next name on the king's list. We have crushed the Viking invaders, and their presence here will crumble. Now that Kvitsr is dead the lesser jarls will either sail away, or are ripe for local Saxon thegns to sweep away. Now we ride against the most pressing name on King Æthelred's list. The leader of the oathsworn traitors.'

'We rode west. It was a fine day. Your men drank late into the night, and took the day to sleep it off. This was no planned rest to freshen the horses. Don't piss up my back and tell me it's raining, Robert. Your men slept off their ale and wine and I took the Saxon warriors out riding.'

Robert de Warenne rubbed his eyes and shook his head. 'You went to Watchet, did you not?'

'He did. He defied your orders, took the Saxons and rode to Watchet,' said Odo de Warenne, sliding to his brother's shoulder like a snake.

Robert de Warenne carefully took in Beornoth's appearance. He saw the sea salt dried into Beornoth's boots and trews, and the mud and blood spattered upon his byrnie. Finally, he gazed at the cut on Beornoth's cheek. Beornoth just stood there, straight-backed and silent. What could he say? He had taken the

Saxons belonging to Robert de Warenne's service, against the Norman's clear orders, and risked their lives.

'Did you free the captives?' asked Robert.

'We did. I killed their commander, Jarl Hvitserk, a man sworn to Kvitsr.'

'How many of our men died?'

'Six,' hissed Odo. 'He lost six of our men, swords we shall miss in the fight to come.'

'You undermine me, Beornoth,' said Robert. 'We have beaten Kvitsr and his followers will be in disarray. Next, we ride to punish Pallig and his men, those who were oathsworn to the king. Traitors who turned their cloak and committed slaughter amongst people they had sworn to protect. Pallig is a cunning warrior, as you know, and our hardest fight is ahead of us. I need the respect of my men if we are to succeed in what we must do.'

'He works against us, brother. At every turn! I've said it before. He wants to lead, he resents it that the king granted you power. This man is your enemy! Is it a coincidence that he and Pallig are friends?'

'I warned you once before,' said Beornoth. He took a step closer to Odo, and Robert moved in between them.

'Enough,' said Robert. He turned to his brother. 'Leave us.'

Odo spluttered, face contorting as his eyes flicked from Robert to Beornoth. He saw the anger on Beornoth's face, and the serious look on his brother's. With clenched fists Odo de Warenne limped away, but Beornoth understood in that moment that there must be a reckoning somewhere down the line. Odo de Warenne had set himself against Beornoth. He was right in some of what he said, for Beornoth had disobeyed Robert, but Odo had already gone too far. Beornoth's warrior's pride could not permit the insults Odo had uttered to pass unanswered. The Norman had suggested that Beornoth was a traitor, had questioned his loyalty. All a warrior had was his reputation, so Odo must be held responsible for the words of his mouth.

'You should not have gone to Watchet,' said Robert. There was no anger in his voice now that he and Beornoth were alone. He watched his brother limp away and turned to Beornoth. 'My men will expect me to punish you for disobeying my order. I should punish you, but I know you would not allow it. We could fight, you and I. We could draw our swords and hack at each other until one of us is dead and the other can lead what remains of this war band. You and I are the strongest amongst us. Is our company stronger if one of us is dead? No. What would you do in my place?'

Beornoth had always looked upon Robert de Warenne as an enemy. He was still intensely loyal to Ealdorman Byrhtnoth, and Robert was a creature of Lady Ælfthryth. Beornoth had expected Robert to fly into a rage when he discovered that the Saxons had gone to Watchet. But he suddenly realised that Robert de Warenne was more than just a warrior, he was thoughtful and clever, as all warlords must be. He had every right to be angry, and just because Beornoth didn't like him, didn't mean that the Norman was wrong. So Beornoth told him the truth. 'If you had disobeyed my order, I would have fought you for it.'

'We ride tomorrow to face Pallig. If I kill you, or you kill me, I fear that our Saxon and Norman warriors will turn on each other. Perhaps when this is done, when we have hunted and killed the men on King Æthelred's list, you and I shall settle our disagreement. Man against man. But for now, we must be aligned. Though my brother would prefer if I killed you.'

'Do you think you could?'

Robert thought about that for a moment. 'Does it matter?'

'No,' Beornoth allowed.

'You hate me because I came to England in the service of Lady Ælfthryth. She was your enemy, so I am your enemy. The lady was good to me, to my family. I make no apologies for my loyalty to her and the king.'

'She killed King Edgar's heir to place her own son on the throne. Your father killed King Edward. Your place here is a reward for your father's king slaying.' It was a hard thing to say, a hard truth which had remained unspoken between them, but Beornoth did not flinch away from it. Robert de Warenne had wisely chosen to try and resolve their differences by talking rather than fighting. There was no use in holding back, just as there was no use in pulling a sword stroke in battle.

'My father struck King Edward down, that is true. He followed orders, and would have done it again a dozen times over. He was oathsworn to Lady Ælfthryth. Æthelred is our king because of what my father did. So, from today's perspective my father was a loyal patriot. He was banished to Normandy, where I was raised amongst descendants of Vikings. I am both Norman and English. I have prospered here in England. I hold lands and titles and you begrudge that of me. I am a warrior, just like you, I follow orders. My orders are to punish Vikings and traitors. I will kill the men on the king's list or die trying. You can either ride with us and follow my command, or return to Cheshire. That is it, plain and simple. You must decide here and now, because we cannot continue to fight together when we are full of hate for one another. I must trust you to protect my right side in the shield wall and you must believe that I will do the same. Without that trust we are weakened. When we fight Pallig's Danes our shield wall must be as strong as Roman stone. I cannot fight worried that your shield does not protect my side when I swing my sword. Would you lower your shield and let a Danish axe hack beneath my sword arm, Beornoth?'

'The king ordered me here. I will fight until my last breath, and I would die to do my duty. Even for you. We have fought together before and you cannot question my loyalty or my honour. I hate you because you are Lady Ælfthryth's man, that's true enough. She tried to kill me and worked against a man I loved like a brother. But when we face the Danes and the shields come together I would give my life to protect your right side and I know you would do the same for me. I will fight, and despite our differences you know I would not betray you.'

'So then you must follow my command.'

'You took Thorkell's axe and made it your sigil.' It was time to get it all out, to lay their differences on the table like food for a feast. The time for quiet grudges had passed, so Beornoth spoke his mind and didn't flinch from its harshness.

'What of it?'

'I fought Thorkell on Lundenwic bridge, not you.'

'I have never claimed to have fought Thorkell the Tall. I saw you fight the giant, and it was a battle worthy of the finest bards. The axe is a symbol of the victory we won together at Lundenwic. Did I not fight in the battle?'

'You did.'

'Did I not fight at the front? Did I not kill Danes upon those high walls? Who fought more fiercely than I to defend the city?'

'We go for Pallig next?' Beornoth could not summon the words to agree with Robert de Warenne. The Norman fought well at Lundenwic, and was now extending the hand of peace to Beornoth. He had never considered the world through the Norman's eyes before, and he admired the man for his ability to rise above the brutal solution of combat to settle their differences. But Beornoth was old, he was grim, and it was too late for him to change his ways. It was easier to change the subject than to give the Norman the satisfaction of acknowledging his bravery. Beornoth had thought Robert de Warenne wanted to steal his valour for the fight with Thorkell, though perhaps there was some truth in the Norman's reasoning for taking the giant's axe as his sigil. Robert stared at him, waiting for Beornoth to back down, for him to concede that he had been wrong to think so low of him. Priests, scops and bards told tales of holy men and heroes who turned the other cheek, who were ready to acknowledge when they were wrong. Stories of magnanimously pious men who forgave their enemies and embraced their foes. Beornoth sniffed and silently held Robert de Warenne's gaze. He wasn't pious, gentle, forgiving or magnanimous. Beornoth was too old to change and he didn't care.

Robert de Warenne smiled sadly at Beornoth. He understood from Beornoth's silence that Beornoth knew he had fought well at Lundenwic, but also saw that the differences between them could not be settled. Robert had tried, and perhaps with another man would have succeeded. It was enough that both men had spoken honestly, that they had laid their grievances bare, even if they had not resolved them. Beornoth respected Robert de Warenne for that, even if he couldn't bring himself to say it. Hate and respect could live side by side, as could enmity and trust in battle. Or so Beornoth hoped. He trusted Robert, even though they would always be enemies. Odo was a different story. Beornoth trusted him less than a starving rat before a plate of food.

'Pallig is at Pinnock on the south coast. His jarls have settled lands there in the south of Defnascir, close to the Roman town of Exanceaster,' said Robert.

'How many men does he have at Pinnock?'

'We'll find out when we get there. Maybe the same men he had at Lundenwic, probably more. Pallig did well in the king's service, he was trusted and fought well at the king's command. Many Viking crews came to England to fight beneath his banner. Pallig became wealthy and paid his men well in silver coins bearing King Æthelred's head. But such crews come and go. They are summer warriors. They sail south in the spring and return home in the autumn. Pallig could have six hundred men or two hundred. Like Kvitsr, he will have sent most of his warriors out in the shire to live and forage for themselves. He had five hundred warriors when he attacked beside Kvitsr. He could not have fed so many in one place over the winter. So they could have sailed home, or settled somewhere in Defnascir to live off the land and stores of the Saxons they have slain.'

'We can fight two hundred, but not six. Luckily we don't have to fight them all, and hopefully you are right and Pallig has not recalled his warriors to gather his army for another summer campaign. But he will surely be aware that the king will not sit by whilst he and Kvitsr take over Defnascir and Somersaete. News will also travel of our attacks against Kvitsr and Hvitserk. So we should expect Pallig to be ready. He won't just sit there perched on a horde of raided silver and wait for us with a force of household troops. He will be hard to kill, and tricky to fight. How many more names are there on the list?'

'Many more. All Danes who have settled in England and grown fat off stolen land. All must die.'

'And the Danelaw?' Beornoth asked because the land north of Watling Street, much of what was north Mercia and Northumbria, was ruled by Danes and had been for a hundred years. If the king wanted those lands purged of Danes, then blood would flow like an ocean, if it was even possible to kill so many without the settled Danes inside the Danelaw rising up to fight back. The scale of such a war was unthinkable. Beornoth had friends there, more than friends. Brand lived there, a man Beornoth loved like a brother. A Norseman, proud Viking and savage warrior who had saved Beornoth's life.

'Only newly settled Danes need fear our wrath. The ones who come with malice, who bring their ships and greedy warriors to plunder England's wealth.'

'Pallig won't just roll over and let us kill him.'

'No, he won't. So we must be ready and we must fight as one force. Normans and Saxons together. We are speaking together as men here beside this fire, so I will speak my mind. You disobeyed my orders and took warriors under my command to Watchet. Whatever the righteousness of that, that you did God's work to free people destined for slavery, your actions undermined my command and you know it. We could fight and settle our differences that way, but that serves only our enemies. So, on the ride south, you must demonstrate to the men that you can follow my orders. That there is no rift between us.'

'I can do that. But you must mind your brother's tongue. Keep him away from me or there will be trouble.'

'I can do that.' Robert extended his hand and Beornoth took it in the warrior's grip.

Beornoth left him and stalked towards the Saxons. Robert de Warenne had swallowed his pride and his anger and made peace, but even that rankled Beornoth and he couldn't say why. Perhaps it was because the Norman had swallowed his pride, that he had risen above a warrior's instinct to reach for his weapons when insulted. Beornoth would have preferred to fight the Norman than trade blows with words. Robert was well spoken, successful and cunning where Beornoth was blunt and brutal. De Warenne had mastered his anger and found a way to see the greater goal above his own pride. He saw glory in serving the king, he saw swathes of green hills and fertile fields as a reward for killing the names on Æthelred's list, and he saw that he needed Beornoth to do it. That made Robert de Warenne a man to fear, a man who had the ear of the king and whose power and influence spread across the kingdom like a plague.

'You still have your head, lord?' said Wigs with a wry grin. The Saxons had expected Beornoth to feel Robert de Warenne's wrath for the ride to Watchet, and so had Beornoth.

'Looks like it. But our Norman friend saw the justice in what we did. Tell the men to get some rest. We have a hard ride south tomorrow.'

The Saxons saw to their horses and cleaned their armour and weapons. Beornoth filled his helmet with sand from the river and scrubbed his byrnie and helmet to a shine. Wigs came to him after the sun had set. He brought a steaming bread trencher and sat opposite Beornoth on a half-chopped log.

'Ecga made a stew from leftovers after the Norman's celebration,' he said, handing the trencher to Beornoth. 'Beef and onion.'

'It's good,' Beornoth replied, blowing on the stew after taking a sip.

'He can work miracles with scraps and old bones. It was a close-run thing today.'

'Aye.' Beornoth took another slurp of the stew and it warmed his chest and stomach. Wigs opened and closed his mouth, glanced up at the twilight darkening clouds, back at Beornoth and then away again, his boots shifting and shoulders twitching. 'Spit it out.'

'Well, lord. Me and the lads were talking. And well... sometimes it seems like you fight reckless. Like you don't care whether you live or die.'

'I am a warrior.'

'We are all warriors, but there are warriors and warriors. You are a king's thegn, famous for the battles you have fought and the men you have killed. We are simple men. Warriors, yes. But also fathers and husbands. What becomes of our wives and children if we die in battle?'

Beornoth took another slurp of his stew and fixed Wigs with a flat stare. 'The risks are the same for every warrior. You chose this life, chose to swear oaths to a lord in return for the status you enjoy. You don't till the fields with bent backs. You don't fear a failed harvest or flooded fields. A warrior fights for his lord and is rewarded with silver and position. Churls bow their heads when you pass. You are wealthy in your byrnie and with your weapons. If the harvest fails the churl's children starve, they weep with swollen bellies and there is nothing the farmer can do. Your family will never starve, and all you must do for that privilege is fight. You must give your life, if required, in service of lord and king. So we fight, and you may die. Your wife will be paid a sum of silver in the event of your death, and then she must find a new husband.

'We have all seen women marry again, and warriors who raise a dead man's children. The ones to pity are the women who are old when their men die, who have lost their beauty and cannot find a new husband to take them in. That is our world. Is it any worse for the warrior who suffers the grievous wound that does not kill? For he who loses a leg or an arm and cannot fight any more and is dependent on gifts and charity for food and ale? A man cannot think of these things when he goes into battle. He must fight without fear, he must charge when the shield wall breaks and he must face his enemies without fear in his heart. I fight reckless because that is how to win battles.'

Wigs held up his hand and bowed his head. 'Everything you say is true, lord. But there is reckless and reckless. You would charge alone into a wall of axes and spears, where another warrior would advance cautiously, efficiently, controlled and considered behind a wall of shields.'

'And?' Beornoth's mouth was dry from talking. He was not a man of words, not a bishop or lord at court. He had already spoken at length with Robert de Warenne, hard, head-spinning words requiring thought and consideration. Now Wigs wanted more talk and Beornoth didn't have the stomach for it.

'I meant no offence, lord. You don't fear death though, do you lord?'

'No.' Beornoth shifted, the question making him uncomfortable. He had never feared death, had always accepted it as part of his life as a warrior. Death could strike in any skirmish or battle, he was ready for it. He hoped for heaven, prayed to be at Eawynn's side in the glory of God when he died. Beornoth suddenly realised that since Eawynn's passing, he was ready to die. Had he sought it amongst the blades and axes? Beornoth wasn't sure. It would be easy to lower his shield, or fail to parry an enemy blow and let a sharp edge end his life. It would be over then. A life of pain, struggle, violence and suffering ended.

'The rest of us do. We fight, and fight well. You've seen us, lord. There aren't many war bands to match us, even if I do say so myself. Just have a thought for the lads, lord, that's all I'm asking. They love you, love fighting for you. They are proud to fight alongside the greatest Viking-killer in the kingdom. You inspire us, not through flowery words or with pouches of silver, but with deeds and courage. But care for them, lord. For we do not all need to die for this company to complete its quest.'

'What man among us seeks death?' Beornoth spoke wistfully. He took a long drink of his stew and wiped the drips from his beard. 'I say I do not fear death, but I fear what comes after it. How can a man be sure if the deeds of his life assure his place in heaven or in the fiery horrors of hell? I have done things in my life. Things I regret. When my children died I lost my way. They were dark days. I have killed heathens, and priests tell me that is the path to heaven. But who can be sure?'

'You are a good man, lord.'

Beornoth finished his food and he and Wigs sat in companiable silence. Beornoth knew what he was. He was what the kingdom needed him to be. A warrior. Good or bad did not come into it. The conversations with Robert de Warenne and Wigs circled around Beornoth's mind like crows above a battlefield. Deep words and thoughts he had not given voice to before. He slept fitfully and was glad to rise early, to ease his groaning bones and aching muscles into the saddle and ride to battle once more and fill his head with thoughts of war.

14

Robert de Warenne led the war band south. They rode through lands ravaged by Danes with slaughtered cattle rotting in the fields and farmsteads burned to ash. They rode beneath deep blue autumn skies with clouds like curds drifting on warm winds. The heat made Beornoth sweat beneath his byrnie and its leather lining, but every warrior rode in full armour and carried their spears in one hand and their shields upon their backs. Odo de Warenne led a splinter force ahead of the main column to scout the path ahead and his departure lightened Beornoth's mood.

The war band crossed the River Parrett at a shallow ford and followed the Roman Fosse Way south. Ripening barley and thick hedgerows flanked the road as they passed Ilchester, a town of lean-tos and hovels built around an old Roman fort with low stone walls. Folk watched them from the walls, people with frightened eyes, and warriors carrying spears glowered over the crumbling ramparts. They were Saxons who had held out against the Viking raids, made wary of all but local people. The war band rode on and stopped to rest the horses at Crewkerne, a bustling village surrounded by apple orchards and pollarded woodland. The track grew narrow as it wound through ancient oak and beech trees, where dappled sunlight flickered across the riders' spear points and riding tack.

Robert de Warenne ordered another brief rest close to Axminster, where men and horses took food and drink. As the sun began its descent after an entire day in the saddle, they spied Pinnock rising among green hills with the towers of Exanceaster's minster visible in the distance. Pinnock was little more than a small village with timber-framed wattle and daub dwellings, grazing meadows and small crofts. All seemed quiet and serene, with lowing cattle and lilting birdsong, but Danes lurked in the fertile valleys and Robert de Warenne ordered the riders to halt whilst he waited for the return of his brother's scouting party.

It was dark when Odo de Warenne returned with ten riders. They carried furs and sacks from their saddlebags and their cloaks and clothes stank of smoke. A column of grey rose like winter breath behind them, rising to join the clouds above a line of undulating hills. Beornoth fed Virtus a handful of oats from his pack and the warhorse nuzzled him with her great head.

'They look pleased with themselves,' said Gis as the riders approached. Laughter and shouts of joy rose from Odo's men like drunk men at a wedding feast as their horses trotted alongside Beornoth and the Saxons.

'That smoke above the hills tells the story of their scouting party,' said Wigs with a shake of his head.

'But is it Danes or Saxons whose furs and silver they took?'

Beornoth listened but made no comment. He strode after Odo and found Robert de Warenne checking the straps on his horse's saddle. Odo reined in and grinned at his brother. He reached into a saddlebag and pulled free a silver and gold cloak pin, which he tossed to his brother. Robert de Warenne caught it and held it up to the sun.

'A fine pin,' he said. He turned it over, examining the craftsmanship.

'A gift for you after a good day's hunting.'

'Thank you. You found Pallig's men?'

Odo waved a hand dismissively. 'They are in the town. We found a long hall, and plump maidens within.'

'Saxon or Dane?' Beornoth asked.

Odo had not noticed Beornoth's approach and his scarred face soured into a scowl. 'Danes.'

'They had their women and children with them?'

Odo's horse sensed his anger, and its forelegs scraped the grass. 'This is war, Lord Beornoth. We take the spoils where we find them.'

'Did you scout the ground between here and Pinnock? How many spears are there on the walls? Do the Vikings have scouts in the hills? Is there a palisade? Is it in good repair? Do local folk say Pallig is within the town?'

Odo spat over the side of his horse and glanced at his brother, but Robert offered no words of support.

'I report to my lord brother, Saxon, not you.' Odo's horse turned and Odo sawed on the reins so that the beast's rump almost knocked Beornoth from his feet.

Beornoth took two steps back. 'Report then, so that we know what we face when we ride against Pallig and his warriors.'

'My brother will report to me, Lord Beornoth,' said Robert de Warenne. He spoke in an even voice, showing neither anger nor concern. 'We camp here for the night. We ride against Pallig in the morning.'

Beornoth left the brothers and felt Odo's stare like a dagger in his back as he returned to the Saxons. They made camp on the edge of dense forest, erecting tents and laying out their armour for the night. Horses chewed grass and Beornoth ate a small meal of oatcakes and dried beef. The camp fell silent as the sun went down, and Robert de Warenne ordered the usual watch around the camp's perimeter. Beornoth fell into a deep sleep, exhausted from a hard ride. His ribs ached and the cut on his face had healed into an itching scab. He went to sleep thinking of Pallig, of how much he had liked the man at Lundenwic. Beornoth didn't savour the thought of fighting his old comrade, even if Pallig had broken his oath to the king. England had changed, its course altered by the king's attempts at redemption. Lady Ælfthryth's return with her Norman allies and the clawing back of land from the Church had changed the country's direction like wind changing a ship's course at sea. That change had turned Pallig against his former masters, and who could blame him? But there was a price to pay for breaking an oath. Beornoth's thoughts cleared, and he drifted into a fitful sleep dreaming of Eawynn. He would wake, roll over and dream instead of men he had killed in battle, their fearful faces and the horror of their wounds.

A stab of pain in his wounded ribs woke him. Beornoth groaned and rolled onto his back, his chest damp with dream sweat. A horse whickered outside and Beornoth sat up. Hairs on the back of his neck stood up. A strange feeling came upon him, like when a person can feel someone looking at them from afar or across a crowded hall. He reached for his sword and seax and slipped both from their scabbards. Beornoth crawled from the tent and stood, the night air cool against his neck. The camp was quiet and the night dark beneath a starlit sky. Campfires glowed orange, almost burnt out. Beornoth stood still, listening, unable to shake off that feeling that he was being watched. A horse whickered again and Beornoth turned slowly, sword in his right hand and seax in his left. A twig snapped inside the woodland and Beornoth walked slowly towards the sound. He was barefoot, wearing only a light jerkin and his trews. A voice came from the woods, hushed and urgent, followed quickly by another.

'Wake up!' Beornoth roared. 'Wake! We are under attack!' He kicked the tent beside him and another one two paces away. Beornoth strode towards the woodland, shouting warnings to the sleeping war band until his throat grew hoarse.

Men came from the trees like the fetches of long-dead warriors. Shadows played their faces and hair, moonlight catching their axes and spears so that they gleamed like fangs in the night. Scores of them came, walking at first, and then running, charging with war cries in their throats and fury in their eyes. They came with braided beards and long hair. Big men, teeth bared and ready to kill. Vikings. It could only be Pallig, and Beornoth cursed Odo de Warenne. The Norman had ridden out to scout around the advancing war band for any sign of the enemy, and instead he had burned, killed and raided. Pallig could have received word of the war band's attack on Kvitsr. More likely, however, was that Pallig's scouts had noticed two hundred armoured warriors riding towards Pinnock and Pallig had prepared as a warlord should.

Warriors charged from the woods, and Beornoth strode towards them. He readied himself, flexing his fingers around his weapons. A big Dane with a scarred face came at him, axe raised above his head, mouth open and bellowing with anger. The axe swung, but it was wild and uncontrolled and in his haste the Viking had misjudged the distance to his intended victim. Beornoth flicked his wrist and his sword came up. The Dane ran onto the point and his own weight pushed it deep inside him, its honed blade stabbing through his padded leather breastplate and into the soft flesh beyond. Despite the wound, the axe kept on coming and Beornoth parried it with his seax. The Dane grimaced and closed his eyes. He fell to his knees and Beornoth tore his sword free of flesh and innards and leapt backwards as another enemy came hurtling towards him with a spear held low in both hands. Beornoth caught the spear point with the flat of his sword and drove it away from him, seax coming around in a wide arc to punch into the enemy's head beneath his ear. Beornoth kept moving, yanking his seax from the wound. He ducked beneath a scything axe blade and cut the legs from another wild Dane.

The camp changed from sleeping calmness to red war in an instant. Norman and Saxon warriors came from their tents and lean-tos with bleary eyes and weapons in their fists. The Danes stabbed and hacked at their enemies and whooped for joy as men who had ridden across to Defnascir to kill them found their own doom instead. A shield hammered into Beornoth and drove him from his feet. He fell into a campfire's embers, rolling as sparks erupted. A boot kicked him hard in the face and Beornoth rolled again. Panic welled inside him, blooming and swelling into anger. If he did not act quickly, the war band would die and Pallig's ambush would send them all screaming into the afterlife.

Beornoth rose with a roar. Another shield came at him, but Beornoth dropped his shoulder and met it. The Dane shuddered and took a step back. Beornoth whipped his seax low beneath the shield's rim and yanked it towards him so that the upper rim smashed into the Viking's face. Beornoth kept moving. He shook his head and found his bearings, recognising his own tent. Wigs and Gis fought there against four howling Vikings and Beornoth charged to their aid. He came up behind the Vikings like a beast, huge and terrifying, hacking with sword and seax with all the strength in his muscled arms. He chopped into their legs and backs and three of the Danes fell screaming to meet their deaths.

'Where's Ecga?' asked Gis, shouting above the din, head twitching frantically from left to right like a startled rabbit.

'There,' said Wigs, pointing his spear to where a group of Saxons formed a makeshift line and fought against the marauding Danes.

Beornoth marched towards the Saxon formation as Danes stormed through the camp. They stabbed and stamped at tents as more Normans tried to join the fight. The Vikings hacked at them with spears and axes and the night air reeked of old leather, sweat and the iron tang of blood. A squat Viking with a thick neck and a bald head jumped over the ash of a burned-out camp fire, swinging an axe at Beornoth. Beornoth caught the axe on the edge of his sword and stabbed his seax into the Dane's guts in six short, sharp blows. Two more enemies came snarling from the melee, spears in their fists. Gis and Wigs met them with pitiless strokes of their swords.

'We are all going to die,' whispered Wigs. He stared wide-eyed at the slaughter. Shadows moved in the darkness, men screamed and weapons chopped and stabbed with relentless fury. The Vikings whooped and called out to one another like men who have caught a deer after a long hunt. Beornoth could make no sense of it in the chaos. Figures surged and milled about him and he could not tell how many of his own men were dead or how many Danes attacked the camp.

'No,' Beornoth said under his breath. 'No,' he repeated, louder. Fists tightening around the hilts of his weapons. 'No, no, no.' The urge to fight the Vikings was deeply ingrained within him, like the need to eat, drink and sleep. So Beornoth summoned all of his rage and all of his strength and went to work.

Four Danes charged from behind a leather tent, faces spattered with drops of crimson. Beornoth went for them. He kicked the glowing embers of a fire so that the faggots and glowing logs crashed into the Vikings. Embers swirled about them and the Danes flapped their arms and weapons to protect their faces. Beornoth cut his sword in a backhand swing that chopped through a warrior's wrist and on into his throat. He slammed his seax into the next man's chest with enough force to drive the warrior from his feet. Beornoth kept moving, turning and cutting the legs from a third Dane. He rose to meet the fourth, but found Wigs and Gis beating the enemy to his knees with cuts of their swords.

Beornoth's chest heaved and his arms burned. He mastered that pain and went on, seeking the enemy amongst the fallen and cutting them down with merciless sword skill. The fight raged beneath a clear night sky, weapons flashing and warriors hacking each other to bloody ruin. A Dane with long golden hair flowing like a field of wheat in summer came at Beornoth brandishing an axe in each fist. He was handsome, broad-shouldered and wore a coat of shining chain mail. Wigs tried to cut at him but the Dane caught the blow with the haft of his axe and kicked Wigs away from him. He pointed his axes at Beornoth and smiled with the arrogance of a warrior who sees an equal, an experienced fighter, a champion to kill and burnish his reputation bright like a star.

'Stay back,' Beornoth said to Wigs and Gis. He nodded to the Dane and set himself in a wide stance, balanced on the balls of his feet. The Viking lifted his axes, beautiful things with hafts wrapped in strips of leather and curved bearded blades engraved with Norse runes of power. He clashed the axes together, rubbing the steel edges around so that they scraped and rasped together. The Viking flashed a wide smile and then hurled himself at Beornoth. He moved gracefully, light on his feet, axes whirling in wide circles. Beornoth kept his eyes fixed on the blades, he swayed away from them, trying to time his parry. If he caught one off balance, the next one would chop into his neck or chest and take his life in an instant. The Viking warlord grunted and his axes scythed through the air with the sounds of a bird's wings. Beornoth stood his ground and parried an axe with his sword and ducked as the second axe flew over his head to find nothing but cold night air. He ducked beneath the axe blow and the Viking slammed his knee into Beornoth's face. He fell backwards, scrambling. The first axe came over-hand and Beornoth stopped the strike with his seax blade a hand's breadth from his face. He could smell the metal and the stink of death upon its wickedly curved blade. The Viking crashed his second axe on top of the haft of his first. The blade edged closer and Beornoth's muscles strained to stop the edge from cutting into his nose and eyes.

Beornoth tried to strike at his enemy with his sword, but the Dane was too close. He leant down onto his axes, using his body weight to press the axe even closer to Beornoth's face. His seax held them away, but its blunt back pressed down against Beornoth's face and all that lay between the axes and his eyes was the width of the seax. Beornoth glanced sideways and saw Gis and Wigs fighting against a roaring Dane who kept them at bay with his shield and axe.

'Die, turd,' the Viking hissed, spittle running from his white teeth into his golden beard as he strained to press his axes into Beornoth's cheek. Beornoth beat at the man with the hilt of his sword, tried to slice the edge at his legs, but there was not enough room to make the blows count. The Dane lifted himself and dropped into the axes. His weight drove them down, and the edge sliced a hair's breadth into Beornoth's face. Panic swamped him, and for a terrifying moment Beornoth thought the axe had cut out his eye. But he blinked and realised that the blade had cut above and below the eye but not taken the eye itself. It was enough to send a flood of strength into his arms, into arms hardened by a lifetime of battle. Beornoth lifted the Dane away from him, using his seax to push his enemy away. The Dane stared at him in surprise, shocked by the power of the Saxon he had come so close to killing. Beornoth wriggled, drove his knee into the Viking's groin and twisted. The Dane groaned and the axes gave way, Beornoth shot his neck forward as his enemy fell beside him and bit his teeth down onto the Viking's ear. He tore at the flesh and the Dane howled in pain. He jerked away from Beornoth's ripping teeth and rolled with his axes clutched tight to his chest. Beornoth turned with him and fell upon the Viking with his knee pinning the axes against his body. The Viking's mouth gaped, flapping, head rocking from side to side as he realised death was upon him. Vikings dream of their glorious afterlife, of Odin's great hall in Valhalla, where they will live forever, fighting and feasting. So Beornoth sent him there with a cut of his seax across the golden-haired warrior's throat.

Beornoth wanted to lie down, to stop fighting, to rest. His body ached and his chest burned. He ground his teeth and spat out a gobbet of blood. The battle raged and Beornoth closed his eyes for a moment, fighting against his aged body and its weakness. A man Beornoth's age should spend his nights warm by a fire, wrapped in blankets and furs, not fighting men half his age on a night-shrouded hillside. He pushed himself to his feet and joined Wigs and Gis as they finished a Dane with swings of their swords. They set off to join Ecga, and the Danes avoided the three Saxons who stalked amongst the carnage with blood upon their blades. Beornoth hurried to where Ecga and a group of warriors fought against a score of the enemy.

'Kill them all!' bellowed a voice in Norse, a fearsome voice full of determined fury. A familiar voice. Pallig. Beornoth could not see his old friend through the flashing blades and charging warriors, but the cunning Viking had brought his warriors to kill Robert de Warenne's company before they could take his life, and had almost succeeded when Robert de Warenne appeared, huge and baleful in his byrnie with a sword in one hand and a shield in the other. He bullied his way to the front of a Saxon line burgeoning with fresh warriors as Normans came to fight beside their Saxon shield-mates.

'Shields to the front,' Robert de Warenne said, 'shields on me.'

The Vikings paused as Robert brought order to the fight, and in an instant a dozen shields flanked the tall Norman as the war band presented a formidable front to their enemies. Robert thrust two Danes away with a mighty heft of his shield. He cut at them with his sword, slicing open an enemy's forearm in a spray of blood. A Viking spear crashed into Robert de Warenne's shield boss with a loud ring. Robert swept his sword through the spear stave, breaking it, and drove the point of his sword into the spearman's chest. The Normans roared support for their thegn and the Danes fell back before Robert de Warenne and his flashing blade.

Beornoth took that chance to charge into the Vikings' flank. A score of them bayed before Robert de Warenne's line like a pack of wolves. They brandished weapons and shouted hate to the Normans and Saxons, but stopped short of an actual charge. It takes courage to charge a force of armed men. Often two armies will stand and hurl insults across the battlefield until they find enough anger and bravery to attack, or they find that courage at the bottom of a skin of ale. Beornoth had never had that problem.

Beornoth smashed into them, shoulder first. He drove three men back and then sliced his blades across arms, legs, faces, whatever of the enemy he could reach around him. Gis and Wigs followed his lead and in five heartbeats ten Vikings dropped wounded to the blood-darkened grass. A spear sliced across Beornoth's shoulder and the haft of an axe crashed into the side of his head. He kicked, slashed and drove his head at the enemy and an almighty roar rose from Beornoth's left. The Danes fell back, running from the fight and Robert de Warenne led the war band in a furious charge, cutting down Vikings with his blood-drenched sword.

'Ecga,' said Gis, and embraced his friend, who for a moment had seemed doomed to fall before the Viking surprise attack. Beornoth breathed a sigh of relief. Ecga was alive and the Danes broke off their attack. Beornoth stalked across the battlefield, finding Robert de Warenne and the company formed into four ranks, poised and ready to fight.

Beornoth pushed his way through to the front where Robert de Warenne stood before his warriors with his sword held high in challenge to the enemy, who had retreated into the woodland.

'Bastards only had two score with them,' said Robert de Warenne through gritted teeth when he noticed Beornoth next to him.

'Enough to hurt us badly,' Beornoth replied. 'Are we fools or churls to be surprised in camp?'

Robert glanced at Beornoth, and they stared into each other's eyes. It was a hard moment. Beornoth saw understanding there. He did not need to say that had Odo scouted the area properly, he would have reported that Pallig had forty warriors in the field, armed and ready to ride against them.

'This is Odo's work.' Beornoth said it anyway. 'Men have died because of his incompetence. Good men killed in their beds.'

A figure came from the darkness, strolling from the night-black woodland as though he had not a care in the world. The man was muscled and broad-shouldered, with a shining bald pate save for two long plaits hanging from the sides of his head above his ears. It was Pallig, wearing a byrnie and swinging an axe as he walked. He pointed the axe at Beornoth and Robert de Warenne.

'Well, well,' Pallig said. 'Look at us. Old comrades reunited. Shame it could not be in better circumstances.'

'Pallig,' said Beornoth in greeting.

'You keep poor company these days, Beornoth.' Pallig pointed his axe at Robert de Warenne, and a fat drop of blood dripped from its hooked point.

'You betrayed the king,' said Robert de Warenne.

'I betrayed nothing. I served King Æthelred well. For many years. He made it clear I was no longer required.' Pallig shrugged. 'I have mouths to feed. Men sworn to my service who expect me to keep them in food, silver and battle. What sort of lord would I be if my men had no silver and bellies growling with hunger?'

'You swore an oath to serve the king. He made you a thegn, even though you are a Viking.'

'An oath works both ways, Norman. Æthelred has you now. He has no need of me.'

'You could have left. Taken your ships and sailed away with your warriors.'

'My ships?' Pallig laughed. 'I have wives here, Norman. Children. So do my men. We settled here, on lands granted to me by the king. Granted to me and my heirs for all time. We cannot simply sail away.'

'You have a new wife?' asked Beornoth. 'What of Gunhilde?'

'Gunhilde is still my wife. My favourite wife. Who would cast aside the sister of Sweyn Forkbeard unless he wished to bring about the wrath of the king of Denmark and Norway? The king of the Vikings! I have other wives, younger wives, but Gunhilde is the leader of my household.'

'My men lie dead and you talk of wives?' said Robert de Warenne with a fierce look upon his hard face.

'Men who came to kill me.'

'You broke your oath. There must be a price to pay for treachery. What are we if we do not honour the oaths we make?'

Pallig rested his axe on his shoulder. 'You came to kill me, and now your men lie bleeding about you. Carrion for the ravens. Just as you would have done to me. We were surprised you didn't know we were coming. Your watchmen were easy to creep up on, and you might have noticed our spears had your men not raided a village of your own people. Dark days when men prey upon their own like feral wolves.'

Beornoth sniffed and glanced around, looking for Odo de Warenne, but Robert's scarred brother was nowhere to be seen.

'There must be a reckoning,' said Robert.

'You have had one,' Pallig replied. He waved his axe around at the carnage of Robert's camp. 'I am going to lead my men away now. You can come and try again, if you wish. All you will find on that road is death. So take your men and ride away. Tell the king I bear him no anger. He broke his word to me and cast me aside, and I broke my oath to him. Tell King Æthelred there needs to be no ill will between us. I have my lands, and I have taken more. It's only what I am owed. That is the way of things in Midgard. The strong take what the weak can't protect. I will put my axe away now and live in peace.'

'What would a Norse whoreson like you know about peace?'

said a high-pitched voice. Beornoth winced as Odo came limping from the darkness. He was a fool and a liability, and his very presence made Beornoth's shoulders taut.

'Does he speak for you?' Pallig asked Beornoth, the good humour vanishing from his broad face. Beornoth shook his head.

'Surrender to me,' Odo spat. 'Throw down your axe and beg for mercy, Viking nithing. Crawl on your knees at my feet and pray to your foul gods for the king's mercy. Or perhaps I shall find your wives, even your old whore of a Viking, and teach them what it means to face the king's wrath.'

'The company you keep shames you, Lord Beornoth,' Pallig said, and the words cut Beornoth like a blade. 'Come for me then, Normans. I'll be waiting.'

Pallig stepped back and disappeared into the forest's darkness.

'Come, we can follow him and kill them all,' said Odo. 'We have the men to do it. He has but forty warriors.'

'And how many of our men died tonight because of your stupidity?' said Beornoth, turning to face the smaller man.

'How dare you talk to me like that, Saxon filth? This attack was none of my doing, but I would lead our men out now and kill that Viking turd. Would you remain here, cowering behind your Saxons?'

Beornoth punched Odo do Warenne so hard in the stomach that he bent double and vomited. Beornoth hooked his leg behind Odo's knee, grabbed the back of his byrnie and threw him to the ground.

'Beornoth!' Robert shouted.

Odo scrambled like a dog on its back, gasping in horrified shame.

'I warned you to watch him,' Beornoth snapped at Robert.

'Men have died, and we suffered a defeat at the hands of enemies we came to kill.'

Beornoth stalked away and left Robert to help his malevolent brother. Pallig had inflicted a crushing defeat upon the war band, and if they were not careful, the hunters would soon become the hunted.

15

The war band spent the rest of that night tending to the wounded and burying the dead. Eighteen men had died, and three score taken serious wounds. Odo de Warenne lounged against a birch tree whilst the rest of the company dug graves and bound wounds.

'He's a devil, that one,' said Wigs as he dug a grave using his spear to shovel clods of damp soil.

'He's going to get us all killed,' Ecga replied. 'We could have died last night.'

'Offa's dead,' said Gis, 'and Hedda, and Rothulf. Hedda was married to a cousin of mine. He had three children. Bloody Norman bastards.'

'They've treated us like shit from the moment we left Winchester. We dig the shit pits, we forage for firewood, whilst they hunt for game and laze around drinking wine. It ain't right. Norman bastards is right.'

'Just dig and keep your teeth together. The Danes killed our lads, not the Normans,' Beornoth warned them both. He felt it too, that Odo de Warenne was a fell spirit amongst them, a man without honour who fouled their luck and brought bad omens upon them. They were right. Odo's failure to properly scout the countryside had allowed Pallig to approach unseen, and so Odo was as responsible for the slaughter as Pallig's blades. But it would do no good to sow more discontent between the Normans and Saxons of the war band, and so Beornoth would hear no talk of it.

Odo glowered at Beornoth, his face already swollen and turning purple where Beornoth had beaten him. Beornoth turned towards him and crossed his arms. They locked eyes and Odo's jaw clenched, the muscles beneath his beard working. They stood there like that whilst the men worked, and Beornoth would not break first. Five Saxons had died because of Odo's incompetence. Beornoth could not forgive that.

A Norman warrior called to Odo. He grinned, spat, looked away from Beornoth and strolled to his Norman friend, ambling around the rest of the company hard at work preparing camp. Traitors to the crown must be punished, but Beornoth wondered if King Æthelred had made a mistake trusting the Norman warriors his mother had brought across the sea. There was an ill taint about the company, like the taste of a sour apple. Beornoth felt it in his bones. He couldn't explain it, but the feeling was there. He could not talk to Wigs, Gis or Ecga about it without fuelling the fire of their discontent, so he kept his mouth shut and instead stretched his aching body.

The following morning was still and cold. Autumn had descended and trees shone like gold with yellowed leaves falling in clumps onto grass heavy with dew. They found Pinnock deserted, its gates open and its people waiting for them with frightened faces. They were Saxons, inhabitants of the town before the Vikings came and who had remained there once Pallig's men had taken control. A fat man with thick lips told them how they had suffered at the Vikings' hands. Women wept as the fat man told how the Vikings had taken men's wives and daughters for their playthings. Pallig had taken no slaves, but his Vikings had not been gentle. Pallig's men had left in the night following their successful raid on Robert de Warenne's camp, so there was little the war band could do to give the townsfolk the justice they craved.

Pallig had left Pinnock with forty warriors. Half mounted on fine horses and the rest on foot. Their tracks smeared the valley leading away from Pinnock as though a great worm had slithered across the land in the dark of night. The fat man told of feasts Pallig had thrown over the winter where two hundred men or more had come from neighbouring farms and towns taken by the Vikings in last year's raids.

The war band followed the trail of Pallig's retreat until they came to the remains of a farmstead. It was a small place, its hall little more than a wattle-walled barn with a pigsty, and a handful of small outbuildings. Those buildings were in ruins. Soot-blackened wooden posts stood from the earth like bent, grasping fingers, the earth about them scorched. Men made the sign of the cross as they rode slowly past corpses visible in the ruins, burned and shrunk by the flames. One body lay outside the burned buildings, a woman's body with her skirts hitched up and her legs bloody.

Odo de Warenne called to the Normans and a handful of them laughed.

'This was his work,' said Wigs, casting a sullen glance in Odo's direction. 'Not the Danes. They had no time to raid this place after attacking us in the night. The devil's work killed these people. Look at what they did to that poor woman. Who knows what tortures those poor burned corpses suffered before the flames consumed them? These are our people. We are supposed to protect them.'

Beornoth knew it too, but he kept silent. As did the rest of the riders who rode through the devastation with bowed heads. The scene brought back painful memories for Beornoth. Memories of his own dead daughters and the harm done to his wife by Viking raiders. His stomach turned and he wanted to kick Virtus into a gallop and ride away from the horror. The pain of the days in the aftermath of his family's suffering was too dark. The deaths of little Ashwig and Cwen had broken him. Crushed his soul and left him a drunken mess, worthless and unable to care for Eawynn when she had needed him most. For years, he could not look at Eawynn without imagining what the Vikings had done to her, and the scar at her throat where they had left her for dead was a constant reminder. He had been a fool in those days, seeking comfort in ale. Eawynn had descended into madness and lived in the care of nuns. It was only in their later years that Beornoth and Eawynn had healed together, had learned to value their final years as husband and wife.

'Wigs is right,' said Gis as they left the raided farmhouse behind. 'These were our people. Good, honest people. If this is why we ride, then we are little better than the Vikings we hunt. How can the king give power to men who would hurt his subjects so?'

Beornoth shushed them and they rode away from the ravaged farm in stunned silence. The shrivelled, burned bodies flashed into Beornoth's mind every time he blinked. He tried to think about Pallig and where the Viking might go next and how long it was before Pallig called his oathmen to his side. Every time Beornoth attempted to consider that problem, sounds of screaming children and weeping women clawed their way to the forefront of his brain, overtaking any rational thought. He was ashamed to ride with Odo de Warenne, guilty that a company he rode with had committed such an act of wanton cruelty, the same ruthless violence for which he hated the Vikings and had dedicated his life to fighting them.

Robert de Warenne led them north-east, following Pallig's tracks as fast as possible without blowing the horses. The urge was to ride hard, to push the horses and chase Pallig and his forty warriors down. But blown horses would cripple the company and leave them open to attack, so Robert wisely chose caution. They rested beside a babbling brook, its waters dancing over slick grey rocks as the water curled its way through a copse of birch and elm trees. Beornoth led Virtus to the water and let her drink. He took off her saddle and brushed her coat with a handful of dry grass. His byrnie lay heavily upon his shoulders, and his shield strap chafed the skin at his neck. He left the shield, his sword and spear beside a grey boulder thick with green lichen and walked towards the woods. Beornoth paused to stretch his back and knead out the aches in his arms and thighs. His ribs still burned and the cut on his face had turned to an itching scab. He ducked beneath a low branch and searched amongst the trees and briars for wild blackberries and purple thistle tops which Virtus loved to eat.

He found a patch of blackberries, picked a dozen and wrapped them in a corner of his cloak.

'All alone in the woods, Saxon,' said a voice behind him. A high-pitched voice tinged with venom.

Beornoth closed his eyes and tried to master the surge of anger he felt at the very sound of Odo de Warenne's voice. Four big Normans crunched through the fallen leaves and twigs to surround him. They wore helmets, carried shields and spears, russet cloaks hanging long and still from their shoulders.

'You really want to do this?' Beornoth said.

'Did you think you could attack me and get away with it, you Saxon pig?' Odo appeared behind two of his men, his scarred face twitching with delight. 'You think you are the great hero? The Dane-killer? You're nothing but a crusty old bastard living off the fat of old glories. You need putting in your place, Saxon.'

'Are you going to do it? Or let these brave men do it for you?'

'I wouldn't lower myself to fight you, dog.' He rested a hand on the shoulder of the Normans to either side of him. 'Don't kill him. Just hurt him enough to stop his yapping.'

The Normans turned their spears around so that the butts faced towards Beornoth like clubs. Odo waggled his fingers at Beornoth to wave goodbye and limped off into the trees whistling a jaunty tune. Beornoth let the blackberries and thistles fall from his cloak. The trees about him creaked and the sound of men's voices rumbled lightly from the stream beyond the trees. He stared ahead into a Norman's angular face, hard and flat beneath the cold iron of his helmet. Blue eyes looked back at him, icy and with no flicker of emotion. Each of the men surrounding Beornoth was thick-chested and muscled, but none were as tall as he. A warrior to Beornoth's left took a step forward and his heavy boot crushed a fallen blackberry. Odo had chosen violence, and these men followed his command. Beornoth doubted he could fight four men with shields and spears and emerge unscathed. All he had was the seax sheathed at the small of his back. If they wanted violence, then they had come to the right place.

A spear butt flashed at Beornoth from the left and he leaned back so that the ash shaft passed harmlessly in front of his face. Beornoth grabbed it and yanked the spear towards him. The wielder came with it and Beornoth drove his fist into the Norman's stomach. He grabbed the man, spun him around and pushed him into the other three enemies. They shouted in anger and pushed their man away. A spear stave came at Beornoth's head and he caught the blow on his forearm. Before he could move, another spear hit him on the knee and a third drove into his stomach. Air rushed from Beornoth's guts and he bent double. A hand grabbed a fistful of his hair and a knee smashed into the side of his head. Beornoth twisted and stamped on one Norman's foot and drove his fist into the groin of another. They grunted in pain and the hand holding his hair gave way. A spear staff smashed into Beornoth's back and he fell to one knee. They surged at him then, raining down blows as Beornoth raised his hands to protect his head.

To cower amongst them was to risk broken bones, a cracked skull, even death. Whilst Odo had ordered his men not to kill Beornoth, a warrior cannot fully control himself in the heat of combat and a stray spear or hard blow to the skull could mean the end. He would not die at the order of Odo de Warenne. Beornoth reached to the small of his back and whipped his seax free of its sheath. The Normans fought to injure and hurt Beornoth, but he had struck no such bargain. The Normans hammered punches and spears about Beornoth's back and shoulders, grunting, cursing and spitting with the effort of beating him.

Beornoth stabbed the point of his seax into the soft tissue behind a Norman's ankle. The wicked, broken-backed blade pierced leather boot and ankle beyond and the injured man howled in pain. It was a terrible blow, crippling and impossibly painful. The sound of his cry was like a soul scratching and clawing to keep out of the jaws of hell. Beornoth pulled his weapon free and rose sharply, crashing his head into the wounded man's face. He slashed about him six times with the seax and the Normans fell back with cuts to their arms and legs.

The battle paused, and Beornoth stood to his full height. His back and torso throbbed with pain, but he swallowed it. Embraced it. The Normans hefted their shields and turned their spears around. The notion of fighting without deadly force was over, and for Beornoth, it had never existed. A spear point stabbed at him and Beornoth parried it with his seax. A shield crashed into him from one side and another bullied him backwards.

'Stop!' shouted a voice from the woods. 'I command you to stop.' Robert de Warenne strode from the trees with a frown like thunder creasing his handsome face. 'Have we not enough enemies without fighting each other? Back to your horses.'

The Normans glanced at the commander, then at one another, and then stalked away. The wounded man rolled and mewed in agony, clutching at his wounded ankle.

'What happened here?' asked Robert, coming close but falling short of squaring up to Beornoth.

Beornoth wanted to shout, he wanted to rage, and he wanted to fight Robert de Warenne and every Norman in camp. He took a breath and closed his eyes, needing to let the rage subside. The fury of combat still pumped through his veins and Beornoth loosened his grip on the seax. He relaxed his shoulders. Fighting Robert de Warenne was not the way to punish Odo. It was a quick way to die. Odo's time would come. He must die for what he had done to the people at the farmstead. He was Beornoth's enemy. Their hatred was now out in the open, and even though they rode together, their enmity was obvious. Beornoth would have to be cunning to complete his task, to bring the king's enemies to justice, and to kill Odo de Warenne. Odo de Warenne would die, but to do that, Beornoth had to remain calm. He had to let the Norman think he had got the better of their enmity. A knife in the dark, or another attack when he stopped to piss, was all Beornoth could expect if he kept up their feud. To defeat Odo, Beornoth must be what he had never been before. Calm and controlled until the time came to take his chance.

He knelt and wiped blood from his seax on the cloak of the injured Norman. He rose and slid the weapon back into its sheath. 'Ask your brother. They came at me.'

'This nonsense ends now. Is that clear?'

Beornoth held his stare, resisting the urge to remind Robert that he was not his superior. 'I should not have struck Odo when I did, and he was wrong to retaliate, so let this be an end to it. Remember, though, I did as you asked. Since we last spoke, I have followed your orders without complaint. The men understand you lead this company, not me. Your brother set these men upon me. I did not seek to hurt this man.' He gestured to the still groaning Norman, who had now sat up and removed his helmet to reveal a pained, sweating face.

'This bickering must end if we are to complete our mission with our lives intact. We must destroy Pallig and his men.'

'Talk to your brother. Did you see what he did to that farmstead?'

'I saw.' Robert kicked a rotting branch and turned away from Beornoth with his hands on his hips. 'I will deal with my brother. We must ride now if we are to catch Pallig before he can round up the rest of his warriors.'

Beornoth followed Robert out of the forest and mounted Virtus as two Normans helped their injured friend from the trees.

'What happened to you?' asked Wigs, leaning forward in the saddle, taking in Beornoth's dishevelled appearance.

'Odo and four Normans attacked me in the woods,' Beornoth said. He stiffened as a stab of pain shot through his back, a reminder of the spear staves and fists which had pummelled him in the forest. 'I don't want any trouble. He set his dogs on me and it could have been much worse.'

'You don't want any trouble?' said Wigs with an astonished look on his face. 'Have you taken a blow to the skull?'

'How was your stroll in the forest, Lord Beornoth?' said Odo de Warenne, trotting by on his horse. He laughed and gave Beornoth a mock salute.

'All shall be settled,' Beornoth said, biting his tongue.

'A pox on these Norman dogs,' said Gis once Odo was out of earshot. He made the sign of the cross in front of his chest to ward off Odo de Warenne's evil. 'We should leave them. Ride to Winchester and tell the king what Odo de Warenne did to those farmers.'

'Do you think the de Warennes would allow us to just ride away?' said Wigs as they urged their horses onwards. 'We'd be just as bad as Pallig. We've sworn oaths to serve the king and kill the traitors. Besides, what makes you think the king would grant you an audience? Talked to him often, have you?'

'All right, smart-arse. You might think it's funny. You won't be laughing when Pallig carves us up the next time Odo the bastard makes a fart of his scouting duties.'

'The king would listen to Beornoth,' said Ecga through a mouthful of cheese he had found in his pack.

'That's enough of that talk,' said Beornoth. 'If the men hear you three talking about riding away, it won't be long before men start to disappear in the night. When the fighting goes well, men are full of spirit. After a defeat is when they melt away. When men yearn for the warmth of their beds and their wives and fear cold enemy steel.'

Beornoth clicked his tongue and cantered to the head of the column. He fell in beside Robert de Warenne and the Norman raised an eyebrow to see Beornoth. The Saxons normally took up the rear of the column, riding separately from the Normans. Beornoth usually rode with the Saxons, but if he was going to be cunning and live long enough to kill Odo de Warenne, then he needed to keep Robert close until the fighting was done. After that? Then perhaps Odo would find the same justice as Kvitsr and Hvitserk.

16

The war band tracked Pallig's force for four days. They left the woodland beneath a pale early-morning sky streaked with fire orange and rose-petal pink. They rode north-east, following the brown smear left by Pallig's horses, and it was four days of blood. Cold wintry days where swirling leaves and bitter, lashing rain mixed with balmy, warm winds which made the horses thirsty and the nights short. Pallig attacked again on the first night, not the brutal slaughter laid down at Pinnock, but short, savage and deadly. The war band woke to find two sentries dead and two more hanging from a tree with swollen tongues lolling from their mouths.

The second attack came the following day as the war band reached the borders of old Wessex. Arrows whistled from a crumbling building at the roadside, struck two horses and injured a Saxon warrior's leg. The archers sped from cover on swift ponies and Odo de Warenne set off in pursuit with ten men and returned with only three. He told a tale of ambush in dense woodland and Beornoth winced to think how Pallig and his Danes must have laughed at the Normans' blundering mistake. The mood amongst both Saxons and Normans plummeted. Men rode with hunched shoulders, cloaks pulled about them to keep out the onset of winter cold. They argued over the smallest matters. Robert de Warenne ordered scouts to both ride ahead and behind the column to watch for more of Pallig's men. On the third day, the war band found four heads waiting for them. Four heads placed carefully in the road, with no sign of their horses or the rest of their corpses.

The riders returned along the Fosse Way, the old Roman road cut straight through swathes of rich farm and woodland. They rode beneath rolling hills crowned with pines still green despite the end of summer and stopped at Ilchester to water their horses in the River Yeo. Robert de Warenne took on supplies at the burh built on the ruins of a Roman fortress. He ordered a score of men too injured to fight to remain within the walls until they were well enough to fight, at which time they were to seek the war band and continue their service. Beornoth bought oats and carrots for Virtus and paid a smith to put a new edge upon his sword.

'We've only six score men left who can fight,' grumbled a Saxon supping ale inside the fortress walls. 'How can we attack the Danes with so small a force?'

'By the time we reach them, there might only be a handful of us left. We're cursed, I tell you, cursed,' said another.

Beornoth listened to them as he waited for the smith to finish his work. Ill feeling will spread amongst fighting men like the plague. He had seen it before. There was little to be done about it until they could catch up with Pallig and put his warriors to the sword. Only a victory would lift warriors' spirits. Ilchester's thegn reported no sightings of a Viking war band travelling through his lands, for Pallig's men had neither raided nor attacked any settlements on their ride north.

They left Ilchester without spending the night, pressing hard and riding through small villages like Martock, Woodnes and Leigh. They camped in sight of the Somersaete hills, and Pallig's men attacked again in the early hours. Thundering hooves woke the war band as six riders stormed through the camp and killed three men with thrown spears. The Danes had killed two sentries, men found with their throats cut, and Beornoth went to Robert de Warenne, who raged at his captains as he stood before the dead warriors.

'How are they able to kill our sentries?' he roared, and kicked a fallen helmet to send it flying across the grass.

'We don't know, lord,' replied a man with a long nose. 'These were good men, vigilant.'

'Vigilant? I'd say they were the opposite of vigilant. Tonight I'll take first watch myself, and you shall take a watch each. Do you understand?'

'Yes, lord,' said de Warenne's five captains as one.

'Clean up this mess and bury these men properly.' Robert de Warenne noticed Beornoth watching and raised a finger. 'Today is not the day, Beornoth. Unless you have something helpful to say.'

'We've left the lands taken by Pallig and Kvitsr in last year's raids,' said Beornoth. 'We are in Wessex now. The Downs are a short ride from here, then we shall reach the chalk hills. Pallig rides for his lands, the lands granted to him by the king after Lundenwic.'

'What of it?'

'He takes the long way around, trying to fool us. But he rides for home. Fighting season is over, winter creeps across the land and men prepare their stores for winter. For weeks we have ridden alongside meadows where shepherds bring their flocks down from the heights to keep them stabled and close for when the ice and snow comes. Pallig must eat and he must feed his men. I doubt much farming took place in Pallig and Kvitsr's conquered lands in Defnascir. They killed or enslaved the churls and left last year's fields untilled. His family must still be on the lands granted to him by the king. Perhaps he left Gunhilde or his children there and brought his younger wives with him to Pinnock. Maybe the greater force of his warriors waits there for him. He could not leave those lands undefended, not with his family and his winter supplies there. So he rides for home to spend the winter months with his family and in the comfort of the greater part of his fighting strength. We have also seen no sign of the twenty-four thousand pounds of silver paid by the king to Kvitsr and Pallig. That horde must be somewhere, unless the warlords gave the largest portion of it to their jarls and warriors. Who can say for sure? But he rides for Oxenforda.'

'Are you sure?'

'Why else would he leave his new lands? Why ride north into Wessex with forty men where all that awaits him are enemies? Wessex is the kingdom's heartland, bristling with thegns, reeves, burhs and warriors. He rides for Oxenforda, and whilst he takes the long road to throw us off his true path, we can ride east and get there before him.'

'Good, Beornoth. Good.' Robert de Warenne stared north and chewed his lip. 'Perhaps we should have struck at Oxenforda first. We could have drawn Pallig out by burning his hall or taking his family captive. You follow Pallig with your Saxons so that he believes we are still on his trail. I shall take the rest of the men to Oxenforda and head him off.'

Beornoth left Robert de Warenne and stood with the Saxons as they watched the Norman warriors ride away.

'Good riddance,' said Wigs.

'What's stopping Pallig from killing us all now that they've gone?' asked Ecga. 'He wasn't afraid to pick us off when there were two hundred of us. We are only forty men now.'

'Bloody hell, Ecga. Do you have to piss on our fire so quickly? At least give us one moment of happiness. We're free of the Norman pigs. Enjoy it.'

'Ecga is right,' said Beornoth, not wanting to dampen the Saxons' new-found smiles but needing to remind them of the danger they faced. 'Our number matches Pallig's, and we don't want to get drawn into a fight with his men. We follow at a distance, riding slow and clumsy. All we need is Pallig to believe that we follow his trail. We don't get close enough for him to spring one of his ambushes or far enough away that we lose track of them.'

'What if they come for us at night?' asked Gis.

'We make camp carefully, in a place Pallig can't catch us unawares. Tomorrow or the day after, he'll swing east to Oxenforda and we'll pin him between our men and the Normans.'

They left Ilchester with packs heavy with hard bread, dried meat, apples and leather skins sloshing with freshly brewed ale. With the Normans gone, the Saxons laughed and talked throughout the day and Beornoth ordered regular breaks to slow the pace. Pallig's band left simple tracks to follow and by the end of that day Beornoth guessed the Danes were at least a half-day's ride ahead of them. They would reach the Thames Valley in the morning and Beornoth ordered his men to camp in the lee of a chalk hill high above a sloping valley close to the ancient earth fortress at Sarum. No Dane could attack that position without marching uphill from the north, and Beornoth scouted the valley himself before dusk to make sure Pallig had left no surprises waiting.

No Saxon slept that night. It was a cold, cloudy night dimly lit by a sliver of moon and men spent it outside beside their campfires with cloaks wrapped tight about them.

'Give us the tale of Forkbeard and the riddles, lord?' asked Wigs as Ecga served a broth made from dried beef.

Beornoth grumbled, not wanting to talk in front of the gathered warriors. But he saw their wide eyes and faces gaping at him and could not refuse. They were simple men, warriors who could not expect to be in the company of great lords, so to hear tell of the great Sweyn Forkbeard and Ealdorman Byrhtnoth would give them a tale to share with their families at firesides for years to come. He was not a great speaker, not like Byrhtnoth had been, or his old friend Aelfwine of Foxfield. Beornoth's skills lay in his hands, not in words. But he cleared his throat, took a sip of ale and told them of the great King Sweyn's deep cunning, of his hall and the fearsome warriors at his back. He told them how he entered Forkbeard's presence expecting a fight, for Vikings are ever fond of single combat and Beornoth had expected to fight against one of Forkbeard's champions for the chance to speak to the king of the Danes. Instead, Forkbeard had challenged Ealdorman Byrhtnoth and his hearth troop for a contest of riddles. Beornoth asked the men the riddles that both Forkbeard and Aelfwine had posed, and they hoomed and struggled to come up with the answers.

'You speak like a northerner, lord,' said Gis when Beornoth had finished his story. 'How is it you came to Ealdorman Byrhtnoth of Essex's service?'

'That's another long story, and my throat is already dry from talking,' Beornoth said, and the men laughed. 'How is it that a force of Saxons comes to ride with Robert de Warenne and his Normans?'

'Rotten luck,' said Gis.

'A kick in the unmentionables more like,' said Wigs. 'We

served a thegn, a great man who died old without an heir. His lands were forfeit to Lady Aelfryth. She granted our lord's lands to Robert de Warenne and us with them.'

'Your lord had no sons?' asked Beornoth.

'He had three. Two died as children and the third died in battle against Vikings many years ago. He had a daughter who married a Mercian lord, but she died in childbirth. So our homes passed to Norman rule.'

'They came and settled in the hall. Robert let his captains choose where they wanted to settle their families and the folk who lived there had to move. We are lucky, we are warriors. Churls and freehold farmers were not so lucky. All we had to do was swear oaths to our new Norman lord and wear his livery. Many men fell from freedom to become slaves, committed to serve their lords forever in return for food and protection for their families.'

'God save us, but they were dark days,' said Ecga. 'People we knew turned out of homes built by their fathers' grandfathers. Even the Church would not turn a man out like that.'

'Gis has seven children,' said Ecga.

'Ecga's wife is a rare beauty,' said Wigs. He jumped up and walked with swinging hips and pouting lips, and the men fell about laughing. Ecga rewarded him with a thump on the shoulder.

'Wigs was once destined for the Church,' said Ecga. 'Believe it or not.'

'I surely do not believe that,' said Beornoth.

'It's true,' said Wigs. 'My father was a reeve and I his third son. My eldest brother was to become a reeve, the second to become a warrior and serve the thegn, and I was to become a priest. Thank the Lord Jesus for his fortune, and God forgive me for it, but the second brother died of the pox and so I took up sword and shield. Though at times, especially when we are about to make the shield wall, I think I would have made a fine priest.'

'Without a wife?'

'How many priests do you know who don't have a woman or two on the side?'

'True enough.' Beornoth smiled at the jest. Other men spoke of their families, spoke fondly of a son or proudly of a daughter and so their night spent watching out for Pallig's Vikings passed quickly, despite the cold. It was a peaceful night of comradeship and relief after so long spent in the shadow of Odo's malevolence and the blood and horror of the hunt for Pallig and his crew.

At first light they picked up the trail, and Beornoth was satisfied to see Pallig's track turn eastwards towards the River Thames and its slow-moving waters. The Saxons sang war songs as they rode, trying each other at riddles as steam rose from horse and riders' mouths in the chill air. The timber spires and crosses of Oxenforda's church came into view over the horizon as the land levelled out, and though the riders and their mounts were weary from so many days in the field, their spirits remained high. King Æthelred had granted Pallig a fine swathe of land in return for his service protecting the crown against fellow Viking warlords. The growing town of Oxenforda lay within those fertile fields and meadows.

The land around the town had turned damp and dour with the onset of winter. Fields stripped bare after the harvest lay in shades of faded gold and earthy brown. Hills washed with dull greens and russet rose above leafless hedgerows, and Beornoth called the column to a halt in a shallow valley where mist rose above a thin stream. A rider cantered across a low peak, spear in hand and a shield slung across his back. A tinge of smoke hung in the air, and columns of grey twisted around the town's tall buildings to smudge the sky like charcoal.

The rider spotted Beornoth's men and led his mount down a slope where a shepherd herded his flock towards a sheltered pasture. A clutch of churls stopped to stare, taking a break from digging furrows and scattering fistfuls of ash over the soil. A chill wind whipped through the valley and the sky hung close, heavy and grey, casting a sombre mood over the company.

'Lord Beornoth,' called the Norman rider. He wore a leather helmet liner on his head and riding gloves to warm him against the cold.

'What news?' asked Beornoth.

'The Danes are in the town, lord. Pallig is there. We have them, lord!' His horse skittered and snorted, casting plumes of smoke into the air.

'Have them how?'

'Trapped, lord. In the buildings. Lord Robert sent me out to keep watch for you, or for any other Danes.'

'How many men does Pallig have in the town?'

'Sixty, lord. Their families are with them.'

'Lead on.' Beornoth clicked his tongue and Virtus followed the scout towards Oxenforda's walls. Beornoth's stomach churned, and he was surprised to feel a surge of nervousness. Not nervous of fighting the Danes, but concerned for Pallig and his family. Even after the ambush attacks and his betrayal of King Æthelred, Beornoth liked the man.

Beornoth rode Virtus through open gates and into a strangely quiet town. Eyes stared at him from behind closed window shutters, and though the lanes and streets were empty, Beornoth felt fear like a fog hanging about the place. A dog barked at the riders and the horses trotted through streets thick with mud, throwing up clods of dark earth. They turned around a long stable with a pinewood roof and found the Normans thronging a wide street before two large buildings.

Beornoth dismounted, and Gis took Virtus' reins. He stalked amongst the Normans who busied themselves lighting fires in iron braziers. Men came from the snarl of paths between houses and stalls, carrying more of the small iron cages gathered from throughout the town to start more fires. They took doors from homes and buildings and hacked them into firewood, which they stacked in the braziers and used smoking faggots to light them. Norman warriors ringed the two buildings, shields and swords ready in a defensive shield wall.

The hall was a Saxon building, not the glorious Viking long halls to be found north of the Danelaw with a keel-like post at the centre of its roof and fine carvings on the door lintel and gable. It was a Saxon hall, so low that its grey thatch almost touched the mud. Its walls were wattle and daub about a timber frame with stout oak doors and latticed shutters closed across small windows. St Frideswide's church sat before the bend of a slow-flowing river which ran through Oxenforda town. It was built of stone up to the height of a man, and then finished in timber. The stone was a mixture of Roman-cut stone plundered from ancient buildings and crudely cut local rock placed about the Roman work, gaps filled with smaller rocks and daub. The church was named after the town's patron saint, St Frideswide, a princess who had died hundreds of years ago. Beornoth remembered the tale from a church sermon, of how she was blind and prayed to God for water and a spring welled up at her feet. The church had straw thatch, and its door, made of heavy oak, was reinforced with iron bands and marked with simple carvings of crosses. Two slim windows stood on either side of the door, covered with thin slices of horn to keep out the cold.

'Where are the Danes?' Beornoth asked a Norman who

walked past him with an armful of firewood. He knew the answer, feared the answer, but needed to hear it.

'A score inside the hall, lord,' he said, a winter cold making his nose run into thick moustaches. 'At least two score inside the church.' He grinned like an excited child and went off about his business.

Beornoth found Robert and Odo de Warenne stood with arms folded, watching their men at work.

'Lord Robert,' Beornoth said in greeting. Robert raised a hand, but Odo sneered and spat into the mud. 'When did Pallig arrive?'

'You were right, Lord Beornoth,' said Robert de Warenne. 'Pallig and his men arrived yesterday and found us waiting for them.'

'They ran like frightened rats,' said Odo, glee stretching his scarred face. 'Ran for the wives and children and walked into our trap.'

'Their women and children?' said Beornoth.

'We herded them into the hall and church, killed a few, and the Danes ran inside to protect them. So now we've locked them inside.'

Beornoth turned to Robert, but he looked away, unable to meet Beornoth's eye. 'You killed their families?'

'Some, yes,' said Odo. 'You missed it, Beornoth. You would have enjoyed the bloodshed. They are scum, traitors. Danes.'

'They have done worse to Saxon folk,' said Robert, and shifted his shoulders as though his byrnie were too tight, unable to meet Beornoth's eye. 'We can't chase Pallig across England forever. It ends here.'

Beornoth glanced again at the braziers. 'Have you asked them to surrender?'

'We asked. They refused. They tried to break out twice during the night and we beat them back.'

'They even handed up a horde of silver,' said Odo. 'What remained of Pallig's share of the gafol. Bastard had buried it beneath the church altar and his men threw it out of the windows.'

'They threw it out of the windows?'

'To save their miserable lives. I told them we would allow their families to come out and leave in peace if they gave up the silver.'

'And did you?'

'Did I what?' Odo raised an eyebrow as though Beornoth had said something preposterous.

'Did you let their women and children go?'

'Of course not. The bastards would fight to the death if they thought their loved ones had gone free. Now they'll wait inside, protecting what they hold most dear. They can't charge us and leave their sweet ones to suffer in the clash of blades, can they? So we are going to burn the bastards. Then, when they come out with the backs of their children ablaze, we shall put them to the sword. Bloody traitors. Make sure you are in the front, Beornoth, for there will be a great slaughter today.'

The words hit Beornoth like a punch to his gut. He looked at Robert, but the big man turned away and shouted at his men to make the ring of shields tighter. Beornoth stumbled away, feeling dazed, as he weaved around the laughing Normans and their flaming braziers.

'Beo?' called a voice from the hall. 'Beornoth?' It was Pallig. Beornoth winced. He trudged towards the ring of warriors before the hall and pushed his way through.

'Get back!' barked a Norman warrior when Beornoth eased

his shield out of the way. Beornoth stopped and stared down at the man, and he looked away, crouching behind his shield.

'I'm here,' Beornoth called in Norse. Pallig was an enemy, and he could sense the surrounding Normans bristling with uncomfortable anger.

'Can you help me, Beo? These Normans have me penned in.'

'You turned your cloak, Pallig.'

'I did, and I told you why. Perhaps my time is up, but can you get my family out of this mess? A favour for an old friend.'

'It's too late for that. They want your blood. It's over, Pallig.'

'What kind of *drengr* burns women and children?'

Pallig had used the Norse word for a warrior, and every Norse warrior strived to follow *drengskapr*, the way of the warrior. 'You took slaves. Your men killed and raped. Did you show any pity for the people who suffered from your wrath?'

'I took no slaves. Find a man who says I killed a child and I will fight him for being a liar.'

'I wish things were different, Pallig. I wish you had not betrayed the king.'

'I wish that too. Try for me, Beo. See what you can do. If there is no way out, then at least try to give me a quick death with a blade in my hand. Do that for me, as a favour. Warrior to warrior.'

Beornoth raised his hand. He couldn't see Pallig. The gesture came as an impulse, and he wasn't sure he waved goodbye or acknowledged Pallig's request. Beornoth felt sick to his stomach. He felt old, tired and dirty. He turned on his heel and marched away from the ring of shields.

'Hall burning?' asked Wigs when Beornoth found his men.

'Hall and church. Today is St Brice's Day,' Beornoth replied. He spoke distantly, staring off into the sky where a bird swooped and dipped above the thatch. Men about him talked and asked questions, but the sound of their words dulled and became like the sound of the sea in his ears. Men made the sign of the cross at the ill omen of burning a church, especially on a holy day. Beornoth's mind drifted away from Pallig's plight and he allowed himself to fall deeper into his mind. He couldn't remember who St Brice had been, nor what he had done to become venerated. Beornoth remembered the date because he had once visited a town where they held a bull-running festival every year on St Brice's Day. His father had taken him as a boy to see the bulls and Beornoth had marvelled at the size and power of the animals and wept at the end when warriors cut the bulls bloody.

Men jostled about him, and Beornoth blinked slowly. He saw Robert de Warenne wave his sword and point the blade at the buildings. A roar went up from the Normans and they grabbed flaming logs from the braziers. Beornoth left the Saxons and rushed to Robert de Warenne, who still stood with his sword pointed at the hall and church with a hard, cold look on his handsome face.

'I saw you talking with the heathens,' Robert said without looking at Beornoth. 'You are too fond of them, Beornoth.'

'You should let Pallig's wife and child live,' said Beornoth.

'We have God's work to do. The king's work. Ready your sword.'

'Pallig's wife is the sister of Sweyn Forkbeard. His children are nephews to the king of the Danes and the Norsemen. Save their lives.'

'They have made their choice. You must make yours.'

'Stop this madness!' Beornoth shouted, and took a step towards Robert de Warenne, which was a mistake.

'Seize him!' Odo screamed in his strangely high-pitched voice. 'Take the Viking-lover, now! Take him!'

Big men crashed into Beornoth at full force. A hard object

clattered across the back of his skull and Beornoth fell to his
knees. There was no rage in him, no anger, and he fell on all
fours. He was tired, horrified at what was about to happen to
Pallig and his loved ones. Fists clubbed him and strong hands
grabbed his arms and hauled Beornoth away from the de
Warenne brothers. His senses swam. He hung loose between his
captors as they dragged him through the press of Norman
warriors. Wigs, Gis, Ecga and the Saxons shouted and cursed at
the Normans, but Beornoth could say nothing. The fight was
gone from him. Ripped away by the shame at what was about to
unfold. Normans dragged Beornoth from the front, heels dragging in the mud as the war band whooped and shouted their
excitement, carrying firebrands towards the buildings. His head
rolled and swam with the warp and weft of it all. With memories
of his own children killed and burned, and sorrow for Pallig's
family and the horror the de Warennes were about to unleash
upon them.

17

'That'll hold the bastard,' said a thick-necked Norman as he hauled on the hemp rope tied about Beornoth's arms and chest.

'Tie his legs,' replied the second Norman, a smaller man with protruding front teeth.

'You tie his bloody legs, Fulk.'

'Just do it. He's dangerous. And if he gets loose, Odo will cut your stones off.'

Fulk cursed under his breath and tied another length of rope around Beornoth's ankles. 'Stay there and don't move,' he said, and tapped Beornoth twice on the cheek. 'There's a good lad. We've got Danes to kill.'

The two Normans laughed and strode from the stable, bumping shoulders and talking excitedly of the slaughter to come. Beornoth's head dropped to his chest. He could find no strength in his body, no will to struggle or try to free himself. He was a king's thegn and the Normans had him tied up like a hog for slaughter in a stinking barn. A scream shook him and Beornoth's head snapped up. It was a child's scream, a shriek of terror. Beornoth caught the waft of smoke through an open horse door, and more screams tore through the air. The hall and church were aflame. Pallig and his family burned, and the Normans cheered with sadistic glee.

Beornoth shook his head to keep the noise from his ears, but the screams grew louder, joined by angered shouts, and the laughter of Norman warriors. Beornoth could hear the crackle and roar of fire. He closed his eyes tightly, unable to keep the image of his own burned daughters from his mind. The battle between his duty to the king and his horror at Pallig's fate raged within him and Beornoth could not reconcile it. His heart told him to break free of his bonds, charge to the hall and free Pallig and his family from the flames. His head told him to stay still, to wait until Robert de Warenne's Normans did what must be done.

The stable door burst open and three warriors stormed in amidst a swirl of smoke.

'Cut him loose,' said the first man.

It was Wigs, Gis and Ecga, but Beornoth felt no relief. He hadn't the heart to break free and fight. He was tired, too old to ride for days across England hunting its enemies. The wyrd of his luck made Beornoth's bones ache. He wished he had stayed at home, resting peacefully beside Eawynn's grave in the company of Alfgar and his family until his time was done.

Wigs bent and cut the ropes tied about Beornoth with his knife. The bonds fell to the straw-covered ground, but Beornoth did not move. His three Saxon friends gaped at him, as though they expected him to surge to his feet and draw his sword. But Beornoth just sat, slumped against the barn wall.

'Come on, lord,' said Wigs. He held a hand out to Beornoth, offering to help him up.

Beornoth shook his head, and the Saxons exchanged puzzled glances.

'The men are busy with the slaughter outside. We have Virtus ready, with your weapons. We can ride away now and nobody will notice for hours,' said Gis.

'Ride where?' said Beornoth, his voice barely audible above the fire and the roar of the war band outside.

'Away from here,' said Ecga. 'We can't be part of this. We are supposed to be warriors, men of God. If we kill these people, if we butcher women and children, how are we any different from the Vikings?'

'We should go to the king,' said Wigs. 'Tell him what happened here. Tell his bishops. They will listen to you, lord. You are Beornoth, a king's thegn.'

Beornoth wrapped his hands around his head and stared at the ground.

'Help me get him up,' said Wigs. He and Gis took an arm each and hauled Beornoth to his feet. He walked with them, feet dragging, in a dreamlike state.

Virtus waited outside the stable and Gis, Wigs and Ecga pushed Beornoth up into the saddle. He pulled himself upwards half-heartedly. Virtus turned as a shriek howled from the church and suddenly Beornoth came face to face with the dreadful events he had no wish to be a part of. Orange flame licked across the hall and church roof, eating up the thatch like a starving beast. The Normans shook their weapons and flames cast their bloodthirsty faces in a dancing light. Pallig's hall burned faster than the church and flames licked about its timber frame so that the entire structure was ablaze. Smoke billowed from the windows and doors in dirty grey columns. Beornoth sat slumped on Virtus' back, sword, shield and spear tied to her saddle.

The hall door smashed open and Pallig himself ran through the thick smoke. He ran with an axe in one hand and a small child held in the other. The child's clothes were on fire and Pallig knelt, frantically patting out the flames with his bare hands. A Norman charged at him and drove the point of his spear into Pallig's back. The Viking roared in fury and rose, teeth bared and ivory-white in his smoke-blackened face. Pallig grabbed the spear and hauled it out of his flesh. He killed the spearman with a swing of his axe and threw the spear at the next Norman. Two more Norman warriors came at him and Pallig stood before his weeping child like a wolf before its cubs. They came with swords and Pallig met them, cutting one down with an overhand strike of his axe and burying the weapon in the chest of the second.

A spear flew from the massed war band ranks and sunk into Pallig's thigh and Beornoth gasped because a Saxon had thrown the weapon. The Saxons had joined the Normans, faces wickedly hungry for blood as they bayed before the burning buildings. Odo de Warenne capered before the Norman lines, screaming like a seiðr witch, and six men charged at Pallig. Odo limped after them. A woman came howling from the burning hall carrying two more children, her shawl and hair ablaze. Beornoth could not tear his eyes away from what he knew would happen next. The six men set about Pallig. He cut at them, but swords opened wounds in his stomach, chest and arms. Three Normans fell before his axe, and Pallig knelt in the mud, weeping like a child and swinging his axe to keep the Normans away from his burning family.

Odo de Warenne cut Pallig's wife down with a sweep of his sword, and Beornoth closed his eyes. A solitary tear rolled down his cheek. He turned away from the slaughter as Pallig's cries of sorrow rang in his ears. Wood creaked and crashed as the fire collapsed the buildings and Beornoth heard more warriors come howling from hall and church.

Beornoth dug his heels into Virtus' flanks and led her away. His three Saxon friends followed and as they reached the gates of Oxenforda, Beornoth clicked his tongue and urged Virtus first into a canter, and then into a wild gallop away from the sickening cries, screams and the chop of steel into flesh. The wind blew Beornoth's hair back and snatched the tears from his face. He rode until Virtus' flanks became lathered with white sweat. He let the horse slow to a trot and released the reins.

'Where are we going, lord?' said Wigs once he, Gis and Ecga had caught up.

'We must go to the king,' Beornoth replied.

'To tell him of the de Warennes' murderous slaughter?' asked Ecga.

Beornoth fixed each of them with a hard stare. 'To tell him that Odo de Warenne has killed the sister of Sweyn Forkbeard, the daughter of Harald Bluetooth. That he burned Forkbeard's nephews and put them to the sword.'

There was an audible gulp from Ecga's throat. 'What will the king do?'

'What can he do? Pallig was on the kill list and now he is dead. But there was an old saying I heard once. Something Ragnar Lothbrok said before King Aelle threw him into a pit of snakes. How the little pigs will grunt when they hear how the old boar suffered. This time it's the other way around. How the old boar will grunt when he hears how the little pigs suffered.'

Beornoth rode hard for Winchester. It took two nights to reach the king's capital, riding along the Icknield Way. They crossed the Thames along a rickety wooden bridge and stopped to purchase food at Wallingaford. It was a hard ride through face-stinging rain tinged with ice and the horses struggled on the cold ground. The four riders reached the gates of Winchester just after midday. A sharp chill bit through the air, and the stink of hearth-fire smoke made Beornoth shudder at the thought of Pallig and Oxenforda. They led their horses beneath the gate and a low sky, heavy and grey, which cast a dim light over the fields outside the city where frost clung to stub-bled crops and the earth lay heavy and dark. A crow cawed at Beornoth from the gate lintel to break the stillness. Beornoth dismounted inside the gates and showed his king's thegn ring to the guards who barred the way with long spears and hands blue from the cold.

Townsfolk bustled about the inner courtyard in heavy woollen cloaks, their collective breath rising like mist in the winter chill. The smell of damp thatch and freshly butchered meat mixed with the heavy pall of burning peat to give Winchester a close, oppressive air. The guards moved out of Beornoth's way and he found a stable close to the gatehouse where he paid a one-armed man a silver coin to take the four horses, brush, feed and hold them. Wigs, Gis and Ecga followed Beornoth silently through the wind and weave of Winchester's narrow streets. They exchanged fearful glances and kept close to Beornoth, hurrying behind his long strides.

Robert de Warenne had not sent riders to pursue Beornoth, and the ride from Oxenforda to Winchester had given Beornoth time to think about what must happen next. He did not doubt that the de Warennes would send a report to Æthelred confirming that Pallig was dead, and the rider who came with that news would also say that Beornoth had left the war band. That he had shirked his responsibilities and rode away from the king's duty. Beornoth had reached Winchester riding hard, and no messenger could have reached the king ahead of him.

A steward in a jerkin bearing the green dragon of Wessex walked along a line of commoners waiting outside the royal enclosure and its stone walls. Beornoth tossed his cloak over one shoulder, making his scabbard easily visible. He then waited behind the line of men who were gesticulating and standing on tiptoes to get the king's attention.

'What are they doing?' asked Gis.

'The king grants audiences once, maybe twice a week,' said Beornoth. 'He will make judgement on disputes and hear complaints and problems. These men should, and may have already sought justice from an ealdorman, thegn or reeve and come to the king to appeal an unjust judgement. Some could be merchants or messengers bearing reports from across the kingdom.'

'The king's ears will burn with complaints by the end of the day,' said Wigs.

'He won't see them all. Perhaps none today, or the day after that. Which is why they protest out here to get an audience.'

'Maybe we should come back another day,' said Ecga. 'When things aren't so busy.'

'They are always busy. We see the king today.' Beornoth took two steps forward. 'You there, steward?' he called in a booming voice, which made the entire line of plaintiffs turn and stare.

The steward, a pinch-faced man with a drooping nose and bright blue eyes, glowered at Beornoth. He was about to shower Beornoth with rebuke until his beady eyes fell upon the green dragon scabbard and the gold ring on his finger. The steward hurried towards Beornoth, barging through the line of waiting men. He frowned as his soft leather shoes trod in a pile of horseshit, and then bowed so deeply to Beornoth that he almost fell over.

'Welcome, my lord,' said the steward in a slow drawl. 'How can I be of service to you, king's thegn?'

'I must see the king,' said Beornoth. 'With urgent news of Robert de Warenne and the hunt for Pallig and Kvitsr War Raven.'

The steward itched at his stubbly jaw, glanced back at the line of men waiting to see the king. His blue eyes flickered up to Beornoth's great height and down at his gold ring bearing the green dragon of Wessex.

'I have orders that the king is not to be disturbed, lord. But I am sure he could make an exception for you.'

'Tell him Beornoth is there.'

'Yes, lord, of course, lord.' The steward hurried away and waved his hands dismissively at the men in line who called to him as he pushed his way through.

Less than an hour later, Beornoth waited inside the royal enclosure in a dusty room lined with tall rows of shelves, upon which lay row upon row of yellowed scrolls. Candles burned in alcoves and upon iron holders, some long and dripping wax, others low with long tails of wax dripped almost to the floor.

Wigs gingerly took a scroll from its place on the shelf closest to him and unrolled it a little to peer at the words scrawled on the parchment in black ink.

'Can you read, lord?' he asked.

'I can read enough,' said Beornoth. His father had paid a man to teach Beornoth his letters and Latin as a boy. He had been a terrible student, and could only remember a few words of the language of the Romans and of the Church. He couldn't write much, but could read.

'I can't read at all, not a word,' said Gis. 'Imagine all the stories and secrets in this place. They say King Alfred was a great reader, that he wrote books of wisdom. A man could become wise in here.'

'What do you need to read for? You're a warrior, not a priest,' said Wigs.

'I'm just saying there is knowledge and wisdom on these scrolls. A man could learn a lot.'

'You just stick to spear work. Your head's as thick as a ship-wright's mallet, so don't get notions of wisdom.'

'You're one to talk. I doubt you could even name ten saints.'

'Of course I bloody could.'

'Go on then.'

The sound of footsteps silenced their bickering as six men came bustling into the room. King Æthelred led them, his long auburn hair dull in the half-light afforded by the library's horn-covered windows. The king glanced at Beornoth, smiled wanly, and then itched beneath the gold circlet upon his brow. He wore a silver crucifix upon his chest hanging from a gold chain and a softly combed beard covered his lantern jaw.

'Welcome, Beornoth,' said the king. He clasped his hands behind his back and forced a thin smile to his lips. 'Fresh from the field of battle. How goes the traitor hunt?' Wrinkles creased Æthelred's brow and dark circles ringed his eyes.

The men about Æthelred glowered at Beornoth from beneath tonsured brows. Each wore the black and brown robes of the Church and wrung ink-stained hands as they cocked their heads to see what Beornoth had to say.

'Lord king,' said Beornoth, and bowed respectfully, as did Wigs, Gis and Ecga. 'Kvitsr War Raven is dead, as is his jarl Hvit-serk and other Danes who raided our shores last year.'

'I had received news of that already, Beornoth. We are all relieved to hear that you killed the sea-wolves.'

'We caught Pallig at Oxenforda, lord king.'

'Good. Is the traitor dead?'

'We pursued him across Defnascir at the cost of many warriors' lives.'

'And then found him at his home,' said a big-bellied priest with a pox-scarred face. The other priests laughed into their baggy sleeves at the sarcasm.

'I come to you with ill news, my king,' Beornoth continued, ignoring the insult. 'Pallig is slain, along with his wife and children and the families of his followers.'

Æthelred clapped his hands and turned to his gaggle of priests who offered the king their congratulations. He cocked an eyebrow when he realised Beornoth had more to say.

'The Normans slaughtered the women and children, lord king,' Beornoth said.

'Then Pallig, the treacherous dog, should not have taken refuge behind them. War can be brutal, Beornoth. There can be...' Æthelred waved to his priests for support.

'Unfortunate consequences,' said the big-bellied priest.

'Exactly. War is brutal, Beornoth. Bloody and brutal. You should know this. What is it the Vikings call you again?'

'Beornoth Reiði,' Beornoth whispered. His stomach lurched. The king had no sympathy for Pallig's family.

'Beornoth the Wrathful,' said the fat-bellied priest, translating for the king.

'That's it,' said Æthelred. 'Pallig should have thought of his family before he broke his oath. Before he put my thegns of Defnascir and the south coast to the sword.'

'There are casualties in war,' the fat-bellied priest said to Beornoth. 'It is not only the warriors who die. Robert de Warenne does God's work. He purges our lands of heathens. Of those squatters who took advantage of our lord king's good nature, took his silver and his generosity and then turned their cloaks. They are believers in false gods and now they writhe and wail in the depths of hell.'

Beornoth stiffened at the lecture in war from a soft-handed priest. 'Is it God's work to kill screaming children as they burn alive?'

'Enough!' Æthelred shouted, putting a hand to his mouth as though he might vomit. 'I am a busy man, Lord Beornoth. There are urgent matters of state to attend to. I did not grant you an audience, nor endow you with the office of king's thegn, to fill my head with such terrible things.'

'We must go to discuss the increase of land to the abbey at Wilmslow, lord king,' said a small priest, leaning and whispering into the king's ear.

'There are more names on the list, Beornoth,' said Æthelred. 'Get back on your horse and punish them. We cannot allow the Danes to taint our nation with their heathen filth.'

'The Normans run amok, lord king. I beg you to...' Beornoth said. Æthelred turned on him and raised a quivering finger to silence Beornoth mid-sentence.

'My wife is a Norman lady. So watch your tongue. Enough of this.'

'Can I be of assistance here, my king?' said a silky voice from beyond Beornoth's sight. A tall, thin man strolled into the room. He wore a tunic of deep red, his golden hair was long and tied at the nape of his neck and his beard combed to a lustrous sheen. He had a long, clever face and rested one hand on the pommel of the sword belted at his waist. Beornoth had surrendered his weapons at the entrance to the royal enclosure, as must all men other than the king's guard.

'Lord Eadric,' said the king with a relieved sigh. 'Explain the nature of war to Lord Beornoth, and the necessity for us to be robust with our Viking enemies. Help him understand the need for us to restore our kingdom to its former glory and purge it of those who would see me cast asunder and our kingdom ruled by Danes. When we finish here, send another hundred warriors to support Lord Robert de Warenne and his noble work on the battlefield.'

'The Danes are a plague,' said Eadric. He sauntered across the room and examined Beornoth up and down as though he were a mare for sale. He frowned at the dirt on Beornoth's boots and the travel stains upon his cloak and byrnie. 'They are cockle in the wheat. Sprung up on this island of ours like rats. They are to be slain with a most just extermination.'

'God wills it!' shouted the fat-bellied priest, and the rest of the clergymen made frantic signs of the cross. Æthelred scowled at Beornoth, turned on his heel and made to walk for the door.

'Pallig's wife, who died protecting her children whilst their backs were ablaze, was the daughter of Harald Bluetooth and the sister of Sweyn Forkbeard,' Beornoth shouted. 'I thought you should know, lord king, for news of how she died is surely winging its way to Norway where King Sweyn is settling the kingdom he so recently conquered from Olaf Tryggvason, who as you know was a fearsome warrior and battle-king to fear. I wonder how the king of the Danes and the Norsemen, the lord of the Vikings, the leader of every warrior in Kattegat, Jutland and the Vik, where the killers lurk, will take the news of his sister's slaying?'

Æthelred stopped, half turned, thought better of it and continued on his way. Eadric came close to Beornoth and seemed surprised to have to look up so far to meet Beornoth's stare.

'You sound like you pity the Danes?'

'You are a young man and are fortunate to have found a

place close to our lord king. Have you ever fought a Viking, Lord Eadric? Ever crossed blades with a man who worships Odin, a war god who promises his faithful an everlasting life of feasts and battle? Have you stood your ground against a Dane who hates you with the utmost intensity and would cut your head off to honour his gods and rip that pretty armour from your soft body to make himself richer? Have you stood in the shield wall, where men die in shit, piss, mud and blood, and traded blows with the champions who braved mountainous waves and treacherous seas to take everything you have?'

'I am trained in the arts of war, and captain of the king's guard. You will show me more respect. Have you seen the list of Danes who must die, Lord Beornoth?'

'No,' Beornoth growled.

Eadric smiled. 'An old friend of yours features prominently. A Viking made into a thegn by the ealdorman of Northumbria. We cannot allow Danes to hold high offices. Brand Thorkilsson, I think, is his name. A survivor of Maldon, I believe, just like you.'

'I have done my duty. Now it's over.' Beornoth slid off his gold ring and pressed it into Eadric's hand. He unbuckled his scabbard and let it fall to the floor. 'I am king's thegn no longer and I wish you luck in the wars to come.'

Beornoth brushed past Eadric, knocking his shoulder hard enough to send the man stumbling. Eadric laughed mockingly but made no effort to stop Beornoth from leaving.

'God help us,' said Wigs as they strode along the corridor away from the library. 'What just happened?'

'I think we just made enemies of the king of England and the captain of his household troops,' said Gis. 'Oh, I almost forgot. And Beornoth gave up his position as a king's thegn.'

'Do we need to run?' asked Ecga, fear making the pitch of his voice rise. 'Will men want to kill us?'

'Nobody wants to kill you,' said Beornoth, striding through corridors fragrant with plants and winter flowers. 'But I must go to help an old friend. I won't force you three to follow where I must go.'

'It's a bit late for that,' said Wigs. 'You could have said before you angered the king and barged over one of his noblemen.'

'We leave today. But first I must speak with a man I trust.'

18

Beornoth led Wigs, Gis and Ecga through the maze of colonnades and dimly lit corridors until they left the royal enclosure. They crossed a courtyard lined with rose bushes into a rectory surrounded by other church buildings close to the lofty tower of Winchester's great minster. Beornoth hurried, concerned that he had gone too far with the king, and with Eadric. The three Saxon warriors sensed his worry and constantly glanced over their shoulders as they marched with quick steps, fearful that the king's guards would burst from a shadowed door and charge across the courtyard to take them prisoner. A man could not be the king's enemy and live, and Beornoth had no desire to become an enemy of the crown he had served bravely for so many years. But the news that Brand Thorkilsson's name was on Robert de Warenne's kill list had hit Beornoth like an arrow to the chest.

Beornoth entered the clutch of cleanly swept stone corridors and brushed past two hooded priests who tutted as Beornoth went by. He found the door he was looking for and knocked three times. It creaked open and Bishop Nothhelm appeared.

'I am honoured to see you again so soon, Lord Beornoth,' he said, and then seemed surprised to see the three warriors flanking him. He waved Beornoth in and served them ale from a wooden pitcher. 'I can only offer a frugal refreshment, I am afraid. Please, sit.'

Wigs, Gis and Ecga sat at Nothhelm's table, thanking him profusely, embarrassed to be in the company of a bishop and unable to meet his eye. He served them dark bread and honey, which the warriors ate hungrily after Nothhelm had blessed both them and the food.

'You saw the king again, Beo?' asked Nothhelm when he had finished fussing around the table.

'Yes, that's why I've come, father... I mean your excellency,' Beornoth said, fumbling over the correct way to address the old bishop.

'In all the time we have known each other, Beornoth Thegn, you have never addressed me as your excellency and I see little point starting now. Nothhelm will suffice quite adequately.'

'Sorry about that father... Nothhelm.' The bishop looked paler than the last time Beornoth had seen him. His skin seemed translucent and thin over his bones. A small fire burned in one corner of his room, but the heat was paltry and not enough to stop Beornoth's breath misting as he spoke. 'The king no longer seeks your advice?'

'Our lord king has not done me the honour of requesting my presence for some time.' He laughed nervously and brushed down his rough-spun brown robe. His bishop's vestments hung on the back of the door, gloriously expensive cloth of green, white and brown sewn with gold. They shone in the dour room as though imbued with the power of God and Nothhelm looked at them with the same fondness a warrior looks upon a notched sword hanging over his hearth. 'I am unfortunate enough to be a bishop with neither church nor flock. I gave them up to serve the king and now find myself... put out to pasture, let's say.'

'Much has changed in Winchester, and not for the better.'

'Who are we to say, Beo? A king's court is a precarious place. Cunning courtiers, rich ealdormen, sons of displaced lords and powerful churchmen will always have the ear of a king. They seek it for their own ends, for the betterment of the kingdom, and for power. The faces and words of such men change over time, like the rolling wheel of a merchant's cart. Different faces, different objectives, but the cart must roll on.'

'I had hoped things would return to proper order when Lady Ælfthryth died.'

'Proper order. What an interesting notion. We live in a world of constantly shifting order, thus it has always been, and thus it will always be.'

'Aye, well, at least in the old days, the kingdom made sense. We had ealdormen, thegns, warriors and the king. Men did what was right for the kingdom. Now there doesn't seem much right in the king's orders. God forgive me for saying it.'

Nothhelm smiled sadly, and a silence passed between them, disturbed only by the sounds of Wigs, Ecga and Gis munching bread from Nothhelm's table and slurping his ale. 'Things often seem like that to old men. Which is what we are, Beo, like it or not. You are lucky to still have much of your old strength and vigour, but we are old and there is no escaping that fact. The world of our youth seems gilded, in some way finer than the place we now find ourselves in. I am not sure that is the truth of the matter. There were king slayings in those days. Ealdormen fought over land. King Edgar's gifts of swathes of land to the church caused a bitterness which lingers even to this day. Æthelred tries to heal those wounds. He takes land from the abbeys and monasteries and grants them to powerful lords.

Including your new Norman friends. My esteemed colleagues in the Church are bitter and resentful of those changes. But the king must keep his powerful lords happy.'

'The Normans are no friends of mine. They slay women and children without honour, and the king's list of Danes who must die includes settlers north of the Danelaw. Men I know. Friends.'

'We must each live according to our own conscience, Beo. War is full of acts of barbarity. Has there ever been a war where the innocents do not suffer most? Warriors take the glory, but it is the women and children who pay the price. Widows, orphans, bastards and slaves are the true face of war.'

'I came to Winchester to tell the king how his Normans make war, but he would not hear me. The kingdom will run red with blood if he allows Robert de Warenne and his godless brother to kill, rape and burn their way north.'

'I dare say I know our good King Æthelred better than most men. I was his confessor for a time. He is a good man, Beo. A man with immense power who strives to do good. The change you feel about Winchester was slow in coming, but now it drowns us like a tide. The Vikings did not trouble our shores during King Edgar's reign, but since Æthelred succeeded to his father's throne, we have known nothing but war. Vikings return each year, and we are beset by the cursed heathens. Many of my colleagues in the Church believe that we suffer because of our sins, that God sends the Vikings to punish us. Æthelred is particularly fearful of such talk because of how he came to the throne. There needs to be no whispers between you and me, Beo, for we both know the hand Lady Ælfthryth played in King Edward's death and Æthelred's accession. Edward was Edgar's named and preferred successor.

'The truth of his power, the actions of his lady mother, the land he took from the Church to enrich the Normans and his nobles weighs heavily upon our king. When my colleagues talk to him of the need to repent, to restore grace in the eyes of God, Æthelred takes it to heart. Those thoughts have festered and become a driving force in royal policy. I spoke against the need for repentance, for the king is God's voice on earth imbued with power by holy decree. That is the nature of kingship. Unfortunately, Æthelred preferred to hear other bishops and their talk of God's punishment. Those men grew in power, their voices kept close to the king, whilst mine fell away. They dripped poison into his ear, of the need to repent and reform. So, he repents for trusting the Danes and bringing them into his service, and reforms his old policy of granting Church land to powerful lords. Unless those lords are new men, men who have Æthelred's favour. Thus we have powerful Normans riding about the kingdom with a mandate to slay our Danish enemies and enriching themselves with the king's favour.'

'There is little I can do to change the king's mind on such matters. I fear I have already gone too far with him. I have resigned my place as king's thegn.'

Nothhelm glanced at Beornoth's hand and at his belt and placed his hand over his mouth in shock. 'Can someone resign from such a high rank? King Æthelred made you one of the most senior warriors in the kingdom, Beornoth. You cannot walk away from such an honour.'

'Yet I have, and I come to you for advice.'

'I wish you had come to me for advice before meeting with the king, Beo.' Nothhelm made the sign of the cross and poured himself a cup of ale. As he drank, his eyes flitted about the room and then came to rest upon Beornoth. 'Please tell me you did not have cross words with King Æthelred?'

'Not as such, no. But I spoke my mind.'

'Then you are lucky to still have your head. There are men

about the king who would encourage him to separate you from your skull and take your title and heriot for their own.'

'Æthelred has a new lord of his king's guard. A man named Eadric?'

'Ah. Eadric. He is a new man, somehow grown close to the king through cunning shadow work. Eadric Streona, men call him. Eadric the Grasper. His rise knows no bounds. Be careful of him, Beornoth, he is both cunning and dangerous. One of Æthelred's new advisors, and one of those responsible for the changes you feel in Winchester.' Nothhelm winced and reached around to rub at the small of his back. Beornoth helped him to sit, and the bishop patted his arm in thanks.

'Eadric told me of a name on Robert de Warenne's kill list. A Dane made into a thegn in Northumbria. How would he know the man on the list is my friend?'

'He knows much and more. Especially of those who wield power in the kingdom. He wants that power, craves it like a starving man hungers for meat. You are, or were, a king's thegn, as powerful as an ealdorman. With that rank, you could ride into any burh, hall or fortress in the kingdom and demand succour and spearmen. You were answerable only to the king himself. What could Eadric Streona do with such power? I imagine he has made his business to know everything about you, who died fighting beside you at Maldon, your friends and your enemies.'

'Is Eadric my enemy?'

'Every man who holds power is his enemy. He has beaten you now. You gave up your ring, which he will now try to take for his own. You were an opportunity, a chance for him to further his ambition. One of dozens of men Eadric has made it his business to know inside out so that when the chances come, when luck shows him with a chink in a powerful man's armour, he can swoop and strike and grasp his way a little further up the greasy ladder to power. That list is mostly Danes who have recently come to power, men who have land and wealth. If a thegn dies in disgrace, what becomes of his land and wealth?'

Beornoth shrugged. 'His ealdorman decides who should take over the heriot, who should now wear the byrnie and helmet. Who should carry the sword and own the land.'

'His ealdorman or his king.'

'So Eadric sees a chance to enrich himself with the lands of men killed by Robert de Warenne?'

Nothhelm opened his arms wide and clapped his hands together. 'Who knows what goes on in the minds of such men? But why else would he know of your friend's presence on the list?'

'The man I speak of saved my life. He dragged me from the blades and blood of Maldon and risked his life to save mine. I can't let Robert and Odo de Warenne kill him.'

'Yet this man's name is on a list of the king's enemies. By helping him, you would raise your sword against the crown?'

'All my life I have fought for my ealdorman, my king and my country. My body is littered with the scars of those battles. But I cannot let my friend die at the hands of men who butcher women and children without fear of God's wrath.'

'You are like Daniel, Beo. Do you remember the tale of Daniel from the good book?'

Beornoth sucked his teeth with shame. 'I do not. I never paid much attention to my Bible lessons as a boy.'

Nothhelm wagged a reproving finger at Beornoth and then beckoned him close, delighted to have the chance of telling a parable to help Beornoth understand the difficulty he faced. Gis, Wigs and Ecga drew their stools towards the old bishop and he smiled, opening his arms to urge them closer.

'Daniel was a trusted advisor in the kingdom of King Darius the Mede,' Nothhelm began, leaning forward with a gleam in his eye. 'Darius was a proud man and believed his achievements matched those of God himself. Darius ordered all men to stop praying to God for thirty days. Anyone caught worshipping any god other than the king was to be thrown into a den of lions. Of course, in such barbarous times, men worshipped all kinds of gods, not only our Lord Almighty.

'Now Daniel, God bless his soul, was a faithful man who prayed daily as all good men should. His relationship and duty to God were central to his life. As I am sure it is with you fine warriors as well.' Nothhelm drank in the guilty looks on their faces, laughed, and continued with his story. 'So Daniel respected King Darius and served him faithfully. But he could not obey the king's decree because it brought him into direct conflict with his deep commitment to God. Daniel knew the consequences and yet continued to pray openly by his window three times a day. Daniel was reported and brought before the king. Darius was distressed because he respected Daniel and valued his loyalty. Darius was, however, bound by his own decree and, with a heavy heart, ordered Daniel thrown into the lions' den.

'God ultimately saved Daniel's life by a miracle. He shut the lions' mouths and Daniel emerged unharmed. Daniel remained faithful to what he believed was right, even at great personal risk. You must follow your conscience, Beornoth.'

'But if I fight against the king's men, if I kill men who ride with the blessing of Church and king, do I commit sin? Will it stop me from entering heaven?' Beornoth feared that above all things. Eawynn waited for him above in the grace of God.

'If you fight against men who kill those who cannot protect themselves, how can that be a sin?'

Beornoth frowned at Gis, Wigs and Ecga, for he would rather they not hear what he was about to say. 'When I look back at my life, I wonder if I have been a cruel man. Am I destined for hell?'

'You are a warrior. You are cruel because you must be. Could I do the things you do? Could I trade blows with the hard champions of Jutland and the Vik? I don't think so. You are God's instrument, Beornoth, and I doubt that protecting your friend and his family is a sin.'

'Eawynn, my wife, passed. She waits for me, Nothhelm. I can't do anything to jeopardise my immortal soul. I fear that I have already done things that make my soul unworthy of heaven.'

'Then let me give you my blessing. Let me do this one thing for you, Beo, just as you have risked your life and fought so hard for us. Let me absolve you and your men here of sin, so that you may ride out in the grace of God.'

Beornoth, Wigs, Ecga and Gis knelt before Nothhelm. The old man donned his vestments. Pallor fled from his skin and he became imbued with light. The cold room seemed to grow warmer and Beornoth closed his eyes and listened to the Latin pour from Nothhelm's tongue like honey. He felt lighter, younger, suddenly clear that he could ride north to Northumbria with a clear conscience. He would not let Robert de Warenne descend on Brand with his bloodthirsty war band and Odo's malice. With the strength left in his aged bones, he would fight for something that mattered beyond the words and whims of an ill-advised king. Brand and his family would not meet the same fate as Pallig and Gunhilde. Not while Beornoth could swing a sword.

19

Beornoth arrived in York eleven days later. Rain laced with stinging sleet lashed his face, numbing his nose and ears. York sat at the confluence of two rivers, the Ouse and Fosse, and had been an important city since before the time of the Romans. Some men believed the Romans had used giants to lift and place the enormous stones that formed the walls and older buildings around the city, and there were certainly no men alive in England who could cut and dress stone as closely as the Romans. In the time of Beornoth's father, the kingdom of York had been a mighty state outside the rule of King Alfred and his descendants. It had ruled at the heart of the Danelaw until the death of Eric Bloodaxe just before Beornoth was born.

The gate guards admitted Beornoth and his three companions through the high walls and they waited beside a brazier inside the gate guard's hut, warming their hands before the crackling flames. One guard went to notify the ealdorman that Beornoth was waiting and the second leant on his spear halfway between the guard hut and the gate, so that he could keep an eye on the four warriors and anyone trying to enter the city.

'I thought my fingers might snap off out there,' said Wigs, hopping from one leg to another as he held his raw meat-coloured hands close to the fire.

'There's a reason men don't fight or ride in the winter,' said Gis.

'Because it is bastard freezing.' They laughed and huddled close about the warmth.

'Have you come far, lord?' asked a guard. He was a short man with a patchy scrap of beard who stared nervously up at Beornoth's great height. His eyes glimpsed the byrnie chain-mail links beneath Beornoth's heavy cloak, and the helmet and sword strapped to the saddle of Virtus, a warhorse worth a king's ransom.

'From Winchester,' Beornoth replied. 'So far enough.'

'Ealdorman Thered is in his hall, lord. With enough timber stacked behind it for a thousand days like this. Have you met the ealdorman before?'

'Once or twice,' Beornoth lied, not wanting to give the man the long history between him and Ealdorman Thered. He stared out at the cobbled streets, where a cold sun broke through the sleet to shine upon the wet stones. Steam rose from wet thatch and a sad-faced dog peered out from beneath a resting handcart. Thered and Beornoth had been enemies, once. Thered's father, the old Ealdorman Oslac, had tried to have Beornoth captured and killed inside York's great hall. Ealdorman Byrhtnoth had saved Beornoth's life that day, along with Leofsunu of Sturmer, Aelfwine of Foxfield and the rest of the ealdorman's old hearth troop. All dead now, slaughtered at the massacre at Maldon. After Thered's father met justice, Thered had joined Ealdorman Byrhtnoth's hearth troop as a hostage. He had fought well and Beornoth and Thered had eventually become brothers of the sword.

'Do you have any ale in this hut, friend?' asked Wigs, searching about the small wooden enclosure which stank of old onions and smoke. 'My throat is dryer than the bottom of a falcon's cage.'

The guard rummaged beneath a pile of cloaks and came up with a flagon of warm mead. He had no cups, so the men drank it straight from the flagon. Droplets ran into Wigs' beard and he belched so loudly that a man approaching the gate with a bundle of sticks tied to his back stopped and stared. The first guard came running across the cobbled street, his spear, helmet and seax clanking as he hurried with one hand held to his slightly too big helmet to stop it falling from his head.

'My Lord Thered will see you right away, Lord Beornoth,' shouted the man, out of breath from running from the ealdorman's hall. Beornoth and his three companions followed the guard through the streets and passed the magnificent walls of the city's great minster. Even in winter, the city bustled with life. Churls, merchants and wealthy ladies in finely woven cloaks wove their way through the bend and warp of tightly packed wattle buildings butted up against larger houses built from looted Roman stone.

The guard led them into the great hall, lit by a roaring fire at its centre which stewards would keep lit day and night until summer returned. Thered waited for them beside his hearth, draped in a heavy bear's-fur cloak, and he laughed for joy when Beornoth walked into the warm hall and raised his hands in greeting.

'Beornoth!' Thered called. He cast his arms wide and ran towards Beornoth.

'Lord Ealdorman,' Beornoth said and bowed his head respectfully.

'Don't give me that, you old wolf.' Thered crashed into

Beornoth and drew the bigger man into a warm embrace. They held each other for a long moment, and it was like Beornoth held the old dead hearth troop close to him. Beornoth wanted to keep him there, to hold on to that warmth a man can only feel for a brother he has fought beside, with whom he has come close to death and come out the other side victorious. They pulled away eventually and regarded each other at arm's length. Thered was as scarred as Beornoth, the marks of Maldon slashed into his face, his missing fingers and the sadness deep within his eyes.

'You look well,' Beornoth said, ignoring the grey showing at the younger man's temples.

'You look old,' Thered replied, and then laughed when Beornoth frowned. 'Still as sour as a crab apple, I see. Ohter?' He called to his steward. 'Take Beornoth's men to the kitchen and find them something hot to eat, and some of that ale we brewed in the summer, and bring food for Lord Beornoth and I.'

'Yes, lord,' said Ohter. He bowed and beckoned that Wigs, Ecga and Gis should follow him through the hall towards the kitchens. Thered waited for them to leave through a side door and then clapped Beornoth on the shoulder.

'So, what brings you to Northumbria?' he asked.

'I bring dark tidings, and wish I came to you in better circumstances.'

'Very well, best get the bad news out of the way first and then we can talk properly as friends.'

'King Æthelred has set a force of Norman warriors to killing a list of Vikings he believes are enemies of the crown. Most are Danes who raided the south coast last summer, and Viking mercenaries sworn to his service who betrayed him to join the raiders. I rode with the Normans for a time, and those Danes are dead now. But there are other names on the list, Vikings who

settled in the kingdom recently and who have become landown-
ers. The crown considers these men enemies, and the war band
is riding to kill them all.'

Thered thought about that for a moment. 'Such men are
south of the Danelaw?'

'Some. Others are north of Watling Street. Some in
Northumbria.'

'I have received no word from the king that men in my shire
are to be killed. But I received a proclamation from the king
earlier this year which said that Danes were to be killed. I
assumed they were all raiders in the south. Northumbria hasn't
been raided in many years.'

'That's because half of your subjects are of Viking descent.
Half the place names in Northumbria are now Norse.'

'True. Did the king send you north with this information?'

'No. I have resigned my position as king's thegn. We
disagreed over the Norman war band's methods.'

'Can you resign from that position? I never had you pegged
as a squeamish man, Beo.'

'They burned and slaughtered women and children. We
who follow the way of warrior cannot fight beside such men. In
the spring they will come to Northumbria, and they come for
Brand.'

'Brand? What has he done to earn the king's enmity?'

'He is a thegn, and he is a Dane. That is enough in the
kingdom we find ourselves in.'

'They would punish him for that?'

'For that and to take his land, your land, and grow rich off
dead men's soil.'

Thered ran a hand through his hair and glanced up at the
hall's high rafters. 'How many will come?'

'Three hundred, perhaps less. Led by Robert de Warenne

and his brother Odo. Normans who came to England from exile at the side of Lady Ælfthryth. Their father was the thegn who killed young King Edward at the lady's request. The Normans come for blood and silver, and they will show no mercy to any who get in their way.'

'Has the king declared you an enemy?'

'No, but we parted on bad terms.'

'Have these Normans attacked you since you left them and went to Æthelred?'

'They sent riders to hunt me down. Those men died on the road deep in Mercia.'

'Have you come to ask me to fight them?' Thered said wistfully, still staring upwards as though his mind were half elsewhere.

'If you fight them, you fight against the king. You are the ealdorman of Northumbria and that cannot be so. The Normans will come to you in the spring with their list and demand succour. They will ask for food and ale and for you to direct them to Brand's home and hall.'

'If they ask it and hold the king's order, I must grant it. Though I wish no harm to Brand and would do anything I can to protect him and his family.'

'I know, and I will not hold it against you. We fought at Maldon, you and I. You came with me when we rode to punish those who betrayed Ealdorman Byrhtnoth. We are brothers, you and I, forever bonded by blood and blade. All I ask is that you let me go to Brand and fight beside him when the Normans come.'

'My love for war died many years ago, Beo. You knew it when we marched against Godric. Maldon stole my warrior's heart. It lies there still on that riverbank, amidst the blood and the souls of our departed brothers.'

Thered itched absent-mindedly at the scar upon his palm, and Beornoth held up his matching scar. 'We swore blood oaths to Ealdorman Byrhtnoth, and we fulfilled those oaths. You fought as bravely as any man I have ever seen that day, and there is no shame in the way you feel. I do not ask you to pick up your sword. Just to turn a blind eye whilst I stand with Brand.'

'Brand owns lands in my shire. Good land. He has his own hearth troop and men in his farms and villages sworn to fight for him when he calls. He has perhaps fifty men. Not enough to stand against three hundred. He could leave. I would give him a fine ship and he could take his silver and his family and sail away to live in peace.'

'He won't sail away.'

'No. He won't.'

'So we'll fight.'

'And you'll die.'

'We have the winter to prepare. They won't ride north until the spring. But they will come for Brand with fire and sword. Not just because he is wealthy, but to hurt me. It is well known Brand fought beside you and I at Maldon.'

'I can't let you die. Or Brand. Not on my land, not whilst there is blood still in my veins.'

'Don't sacrifice your shire for us. I ask nothing of you, Thered. I only came out of respect. To tell you what is coming when the buds return to the trees and the birds sing again. Do you have a family?'

'I do. A wife, two daughters and a son. They are east of here, warm and safe and beautiful.'

'I am pleased for you and wish you nothing but happiness. So when the Normans come, tell them where to find Brand. Do as they ask and live your life in peace.'

Thered smiled sadly and walked towards his fire. He moved

slowly, hands clasped behind his back as though he sought guidance or wisdom in the flames. 'I'll send men with you. My men. Good men.'

'You cannot. The king will punish you if he believes you aided Brand. I can't allow that. You must put your own family first.'

'The men I will send are Viking. They came to me five years ago looking for service. A summer storm wrecked their ship off Lindisfarena, driving them ashore. Their jarl is a man named Bjornulfr One Ear, and he has twenty men. Twenty men from a crew of sixty. They fought for me against a band of masterless men, remnants from a war in the lands of the Scots who came to my lands looking for plunder, food, silver and women. Bjornulfr and his men put those warriors to the sword, and I paid them well in silver. Bjornulfr offered his men a choice: they could stay in my service as warriors of my hearth troop, receiving silver, regular meals and a home in York, or they could seek a new lord and a new ship and return to the Whale Road. Twenty stayed. They have never let me down and they fight like starving bears. I will send them with you, for they speak Norse and do not wear my livery. That is the best I can do for an old friend, though I wish I could do more for you, brother.'

'That is enough, and their axes will be welcome. Are they oathsworn to you?'

'Bjornulfr would only swear to be my man for one season, but he stayed and swears a fresh oath each spring.'

'Then he is an honest man.'

'Honest, brave and fierce, but not gentle. He is a hard man, a raider and a killer. A man of the sea. You can trust him to fight, but he must agree to it first, for I cannot command him and his men to fight for you next spring. His oath expires with the year.'

'Where is he, and I will ask him.'

'Here in York.'

Thered sent a man to find Bjornulfr. Whilst they waited, he and Beornoth shared a meal of freshly smoked fish, bread, roasted onions and ale. Beornoth listened as Thered spoke warmly of his family and it warmed his heart to see his friend, haunted by the demons of war, find joy in the happiness of family. Beornoth himself had experienced that joy, the fulfilment of being a father and husband. They spoke no more of Maldon or of the hunt for Godric. Those ghosts were best left in the past. Beornoth knew of other men like Thered, men with minds broken by the horror of battle. When a man spends too long amongst axe blades, swords and knives and sees men killed and injured, the memories haunt him and damage his mind. The blood, devastated limbs, torn flesh, the screaming and the rank stench of bowels voided in terror, live inside that man's thought cage like a curse. Beornoth understood it, even though he had never been struck by that curse. The men he had killed haunted his dreams, but had never stopped him from fighting. As a man of war and a veteran of countless shield walls, Beornoth would never judge a man who had fought and could fight no more.

Beornoth listened to Thered talk, marvelling at the contrast of his battle scars and the smile when he spoke of his loved ones. Stewards kept the fire blazing with logs and the flames sent shadows dancing on the high stone walls. When the food was gone and the table cleared, the heavy hall doors opened and a man filled the space. He stomped into the hall, boots thumping on the floor, the iron of his war gear clanking about him.

'Lord Thered,' said the man in a thick Norse accent. He came from the shadows into the firelight and stopped ten paces from where Beornoth and Thered waited. Beornoth stood and looked eye to eye with a man his equal in height and breadth of shoulder.

'Bjornulfr, this is Lord Beornoth,' said Thered.

'I have heard of you, Beornoth Reiði,' said Bjornulfr. His voice was like a ship's hull dragged across jagged shale and he ran a tongue across his top teeth. Bjornulfr had thick red hair the colour of Thered's fire, tied back from his scalp in a long braid hung with iron symbols. Beornoth saw a hammer, a fish, a spear, amongst others. Symbols of his gods, harsh gods, gods of war. Odin, Thor, Njorth and Týr. Strands of white streaked his red hair and shot through his beard, which he wore long and combed. His right ear was a nub of skin, lost in some distant battle, and a white scar ran from that missing ear down towards his jaw, cutting into his beard like a line of marble. The beard rested on a gleaming byrnie which reached to his knees above worn leather boots. His thick forearms shone with gold and silver warrior rings and he carried two magnificent axes in loops at his belt. Their bearded blades shone with carved runes and the leather-wrapped hafts were oiled and well cared for. His face was a cliff of flat cheekbones on either side of a broken nose, with small blue eyes unflinching and fierce. His neck was as wide as his skull and his shoulders round above a back made broad by a lifetime at the oar.

'Some men call me that,' Beornoth replied in Norse.

'Men are coming to Northumbria to kill Brand Thorkilsson. Three hundred Normans will arrive in spring and Beornoth needs men to fight beside him and Brand when the riders come.'

'I know Brand,' said Bjornulfr, and rested his cold killer's eyes on Beornoth. 'He does not have three hundred men.'

'They will outnumber us. But we will fight.'

Bjornulfr sniffed and turned his gaze to Thered, waiting for the ealdorman to tell him how much he would pay for the Viking to risk his life.

'You are free of your oath to me in a month's time,' said Thered. 'Free to stay and swear again, or go where you please with my blessing. If you ride now with Beornoth and spend a winter with Thered and fight for him in the spring, I will buy you a new warship. I will pay the shipbuilders at Grimesby to make you a *drakkar* from oak cut from my land, with sails made from Northumbrian fleeces, seal-hide ropes. A ship as fast as an eagle on the wing.'

Bjornulfr's mouth turned at the corners into an upside-down smile. 'A vast prize. One I cannot spend if my corpse rots beneath a Northumbrian field. I lost my ship in a vicious squall, a ship built by my father's father. Its keel cut from a single piece of oak from our island home in the Skagerrak, where the warriors live. If I bring my men to fight for you, Beornoth Reiði, can we win?'

'I can make you no promises, and give you no assurances,' said Beornoth. 'Three hundred men will come north in spring, men in good mail with sharp swords. They come to kill a man I love like a brother, so I will stand and fight for him. If you meet your end, then it will be an end worthy of a song the bards can take to the Skagerrak. They can tell your people how Bjornulfr One Ear stood with few against many and earned his place in Odin's hall.

'If you die fighting, then I will be beside you. Odin will see your courage, and the Valkyrie will surely descend to carry your glorious souls to Valhalla. I will go to my God's heaven, and you will take your place beside your forefathers and the men you have slain in battle. You will sit beneath Odin's ceiling made of cloven shields and drink the god's ale all night and fight against heroes all day. A glorious death is all I can give you. But yes, we can win. We have the winter to prepare and ready ourselves for battle. If you know Brand, then you also know he is not an easy man to kill.'

'No, Brand has fair fame and no man can deny that. For a worshipper of the nailed god, you talk like a Viking.'

'I have been around Norsemen my entire life.'

'You have killed many of them, or so men say.'

'I have. I've killed Vikings, Danes, Norsemen, Svears, Frisians, Normans and Franks. I killed Palnatoki and Skarde Wartooth and crossed blades with Thorkell the Tall on Lundenwic bridge. I am old, but there is strength in me yet.'

'Just so. I'll march with you and fight these Normans, Beornoth Reiði. When it's done and enough men have bled and died, I will come back to York and Ealdorman Thered will have a fast ship waiting for me. Or I will be dead and will laugh about the doom of our meeting with the champions in Valhalla.'

20

'Can they speak our language?' said Gis as they rode north from York through Northumbria's rolling countryside. He glanced over his shoulder at Bjornulfr and his twenty Vikings, who rode ten horse lengths behind the Saxons.

'They understand it well enough,' said Beornoth. 'But they won't speak it.'

'Because they despise us?'

'Because they are proud and arrogant, as warriors should be.'

'One of them carries a dead man's scalp in his belt,' said Ecga.

'Why are they all so big?' asked Wigs. 'Can't some of them be short with little stumpy legs and thin arms like a priest?'

'They aren't so much different to you and I,' said Beornoth. 'A little harder, perhaps, grimmer. But Bjornulfr gave Thered his oath before we left, so he and his men will fight beside us and die if they have to.'

'If they don't cut our throats in the night, take our horses and our weapons and leave us naked in the hills,' said Gis.

'Nobody wants to find you naked in the hills,' quipped Wigs.

'I ride to help my friend,' said Beornoth. 'You three are good men, fine warriors. You've done enough for me and I won't hold it against you if this is the end of our journey together. I give you a chance now to turn around and ride south, back to your homes and live out the rest of your lives in peace.'

'What a thing to say after all we have been through,' said Wigs. 'We left our war band and went with you to Winchester to argue with the king himself. We've fought and killed Normans who came to hunt us on the road and followed you to Northumbria. Slept wet-arsed in the heather for countless nights, riding north in the heart of winter. I could go on.'

'What he means to say,' said Ecga, 'is that there won't be any turning back now, lord. We're with you until the end, if that awaits us.'

'Then you have my thanks,' said Beornoth.

'Do we get a ship each if we kill the de Warennes and their three hundred bastards?' said Wigs with a broad grin.

'You'll get my boot up your arse before we meet any Norman blades if you carry on like that.' Beornoth smiled with them and was glad to have the three Saxons at his side.

The sky above them turned ashen grey and bloated clouds hung low to the hills. The company rode north-west into Northumbria's heartland, following deep valleys and high crags. Beornoth knew the way, for he had been to Brand's home at Stag Hall before. It had once belonged to Brand's father-in-law, a savage Viking warrior named Vigdjarf. Thered had recruited Vigdjarf and his war band, including his daughters, to join the hunt for Godric after the battle of Maldon. Vigdjarf died fighting Godric, Brand married Vigdjarf's daughter, Sefna, and inherited Stag Hall.

Beornoth followed the trail of farms, marked by familiar

rivers, hedgerows, forests, streams and hills. He was born in the harsh northern lands, west across the high Pennine hills. He felt at home here, as if the air was cleaner, more wholesome than the fens and flatlands of the south. Beornoth led Virtus through the shallow ford of a fast-running stream above which a curving hillside swept away into a plateau of sharp, dark rock. These were the lands of the ancient folk, the hollows and springs where wiccan, thurses and eutons dwelled. Those witches, trolls and giants felt close enough to touch, just like in the stories Beornoth's mother had whispered to him on dark, stormy child-hood nights.

They crested the rise and Beornoth's heart felt lighter as he looked down upon a shallow, curving valley where a sliver of gleaming water ran alongside a huddle of buildings topped with thick green turf. Sheep huddled about the farmstead, braying and eating from a bundle of grey grass cut in summer. A dozen horses trotted in a paddock and behind it all rose a hall roofed with damp thatch and a bone-white ox's skull hung upon its gable end.

Ten men came from a low building, men with spears and leather breastplates. One whistled, and they ambled carelessly to a chest-high fence running around the perimeter. Another four men came from behind a long stable and together they formed up at the gate. Beornoth smiled because the men tried to look lazy, like they did not care that twenty-four riders carrying shields, spears, axes and swords approached the hall they were oathbound to protect. They formed up in two ragged ranks, so that none but an experienced warrior would notice that they were ready to form a formidable wall at a moment's notice.

'Wait here,' said Beornoth.

'Is this the place?' said Bjornulfr, bringing his horse along-side Virtus.

'This is the place. Stag Hall. I'll go down alone, so we don't get their backs up.' Beornoth rode halfway towards the men and then dismounted. He grunted as his boots hit the cold ground, old bones and old wounds complaining after a day in the saddle. Beornoth left Virtus to crop at what remained of the wild grass in the depth of winter and ambled towards the huddle of warriors. He carried his shield across his back, over his heavy russet cloak, sword strapped to his waist, and his seax at the small of his back. He left his helmet strapped to Virtus' saddle, along with his spear. Beornoth opened his arms and held them wide to show he came in peace.

'Are you lost, grandfather?' called one man in Norse. He was slim with long dark hair worn in two tails hanging on either side of a sharp face.

'I seek Brand Thorkilsson, thegn and lord of these lands,' Beornoth replied.

'You come with twenty spears, grey beard. Are you here for trouble, or shall we show the way to the nearest town where you can find a soft bed and stabling for your horses?'

'Is Brand here?'

'Maybe, grandfather. What is your business?'

'Call me that again and it will be the last thing you ever say.' Beornoth had not intended to lose his temper before meeting his old friend, but an insult is an insult.

'Apologies. I did not mean to offend you. Greybeard.'

Beornoth's hand fell to the hilt of his sword and the men at the gate bristled with blades.

'That's enough, Orm,' called a voice from behind the men. A familiar voice. Brand Thorkilsson eased his way between the warriors and clapped Orm on the back. 'This man will kill you and six of our friends here before we could lay a blade upon him.'

'You got fat,' Beornoth said, pointing at the paunch stretching Brand's green jerkin.

Brand threw his head back and guffawed, his golden braid swinging behind his head. 'You are too old to be riding in winter. Have you got any teeth left in that grizzled head of yours?'

'I've still got teeth. Have your hands grown soft with all this wealth, or can you still hold an axe?'

'Come here, you old boar.' Brand strode forward and wrapped his muscled arms around Beornoth. It was a warm greeting for five heartbeats until Brand shifted his feet and his arms hooked in tighter. Beornoth moved his hips and stepped in to the Viking just as Brand tried to wrestle him to the ground. Stumbling and heaving at each other, the two men grunted and snarled, searching for holds, each trying to shift their feet and get enough leverage to throw the other to the cold earth.

Beornoth lifted Brand from the ground and the Viking laughed, wriggled like a landed fish. Brand came down and hooked his foot around Beornoth's ankle and Beornoth had to lean in to stay on his feet. Something struck Beornoth's leg, and then again. A small foot kicking at him, then a tiny fist thumped into his ribs and Beornoth looked down to see a pugnacious little face scowling up at him.

'Let go of my father or you'll have to face me,' said a little boy with a tangle of blond hair around a round face with a turned-up nose. His cheeks were ruddy with dirt, and he raised a fist to Beornoth as a warning.

Beornoth let go of Brand and backed away with his hands held up in surrender. 'Forgive me, little warrior,' he said, and turned to Brand. 'Who is this fearsome champion who saved you just in time?'

'This is my son, Vigdjarf,' said Brand. 'Named after his grandfather. Watch him, Beornoth, or he'll have your head.'

'I can see that. Do you have any brothers or sisters, little warrior?'

'Three brothers, but I'm the strongest.'

'I do not doubt it.'

'Lord Beornoth,' called a woman's voice. Beornoth smiled as Sefna strolled through the men at the gate with a baby on her hip and a glow about her that warmed Beornoth's heart. 'Welcome.'

'Thank God you came, lady. This little warrior was about to put me on my behind.'

'Vigdjarf, leave Lord Beornoth alone.' She beckoned to Vigdjarf with a hooked finger and he scowled, folded his arms and went to hide behind her skirts. 'What brings you to Northumbria, Lord Beornoth?' She was a tall woman with a round face and bright blue eyes. In her billowing dress, Sefna looked the picture of motherhood. A stiff wind blew down from the hills to whip her long hair away from her face. She was, however, a fearsome warrior who had fought like a demon in the battle against Godric.

'I wish I came to you with better tidings,' said Beornoth, the happiness falling away from him like leaves from an autumn branch.

'You bring twenty-three growlers to my home in the depths of winter, Beo,' said Brand. 'So I assume you haven't come to celebrate Yule.' He was a tall man, not much shorter than Beornoth, with straw-gold hair and a faded tattoo of a raven etched onto his face. 'Orm, see to Lord Beornoth's men. Have the churls take care of their horses and make sure they are fed and given ale.'

'Come on, lads,' said Orm, bowing his head respectfully to Beornoth despite his earlier tone. He waved at the three Saxons and Bjornulfr's warriors to follow him.

'Come inside, Beo,' said Brand, 'let's talk in peace.'

Beornoth sat with Brand on two great chairs swathed in furs. A churl woman brought them each a wooden plate of strong-smelling cheese and pork and a flagon of ale to share. A fire roared at the centre of Brand's longhouse, its smoke disappearing through a hole cut into the thatch. Skulls of wolves, bulls and more than a few men hung upon the walls, along with shields, spears and crossed axes. Feasting benches filled the hall's length, and a platform ran around the upper level where Brand and his family slept. His hearth troop and their families lived around the hall's lower edges, and they had carefully folded furs, bowls, cradles and cloaks in shadowed corners.

'You have a beautiful family,' said Beornoth, and raised his cup to toast his friend's happiness.

'I have been lucky,' Brand replied. 'I am glad you are still alive.'

'Eawynn died.'

Brand set his cup down, placed a hand over his heart, and bowed his head. 'I am truly sorry. She was a fine woman, and surely lives on in your Christ God's heaven.'

'Yet I linger on without her.'

Brand kept his head bowed for a long, respectful moment. 'We shall drink to Eawynn tonight, remember her, talk of her grace and kindness. As long as she lives on in our hearts, something of her soul remains with us in Midgard.'

'Thank you, Brand.'

'Do you still fight for the king?'

'I did until recently. That service led me here with bad news. I am sorry to bring such tidings to your hearth.'

'Well,' said Brand, leaning back into his chair. 'Better give it to me straight.'

Beornoth told him of the changes at King Æthelred's court. Of Kvitsr and Pallig, of the Normans, and the persecution of the Danes. He gave Brand the story of the St Brice's Day Massacre and King Æthelred's kill list. 'All Danes risen to power, men who hold land and wealth, have become targets of the crown. Robert de Warenne and his war dogs ride to slay every man on that list. A list scrawled on parchment by priests and greedy lords in Winchester.'

'My name is on the list?'

'Yes.'

'What have I done to earn the enmity of a king?'

'You are a thegn, and you are a Norseman. That is enough in these dark days.'

'Will they really ride north of the Danelaw?'

'They are coming, Brand. With fire and sword and black hearts.'

'Do the men in Æthelred's court want my land so badly?'

'Men want power and wealth. They look upon those who have it with avarice, and it does not matter where it lies. They will take it and cast down those who get in their way.'

'How many will come?'

'Three hundred.'

Brand blew out his cheeks. 'Three hundred. A lot of spears.'

'I went to Thered before I came here. He says you can raise fifty men?'

'Will Thered fight?'

'He can't fight against the king. But he sent Bjornulfr and his twenty.'

'Bjornulfr is a hard man, and his men won't flinch when the blades are flying. I fought with him before, against the Scots. The Scots are wild, fierce bastards and so any man who has crossed axes with them is worth his sand. I can raise perhaps fifty warriors, and then another twenty farmers.'

'It will have to be enough.'

'When will they come?'

'Spring.'

'I sense from the way you gave the tale of Robert de whatever his poxed name is, that you are none too fond of the man?'

'Robert de Warenne is a warrior, but his brother Odo is a piece of goat shit.'

'If there is a list, how can you be sure they come for me in spring?'

'Because they know you are a friend of mine.'

Brand took a long pull at his ale. 'So three hundred Normans will come to kill us.'

'They'll come. Not just for the fight, either. They'll come with fire, Brand. To hurt Sefna and kill your children, and the families of your men. They come for slaughter, and when it's over, they'll have your land and your silver and would trample over the corpses of everything you love to take it.'

'Any man who comes here to kill my children will find me waiting.'

'And me with you. We've winter to prepare ourselves. We'll be ready.'

'Thank you for coming, old friend.'

'You saved my life after Maldon. I won't let them hurt your family.'

'Seventy men against three hundred. I like those odds. I'm more worried about how I'm going to feed twenty-three hungry warriors through the winter. Sefna will have kittens at the thought of it.'

'You look like you've eaten your winter stores already?'

'This is all muscle.' Brand patted his paunch and smiled. 'We can't just wait here for them to come. A shield wall with three hundred spears would just wrap around our line and cut us to pieces.'

'We won't wait for them. We'll ride out and meet them. Pallig did it to us down in Defnascir. He dogged us at every turn, small ambushes, hit, run and hide. We'll whittle them like a stick.'

'There is no *drengskapr* in running and hiding.'

'I follow the way of the warrior, same as you. We can either stand with honour and fight whilst your children burn, or we can put *drengskapr* to one side and kill the murderous bastards whilst they sleep. Cut their throats whilst they shit. By the time they reach your home, they'll be angry, bloody and desperate.'

'It will be a busy winter.'

For four weeks leading up to Yule, the men prepared for spring. Brand gave Orm and his household troops to Bjornulfr, and the grizzled Viking drilled them daily in shield-wall work and battle formations. They wrapped their axes and spear points in old cloths and spent the wintry days shifting forward in perfect time, retreating five paces to create a gap, and a dozen other cunning shield-wall tricks Bjornulfr knew like the back of his axe. Beornoth, Brand, Wigs, Ecga and Gis spent their days riding the hills and dales trying to predict the route Robert de Warenne's war band would take north. Robert would go to Thered first. He must. Even riding beneath the king's banner, Robert could not fight in the ealdorman of Northumbria's shire without doing him the honour of asking his permission. Thered could not refuse, of course, but there must be some semblance of respect for the ealdorman's position. Beornoth and his Saxons explored every valley, wood, stream, copse and gulley in search of places to hurt the Normans before they reached Stag Hall.

Sefna had the churls and stewards strengthen the wall around the settlement. They turned the fence into a palisade ringed by spiked posts with a ditch dug in front of the wall, and a bank behind it which the defenders could use as a fighting platform. She also called in supplies from the estate, and churls came by each day for a fortnight carrying eggs, wheat, grain, smoked meat and cheese. Sefna paid them in hacksilver, but they still went away sad-faced at giving up their winter surplus to feed Beornoth and Bjornulfr's men.

Yule itself was a grand affair, as good as any Viking new year celebration Beornoth could remember. The family gathered in the long hall as the fire roared and crackled to cast dancing shadows across the smoke-darkened roof beams. Outside, winter held the valley in a still, icy grip, but inside Brand's hall warmth and good spirit abounded. The children laughed and ran between the feasting benches. Little Vigdjarf, who, since their first meeting, had taken a shine to Beornoth, bounced on Beornoth's knee and laughed as Beornoth threw up scraps of beef and caught them in his mouth. Beornoth had grown close to the lad, warming to his wildness and boisterous nature. Vigdjarf would come to Beornoth every evening and ask for war stories, and Beornoth would give him tales of old battles and fearsome enemies.

Sefna had decorated the hall with pine branches, holly and ivy to celebrate everlasting life, to remind them all that life would grow anew in the fields come spring, which seemed so far away in the depths of winter. The stewards lit rushlights which bathed the hall in a soft, flickering light and Beornoth played with Ulf, Brand's oldest son, and Vigdjarf as they ran around the tables and poked fun at Beornoth's grim demeanour. The family shared a small meal. Sefna and Brand said prayers to Odin and Frey and thanked the gods for their land and children's health. Once that part of the celebration was over, Sefna and Brand welcomed Orm and the hearth troop into the hall, along with Bjornulfr and his crew. Sefna and Brand also welcomed Wigs, Ecga and Gis, and they sat with Beornoth at a feasting bench close to the fire where a pig roasted over the flames.

The warriors came in with bowed heads, respectful and thankful for their hosts. Every man came in with clean boots, polished mail, combed hair and beards. Bjornulfr brought gifts for the children, a carved horse and a wooden sword, and the men enjoyed a hearty meal of salted pork, lamb, pheasant and goose. Platters came out laden with onions and leeks, preserved apples and honeyed breads. Ale and mead flowed like a river and, before long, the warriors' respectful manners gave way to table thumping, raucous cheers and bawdy rowing shanties.

Brand brought in a small wooden Yule log which he reverently placed to burn in the hearth as a symbol of light returning after the winter's short, dark days. Night drew in and the celebrations moved outside. They gathered around sputtering torches and Brand emerged, stripped to the waist, carrying his war axe in one hand. The crowd fell silent, and little Vigdjarf bullied his way to the front to stand between Beornoth's legs. Beornoth ruffled his hair and Vigdjarf stamped on his foot to return the gesture. Brand began a chant to Odin in a deep voice and the warriors banged closed fists to their chests to keep time. Orm came from the stable, dragging a reluctant goat as it brayed and pulled at the rope around its neck.

Brand took the goat and cut its throat in the blót, a sacrifice to Frey for fertile fields, lambs, calves, and for peace. Brand lifted his bloody axe to the deep black sky and asked Odin for battle-luck when his enemies came in spring. Sefna collected the goat's blood in a bowl and took it to each man. She pressed her finger into the warm blood and smeared it on each warrior's forehead to bless him with luck for the year ahead. Beornoth,

Wigs, Gis and Ecga were Christians, but they let Sefna bless them in the Viking fashion.

'We'll take all the bloody luck we can get,' Wigs said, though each man made the sign of the cross as soon as Sefna moved along the line.

The warriors returned to the hall and drank until their words slurred and fell asleep with their heads resting on benches in puddles of ale and breadcrumbs. They sang songs and told stories of their ancestors and the sagas of the gods. Vigdjarf and the other children listened with wide-eyed fascination as they heard of Thor's battles with frost giants, and Odin's wisdom. Bjornulfr gave a tale of a battle he and his men had fought in the lands of the Rus. Of Druzhina warriors in fish-scale armour and drooping moustaches. He told of sailing down impossibly wide rivers and through crashing rapids in search of treasure and glory.

'My throat's dry after so much boasting,' said Bjornulfr, taking a seat next to Beornoth when his stories were over.

'Do you miss the Whale Road?' Beornoth asked.

'Every day. But my destiny brought me here. Njorth took my ship, my beautiful Wave Falcon, and left me ashore with my men. I thought my luck was gone, left in those battles we fought on the banks of the river Volkhov. If we fight for you and kill the Normans, I shall have a ship again.'

'Where will you go?'

'North. South. East. Anywhere.'

'Can I see your knife?' Vigdjarf said, his rosy-red cheeks appearing between Beornoth and Bjornulfr, wide eyes staring at the knife tucked into Bjornulfr's belt.

'Here, lad.' Bjornulfr pulled the knife from its sheath and handed it to the boy. It was a beautiful weapon. Its thick blade curved into a wicked point, and its hilt was set with a glowing ruby and a blue stone Beornoth had never seen before. 'Careful, though. I took this from a prince. It comes from far in the east, so far away that we almost fell off the edge of Midgard.'

Vigdjarf turned the knife over in his little hands, marvelling at the jewels and the craftsmanship of the exotic weapon.

'If I die in the spring,' Bjornulfr said to Beornoth, his hard blue eyes boring into Beornoth's like those of a wolf. 'Make sure my men find a new lord. Do not leave them alone in this place.'

'If you die,' Beornoth replied, 'and I live, then I will do my best for them.'

'Thank you, lord.' Bjornulfr winked at Vigdjarf and took his knife back. He went to join his men, who were in the middle of a raucous war song. Some of those dangerous men wore baggy, striped trousers tucked into supple leather boots. Others wore leather trews and baggy woollen tunics, some even possessed heavy chain-mail byrnies. Talismans from their distant journeys hung in their hair and beards and one warrior gave each of Brand's children a coin inscribed with the strange writing of the Mussulmen.

The night wore on, and as more of Bjornulfr's men fell to snoring on the feasting benches and Orm's men took their places around the hall's edge, huddled beneath warm furs with their wives, Sefna put her children to bed on the high plat-form. She returned down the timber stairs and laughed as two of the household troops wrestled before the dwindling hearth fire.

'Thank you, lady, for your hospitality,' said Beornoth, crossing the room to stand beside her.

'You don't have to call me lady,' she said, and dug an elbow into his ribs. 'Lord Beornoth,' she quipped with her nose in the air. 'We've bled together and killed enemies together. You were there when my sister died, when my father died.'

'I was. They would be proud to see your family. They were both fine warriors. It was my honour to fight beside them.'

'Thank you.' She placed a hand on his arm. 'I am sorry about Eawynn.'

'She was my life. My queen.'

Sefna stood on her tiptoes and kissed his scarred cheek. 'We should leave. Me and the children, at least. We should go before the Normans come.'

'You should.'

'But where would we go? Thered cannot offer us protection, not if the king has declared Brand his enemy. Nobody could let us into their hall, for they risk becoming enemies of the crown themselves.'

'So you'll stay.'

'I'll stay and fight to protect my family. I still have my axe and my bow.'

'Then we shall be stronger to have you fight at our side.'

'When it's over, if we kill these men, will the king send more to hunt us?'

'Times are changing. I left the Normans because they burned a Dane, Pallig, in his hall along with his family. Pallig's wife was Gunhilde Haraldsdottir. Daughter of Harald Bluetooth and sister to Sweyn Forkbeard.'

'Forkbeard won't like that.'

'No. Not so long ago Forkbeard fought a great battle against his old ally Olaf Tryggvason and won the kingdom of Norway, so he is king now of both the Norse and the Danes. Brand came to England with Olaf's fleet.'

'So Forkbeard will come back to England?'

'If he does, it would be no bad thing for you and the rest of the Vikings in the Danelaw.'

'Then I shall ask Odin to whisper of it to Forkbeard and lure his army here so that my children can be safe.'

Beornoth smiled and went to find a warm fur to sleep beneath. In the short time he had spent at Brand and Sefna's home, he had grown fond of their family. It was a good place, a happy place, and soon Robert and Odo de Warenne would come north with sharp blades and dark malice to slash and burn it all to ruin.

21

The Normans came ten weeks after Yule, just as the first green leaves sprouted in the woods above Stag Hall. A rider came from York, a young messenger on a quick pony with news of a war band pounding north along Ermine Street, the Roman road to York. Word of the messenger's arrival spread through the warriors like wildfire, and within an hour every man at the farmstead gathered in the field before Stag Hall.

'We are ready for the bastards,' Brand said. He stood on a cut tree trunk and raised his hands for calm. 'We'll dog their path like starving wolves stalking prey and make them pay for every mile. By the time they get here, they'll be ragged and furious. Orm, take five warriors and ride to every corner of my estate. Send for the men who owe me their oaths, and call in the men of the fyrd. We must be ready within the week.'

'How many men will you leave here to protect us?' called a warrior's wife, a wide-hipped woman with a bonny baby on her hip.

'We will protect you, Gytha. We won't leave our families here alone.'

'Should we not take to the hills?'

'We could. But it's harder to protect you in the wild. Here we have a ditch, bank and palisade to fight behind. We have prepared the countryside leading to our home with surprises for our enemies. Our best chance of beating these men is here. Protecting our home together.'

A rumble passed across the crowd as Brand's people whispered both support and questions about his plan. Brand was their lord, and he had been patient in his explanation to Gytha. Beornoth doubted he could be so gentle with those who were bound to follow his orders, whether or not they agreed with them. Orm set about his orders. He and five men rode away from the hall in different directions to round up those who owed Brand their service.

Beornoth spent that day sharpening his sword and preparing his armour and weapons for battle. He stretched his arms and legs, old wounds groaning and bones creaking. He had practised with spear, sword and shield every day over the cold weeks, trading blows with Brand's and Bjornulfr's men. Some days he tired quickly, and others he felt he could fight all day. That he was the oldest man in the war band was not lost on him, but he would need all of his old strength to help Brand defeat the de Warennes. He scraped a whetstone down the length of his sword: the sword gifted to him by the king, along with the horse and weapons he still carried. Beornoth sharpened his seax and used its broken-backed blade to cut the leather cover from his shield, the cover which bore the dragon banner of King Æthelred. Was it right to still wield the heriot granted to him by the king? Beornoth recalled his conversation with Bishop Nothhelm. It was not right for a king's thegn to raise his sword against the king's men, but it was right in the eyes of God to protect the weak and innocent against the wicked.

Beornoth wondered if he would meet his end in this battle deep in the Northumbrian hills. If this was to be the fight where he perished, and hopefully ascend to Eawynn's side. It seemed strange, after all the pitched battles he had fought, that his death might come defending a thegn's farm. But Brand was no ordinary thegn, and Beornoth's heart was full and ready to fight until the end. Whilst it was no great battle to defend a city or throw back Viking raiders, this was the most important fight of Beornoth's life. A battle to protect a family he loved like his own. He would not let Brand's children suffer the same fate as his own long-dead daughters.

It was a long, quiet day of preparation. Men checked the straps and boards of their shields. They put fresh edges on their blades and walked the palisade's perimeter to check the sturdiness of its posts. Men found a silent corner to prepare their weapons and prepare their minds for what must come. Each man left the others alone, for it takes great courage to face enemy warriors. It takes bravery and belief to stand fast when the blades come, when sharp edges hack at a man's head and body, when friends die and scream and the horror of battle descends. The warriors spent a last night with their families, there was no feast, no drunken singing. Bjornulfr's men kept apart, talking together, exchanging gifts, talking of brave deeds and old battles. Beornoth slept little, restlessly thinking of their preparations, mind turning with thoughts of what the Normans would do and how the battle would unfold. Six of Brand's men ran that night, taking their wives and children in the depth of a half-moon's darkness to flee eastwards.

'I thought they were loyal,' Brand said in the morning. 'They swore oaths.'

'Better they run now than when battle starts,' Beornoth replied. 'When men break from the shield wall, it breaks courage across the entire line like a rotten branch snapping in a storm.'

'We should follow the runners and kill the bastards. It is my right as their lord. I fed them, their wives and their whelps all winter. At first word of the enemy, they tuck tail and run like whipped dogs. They took food last night. Ungrateful bastards.' Brand sighed, head low and shoulders slumped.

'We can ride them down before sundown. Kill the faint-hearted bastards for their betrayal. Bring their families back, but leave the warriors to rot in the field like carrion. I'll do them all, if it is what you desire.' It was a punch to the gut after all their winter preparations. It wasn't just the men they would miss, but the malignant feeling their flight spread amongst the men and their families. Wives had lost friends, children their playmates, and warriors men they had prepared to stand and fight beside.

'Leave them. Let them go. We are better off without them.'

That afternoon Beornoth rode out with Wigs, Ecga, Gis, Brand, Bjornulfr and ten of his men. They carried their weapons, and each took a hunting bow and quiver of arrows. They brought enough food for three days in the saddle, though it was only a day's ride to York. The riders followed the path they knew Robert de Warenne would take, the only road he could take, a path they had ridden many times across the winter months.

They reined their horses in on the edge of a thick wood where the road ran into a gulley between two slopes. It was the first choke point the Norman war band must pass through on their journey to Stag Hall. The road, little more than a track worn muddy by boots, hooves and wagon wheels, wound along a shallow basin edged on one side by a woodland of birch, elm and willow trees. On the opposite side of the track, the slope was steeper, covered in grass and clutches of marble-white rocks, too steep for a horse to climb.

Gis and Ecga tied the horses on the woodland's edge and Beornoth left the men to rest whilst he took Virtus further south, skirting the high ground in search of the enemy. He found the Norman column winding north in pairs across a mud-brown scrape of heather. Three hundred riders in cloaks, carrying spears in their hands and shields resting upon their backs. Beornoth kept low, for he did not want the de Warennes to see him. Yet, their horses came slowly, trotting, picking their way through coarse, wild grasses. His enemies came towards him, riding towards his sword, and Beornoth was ready. Ready to fight. Ready to die. He wheeled Virtus around and led her away from the advancing column, riding tall in the saddle, body imbued with power at the prospect of fighting his enemies.

'Are they here?' Wigs asked when he saw Beornoth approaching.

'They're here. Two scouts ride ahead of their column. They die first,' Beornoth replied. 'Ready yourselves. Do it like we planned and none of us need to die this day.'

Brand came to Beornoth and stroked Virtus' long nose. 'Are you sure you want to do it like this?'

'I'm sure.'

'You are old. You might fall asleep before the scouts reach this part of the road. I should do it. You stay here with the men.'

'Lack-witted bastard.' Beornoth kicked Brand in the shoulder and he hopped away, laughing. No fear showed on the Viking's face, and Beornoth knew his friend would be ready.

Beornoth led Virtus into the trees, letting her find her own way around the trunks and through the brambles. She dragged her hooves through fallen leaves and chewed at a patch of grass. Beornoth rested in the saddle and waited. He held his spear, and his shield rested across his back. He took his helmet from the leather strap on Virtus' saddle and pressed it over his head. The helmet liner fit snug over his hair, and the leather smelled of old sweat. The iron came down over his face; boar-shaped nasal cold against his nose. He pressed the cheekpieces closed, and his breath sounded metallic. He had polished the metal rings of his byrnie to a bright sheen and waited to fight garbed like a lord of war. The woodland about him creaked and an unseen animal scrabbled in the undergrowth. Beornoth checked the edge of his leaf-shaped *aesc* spear with his thumb and was happy with the sharpness.

Men's voices cut through the quiet accompanied by the sound of hooves clopping and slopping upon the muddy road. It was time. Beornoth stiffened, taking deep breaths, turning himself from a resting old man into a beast. A merciless killer. A warrior. Beornoth leaned forward, leather saddle creaking, and scratched behind Virtus' ear.

'Be brave, girl,' Beornoth whispered. Virtus whickered, and Beornoth urged her forward. He stared through the trunks and branches and spotted two riders coming along the path at a quick trot.

'We'll have to go up there,' said one of the Normans, speaking Norse. They glanced into the trees and up the slope as they came. 'I'll go. You skirt around the trees and we'll meet at the other end of the hills.'

They knew their business, sent out by Robert de Warenne to scout places just like this. Points of ambush and choke points where any enemy might lie in wait. But it was too late for them, because Beornoth was moving. He timed it, digging his heels into Virtus' flanks as the riders drew close. She snorted and Beornoth clicked his tongue. Her strength surged beneath him, the bunched muscle of a mighty horse trained for war. She could sense Beornoth's excitement, and her ears twitched as she surged ahead. The two Norman scouts appeared in front of Beornoth just as he came crashing through the trees, teeth bared in a snarl, warhorse crushing fallen twigs and charging at the enemy.

'Shit!' gasped the closest man, turning to see a monster of a man wrapped in a full-faced helmet, snarling, spear poised, astride a warhorse charging like a storm wave. The Norman's mouth gaped within a close-cropped beard and his dark eyes flashed with fear.

Beornoth dug his heels in again and rose in the saddle, bracing himself for impact. Virtus crashed into the closest horse, her thick chest driving into the chestnut gelding, causing the beast to stumble and panic. Virtus' teeth snapped at the gelding's face and tore at its ear. Beornoth stabbed with his spear and the blade punched into the Norman's side. Beornoth felt the resistance of ribs, and put his strength behind the weapon, breaking bone and rending flesh. Anger flooded him, familiar and welcome. Blood rushed in his ears and he yanked the spear towards him. The gelding reeled away from Virtus and the warhorse reared, clattering the enemy mount with her forelegs. The first Norman cried out in pain and toppled from the saddle in a pile of cloak and tangled shield and blood showed dark red on Beornoth's spear point.

The second Norman didn't wait for Beornoth to attack. He kicked his horse and left his comrade to his fate.

'Go, girl!' Beornoth growled, and Virtus set off after the fleeing Norman. The two horses powered into a gallop, throwing up clods of muddy earth. The Norman glanced over his shoulder at Beornoth, his shaven scalp twisting, fear in his dark eyes. Beornoth raced after him, low in the saddle, spear at the ready. He could not risk the man getting away. If the rider outpaced him, he would return to Robert de Warenne and the Normans would know that Beornoth waited for them. Beornoth had another surprise waiting for them, and he didn't want to spoil it. So he cracked the reins and drove his heels into Virtus' muscled flanks. They galloped along the mud path, Virtus opening up her stride, but the gelding was lighter and faster. If the pursuit went beyond the wooded valley the Norman would escape.

Beornoth gave Virtus another five heartbeats, and she gained on the gelding. The Norman risked a terrified look over his shoulder and he shifted slightly in the saddle and his horse swerved, slowing slightly, enough for Beornoth to strike. Beornoth switched his grip on the spear and hefted it overhand, the shaft close enough to his face so he could smell the pine oil in the wood. He rose in the saddle and threw the spear, leaning forward as he released the long ash shaft. The spear flew across the gap between the horses and struck the rider between his shoulder blades. He groaned, slewed, but clung to his horse's back. The Norman leaned against his gelding's neck and the spear waggled, still stuck in the man's back, shaft bouncing against the horse's rump.

The gelding slowed, and the rider fought for his life, clinging on to reins and saddle in his desperate bid to escape. Beornoth came alongside the Norman and he turned to look into Beornoth's implacable face, and Beornoth snarled at him. He reached over, grabbed the spear and pulled it free. He swung the weapon around his head, allowing the heavy iron point to give it momentum. It came around and cracked across the Norman's skull. He swayed and pitched from his mount to fall, rolling in the mud. Beornoth slowed Virtus and brought her around.

The two Normans crawled with desperate looks on strained

faces. They were fifty paces apart, each man leaving a smear of their blood in the mud.

'William!' cried the second Norman. He tried to rise, howled in pain and flopped back into the mud. 'William, help me!'

Beornoth climbed out of the saddle and patted Virtus on the rump. He turned and strode towards the second Norman. He heard the sounds of Beornoth's boots and turned.

'Help me, William!' he shouted again. He got on all fours and crawled towards William, the first Norman who was crawling on his side, one hand clutched to the wound in his ribs. William ignored his shouting comrade and carried on crawling away.

Beornoth grabbed the hilt of his sword and drew the blade from its new scabbard, crafted by Brand's churls over the winter. The anger was gone. All that remained was the desire to punish men who came to hurt his friend. He reached the second Norman and tapped the edge of his sword against the man's throat. The Norman whimpered and rolled onto his back. He shook his head, clenched his eyes closed and wept.

'Do you know who I am?' Beornoth asked.

'B... B... Beornoth, lord,' he replied.

'You came north to kill Brand Thorkilsson?'

'Yes, lord. Please don't hurt me, lord.'

'I remember you. You rode with Robert de Warenne when we fought Kvitsr?'

'I did! We fought together. We are brothers in arms. Don't hurt me, lord.'

'You were there when we killed Pallig?'

'Yes, I was, I was there.'

'Did you laugh when his children burned?'

'What? Me, lord? No, lord. Please, my back. It hurts. Why did you attack us? We are on the same side, lord.'

'No. We are not.' Beornoth kicked the Norman hard in the stomach. He doubled over and Beornoth rammed his sword down into the Norman's gullet. Blood welled around the blade and the Norman coughed up a gout of crimson. Beornoth left him there to die and walked towards William the Norman.

A slick trail of blood led from where he had fallen from his horse and crawled ten paces along the track. Beornoth needed no information from the wounded Norman. He knew how many men were coming and he knew why. He knew Robert and Odo de Warenne were his enemies and he knew what he had to do. Beornoth reached William the Norman and killed him with a swing of his freshly honed sword.

An hour later, Beornoth waited on his horse, hidden from view further along the path. Brand sat upon his mount chewing on an oatcake.

'You're sure they won't all come?' said Brand between bites.

'They won't all come,' Beornoth replied, scowling at Brand for asking the same question over and again. 'For the third time.'

'How many? Ten?'

'When the scouts don't report back to the column, Robert will send riders looking for them. He won't commit his entire force in case there is something bad, something like us, waiting for him ahead. Robert doesn't expect to be attacked on the road. He thinks I left the king's service and returned home. He tied me up after the St Brice's Day Massacre, so he knows we are enemies, but he won't expect to find me in Northumbria. Thered won't have given the game away. So Robert rides to your home believing he will catch you by surprise, and instead he will find us waiting for him.'

'If it's going to be so easy. Perhaps we should have brought all the men and attacked the enemy force in the forest here. Kill them in one swoop.'

'We could. If we had another three hundred men. I wouldn't attack a similar sized force, even in an ambush. So we must outnumber them. They are all mounted and could ride away from our first attack. With the men we have, they might lose thirty, maybe forty warriors in the first fight. Robert is cunning. He'd simply order his men to ride away, regroup, then use their larger force to slaughter us.'

'Fair enough. So we'll pick them off. Make them suffer.'

Beornoth looked up towards the hillside above the steep, rocky side of the passage. Wigs waved down at him. The rest of their party waited up above the hill with their bows, and Beornoth returned the wave to show he was ready.

'Here they come,' said Brand, cocking his head to listen.

'I can't hear anything.'

'Neither would I if my ears were as old as yours.'

Moments later, a band of horsemen cantered into the path between the trees and the slope and reined in sharply when they spotted the two heads waiting for them in the middle of the muddy road. Beornoth had cut the heads himself and placed them facing the way the enemy would come. It was grisly work, but he wanted this second group of Normans to stop just where he wanted them.

'There are twelve of them,' said Brand, smiling at Beornoth.

'So?'

'You were wrong. I should have made you wager on it.'

'Turd.'

The horsemen reined in, swirling, trying to bring their mounts under control in the path before the severed heads. Shouts of surprise peeled from their ranks and Beornoth rode slowly from cover, followed by Brand. The horsemen saw him, looked nervously at each other, and Beornoth lifted his hand, and then let it fall.

Bjornulfr, his ten men, Wigs, Ecga and Gis appeared above the slope with bows in their hands. Thirteen arrows fletched with white goose feathers whistled down from the high ground and thumped into the Norman horsemen. Five arrows slapped into the mud, the rest thumped into horse and man flesh. The Normans shouted at each other in alarm. The Norman horsemen pulled on their reins, trying to turn their horses, but they were too close together. Another thirteen arrows hurtled from the hilltop, one tonked off a shield boss with a loud ring and a Norman fell dead from his horse with an arrow in his eye.

Brand whooped and charged, spear couched and his golden hair flying behind him as he let his horse canter. Beornoth followed, charging towards the swirling mass of dying riders. Arrows continued to sing from the hillside as each of the thirteen men loosed as many arrows as possible before Beornoth and Brand reached the enemy. Two Normans broke away from the carnage and rode away with arrows jutting from their backs and the rumps of their mounts. One Norman's horse rode over the severed heads and bore its rider towards Brand. The horse ran wild, the whites of its eyes showing. Two arrows jutted from his back leg and all the Norman rider could do was cling to the saddle. Brand held his spear underhand, keeping the shaft close to his armpit, and he charged at the fleeing Norman. The spear point took the enemy rider in the chest, sending him flying backwards from his mount. Brand shifted the grip on his spear and rode at the remaining riders, hollering his war cry to Odin.

Beornoth followed Brand into the fray, clutching his spear, helmet impairing his vision so that he had to turn his head fully upwards to see Bjornulfr and his men cast their bows aside and come racing down the hillside. They skidded and slipped on the steep slope, axes in their hands and hunger for war etched upon their sea-hardened faces. Beornoth led Virtus towards the edge of the riders, always concerned about fighting on horseback, much preferring to cut at his enemies with his feet on solid ground. A Norman warrior swung his sword at Beornoth, but the blade missed by some distance. He slid in the saddle as he tried to bring the sword back, but Beornoth lunged with his spear and raked the point across the man's face. The Norman howled and twitched away and a heavy blow clubbed into the shield slung across Beornoth's back. He turned, unable to see behind him with the cheekpieces of his helmet closed. The blow came again, accompanied by a desperate war cry. Beornoth cursed and leapt from the saddle, landing heavily and forced to take three steps back.

'Odin!' bellowed Bjornulfr as he and his men tore into the Normans like demons from the Norse hell-world, Niflheim. Their axes chopped into the Normans, using the hooked bearded blades to haul the men from their horses. Wigs, Ecga and Gis remained on the hilltop, picking targets with their bows and raining down arrows from above. The Norman who had struck at Beornoth's shield came at him again, leaning over his horse to cut down at Beornoth with his sword. Beornoth deflected the blow with his spear, ducked to come out the horse's left side and jammed the point of his spear at the Norman, so that the tip pushed beneath the rim of his byrnie and into the Norman's groin. He screamed in pain and his horse panicked at the sound and at the smell of blood. It reared and set off running, leaving its wounded rider toppled and sprawling in the mud.

A rider tried to break away from the fight and his horse cantered north along the path, but one of Bjornulfr's men threw his axe and the weapon turned blade over end as it flew and slapped into the fleeing rider's back. The skirmish was over in moments, and ten Normans lay dead or dying in the mud. Bjornulfr and his men went among them, cutting the throats of any Normans still alive. They ripped silver chains and rings from the dead and searched their purses for hacksilver and silver coins.

'No point leaving wealth here for the crows,' said Bjornulfr with a shrug when he noticed Beornoth staring at him. Which Beornoth thought was fair enough.

'What about the horses?' Brand asked.

'We don't need them,' Beornoth replied. 'We've killed a dozen of the bastards today, but there are still many more to come.'

Beornoth wished he could stay and see the look on Robert and Odo de Warenne's faces when they found their scouting party slaughtered, but he must ride on. The Normans had spent a year riding across King Æthelred's kingdom, slaying Danes and punishing men listed as enemies of the crown. It was time for the reckoning. Beornoth hadn't forgotten how they had taken him prisoner, and knew that if Wigs, Ecga and Gis had not freed him from the stable, he would have died on St Brice's Day along with Pallig and his family. So Beornoth felt no pity for the twelve corpses laying still on a Northumbrian road, and he rode away from the blood-soaked path surrounded by Bjornulfr's men who cheered and sang of the victory.

The day grew long, but the sky remained bright. There was time for one more strike at Robert de Warenne's war party before nightfall. Beornoth led his men to the next location, to the next place they planned to strike at the hunters and soak the Northumbrian soil with their blood.

22

'How many will we kill this time?' asked Gis, waiting crouched in a field of long, coarse grass.

'Maybe another dozen,' Beornoth replied, shifting his position. Crouching made his leg ache, an unwanted gift from an old spear wound.

'At this rate, we'd have to attack them every day for a month to kill the bastards,' said Wigs.

'If you've any better ideas, let's have them,' said Gis. 'There's a donkey in my old granny's stable with more sense than you, Wigs.'

'There's a granny in my old donkey's stable who can wield a sword with more strength than you, Gis.'

'That's enough, lads,' said Ecga once he had stopped laughing.

Bjornulfr sidled over to Beornoth and huddled beside him in the heather. 'Your Saxons prattle like wives by the milk churn,' he said, jutting his chin to where Wigs and Gis had begun to roll about in the grass, punching each other and wrestling playfully.

'They'll fight just as well as any of your Norsemen when the time comes,' Beornoth replied.

Bjornulfr raised an eyebrow and scratched thoughtfully at his missing ear. He held up one thick finger and the gold and silver rings stacked upon his forearms jangled as they slipped down his forearm. 'One Viking is worth two Saxons in battle. Except you. But you fight like a Viking, not like a worshipper of the nailed god. The Christ makes his people soft. Our gods encourage us to be hard, to take to the axe and seek reputation across Midgard.'

'A Saxon will fight just as bravely as any Dane when he fights to protect his home. Those three will fight well, trust me.'

'Just so. Where do you want my men when the Normans come?'

Beornoth pointed through the grass to where a river ran through the field, curving around a sprawling oak tree, beneath a bank heavy with waving reeds. The water came out of the bend and thinned across a wide swathe of stony riverbank. The water jumped and babbled around a grassy eyot at the centre of the ford, and wagon ruts led to and from the shallows where users of the road had forded the water for generations.

'Wait here,' Beornoth said. He dug into the leather pouch at his belt and fished out an iron caltrop the size of his fist. It was little more than nails melded into a nugget of old iron. Brand had a smith make fifty of them over the winter for use at this very point in the road. 'I love horses. I would rather kill ten men than one horse. But today we must hurt the Normans' horses. We've dropped dozens of these little monsters in the ford. When the horses' hooves trample over them, the beasts will scream and buck and cause chaos in the river. When that happens, you and your men kill as many Normans as you can in one hundred heartbeats. Don't fight any longer than that. Break off and return to this side of the river where our horses will be waiting. We ride away and leave them bleeding in the shallows.'

'I can't count to one hundred.'

'I'll let you know when it's time to stop fighting.'

'They could ride after us. There are three hundred of them.'

'They won't ride over the caltrops. They can't. The spikes will ruin the horses' hooves, like walking on fire. The Normans will have to clear the river before they can follow. Unless they follow on foot, but we have our horses.'

'So let's kill some more of the whoresons then.'

Beornoth smiled at the Viking's laconic manner. 'Did any of your men take a blow in the ambush today?'

'Not really. One took a spear wound to the shoulder, another took one to the back. If they keep the wounds clean, they'll live.'

'Can they fight again?'

Bjornulfr's eyebrows knitted as though Beornoth had asked an impossible riddle. 'Of course. If they can stand, they can fight.'

'Then let's prepare.'

The sun hung low when the Normans arrived. The sky broiled. One mass of seething cloud without break so that the sun was little more than a smudge of light fighting its way through the morass. Beornoth waited on the far side of the river with his hand resting upon the hilt of his sword. His shield rested against his leg. He had left his helmet strapped to Virtus' saddle because he wanted the de Warennes to see who had dogged their journey north. The ground beneath Beornoth's feet rumbled beneath the pounding hooves of three hundred horses, three hundred less the men Beornoth had already killed. The caltrops lay beneath the water's surface, and Beornoth's warriors hid in the long grass.

The first riders appeared around a bend in the road and

reined in, hollering back to the main column and pointing in Beornoth's direction. Three hundred horses ridden by men in mail are a fearsome sight. The noise of hoofbeats, traces, weapons, men and barked orders filled the riverbank to drown out the sound of the babbling river and the wind across the grass. Beornoth stood strong and silent, waiting for the heaving mass of iron and wickedness to reach the opposite bank. His heart thumped in his chest and he gnashed his teeth to keep calm. The lead riders reined in beside the water, Robert and Odo de Warenne at the fore. Robert raised a hand to quieten his men, and they fell as silent as folk at Sunday mass.

'Lord Beornoth, I am surprised to find you in Northumbria. What are you doing here?' Robert called across the river.

'Lord Robert,' Beornoth said. 'I'm here to protect my friend from your men and your stinking whoreson of a brother.'

'You would raise your sword against the king?'

'Not against the king. Against dogs of war who persecute men who have committed no crime.'

'You're a coward and a traitor!' said Odo de Warenne in his curiously high-pitched voice. His scarred face twitched and his horse shifted nervously beneath him. 'You piece of goat shit. I knew you would turn your cloak.'

'Stand aside, Lord Beornoth,' Robert said. 'We are about the king's business. I won't give another warning. Don't be there when we cross the river.'

'I ask you to turn back,' Beornoth lied. 'For the sake of the battles we have fought together. Seek the other men on the king's list, but leave Brand Thorkilsson in peace.'

'Beg!' Odo spat. 'Get on your knees and beg for your Viking friend's life. In fact, cross the river and kiss my boot. Then you can beg.'

'I wasn't asking you. This is a conversation between warriors.

Not for a child killer, a murderer of women, a man without honour who swings his sword behind the protection of his brother.'

'Honour? What would you know about honour? You left us at Oxenforda. You ran like a dog when the work became difficult, when we did what had to be done. Have you never seen the face of war before, Saxon?'

'Why not settle this between us, Odo the Whoreson? Faint of heart, weak in courage. I'll fight you on that little island there. Just me and you. If I win, you ride away and leave Brand and his family to live. If you win, I'll be dead and you can do as you will.'

'Oh, you'd like that, wouldn't you? We've three hundred men! What have you got, some half-starved churls and a bunch of crusty masterless men? Why would I fight you when we can ride you down like a mangy dog?'

'I killed a dozen of your men back there at the pass. Did you find them?'

'Bastard!' Odo's face turned scarlet, anger seething from him like steam from a boiling pot.

'I'd kill you too, if you can find the courage to fight.'

'Turd! Spawn of the devil!' Odo sawed at his horse's reins as the beast turned beneath his rage. He reached for his sword, and Beornoth knew his job was almost done.

'Why should your men fight and die for a man who won't risk his own life to fight for them?'

'Move aside, Beornoth,' Robert de Warenne said, but it was too late.

'Charge!' Odo yelled. His sword slid free of his scabbard and he waved it around his head, spittle flying from his mouth like a madman. 'Ride the bastard down! A pound of silver for the man who takes his head!'

The Norman riders shouted their approval at the reward,

and their horses pulsed forward as one. They saw Beornoth alone on the opposite side of the river. One man against three hundred and they saw a chance to win themselves a fortune in silver.

Beornoth bent and picked up his shield. He drew his sword and closed his eyes against what must happen next. He could not look as hooves splashed into the river and he winced as horses screamed and thrashed in pain. The wicked caltrops cut their hooves to ribbons. Horses bucked and tossed their riders into the shallows so that the ford became a churning mass of shouting, panicking Normans and screaming, petrified horses. Beornoth hated to hurt the beasts, but this was war. Beornoth lifted his sword, let it drop, and a dozen arrows whipped from the tall, wild grass. The arrows flew low and vicious, crashing into the chaos like murderous rain. Another volley flew, and then another.

Robert de Warenne roared at his men to stay back, to keep more horses from charging into the maelstrom, but it was too late. Twenty horses kicked and thrashed in the water, and more came behind them, pushing into the river, crushing the men thrown from their injured mounts. Beornoth strode forward and Bjornulfr's men came hurtling behind him, howling their Viking war cries like demons. A Norman crawled from the river, dripping water from his hair and beard, mail and leather liner wet and heavy. He rested on all fours, gasping for breath, and looked up just in time to see Beornoth's sword arcing towards his throat. It was a wild swing, full of anger and bloodlust. Beornoth swung like a churl chopping wood and his blade bit so deep into the Norman's neck that it almost severed his head. He dropped to the ground, blood spurting from the awful wound to stain the riverbank red, and Beornoth marched into the water looking for another man to kill.

One of Bjornulfr's men ran past Beornoth at full tilt. He carried an axe in each hand and when he reached the river's edge he leapt into the air with all the litheness of a young, powerful warrior. The Viking landed lightly on the eyot and chopped his axe down into the chest of a struggling Norman. More of Bjornulfr's men came, and then their jarl himself joined Beornoth and they strode into the churning water, avoiding where they had lain the caltrops, cutting and hacking at the helpless Normans like butchers.

Robert de Warenne's voice rose above the din, loud and desperate, bellowing at his men to pull back, regroup and find some order. Beornoth crushed a warrior's face with the boss of his shield and drove the point of his sword into the spine of a Norman who found his feet and tried to run from the river. All about him, horses thrashed, hooves cracking men's bones like firewood. A Norman recovered and cut one of Bjornulfr's men down with a sweep of his sword and then died as Bjornulfr opened his belly with a cut of his axe. The river turned red with blood and Beornoth cut down another Norman who cried out to him for mercy when there was none to be had. It was grim work, pitiless slaughter, and when Beornoth saw that a score of men had died in the chaos, he roared at Bjornulfr to pull his men back.

The Viking ignored him at first, lost in the lust of battle. Beornoth strode to him and grabbed his shoulder.

'Fall back!' he shouted. 'We must go now.' Bjornulfr shook him off and Beornoth saw the fury in his eyes. For a moment Beornoth thought Bjornulfr would strike him, but then the madness cleared. Bjornulfr remembered the plan, and he ordered his men to retreat. They ran dripping from the river, whooping and shaking their weapons at the Normans. Two

Normans followed them and died with arrows in their chests, loosed by Wigs, Ecga and Gis from the grass.

More Normans emerged from the water, faces twisted by hate as they stumbled and clambered over the corpses of their friends and comrades. One of Bjornulfr's men, a big man with striped trews and a seax in his fist, ran at them.

'Odin,' he bellowed, deep in the war-madness. 'Odin, see me, see my blade!'

A Norman stabbed a spear at him, but the Viking caught it in his left hand, dragged the Norman towards him and cut his throat with a slice of his seax. The Viking let the corpse fall and drew an axe from his belt. He fought the Normans like a champion, dancing between their spears and swords and cutting at them as though possessed by the Viking gods of war themselves. Beornoth and the rest of Bjornulfr's men mounted their horses. Virtus turned as Beornoth climbed into the saddle and he pulled the reins to bring her around to face the river. Dozens of Normans came from the water to attack the single Viking champion, and Beornoth knew he must die beneath their blades. Their numbers suddenly parted and Robert de Warenne came from the river, seething with anger. His face was a mask of fury, muscles working beneath his beard, eyes blazing and his sword twitching in his hand.

The Normans fell back and Robert de Warenne faced the Viking warrior alone. Bjornulfr's man set himself, seax and axe poised to strike. Robert de Warenne raised his sword until it paused before his face, hilt and crosspiece level with his ears and nose so that the weapon resembled a crucifix. The Viking attacked quickly, his thick frame launching forwards with a speed belying his size. Axe and seax whirred, feinting, stabbing and scything low and high, but Robert de Warenne held his sword firm in two hands and parried with the clang of clashing weapons. He swayed away from an upward axe blow and chopped his sword blade down, hacking into the Viking's fore-arm. The axe fell and white bone showed through bloody, ragged flesh.

The Viking cut with his seax, but Robert de Warenne's sword caught it low and the weapon flew from the Norseman's grip. It sailed through the air and fell into the riverbank's long grass. Bjornulfr's mounted men let out a collective gasp at the horror of that ill-fated blow. The Viking dived to his right and picked up his axe. He landed on all fours and Robert de Warenne plunged the blade of his sword in between the warrior's shoulder blades. The Viking twitched and clutched his axe close to his chest. Robert de Warenne wrenched his sword free, and a spray of blood followed it.

'Odin!' The Viking roared long and loud, so loud that Bjor-nulfr winced at the glory of it. Robert de Warenne snarled and plunged his sword through the shouting Viking's heart, killing him instantly.

'We are coming for you, Beornoth,' Robert de Warenne said, pointing his bloody sword at Beornoth. His face was pale and drawn, dark circles showing beneath his eyes. He glanced at the river and could not keep the look of desperate frustration from his face. A dozen of his men lay dead or dying in the ford, and worse than that, Beornoth had ambushed him twice and the morale of his warriors dwindled with the retreating daylight.

'I'll be waiting,' Beornoth replied. He wheeled Virtus around and galloped away from the riverbank.

'Why did he do that?' asked Wigs once they were far enough away from the river that the Normans could not catch them and the horses had slowed to a canter.

'Bjornulfr's man?'

'Aye, why did he charge, and then give up his life to grab his axe?'

'For Valhalla. He could not go to Odin's hall if he died without a blade in his hand. He died as all Vikings dream of dying, with slain foemen all about him and his axe in his fist.'

'How could our kingdom survive if an army of such men came to our shores?'

Beornoth left that question unanswered because it was the nightmare of Saxons who knew the ways and the implacable, warlike nature of Norsemen. The Vikings had come with a great army once before, when King Aelle threw Ragnar Lothbrok into the orm-garth, the pit filled with the snakes the king of Northumbria had prepared for that very purpose. Ragnar's sons came for vengeance with a seething horde of Danes. Their warships so numerous that their sails had spread as far as a man could see. Ivar the Boneless, Sigurd Snake-in-the-Eye, Ubba and Halvdan Ragnarsson came and conquered Northumbria, and Ivar cut the notorious blood eagle into a screaming King Aelle's back. After that East Anglia fell, and the sons of Ragnar martyred its King Edmund by loosing arrows into his stricken body. That army ultimately fell apart, laden down with silver and lands won by conquest. One of its members, Guthmund, became a king and the Danelaw was born. Beornoth doubted England could survive if another such army came and allied with the Vikings already living north of Watling Street. As he rode through the twilight with the wind whipping his face and beard, Beornoth wondered if Sweyn Forkbeard knew Æthelred had killed his sister, and what the great Viking battle-king would do to avenge his slaughtered kin.

23

Darkness fell heavy like a black tapestry, extinguishing the sun to leave a low, heaving sky. A driving, merciless rain soaked the land, sheeting and seething against briar and heather.

'They could be waiting for us,' said Gis, stood next to Beornoth as they peered into the gloom. Rain dripped from his beard and he wore his leather helmet liner to keep the worst of the wet off his head.

'They will be waiting for us,' Beornoth replied. He shivered, too wet to bother hiding from the relentless downpour. Rain had seeped through the iron rings of his byrnie to soak the chain mail's leather liner and the linen shirt he wore beneath it. His cloak hung heavy and soaked from his shoulders, but his sword remained dry in its fleece-lined scabbard.

'But let me guess,' said Wigs. 'We're going to attack, anyway?'

'We go when the moon is overhead. Get some sleep now if you can.'

Wigs peered upwards into the pounding rain and shook his head.

'Don't engage them,' Beornoth said, turning to Bjornulfr. 'We kill the sentries, then run through their camp, cutting at anything that moves or snores. Wigs and Gis will lead our horses to the far side, going wide about the camp so the Normans don't hear them. After that, we ride for Stag Hall.'

'Why just run through and stab at them with spears?' asked Ecga.

'Horses loud,' Bjornulfr replied in his broken Saxon. 'Heard for miles. Better like this.'

Which it was, and Beornoth crouched in the rain, waiting for the moon to creep overhead like a great silver spider. It barely showed in the water-soaked clouds, offering mere glimpses of its shining, ethereal glory. After what seemed like an age the glowing crescent peered down at him from above and Beornoth roused the men. Most of Bjornulfr's warriors snored beneath the boughs of three elm trees. They sat up cursing at their tiredness, reached for their weapons and prepared for the march towards the Norman camp. They coughed, pissed, joked and laughed, hefted shields, axes and ran bone combs through their beards and hair.

'When you lot are ready,' said Wigs, waiting for them with his hands on his hips.

'Who wants to die not looking his best?' said a gap-toothed Viking, re-plaiting his beard.

'Who wants to die at all?'

The Vikings looked at Wigs like he was a simpleton and then finished their preparations. Beornoth led them through the darkness as Wigs and Gis rode away, leading a line of horses behind them. They rode gently, taking their time because riding at night is a dangerous business of unsure footing and frightened beasts. Beornoth led Ecga, Bjornulfr and nine of his men.

Their belts, weapons and chain mail jangled in the quiet of night and the Vikings told jokes and old war stories as they crossed the fields and meadows to where Robert de Warenne's men camped at the top of a rise above where they had fought at the ford. They camped on the high ground to give them the best view of the surrounding countryside. The Normans didn't care who saw their campfires. Brand already knew they were coming and now the de Warennes knew Beornoth stood with him.

Beornoth's soaked boots squelched in the waterlogged grass and he paused the advance every three score steps to listen for any sounds of the enemy. Robert de Warenne would expect and fear another attack, as would his men. But they would also be tired after riding and fighting all day, after digging graves for their friends and building camp. Beornoth hoped that their vigilance had dropped. It was so deep into the night that even men who had vowed to stay awake and watch for another attack had succumbed to exhaustion. He imagined them sat by their shields, eyes growing heavier as the night drew on. Fighting back nodding heads, rubbing at stinging eyelids until one by one they drifted off to sleep.

'Ecga, Bjornulfr,' Beornoth said. 'They'll have scouts all over the fields surrounding that hill. Ecga, take your bow and kill any you can find. Bjornulfr, send two of your men out hunting.'

The three men set off loping through the wet, disappearing into the night. Beornoth followed, marching past the corpse of a Norman scout lying at the base of the hill with an arrow in his throat. Ecga waited for them, sat at the bottom of the slope with his bow resting across his lap, and joined the march, grinning at a job well done. Bjornulfr's two warriors came running around the hill with axes in their hands.

'How many?' Bjornulfr whispered as they drew close.

'Only two,' replied the first man, a squat, barrel-chested Viking with a badly broken nose.

Bjornulfr glanced at Beornoth, and the two men exchanged a shrug. Beornoth expected to find the base of the hill crawling with Norman scouts protecting the camp. A pang of fear twisted deep in his belly, a warning that something wasn't right, but he was too close now. Beornoth could smell the garlic stink of the Normans' evening meal, see the glowing embers of their camp-fires. He only wanted to kill another handful of Robert's men. Another half-dozen dead to further dent the Normans' morale.

Beornoth drew his sword and the rest of his company readied their own weapons and followed him up the hill. He quickened his pace, striding up the slope ready to kill as many Normans as possible and then get away into the night like a fox attacking a chicken coop. He drew the seax from the small of his back and went to the slaughter with a blade in each fist. They came in a wide, ragged line. Saxons and Danes with sharp weapons ready to strike at sleeping men. Beornoth strode so fast that he almost broke into a run when he reached the summit. A leather tent rose in front of him and Beornoth stabbed his sword into it twice, feeling no resistance but leaving it to continue through the camp. He kicked the embers of a fire into another tent and stabbed his sword again, but found no Norman body inside.

'Wait,' Beornoth said, raising his weapons to stop the advance.

Ecga and six of the Vikings were already deep into the camp, eagerly searching for something to kill but finding only empty tents and rolled-up cloaks.

'Retreat!' Beornoth shouted. The need for quiet passed, and Beornoth knew what must come next.

A clipped roar came from the camp's far side, and a seething horde of Norman warriors appeared from the darkness, moonlight catching their helmets and the tips of their blades.

'Charge!' shouted a voice. 'Kill them, kill them all!' It was Robert de Warenne's deep voice.

'Ecga, run!' Beornoth called, but his heart sank because it was too late. Fifty Danes sprinted ahead of the rest, running with lithe limbs and reaching Ecga and the six Danes before they could turn and run. Ecga made three strides before a sword slashed across the backs of his legs to send him sprawling. The six Vikings made a brave stand. They did not run, but stood with weapons ready. Each of them killed two Normans before the sheer number of swords hacking at their bodies overwhelmed them and their bodies fell beneath the rise and fall of honed steel.

Odo de Warenne stalked amongst his men, scarred face grinning beneath rain-soaked hair, so that his teeth glowed in the moonlight. He pushed his men out of the way and leaned over Ecga with a cruel, curved knife in his fist.

'No!' Beornoth howled as Odo de Warenne went to work on Ecga. The Saxon cried like a woman in childbirth as Odo cut at his groin and stomach, torturing him with practised cuts designed to inflict maximum pain, humiliation and suffering before death. Beornoth could not bear it and he charged forwards but Bjornulfr and two of his Vikings held him back.

'Now is not the time,' Bjornulfr hissed into his ear. 'If you want to help Brand, we must live. We must go.'

Beornoth snarled and turned away. They ran down the hillside and Bjornulfr cried out for joy when Wigs and Gis came riding towards the base of the hill leading their horses. Hundreds of Normans flooded down the hill, bellowing with murderous rage. Beornoth mounted Virtus and rode away from the hill at a gallop. Ecga was gone, along with six brave men of Bjornulfr's oathsworn warriors. Beornoth's night raid had failed, and Ecga, a man he thought of as a friend, had perished under the terror of Odo de Warenne's knife.

'Where's Ecga?' asked Wigs as they rode through the night, keeping to wide fields to protect the horses.

'Gone,' Beornoth said, almost unable to drag the words from his mouth.

'God save his soul.'

'God save us all,' said Gis.

They rode as far away from the Normans as possible before needing to stop and rest the horses. Beornoth halted the war band beneath a jutting crag that leaned over a heath drenched by midnight rainfall. A pallid slip of sunlight clung to the distant horizon, casting a reluctant light over distant mountaintops still white with winter snow. They rested in silence, exhausted from lack of sleep, tinged with the sour sting of defeat, and bereft at the loss of their dead friends.

'I hope they bury him properly,' said Gis, teeth chattering.

The rain had given way to a freezing night wind which stung Beornoth's face and hands like a nettle sting.

'He wore a cross about his neck,' said Beornoth. 'They'll bury him.'

'What about the Vikings?'

'Them they'll leave for the crows.'

'Poor Ecga. I'll have to tell his family what happened when we get home,' said Wigs.

'If we get home.' Gis stared back across their tracks in the direction which the Normans would inevitably follow.

'His mother still lives. A kind old woman famous for her chicken broth. You should taste it, like eating a piece of heaven it is. She'll weep for the rest of her days. She taught Ecga to cook.'

'He could cook, could Ecga, and he was a stout man in the shield wall.'

'We'll miss him when the Normans come,' agreed Beornoth.

'What the hell are they doing?' asked Wigs after the three Saxons stood in silence for a time, thinking of their dead friend.

'Saying goodbye to their shipmates like we just did for Ecga,' Beornoth replied. Bjornulfr and his four remaining Vikings in the war band stood in a circle with their arms about one another's shoulders, talking in hushed tones. Each said a few words about their fallen friends. When that was done, they kissed their axe blades and raised the weapons to the sky to ask the gods to honour the fallen with a place in the glorious afterlife.

'We've lost a lot of men this last day,' said Gis to Beornoth, though he would not meet Beornoth's eye.

'We have,' Beornoth replied. 'But we need the Normans angry when they reach Brand's home. We need them so furious at the blows we have dealt them that they charge at us full of rage.'

'Let's hope that all our preparations were not for nothing.'

'If they were,' said Wigs, coming about the sombre moment with a cheerful smile, 'we won't care. We'll be dead.'

'Close your cheese pipe, Wigs. You are making me feel worse. We rode with the bloody de Warennes, and now they've come to kill us.'

'We are not dead yet. I don't regret leaving that arrogant turd, Robert, and his badger-shit mad brother. We're on the right side. Surely that counts for something?'

'Badger shit?'

'Yes. Have you ever smelled badger shit?'

'Move out,' said Beornoth to cut through the banter. He was glad to hear them jest so quickly from Ecga's death. That was the way with warriors, finding humour in the most unlikely situations. Their greatest challenge lay ahead of them and laughter helped bury fear in the pit of man's stomach. There would be time to mourn Ecga properly when the fighting was done, but now it was time to return to Brand and the defence of his home.

Beornoth found Brand and his oathman Orm in the field outside Stag Hall. They drilled thirty men in the basic art of shield-wall fighting.

'Men of the fyrd,' said Gis with a sour look on his face as the riders drew close. The fyrd stood in a stubbly brown field outside the ring of Brand's palisade, some with spears, but most with scythes, reaping hooks or clubs. Half of them held battered-looking shields.

Brand raised a hand in greeting as the riders approached. 'So few?' he called, taking in the paltry number of warriors returned from Beornoth's raiding party.

'Good men died,' Beornoth replied, 'but we have stung them. They'll be here before midday. So we'd best be ready.'

'We're ready,' said Orm, wearing a hard-baked leather breastplate, leaning on a spear.

'Can they fight?' asked Wigs, nodding to the men of the fyrd.

'They'll fight. Because if they don't, the Normans will ride to their homes, wives and children once they've finished with this place.' He spoke loud enough for the churls to hear, and they exchanged fearful glances.

Brand led Beornoth into his hall, where Sefna greeted him with a bowl of last night's stew. Beornoth thanked her, and she placed a chunk of dark bread and a cup of ale on the bench beside him.

'Are there three hundred of them?' she asked, sitting beside Beornoth.

'There are,' he replied between slurps of stew. 'Though we have whittled them a little and hurt their pride.'

'Uncle Beo!' called a little voice, and Vigdjarf came bounding into the hall. Brand's son leapt at Beornoth, landing in his lap and wrapping his arms around Beornoth's midriff.

'Careful, Vigi,' Sefna scolded, straightening the bowl her son had rocked in his enthusiasm to greet Beornoth.

'Uncle?' asked Beornoth, and Sefna shrugged with a smile.

'My father tells me you are my uncle. He says you are the bravest and strongest warrior in all England.'

'Does he now?'

'He does. He also said that if I practise my weapons every day, one day I could be as big and as famous as you.'

'You should listen to your father and your mother, even if your lord father is prone to exaggerating.'

'Last night, he told all our men how you fought at Maldon. He told them how you killed Skarde Wartooth and other great champions. The men all believe that you are going to save us, that you can kill a hundred of our enemies alone.'

'I must have a word with your father.'

'Run along now, Vigi,' said Sefna, ruffling her son's hair. 'Let Beo have his meal in peace.'

'Why are the bad men coming to hurt us?' asked Vigdjarf, staring up into Beornoth's face.

Beornoth glanced at Sefna, and she shrugged. 'The reason your father teaches you axe and shield work is because our world, Midgard, is full of bad men. When you grow up, you must decide for yourself if you will follow the ways of *drengskapr*, or if you will hurt innocent people who cannot protect themselves.'

'A *drengr* protects the weak.'

'He should. The men who will come today are why warriors exist. You must make yourself strong, little warrior, because men will always want your land, your woman, your silver and the reputation in taking your life.'

'Are you going to kill them, Uncle Beo?'

'Your father and I will protect you.' Beornoth let Vigdjarf down from his lap and wished he had not made that promise, for he was not sure he could keep it.

'We have sixty men?' Sefna asked.

'Aye. Each must kill three Normans if we are to live. But we don't have to kill them all. Just enough to put the fear in them, to make them surrender or run. But we'll have to kill a lot of the bastards, for they are not new to war.'

'I'd better get my bow and my axe, then.'

Beornoth found Brand stalking along the palisade, testing its strength by yanking on the fence posts.

'It's a bit late for that,' Beornoth called.

Brand turned and nodded. 'Trying to pass the time. I hate waiting for battle.'

'It's always the same. This is when the fear grows, when it gnaws at a man's mind like the corpse ripper.'

'You know more about our gods than most Danes. The corpse ripper is the serpent who gnaws on the corpses of the oathbreak-ers, women killers and nithings who writhe at the foot of Yggdrasil, the world tree. We must send these Norman bastards there to meet their fate, for they are men without honour. I thought I had seen my last battle when I came here with Sefna and Thered made me a thegn. I thought I could live here in peace and raise my family.'

'At least this time we fight for something worth dying for. We fight for your children, to protect what you have built here, not at the whim of a king or lord.'

'Then let this be the last battle, the last time we must stand together, shield over shield.'

'There will never be a last battle. Men will always crave what the men in the next valley own. There will be no end to it as long as the sun rises and sets.'

'Which is why the gods create men like you, Beornoth.'

Beornoth lifted his head at the sound of hoofbeats. 'It looks like your wait is over. Here they come.'

24

The Normans slunk from the east, lumbering across a rolling field with their spear points wavering above them like a forest. A spring sun shone down through strung-out clouds and the enemy came on horseback and on foot, having lost many of their horses to the caltrops hidden beneath the shallow ford. Beornoth could not count them, but over two hundred warriors came across the field, silent but for the whicker of their horses and the clank of their war gear. They came grim-faced and determined, tired from lack of sleep and shaken by the loss of their dead comrades. Brand and Beornoth stood upon the ditch behind the palisade watching the Normans advance. Brand's hearth troop and his fyrd manned the right and left flanks, and Bjornulfr and his remaining crew stood behind Beornoth to defend the gate.

'They won't waste time,' said Beornoth. 'They hate us for the pain we've caused them since they left York. So the fight will come quickly.'

'Good,' said Brand. 'If it's coming, best to have it now.'

'Your family are in the hall?'

'They are. Sefna is on the roof with her bow. We'll fall back there if they breach the wall.'

'They've got to cross that field first.'

Brand grinned and loosened his axe in its belt loop. 'Thank you for coming, Beo.'

'You would have done the same for me.'

'I might. If you weren't such a cantankerous old beast.'

'Remember, we just have to kill enough of them to make the rest afraid.'

'So we go for the leaders?'

'Yes. Just kill as many of the bastards as you can.'

'Looks like they want to talk.'

Robert and Odo de Warenne dismounted and walked from their troops, who had halted fifty paces from Stag Hall's gates. Four captains came behind men, helmets on and dark cloaks about their shoulders.

'Brand Thorkilsson,' called Robert de Warenne. 'The king has declared you an enemy of the crown. By order of the king...'

'Take your men and leave,' Beornoth shouted, cutting Robert off, hoping to antagonise him further. 'Leave now and we won't kill you all.'

'By order of the king you must—'

'Get you gone, child-killing whoresons,' Brand shouted, and turned to wink at Beornoth. 'Your mothers are ashamed of you, your fathers roll in their graves grieving at what has become of their bloodline. You are cowards, nithings and murderers. Your Christian hell beckons to you. Dogs, curs, pig-shit-eating turds.' He leaned into Beornoth and whispered, 'Might as well insult them properly.'

'Heathen scum!' Odo de Warenne called in his screeching voice. He shook his fist at the defenders like an angry child. 'Prepare to meet your doom.'

'Enough talk,' Beornoth said, half to himself and half to Brand. He picked up his spear from where it rested against the wall. He hefted the ash shaft overhand, took aim and launched it with all the strength in his old warrior's body. The spear flew in a flat arc, vicious like an eagle diving at its prey. Odo de Warenne dropped to the ground just in time for the weapon to flash over his head and thump into the chest of the Norman stood behind him. That man had not seen the spear, hidden as he was behind Odo, and he flew backwards as though kicked by a horse. The Normans erupted in a shouting, seething rage. They surged forwards, clashing spears against shields and calling for the deaths of Brand and Beornoth.

'Spears and shields!' Brand ordered, and the men behind the walls responded with a single curt shout. They climbed the ditch and stood ready to defend the palisade, even the farmers who held only reaping hooks and clubs.

'Now we'll see if the work we did in winter was worth the effort,' said Bjornulfr, taking his place beside Beornoth.

As if to answer his question, one hundred Norman horsemen charged from their line in a mass of muscled horse-flesh, iron and hateful men. Odo de Warenne had scrambled to his feet and bellowed at his men to kill Beornoth. Robert de Warenne waved his sword, the sounds of his voice lost beneath the thunder of hooves. The wall of horsemen came on, spears ready. They meant to charge and wheel alongside the palisade and hurl their spears over the walls, and Beornoth drew his sword.

The Normans raised their spears and passed the shrieking form of Odo de Warenne. They came within fifty paces of Stag Hall's palisade, and then fell into a mass of howling, thrashing, bloody ruin. The riders had urged their mounts into a fast canter, almost an all-out gallop, and so there was little they could do to stop their mounts from careening into the pits the defenders had spent eight cold weeks digging and filling with sharpened stakes. They had covered the death pits with turf cut from a mile away so that, to the unknown observer, the land leading to Stag Hall seemed nothing more than a flat, wild field.

Norman warriors tumbled from their mounts and crashed to the earth, breaking bones or falling headlong into the death pits where sharpened oak and ash stakes tore into their flesh to skewer their heads, limbs and torsos. What had been a rumbling thunder of hoofbeats and bellowed defiance became a wretched howl of screaming horses and the terrified bawl of injured warriors.

'Loose!' Beornoth shouted as a dozen Norman horsemen who had, by luck, made it through the maze of hidden death pits came alongside the palisade. The first rider stared at the defenders, his face ashen and his spear lowered. He glanced back towards his dying brothers and then fell from his horse with an arrow in his gut. Every man on the wall carried a bow and a quiver of goose-feather-fletched arrows.

Beornoth raised a bow, which he had never been much use with, nocked an arrow to the string and loosed it at the horsemen. The arrow flew high over the men, but more found their mark and within five heartbeats twelve riderless horses cantered away from the walls, eyes wide and ears pushed back at the stink of blood.

Bjornulfr placed a hand on the palisade and was about to leap over before Beornoth put a hand upon his shoulder.

'Hold,' Beornoth growled. Bjornulfr snarled at him and down at the wounded Normans who writhed on the ground beyond the ditch and palisade. He wanted to kill them, but to leave the walls was to die, and Bjornulfr fell back and nodded his understanding.

The Normans dismounted and came on foot, Robert de Warenne leading them carefully amongst the death pits. They winced as their comrades wept and reached out to them, men with bloody spikes jutting from thighs and shoulders. The advancing Normans tried not to look at the corpses staring up at them from the pits. An injured mare found its feet and bucked, back legs hammering into a Norman warrior and crushing his chest like a smashed chestnut.

'Loose every arrow you have,' Beornoth ordered, shouting so that the defenders could hear him over the din. 'Do it now!'

Bows creaked, and arrows whistled into the air. The deadly shafts rose and fell like a murderous rain, some tonking off helmets or slamming into shields, others tearing into necks, feet, faces and chests. Brand had ordered his smith to make the arrowheads long and thin like a finger, so that the arrows cut through the interlocked iron rings of the Normans' chain mail and dozens of Normans fell beneath the deadly hail.

'Shields!' Robert de Warenne ordered. His men raised their heavy shields above their heads and came together so that they advanced beneath a roof of shields, like the ceiling of Valhalla itself. The Normans came on, grunting with each step, two hundred of them marching as arrows crashed into their raised shields. Some arrows still found their mark, and the Norman formation left a trail of corpses and wounded behind it. More trod on fresh death pits and howled as they slipped through the loose covering of turf and sticks and stakes skewered their feet, legs and groins.

'Time for the last gift for our Norman guests,' said Brand, and waved to Orm, who came carrying a flaming torch.

'Burn the whoresons, lord,' said Orm, a feral grin splitting his face.

Brand took an arrow wrapped in cloth and touched it to the

torch. The cloth caught fire, and he set it to his bow. Brand pulled the string back to his ear and loosed the flaming shaft. Stag's Hall had gone without night light for a week, as every scrap of oil, every ounce of anything flammable, lay in the fields outside the walls. Beornoth had worried that the rains might dampen the oil, but Brand's arrow landed in the grass twenty paces from the wall, flickered for a moment, and then with a crackling whoosh the field caught fire.

Flames licked across the field beyond Stag Hall like dragon's breath, licking about the Normans' boots soaked in oil during their march across the grass. Their shields dropped as they beat at the fire, hopping and howling like madmen.

'Spears,' Beornoth ordered, and every man on the walls with a spear launched it at the burning Normans. A score of them fell with spears jutting from their bodies, and Beornoth picked up his sword. He flexed his hand around the soft leather grip, felt the pulse of war from the blade as it sang to him for blood. His chest heaved, and he left his shield resting against the wall and drew his seax from its sheath at the small of his back.

Robert de Warenne strode amongst his men, marshalling those who were untouched by the flames or had beaten them out. Smoke rose from their boots and trews. Men trembled, staring at their hands burned in the effort of putting out the flames on their own legs. A score of small fires crackled and danced across the field and the air reeked of oil and burned flesh.

'This must be what hell is like,' Beornoth said wistfully, staring out at the carnage.

'We've whittled them down,' said Brand. 'But there are still more than a hundred and a half who can still fight.'

'Now we only need to kill two each,' said Bjornulfr, and Brand laughed.

Robert de Warenne shifted his men into a wide arc two ranks deep and five paces apart. They advanced carefully, prodding the ground in front of them with spears and swords to find the remaining death pits. They came wide to spread their attack around the palisade, to stretch the defenders thin on the walls.

'So now it begins,' said Brand, hefting his axe in one hand and a bone-handled knife in the other.

'Remember,' Beornoth called over his shoulder so that the defenders could hear. 'If we lose the wall, fall back to the hall. Fight for your lord, fight for your lives!'

'And fight for Odin!' Bjornulfr roared and lifted his axe high. 'Odin All-Father, honour us with battle-luck. Let our enemies tremble and die beneath our blades, let their feet slip and their spears shiver. See us, Lord Odin!' The Vikings roared their approval at Bjornulfr's battle cry, and Brand beat his axe against his chest. He turned and waved to Sefna, and she nodded grimly from where she crouched in the thatch above the hall where they had made their home.

The Normans reached the ditch, coming not in a rage now, but carefully, peering over the rims of their shields with hate-filled eyes.

'As one!' Robert de Warenne shouted, and leapt across the ditch, as did every man remaining under his command. He attacked a section to Beornoth's right, and he thought about shifting position to meet the Norman warlord, but there was no time. Six Normans came at the gate, snarling and stabbing with their spears as they leapt into the ditch and scrambled up its side. Beornoth caught a spear shaft with his seax and stabbed down with his sword into the gullet of a black-bearded Norman. Another spear came at him and glanced off his chain mail to open a cut in Beornoth's shoulder. Brand killed that spearman with a chop of his axe.

Bjornulfr hacked at the Normans with his axe and fended off spear thrusts with his shield. All along the palisade, battle raged as the Normans clawed their way up the ditch and tried to climb over the palisade. Beornoth caught a sword blow with his own blade and exchanged blows with a fierce-eyed Norman who spat curses at him from below.

'The fyrd!' Orm called from behind, where Beornoth, Brand and Bjornulfr fought to defend the gate. Beornoth risked a glance to his right and saw that the churls had fallen back from the walls, that Robert de Warenne himself had breached the wall there with a dozen of his warriors and was inside the palisade.

'Go, Orm!' Beornoth ordered. 'Hold them there.'

The Norman stabbed at Beornoth again, and he parried the stroke with his sword and drove down hard with his seax. The point skewered the Norman through his eye with a spurt of blood and filth and Beornoth yanked the blade free and slashed it across the neck of another enemy who fought with Bjornulfr.

'We can't hold them,' said Brand. A livid red slash had cut through the raven tattoo on his face and blood spattered his axe and byrnie.

Pockets of Normans had breached the wall, finding weaknesses and pouring into the gaps like a plague.

'Fall back,' Beornoth said bitterly. He had hoped to hold the walls longer, to kill more of the Normans as they came from the ditch. But Robert de Warenne's men had taken the walls.

Beornoth sheathed his seax and picked up his shield. He dropped back from the ditch and made a shield wall alongside Brand and Bjornulfr. Bjornulfr's men flanked them, clashing their axes upon their shields' iron rims to make grim war music. Orm ushered the surviving fyrd men to the hall, and they fled behind the safety of Beornoth's shield wall.

Robert de Warenne cut down two of Brand's oathmen with deft cuts of his sword and ordered his warriors to form up before the shield wall. Odo de Warenne capered amongst the Normans, stabbing down with his sword to kill any injured defenders he could find. The Normans made a shield wall of their own and charged. Beornoth braced himself, shoulder behind his shield, and took the charge. The Normans thundered into him like the punch of a giant fist and he stabbed over the rim of his shield with his sword. Men grunted with the effort. Blades slid below and over shields, looking for any way to kill an enemy.

'Hold them,' Beornoth bellowed, using every bit of his lifetime of experience. He counted to ten. 'Two steps back.'

They shuffled backwards, and the Normans stumbled as the resistance they heaved against vanished. Beornoth stabbed down into the back of a Norman's neck, and Brand crashed his axe into another foeman's face. Bjornulfr and his crew killed with ruthless efficiency and the Normans fell back from their wrath. Robert de Warenne waved his sword and ordered his men to attack and fell to one knee as one of Sefna's arrows slammed into his thigh. More arrows whistled from the hall roof, each one loosed with an archer's precision. Sefna found unprotected necks, faces, armpits and legs and the Normans fell further back, crouching behind their shields in fear of her deadly shafts.

Brand and Beornoth locked their shields together to allow the rest of their shield wall to run through the open hall doors and then retreated themselves, taking careful backward steps. The last thing Beornoth saw as the oak doors of Stag Hall creaked closed was Odo de Warenne's wicked, scarred face grinning at him.

25

Beornoth dropped to one knee, his body screaming at him to rest. His wounded shoulder stung, and he had taken another cut to his forearm and one across his cheek. Old wounds felt like fresh injuries and his bones were as heavy as lead. Sefna dropped agilely from the rafters and went to hug her children, who huddled in a corner with the wives and children of Brand's warriors.

'We'll have to break out,' said Brand, reaching down to help Beornoth stand. He handed Beornoth a cup of ale, which he drank so quickly that drops of it spilled down his beard. 'Perhaps at nightfall.'

'We'll have to do it sooner than that,' said Beornoth. A vision of Pallig's wife and children running from their hall with their backs on fire stung his thought cage like a whip.

'Fire!' called Orm, peering through a crack in a closed window shutter. 'They come with flame.'

Beornoth closed his eyes, because it was as though the de Warennes had read his darkest fears. Perhaps Brand's people should have fled. Used their horses to flee across the dales and find safety elsewhere. But the Normans would never give up. Brand and his family would be fugitives, looking for a fast ship to take them north, and would find only death.

'Uncle Beo,' said a little voice. Vigdjarf came hurtling at Beornoth and wrapped his arms about Beornoth's leg. 'They are going to burn us. I'm scared.'

Beornoth knelt, groaning at the pain in his aged knees. 'You must be brave, little warrior.' He cupped a hand around Vigdjarf's round face and took his seax from its sheath. 'Here, take this. I have killed many warriors with it, and it will bring you luck.'

Vigdjarf wiped tears from his face on the sleeve of his jerkin and took the blade, turning it over and marvelling at the gleaming point and fine bone handle. 'Is that blood?' he said.

'It is, but do not shirk from it. You will be a warrior one day, so take this seax and use it to protect your brothers and sisters.'

Vigdjarf puffed out his chest and strode towards his siblings like he was the champion of the northmen. Beornoth swallowed a lump in his throat as he watched Brand's son. Churls and women cried out as smoke drifted through the thatch. They grabbed each other and huddled in the dark corners of the hall.

'They've lit it,' said Brand, coming alongside Beornoth and staring up at the thatch.

'What shall we do?' cried Sefna, eyes full of tears for her family.

'Orm. How many men do they have left?' Beornoth called.

'Over one hundred, lord,' Orm replied, still peeking through the shutter. 'They're tossing flaming torches on the roof!'

'We've killed a lot of the bastards,' said Bjornulfr, limping towards Beornoth and leaving a trail of blood behind him. 'I only have four of my men left.'

'You are wounded?' asked Beornoth.

'In the gut and the leg.'

'We can't wait for the fire to burn us. Their plan is to cut us down as we run through the doors, which we will when the smoke and the flames become too much.'

'If we charge, my family will die,' said Brand.

'They will not die,' said Beornoth. 'The Normans have lost two-thirds of their force. We can break them.'

'How?'

'I need a distraction. Some of us must go through the doors and attack the Normans, but those men will surely die. The others will crawl through the thatch where Sefna loosed her arrows. The Normans will be drawn to the fight at the doors and will not notice as we climb down the hall's side and attack them in the flank.'

'Good,' growled Bjornulfr. 'Most of my crew awaits me in Valhalla. I am ready to join them.'

Beornoth nodded and Brand stepped in to the Viking jarl and touched his forehead to Bjornulfr's in thanks.

'Halvdan, Fjolnir, Toki and Kvasir,' Bjornulfr barked at his men. Four broad-shouldered, big-bearded Viking growlers stood to attention. 'Are you ready for Valhalla?' Each of them nodded without hesitation, clasping their axes to their chests. Their byrnies were torn and bloody, and one man carried a useless, mangled arm at his side.

'Wait until I give the order. Brand and Orm, get the best of our fighters and come with me. Wigs, Gis, are you ready?'

The two Saxons gulped, glanced up at the smoke in the rafters, and nodded.

Twelve men followed Beornoth up the ladder Brand's family used to reach their sleeping platform every night. Beornoth coughed and cuffed at watering eyes as he crawled through the heavy smoke. Fire licked at the thatch and he struggled to find the hole Sefna had cut into the roof to use her bow. Prayers to Odin sang out below as Bjornulfr and his Vikings prepared to make their stand. Beornoth climbed and Brand followed him, then Orm, Wigs, Gis and the rest of the surviving warriors.

'Mamma, no!' cried a child's voice. Vigdjarf's voice. Beornoth growled and backed up. Unable to leave Brand's son to suffer alone as flames licked about him.

'Keep going,' Beornoth said, grabbing Brand by the arm. Brand had turned to climb down the ladder to get to his son. He stared at Beornoth and there was fear in his hard Viking eyes. 'Go through the thatch. I will go to your family. The men who go through the hall doors will die. Live, Brand. Attack the Normans from their flank and kill as many as you can so that they lose the will to fight. Live and protect your children.'

Brand bared his teeth and nodded. He came back up the ladder and Beornoth descended. He leapt the last few steps and landed heavily. Beornoth rushed to Sefna, who cradled her baby whilst her sons Vigdjarf and Ulf clung to her skirts. Flaming clumps of thatch fell to the hard-packed floor about them and Vigdjarf howled with fear.

'Don't rush out,' Beornoth said. 'No matter what happens.'

'I won't stand by whilst my children burn,' Sefna said, tears upon her cheeks.

'Then give your children to the ladies and fight beside me now.'

Sefna snarled, pushed her weeping children into the hands of frightened warriors' wives, and readied her axe.

'Odin!' came Bjornulfr's cry as he kicked open the hall door. Smoke billowed from the hall as the doors swung open and the Normans let out a feral roar. All the Normans had crowded to the hall's front leaving the rest of the building unguarded. Bloodthirsty warriors desperate to strike a blow against the enemy who had caused them so much suffering. Brand and the others crawled through the thatch, and Beornoth readied his sword and shield. Smoke grew thicker in the hall, stinging Beornoth's eyes and clogging his throat. Women screamed, everybody beneath the rafters coughed as more clumps of burning thatch fell about them.

Bjornulfr's men charged into the courtyard and Beornoth followed. He waited, counted ten heartbeats, and then strode through the smoke, sword and shield in hand. Sefna marched at his side clutching her axe and a long knife, teeth bared with hate for the men come to burn her children alive. Beornoth waved his sword to clear the smoke and marched into a brutal fight. Bjornulfr's Vikings fought like champions of legend, hacking at the enemies, battling an enemy who vastly outnumbered them. One by one, they fell beneath a storm of Norman blades until Bjornulfr and one last Viking champion stood against a heaving mass of vengeful enemies. Dozens of swords hacked at their shields and Bjornulfr and his man cut at the Normans with war-skill and brutal savagery. Odo capered in the second rank, screeching at his men to slaughter the Danes, his eyes feral and scarred face taut with fury.

Ten Normans streamed from the fight and charged towards the open hall doors. They came with shields raised and smashed into Beornoth and Sefna like a battering ram, driving them back into the burning hall. Beornoth fell over a feasting bench and landed heavily on the ground. Women and children screamed and Odo's bloodthirsty screech of triumph tore through Beornoth's senses like an eagle's claw.

'Father!' howled little Vigdjarf. 'Uncle Beo, help!'

Beornoth's heart broke to hear the fear in the boy's voice. He took a breath, thought of Vigdjarf and the rest of Brand's family, of his own dead daughters, and filled himself with rage.

Beornoth let it overtake him, swarm him, subdue the aches and pains of an old man's body. He felt only hate in that moment, for the men who came to burn another family in their home.

'Bastards,' Beornoth growled. He surged to his feet, shield and sword in hand. Fire rained down from above to fall around a clutch of women and children huddled in a smoky corner of the hall. Only Sefna stood before them, axe and knife dripping blood and two dead Normans at her feet.

'Kill the bitch!' Odo barked, and his men advanced towards Sefna, who crouched low like a wild beast, weapons ready to protect her precious family.

Beornoth charged them. In their bloodlust, the Normans had forgotten about him, and Beornoth hammered into their rear with his shield and sent six Normans flying into the smoke. He cut one enemy down with his sword, and reverse cut the blade across a second man's face. Sefna screamed and hacked into the fallen Normans, cutting her axe at their necks, faces and groins. A cloud of smoke enveloped Beornoth, and he stepped back into it, allowing its thickness to hide him. He held his breath, took four long strides and emerged from the gloom to cut down two more of Odo's men with stabs of his sharp sword.

The women in the hall found their strength, they howled their hate and grabbed whatever weapons they could find. Women with smoke-darkened faces hacked at the Normans with eating knives, swords snatched up from the fallen, even clawed with their nails where no weapon could be found. The Normans died screaming and Beornoth advanced on Odo de Warenne, who stared at him with a look of utter fear upon his face. Beornoth lifted his sword and Odo ran. He dropped his shield and ran from the hall like a hare from a hunting dog.

Beornoth followed, coughing, eyes streaming from stinging fire smoke. Odo dashed across the courtyard where Bjornulfr stood alone before the gates, cut to ribbons but still swinging his axe with a score of dead Normans lying about him and his slaughtered crew. Robert de Warenne fought Bjornulfr, the two big men trading blows as blood seeped from a dozen wounds. Bjornulfr's axe flew wide and Robert de Warenne drove his sword deep into Bjornulfr's belly and the jarl fell to the earth, ready to take his place with the heroes in Valhalla.

Brand and his party charged suddenly from behind the hall, Orm, Wigs and Gis with him as they cut into the Normans' flank. So focused were the Normans on the burning hall and distracted by Bjornulfr's heroic stand that they had not noticed the men climbing through the thatch. Orm killed a man and howled his anger at the sky. Wigs and Gis fought with practised efficiency, striking at enemies with the points of their swords. Beornoth ran to that flank and cut at the Normans, opening a man's bowels and smashing him to the ground with the edge of his shield.

The Normans fell back at first and then rallied, cutting down two of Brand's oathmen and halting the wild charge. Odo de Warenne found his way to that flank, spitting and cursing at his men to fight, and Beornoth saw his chance. He parried a sword cut with his own blade and opened a Norman's chest with a sword cut so powerful that it smashed the links of the enemy's byrnie. Beornoth stepped into the gap and punched the hilt of his sword into another enemy's nose and sent him reeling, face mangled and bloody. Beornoth was amongst them then, stamping, elbowing, butting and slicing with his sword. A man grabbed his shield and Beornoth let it go. He punched that Norman in the face and drove his sword through the man's thigh. The Normans shrank back from his ferocious attack until Beornoth came face to face with Odo de Warenne. Odo tried to get away, but the press of warriors behind held him fast as more Normans fell away from Beornoth's wrath. He grabbed a fistful of Odo's byrnie and hauled him out of the battle line, flinging him towards the hall.

'Hold!' Beornoth roared. 'Still your blades. Enough of you have died today. You can all leave this place alive. Let the de Warennes fight for you. This is Brand Thorkilsson.' Beornoth pointed his sword at Brand. 'The man you came for. The enemy of the king. Let Odo de Warenne fight him and kill him if he can. But if Brand wins, you ride away and leave us in peace.'

'Kill them!' Odo shrieked. He tried to run, but Beornoth grabbed him again and wrenched him close like a bundle of rags. The Normans stared on, their faces crimson-spattered, eyes ringed with tiredness and the ground about their boots soaked with dark blood. Robert de Warenne tried to force his way to the flank, towering above his men, eyes fixed upon his brother. Thick clouds of charcoal-coloured smoke billowed from the hall and coughs and cries of those inside filled Beornoth with urgency.

Brand came forward and Beornoth stepped away, leaving Odo to face the man whose family he had tried to slaughter. Odo looked for his brother, but there was no time for Robert to come to his aid. Brand sprang at him like a wolf, cutting with his axe, bellowing his hate. Odo parried the blow with his sword, but fell backwards. Brand kicked him in the face and sliced a cut across Odo's back with his knife. Beornoth kept the exhausted Normans at bay, glowering at them, huge and baleful in his blood-smeared byrnie. They were not sure what to do, and just stared on as Robert de Warenne reached the front. Odo de Warenne curled into a ball and wept like a child. Unable to rise and fight the man whose family he had come so close to murdering. Brand spat at him and ended his life with a contemptuous sweep of his axe, opening the back of Odo's skull like a boiled egg.

'Brother,' Robert de Warenne said, jaw falling open and sword hanging limp at his side.

'He was a coward and died like a dog,' Beornoth snarled.

'You must all die,' Robert said quietly, almost whispering. He met Beornoth's gaze. 'Every soul in this place will die.'

Thunder rolled across the southern hills, drumming over the land as though a mighty storm was about to break and wash the bloody battlefield clean with rain.

'Riders,' said Brand, pointing his scarlet-stained axe at the hills. 'Hundreds of them.'

The Normans shuffled and shifted, staring across the corpses and men writhing with horrific injuries. Robert de Warenne kept his eyes on Beornoth, as though nothing else in the world mattered. Beornoth looked over his enemy's shoulder and realised that the thunder was in fact an army of horsemen approaching, and at their head came Thered, ealdorman of Northumbria. A silence fell over Stag Hall, disturbed only by the rumble of hoofbeats, the crackle and spit of fire and the coughs and cries of Brand's family. Thered halted his men beyond the death pits and rode his white stallion alone through the carnage. He reined in beside the Normans and glowered down at Robert de Warenne.

'This is over,' Thered said. 'I am the ealdorman of Northumbria and your ill-advised king has caused enough bloodshed in my shire. This man is a thegn, sworn to my service and under my protection. Brand, get your family out of that hall before the fire takes them.' He closed his eyes and whispered a prayer at the horror of it all. 'You Normans, throw down your arms or I swear to Lord God Almighty, every man of you shall die here today.'

The Normans glanced at each other, then at Robert de Warenne. Robert had eyes only for Beornoth, and he didn't flinch as the first of his warriors dropped his sword, followed by another, until all the Normans laid down their weapons and knelt before Ealdorman Thered. Brand dashed into the hall, followed by Orm, Wigs, Gis and the rest of his men. They emerged moments later with weeping women and children clutched to them. Beornoth rolled his shoulders and pointed his sword at Robert de Warenne.

'No surrender for you,' Beornoth said.

'No,' replied Robert. Understanding what must happen.

'No more blood, Beornoth,' Thered shouted, his scarred face furious. The ealdorman had come unlooked for, riding with his hearth troop to save Brand and Beornoth from Robert de Warenne's war band.

'There must be more. Just one.' Beornoth bowed his head in thanks to Thered, his brother of the sword. The ealdorman had come despite the risk of incurring King Æthelred's wrath and Beornoth hated to disobey Thered's command, but there must be a reckoning with Robert de Warenne.

Robert de Warenne tore his eyes from Beornoth and stared at his brother's corpse. 'He was my only friend. We grew up in a foreign court, outsiders, sons of a man everybody believed to be an assassin and a traitor. Everywhere we turned, people whispered around corners, sniggered behind their hands. Sneering, mockery and accusation dogged us at every turn. Odo was impetuous, but I loved him. He was my brother.' He spoke sadly, as if there were no one else around.

'Then join him,' Beornoth said, without pity.

Beornoth's harshness hit Robert de Warenne like a slap, and he jerked as if waking from a dream. His lip curled and his sword came up, feet widening in a fighter's stance. Thered shouted to his men to help Brand and his family, and turned his back on what Beornoth must do. Beornoth rolled his shoulders and set himself, sword held out before him. Robert de Warenne circled him, moving to Beornoth's left, as a fighter should. Beornoth turned to follow his enemy, and Robert de Warenne darted forward with the speed of a serpent. His blade licked out, faster than Beornoth could parry, and opened a cut on Beornoth's chin. Beornoth followed it, cutting with his own sword, but Robert de Warenne sprang away with the lightness of a dancer, as though he wore no armour at all. He was young and strong, a warrior in his prime. Beornoth lunged and swung his blade, but found only air as Robert de Warenne swayed and dodged. De Warenne waited for Beornoth to overstretch in his desperation to land a blow, and then struck, clattering Beornoth over the head with the pommel of his sword.

Everything went dark for a moment, and Beornoth staggered as the blow rang his helmet like a bell. Light came back, with a ringing sound in Beornoth's ears. De Warenne's sword struck Beornoth across the back, his chain mail held the cut, but the strength in it drove Beornoth to his knees. He scrambled, vision returning in flashes, and Robert de Warenne kicked him hard in the ribs. Beornoth rolled, trying to rise but unable to gather his senses. A glint of sun on steel caught his eye, and he jerked his head just as the point of de Warenne's sword plunged into the ground where his face had been. Beornoth rolled and the sword bit the ground again. The blade swept from the dirt and clattered across Beornoth's helmet. He rose to his knees, needing to stand and fight, but de Warenne stamped down hard upon his chest. Beornoth panicked, pinned to the ground by Robert's heavy boot. Death was close and Beornoth swept his sword at his enemy, but Robert de Warenne parried low. The Norman's blade caught Beornoth's sword close to the hilt, and it flew from Beornoth's hand.

Beornoth struggled, but could not move beneath Robert de Warenne's boot. A sword blade rested against Beornoth's gullet, cold against his skin. He closed his eyes, feeling the chill of death upon him. He was ready to go to Eawynn, to rest and be at peace.

'Uncle Beo!' screamed Vigdjarf, and Beornoth snapped awake. Strength flooded him, power born of rage pumping from his heart into his muscled arms and legs, flowing across his broad back and thick shoulders. Robert de Warenne had come north to burn and kill Brand and his family, and Beornoth could not let him live. His hand snapped up like a predator's jaws and he grabbed Robert de Warenne's sword. The blade tugged, slicing through Beornoth's hand, and Beornoth yanked the sword away from his throat. With his left hand he grabbed Robert de Warenne's foot and tore it from his chest, heaving the Norman away from him. Robert took two paces back and Beornoth surged to his feet. He punched de Warenne in the stomach and grabbed his sword hand. Beornoth butted Robert de Warenne, his helmet crushing the gristle of his nose. He butted again, driving the boar-shaped nasal into the soft skin around Robert de Warenne's eye. The Norman jerked away from Beornoth's savagery, his face a ruin of cut, ragged flesh. Beornoth ripped the sword from Robert's grip, reversed the blade, and drove the point deep into Robert de Warenne's guts. The point broke through the chain-mail links and drove on through skin and muscle. Robert gasped and Beornoth grabbed him by the throat with two bloody hands. He squeezed with all the strength in his old warrior's arms, throttling the Norman until his eyes bulged. Beornoth shook him and snarled. He roared into Robert de Warenne's dying face and watched as the light went from his eyes.

Beornoth dropped the corpse and fell to his knees. Wigs and Gis ran to him, lifting him and holding his exhausted body between them.

'Now it's over,' said Thered. The ealdorman had dismounted and stood before Beornoth, his mouth twisted in disgust at the bloodshed.

'You should not have come,' Beornoth said. 'Though I thank you for saving our lives. When the king hears you stopped his men from what they came to do...'

'King Æthelred has bigger problems, Lord Beornoth.'

'What do you mean?'

'Word comes from the north. Sweyn Forkbeard sails for England with one hundred warships. He comes with his son Cnut, his champion Thorkell the Tall, and an army of Vikings to avenge the slaying of his sister.'

* * *

MORE FROM PETER GIBBONS

Another book from Peter Gibbons, *Excalibur*, is available to order now here:

https://mybook.to/ExcaliburBackAd

HISTORICAL NOTE

The *Saxon Warrior Series* deals with events up to and following the historical Battle of Maldon. In *Brothers of the Sword* we saw the events of Maldon unfold, including the death of Ealdorman Byrhtnoth. In *Sword of Vengeance* Beornoth exacted his revenge upon Godric and others who led the great ealdorman and his war band to their famous doom. The Battle of Maldon itself is well documented in the poem of the same name, as I have summarised in the previous books in this series. This novel picks up on events after the battle, and the portentous events later in King Æthelred's reign. A number of different historical texts exist to help try and build a picture of those events, which include the account of the battle in the *Anglo-Saxon Chronicle*, *The Lives of St Oswald and St Ecgwine* written by the monk Byrhtferth, and the *Book of Ely*.

In the years after Maldon, signs of anxiety and fear spread through King Æthelred's court. Those worries came not just from increasing Viking raids but also from what they represented to people at the time. With the turn of the millennium, increasing Viking attacks became a symbol of a perceived lack of

God's favour. The ill-advised gafol to pay off the Vikings did not work and, if anything, invited more attacks. In this period King Æthelred embarked upon a comprehensive programme of repentance and reform. He turned his back on some members of his court, admitted to wrongdoing and rehabilitated the legacy of his mother. In a move to assuage the moral concerns and God's disfavour, Æthelred tried to be a godly king. He martyred his murdered brother and restored land to the Church. Many of the Viking raiders found safe harbour in northern France with the Normans, themselves of Scandinavian descent and the Norman court was probably still bilingual. As part of a defensive strategy, Æthelred married the Norman Duke Richard the Fearless' younger sister Emma in 1002, and so the Normans and the English became allies for a time. In this novel I have used that as a premise for the return of Lady Ælfthryth, along with the fictional de Warenne brothers.

The book begins with Sweyn Forkbeard's attack on Lundenwic in 994, accompanied by the historical figure of Thorkell the Tall who was the leader of the Jomsvikings. We have met the Jomsvikings before in the series and both Sweyn and Thorkell will return in the next book in the series. Pallig is a historical figure, a Dane who came into Æthelred's service in 994 and then defected in 1001. The *Anglo-Saxon Chronicle* stated that Pallig deserted the king 'in spite of all the pledges he had given to him' and without regard to the gifts 'in estates, and in gold and silver' he had received. The *Chronicle* goes on to say that 'in this year the king ordered all the Danish men who were in England to be slain, this was done on St Brice's feast day, because it was made known to the king that they wanted treacherously to deprive him and then all his counsellors of life and to possess this kingdom thereafter.'

There is much evidence to support the St Brice's Day

Massacre, which features heavily in this novel. The massacre on St Brice's feast day was a historical event, about which there is much historical debate. Æthelred attracted his famous epithet, the Unready, based on the old English word Unraed, or ill-advised. Some historians see the massacre as both a crime and a blunder, others as a cleansing of rogue Viking mercenaries who came to England in 994 to serve the king but ultimately betrayed him. Archaeologists found a mass burial from the time of around fifty skeletons where the individuals were all male and mostly aged between sixteen and twenty-five. All the skeletons show signs of injuries inflicted at the time of death. These were mostly multiple blade wounds to the back; several showed evidence of charring, indicating that they had been burned. All evidence points to a mass execution.

We can gain insight into the thinking of the king and his advisors through charters issued at the time. In 1004 a charter issued to St Frideswide's in Oxford from the king states that '...a decree was sent out by me with the counsel of my leading men and magnates, to the effect that all the Danes who had sprung up in the island, sprouting like cockle amongst the wheat, were to be slain by a most just extermination, and this decree was to be put into effect as far as death...'. In the novel I have Robert de Warenne repeat some of this wording, such as the reference to cockle in the wheat. Cockles are a form of weed.

King Sweyn Forkbeard successfully fought the naval Battle of Svolder against his former ally Olaf Tryggvason in the year 1000, and became the ruler of both Denmark and Norway. Pallig was indeed married to Forkbeard's sister, and her death during the St Brice's Day Massacre was a convenient pretext for the great Viking king to launch an invasion of England.

By this point, Beornoth has become old and tired of war, but finds himself at the centre of events which drive King Æthelred towards a war with Sweyn, his son Cnut and Thorkell the Tall. Though Beornoth wishes to join his wife Eawynn in heaven, the greatest war of his life is yet to be fought. Forkbeard comes with a vast army, and Beornoth must stand in the shield wall once again...

GLOSSARY

Aesc spear – A large, two-handed, long-bladed spear.

Burh – A fortification designed by Alfred the Great to protect against Viking incursions.

Byrnie – Saxon word for a coat of chain mail.

Cantuctone – Cannington, Somerset.

Danelaw – The part of England ruled by the Vikings from 865AD.

Defnascir – Devon.

Drakkar – A type of Viking warship.

Dumnoc – A town in Somerset.

Ealdorman – The leader of a shire of the English kingdom, second in rank only to the king.

Exanceaster – Exeter.

Euton – A supernatural being, like a troll or a giant.

Gafol – The Danegeld, or tax raised to pay tribute to Viking raiders to save a land from being ravaged.

Grimseby – Grimsby.

Heriot – The weapons, land and trappings of a thegn or other noble person, granted to him by his lord and which becomes his will or inheritance.

Hide – An area of land large enough to support one family. A measure used for assessing areas of land.

Jomsvikings – Viking mercenaries based at their stronghold at Jomsburg who followed a strict warriors' code.

Lindisfarena – Lindisfarne.

Lundenwic – London.

Mameceaster – Manchester.

Nástrǫnd – The afterlife for those guilty of crimes such as oathbreaking, adultery or murder. It is the corpse-shore, with a great hall built from the backs of snakes, where the serpent Níðhöggr gnaws upon the corpses of the dead.

Níðhöggr – A serpent or monster who gnaws at the roots of the great tree Yggdrasil, and also gnaws upon the corpses of the dead at Nástrǫnd.

Nithing – A coward, villain or oathbreaker, not worthy of the glorious afterlife.

Njorth – The Viking sea god.

Norns – Norse goddesses of fate. Three sisters who live beneath the world tree Yggdrasil and weave the tapestry of fate.

Odin – The father of the Viking gods.

Oxenforda – Oxford.

Ragnarök – The end-of-days battle where the Viking gods will battle Loki and his monster brood.

Reeve – Administer of justice ranking below a thegn.

Seax – A short, single-edged sword with the blade angled towards the point.

Seiðr – A type of Norse magic.

Skuld – One of the three Norns who sit at the great ash tree Yggdrasil and decide the fates of men.

Somersaete – Somerset.

Thegn – Owner of five hides of land, a church and kitchen, a bell house and a castle gate, who is obligated to fight for his lord when called upon.

Thor – The Viking thunder god.

Thruthvangr – Thor's realm in the afterlife, where he gathers his forces for the day of Ragnarök. Similar to Valhalla.

Týr – The Viking war god.

Valhalla – Odin's great hall where he gathers dead warriors to fight for him at Ragnarök.

Vik – Part of Viking Age Norway.

Wallingaford – Wallingford.

Whale Road – The sea.

Wyrd – Anglo-Saxon concept of fate or destiny.

Yggdrasil – A giant ash tree which supports the universe, the nine worlds including our world Midgard.

ACKNOWLEDGEMENTS

Thanks to Caroline, Claire, Nia, Ross, Gary, and all of the team at Boldwood Books for their unwavering support and belief.

ABOUT THE AUTHOR

Peter Gibbons is a financial advisor and author of the highly acclaimed Viking Blood and Blade trilogy. He originates from Liverpool and now lives with his family in County Kildare.

Sign up to Peter Gibbons' mailing list for news, competitions and updates on future books.

Visit Peter's website: www.petermgibbons.com

Follow Peter on social media here:

facebook.com/petergibbonsauthor

x.com/AuthorGibbons

instagram.com/petermgibbons

bookbub.com/authors/peter-gibbons

ALSO BY PETER GIBBONS

The Saxon Warrior Series

Warrior and Protector

Storm of War

Brothers of the Sword

Sword of Vengeance

Enemies of the Crown

The Chronicles of Arthur

Excalibur

Pendragon

WARRIOR CHRONICLES

WELCOME TO THE CLAN ✕

THE HOME OF
BESTSELLING HISTORICAL
ADVENTURE FICTION!

WARNING:
MAY CONTAIN VIKINGS!

SIGN UP TO OUR
NEWSLETTER

BIT.LY/WARRIORCHRONICLES

Boldwood

Boldwood Books is an award-winning fiction publishing company seeking out the best stories from around the world.

Find out more at www.boldwoodbooks.com

Join our reader community for brilliant books, competitions and offers!

Follow us
@BoldwoodBooks
@TheBoldBookClub

Sign up to our weekly deals newsletter

https://bit.ly/BoldwoodBNewsletter

Made in United States
Orlando, FL
28 April 2025

60858083R00186